New Beginnings

Fern began her career as a television presenter in 1980 after completing a stage management course at Central School of Drama. In 1985 Fern became the presenter of the popular *Coast to Coast*, which lead to presenting roles on prime time television shows, the most iconic of which was ITV's flagship show *This Morning*. Fern's warmth, humour, empathy and compassion have made her incredibly popular and she has become a much sought-after presenter. In 2008 Fern released her autobiography *Fern: My Story*, which was a huge bestseller. Fern is deeply committed to a number of charities, in particular those working with and for women, children and childbirth. She lives with her husband Phil Vickery, the well-respected chef, and her four children in Buckinghamshire.

Also by Fern Britton:

Fern: My Story

FERN BRITTON

New Beginnings

HarperCollins*Publishers*

HarperCollins*Publishers* Ltd
1 London Bridge Street,
London SE1 9GF

www.harpercollins.co.uk

This paperback edition 2011
12

First published in Great Britain by
HarperCollins 2011

A catalogue record for this book is
available from the British Library

ISBN: 978 0 00 736270 7

Set in Birka by Palimpsest Book Production Limited,
Falkirk, Stirlingshire

Printed and bound in Great Britain by
CPI Group (UK) Ltd, Croydon CR0 4YY

To you, the reader – thank you! Xx

ACKNOWLEDGEMENTS

I'd like to thank my agents John Rush and Luigi Bonomi for all their support and encouragement, my publisher Lynne Drew, my editor Kate Burke and all the rest of the fantastic team at HarperCollins. I also thank Fanny Blake whose guidance and expertise mean this book exists at all. Her excellent advice 'once you have started, don't stop till you get to the end' should be the writers' motto. Not forgetting my many colleagues over the years who have given me a fund of scurrilous stories – none of which I could possibly use!

THEN . . .

'I want Marmite on my toast. Not Dairylea,' Libby yelled downstairs at the top of her voice.

The day Christie's life changed for ever, began just like any other. Her nine-year-old daughter was sulking on her bed.

Nick called up to her: 'Darling, we don't have Marmite. Mummy's told you she'll get some later. How about honey? Now, come and give your old dad a kiss goodbye, gorgeous girl.'

'No.' Libby already had a very definite mind of her own.

'Well, you'll have to go hungry, get weak and feeble, and you won't be able to go out on your bike with me at the weekend.'

'Don't care.'

Christie came out of the kitchen, drying her hands on a teatowel. 'Libby! Come down here right now and eat your breakfast or you'll be late for school.'

'I hate you.'

'Don't speak to Mummy like that, madam.'

'And I hate you too.'

'She's definitely from your mother's side.' Nick slid an arm around Christie's waist. 'See you later, my beautiful, clever wife. Love you. 'Bye, Freddie.' He kissed them both, and Christie watched the back of his familiar head as he walked away down the mews.

Her morning happened as every morning happened. Wrestling with Libby's stubbornness, coaxing both kids into the car and getting them off to their schools. By nine forty-five she was back indoors and ready to clear the breakfast debris. It was then that the phone rang.

The rest of the day was filled with such pain that much of it she couldn't recall. She had been told that Nick had died, suddenly, on the pavement two hundred yards from his office and that bystanders had attempted to revive him while calling for an ambulance. She remembered the hospital doctor: young, inexperienced at breaking this kind of bad news to a wife who needed to know exactly what had happened to her husband. 'It was a pulmonary embolism,' he explained. 'It could have happened to anyone.'

How? Why? Why? Why?

At last she was taken to the mortuary, where Nick lay in a silent, nondescript room that she supposed had housed many corpses and heard many tears and farewells.

He was cold and gone from her, with a bruise on his cheek where he'd apparently hit the pavement. Had he been dead before he hit the ground? Had he had any warning?

She climbed up next to him and put her arms round him. He was cold. If only she could have closed her eyes and let go of her own life, right there and then, she would have. She stayed there, feeling utterly empty, hopeless. Her sane self stayed outside her body, looking down at the sad sight she made, lying next to him. Someone opened the door, asked if she was all right. Of course, she wasn't bloody all right. She kissed Nick goodbye for the last time, then sat outside waiting to be told what to do next as she let the silent tears spill onto her coat.

Later, Fred stared at her, silent, his eyes big with incomprehension. Libby wailed, clinging to her as if she was the only life-raft in a stormy sea. 'Mummy! I didn't kiss him – I didn't kiss him. I told him I hated him. It's my fault. I love Daddy. I want him to come home.'

Libby's grief was so huge and suffocating that Christie wanted to slap her, to shout at her. In more pain than she had ever experienced, what she wanted to say was right on the tip of her tongue: 'Don't you think I want him home too? He's my husband. The love of my life. I'm his wife. I need you to comfort me.'

But what she actually did was cuddle and kiss and console.

NOW . . .

1

'Why do we have to stay with her?' Libby slammed the door of the battered Peugeot estate. 'I don't want to.'

Christie, lugging overnight bags into the car boot, bit back her reprimand about the door, not wanting to provoke her daughter's temper any further. Instead she forced herself into her best unruffled-mother mode. 'You know that I'm staying the night with Auntie Mel so she can help me sort out what I'm going to wear tomorrow. You're going to stay with Granny, who can't come here because she's got an early-morning Pilates class tomorrow.' She tried to keep the amusement out of her voice. The idea of her mother and her friends as Pilates devotees always made her smile.

In the rear-view mirror she could see Libby looking thunderous, her straight hair cut into a neat bob with a fringe that almost hid her frown. Across the bridge of her nose was a smattering of freckles that ran into her flushed cheeks while her rosebud mouth was drawn into a tight line.

'Can't we come too?' nine-year-old Fred begged, as they began to reverse down the drive towards the lane.

'Freddie, I've already explained.' Christie spelled out what was happening for the umpteenth time. 'You've got to go to school tomorrow and I've got a TV show to do. It's really important that I look good, so I need to see Auntie Mel. If it goes well, there might be more work for me. Then there'll be more money. And we can do all sorts of things.'

'Can I have an iPod Touch, then? Ouch!' he yelped. 'What did you pinch me for?'

'Because you're stupid. You're far too young for one.' Libby mustered all the scorn of a twelve-going-on-twenty-five-year-old. 'Don't!' she yelled, as Fred lashed out. She dodged the blow, jabbing him in the leg at the same time so that he squealed.

'For God's sake! Can't the two of you behave like human beings just for once? Is it too much to ask?' Christie yelled at the top of her voice, shocking the children into quiet.

The two of them kept a sullen silence, punctuated by the odd 'Stop it,' or 'Owww,' as one poked at the other.

Christie tried to ignore them. What was it with kids? You love them, care for them, anticipate their every whim – but did they consider her? Never. Was it all right occasionally to feel such ambivalence to the two people she loved more than anyone else in the entire world? Yes, she decided, if they were so selfish as not to understand how important the next two days could be for her. For them. The last two and a bit years since Nick had died had been a dark chaos. She had managed to exist and bring up the children as best she could. They were at least fed, clothed and relatively balanced. But she was still a jelly, slopped out of its mould and left spreading on a slippery, edgeless plate.

However, she had made some big decisions. She had given up her appearances on *MarketForce*, the afternoon TV consumer programme where she was beginning to make something of a name for herself as a good, solid watchdog journalist. After Nick's sudden death, she couldn't concentrate on anything other than the children's day-to-day needs. She had sold up the little mews house full of so many memories and moved back to her mother's village in Buckinghamshire, where she had found an old, dilapidated money-pit of a Georgian farmhouse. Her mother had told her she'd be mad to buy it so, to prove her right, Christie had blown Nick's life insurance on it.

'It'll be lovely when it's done,' said those friends who had left London to brave the countryside.

Only it hadn't been done. The chimney was cracked, the conservatory was leaking, and the wind whistled through every rattling sash window and door. She was skint. Even though she had Nick's modest pension and a little from the weekly column she now wrote for the *Daily News*, plus occasional features for the paper and the odd women's mag, that didn't do much more than keep the family in new school shoes and petrol.

Now, though, something exciting and scary had happened. *Tart Talk*, the irreverent daytime TV7 show, had asked her to be a guest. Her stomach flipped with fresh nervousness. She wasn't any longer just a widow, with all its connotations of death and sadness, but a woman who had a life of her own to lead. Nick would have wanted that. Wouldn't he?

'Come on, Christie. You can do it,' she heard his voice tell her.

At last, she turned down the road that led to her mother's neat little brick bungalow. She pulled up outside the low wall that fronted an immaculate garden with a manicured moss-free lawn and regimented borders. Christie turned to the children. Libby was busy texting but Fred was fast asleep.

'Come on, guys. Time to get out.' As Libby looked up at her with her big dark eyes, so reminiscent of Nick's, Christie's heart melted. 'Oh, darling, please don't make me feel bad. This could be really good for us all.'

'Yeah, I know. I hope Granny's made one of her sponge cakes.' Her mood had changed with the fickleness of youth as she hopped out of the car and gave her mother a kiss. 'Come on, Fred. We're here.' She pulled out the bag he was leaning on, waking him with a jolt.

Fred clambered out behind her, bleary with sleep. Christie gathered him up in a bear-hug. 'Be good, darling. I'll see you tomorrow after school.'

She had noticed one of the lace curtains in the bay windows move, and knew her mother would open the door at any moment. Not wanting to miss the train by getting caught up in conversation or complaint, she waited till her mother appeared on the doorstep then, as the children waved at her, she locked the car and shouted, 'Can't stop, Mum. I'm going to be late. Wish me luck. I'll see you tomorrow and thanks a million.'

Then, with a wave, she started walking briskly towards the station. As her steps took her further away from her mother's, she couldn't help thinking back to a time when she thought she'd never be able to move on.

The hours and days after Nick's death were wiped from her mind. Christie was visited by waking dreams of him. When the phone rang, it must be him. When the doorbell rang, it must be him. But, of course, it never was, and the blow to her solar plexus felled her more painfully each time. The agony of telling people that she was no longer part of 'NickandChristie' was something she began to avoid. The look in their eyes, the sound of their voices on the phone made anger roar into her brain and scorch the backs of her eyeballs. Instead, she asked Mel to tell everyone they knew.

One morning a postman delivered two letters for Nick. She heard them drop through the letterbox and just managed to open the door and give the innocent man an earful of grief-sodden abuse before he disappeared through the gate. She sagged onto the doorstep. As she wept, she seemed to float outside her body and, looking down on herself, she was filled with compassion and disgust by what she saw.

'Get up, you stupid excuse for a woman. Get up! Comb your hair, get dressed, brush your teeth. Be a credit to Nick. Nick, you bastard!'

She only emerged from this altered state when a small hand

smoothed her hair and a little boy's voice said, 'Mummy, I'm hungry.'

The words lasered through her. Yes. She was literally the bread-winner now, the one to put food in the children's mouths, to clothe them and guide them through life. She had to be both mother and father to them from now on.

The protective shell that had enveloped her that day kept her strong as she organised the funeral. Her mother tried to help with the catering. 'You must have everybody back to the house and feed them, Christine. That's what I did for your father and it's what people expect. I suggest sandwiches, nothing too fancy. A big bowl of cocktail sausages always goes down well. What man doesn't like a sausage? That's what your father always said. And what about drink? Just a little sherry and lots of tea, I think. You don't want anybody getting drunk. And make sure they know when it finishes. If people hang about they'll expect more food. Christine? Christine? Christine?'

But Christie had gone. She couldn't take her mother's wittering any longer so she had opened the front door and just walked out. For a brief moment in her life she wanted to be free of responsi-bility. No more widow, no more mum. Just Christie.

Her escape didn't last long – half an hour at most – and when she got home, the children were in the middle of supper, eating chicken nuggets at the kitchen table. Maureen was at the sink, making a jug of Ribena. Christie went to her and hugged her. 'Thanks, Mum.'

'That's all right, darling.'

And nothing more was said.

Somehow the funeral drew a line through the chaos of the days preceding it, and gradually Christie's life began to take on a rhythm of sorts. Not the same as before, but almost bearable. Now that she was solely responsible for the children and could think of nothing else, she gave in her notice at MarketForce and devoted herself to them, so money was tight. When Libby and Fred were settled, she would start working as a journalist again. The one thing hanging over her head was the bank loan Nick had taken out to help his father, not long before he died. The debt was part of his legacy to her. She had promised him that she would never tell Maureen about its existence, and there was no way she would tell her now.

2

Deep breathing was not producing the desired effect. Christie's heart was still racing as fast as if she'd been rigged up to an intravenous caffeine drip. Her palms were clammy and she knew that if she unclenched her fists her hands would be shaking. She inhaled again slowly, trying to focus her thoughts. Catching sight of herself, she immediately wished she'd stuck with the simple black round-necked dress, her original choice, instead of giving in to her fashionista sister. After last night's couple of glasses of wine, Mel had insisted she went for something more 'out there'.

'Chris! I'm not going to allow you to disappear into the scenery . . . as normal. This is your big chance, the one time when you want people to notice you, and you're dressing in your usual widow's weeds. Try this.'

She held out a funky, figure-hugging aquamarine and yellow silk sheath dress, which they both knew Christie would never wear in a million years. The neck, hemline and lack of sleeves meant there was way too much on show. Only two years younger, Mel had always been the risk-taker, edgier, unafraid of others' opinions, and her dress sense reflected that. She had been the highest-marked student of the year when she graduated from the London College of Fashion and was now making a name for herself as a freelance stylist for the glossy mags. Although the sisters were the same size, there was little in their separate wardrobes that would happily cross over. In any case, Christie wasn't sure she wanted people to notice her because of what she wore.

In the end, they had settled on a compromise, dug from the back of the wardrobe: a maroon wrap dress that reached to just above her knees and whispered, 'Look at me. I'm sexy *and* smart.' Even Mel didn't know how this piece of good taste had got into her wardrobe, but they'd agreed that, zhooshed up with very sheer tights, a simple but gorgeous necklace and some killer heels, this was the look that was just right for Christie and for the show.

However, now, standing at the side of the studio, surrounded by the controlled chaos of cameramen, runners, researchers, editor, producer and the other presenters, Christie suddenly felt less confident. Instead of distracting attention from her modest bosom, the large milky amber pendant they'd chosen seemed to accentuate it. To fill out what now seemed an inappropriately skimpy neckline, she needed the breasts of Sharon Barber, the bosomy ex-soap star and *Tart Talk* regular who was standing a few feet away, chatting to the floor manager. Christie pulled at the jersey fabric, trying to close the V, then reminded herself of how the girls in Makeup had complimented her. Under those super-bright lights, her reflection was of someone she hardly recognised. Instead of the usual dressed-down mother of two, she saw someone elegant but not intimidating, well-groomed but not over the top. They'd given her a bit more eye-shadow and lip-gloss than she was used to and her hair was bigger and more flicked out, but she had to admit that, against her expectations, she quite liked the new her. She took another deep breath.

She felt a hand on her arm and turned to see Marina French smiling at her. An experienced news reporter, now deemed too old for the mainstream news, Marina was respected for her popularity and her ballsy attitude to life, which made male presenters quail. She was still the anchor of *Tart Talk* because of the much-needed gravitas she lent to the otherwise unpredictable fast-talking show. 'Christie, don't worry. You'll be fine,' she murmured, as she nodded towards the audience. 'They've come to have a good time. They want to like you.'

Christie nodded and swallowed. 'Hmm. If you say so . . .'

'Every guest presenter feels nervous their first time on live TV. I'd be worried if you weren't. But once you're out there, the time'll whizz by. Try to enjoy it. You'll soon be an old hand.'

'I hope so.' And she truly did. However nerve-racking the experience so far, she was feeling an excitement that she hadn't known in years. Last week's phone call from the show's producer had come at exactly the right moment. She had read and loved the one-off piece Christie had written about Nick's death, her enforced single motherhood and subsequent move to the country.

After two years, Christie had at last found she was able to look back and understand that she should celebrate the time she had been given with Nick. As the children grew older, she was even beginning to enjoy being single again as she gained a new perspective on her life. When she had said as much to her editor at a drinks party, he had immediately reacted: 'I've never heard you talk like that. You must write about it for me.' So she had. She had poured her emotions into the piece, excited to be exploring something so close to her heart, such a welcome change from the usual consumer-based features that had become her stock-in-trade. When her editor had criticised it as 'too cerebral for our market', and asked, 'Where's the sex?' she had almost despaired.

To be asked to come on *Tart Talk* to talk intelligently about women surviving the loss of the love of their lives was a huge compliment. But today she was feeling rather differently. She had been up since five thirty, unable to sleep, not even in the back of the sleek Mercedes sent to take her to the TV7 building, home of *Tart Talk*, as it crawled through traffic held up by roadworks on the Euston Road. Sitting on the uncomfortable leather sofa in her dressing room, leafing through the pile of the day's papers as she waited to be called to Makeup, there had been plenty more time for the nerves to kick in. She had been thankful when a runner finally took her along to the green room to meet the three regular presenters.

She had immediately sensed the great rapport that existed between Marina, Sharon and Grace: Grace Benjamin – the thin, gap-toothed black comedian with a big laugh, whose bisexuality was often the butt of her own jokes. Their camaraderie meant they had welcomed her without reserve, offering her coffee before they went through with the producer the subjects they might be going to cover on today's show. How much would Christie be able to contribute to a discussion about middle-age binge drinking and subsequent one-night stands? Staying up late to watch *Newsnight* just in case had been a complete waste of time. She'd have to wing it and focus her efforts on the reason she was there.

Just before they were due to go on, a fourth woman had sashayed in, finishing a conversation on her BlackBerry. Tall and well-padded but dressed in a stylish tailored cream suit, not a hair out of its coiffured place, she sat down beside Marina. 'Hello, darling,' she breathed. 'I was in the studios so thought I'd pop down and see how you were.' Her energy and presence immediately refocused the room so all eyes were on her. Christie was wondering where she'd seen her before when Marina introduced her.

'Julia, you must meet Christie Lynch. Remember she used to be on *MarketForce*? She's going to be talking about bereavement on the show today. Christie, this is my very special agent, Julia Keen.'

Christie immediately knew who she was. Julia Keen was one of *the* talent agents in London, a name known to most magazine readers, loved and feared in equal measure by those in the business. She had made her reputation by poaching high-earning clients from other agents, often appearing with them at all the most prestigious showbiz events. Christie had read one or two profiles about her in the press. About a year ago Julia had been the subject of much media interest when one of her clients, the TV presenter Ben Chapman, had drowned in her indoor swimming-pool: coroner's verdict, misadventure. But the press had been free and frequent with speculation about their relationship and the real reason for Ben having been there without his girlfriend, as well as about what had really happened. He had been the co-host of *Good Evening Britain*, a news/magazine show that had actors, writers and MPs queuing up to appear. *Newsnight* meets *The One Show*, it had the six to seven p.m. slot on TV7 five nights a week. When Ben died, his on-air partner, Gilly Lancaster, had made a tribute to him so moving that it was printed on every red-top front page the following day. His long-term partner, Laura, was devastated at losing him, while Julia had absented herself from the red carpets and all that went with them. Success breeds success but scandal can be a dangerous enemy.

Christie remembered the photos splashed in the press of Ben, Laura and Julia, as well as of an indoor pool that had come straight from a scene out of *Footballers' Wives*: colonnaded french windows leading back into the house, white loungers, tropical ferns in large ceramic pots. Julia clearly knew how to enjoy the fruits of her success. Smiling, Christie offered her hand – to find it gripped firmly, as Julia's clear blue eyes assessed her in an unnerving and not altogether pleasant way.

'A pleasure to meet you,' Julia said. 'I've read your *Daily News* column. Good luck today.' She gave her another look of appraisal.

'Thanks.' Christie, feeling a little uncomfortable, was relieved when, at that moment, the green room door opened and they were called to the studio.

As she stood in the dark, behind the set, she could hear the large audience of students and pensioners filing in. Who else had time to go to a daytime show? Bussed in for the occasion, they found their seats and the buzz subsided as the warm-up man welcomed them. Christie strained to hear what he was saying.

Then someone else caught her attention.

'Christie, my darling. Hi. I'm Tim, the floor manager.' A young casually dressed man wearing headphones was at her side. 'Welcome. Nice to have you. In two minutes, watch Marina and just follow her onto the set and take the second stool on the left, behind the desk. OK, love? Good luck.' He patted her shoulder in encouragement.

Oh, God, Marina was walking onto the set. They want to like me, Christie repeated to herself, and followed, as confidently as she could, to the sound of applause. Why did I say yes to this? She could feel the heat of the lights on her face and a prickle of perspiration on her back as she went out into the bright lights. She hitched herself onto the stool, which was high enough to make the women sit up straight or fall off, and wondered what to do with her heels: let them hang or tuck them in? She tucked them in and pulled down the sides of her skirt.

'Look as if you're enjoying yourself,' whispered Grace. 'They won't eat you.'

Switching on a smile as the warm-up guy introduced the team, Christie looked up and out towards the audience where her eyes fell on Mel in the second row, resplendent in a to-be-noticed-by-my-sister neon pink scarf, grinning like a maniac and giving her the thumbs-up. If only Nick could have been there with her. He would have been so proud. She twisted her wedding ring round her finger, then swiftly reminded herself that she had to stop thinking like that. This was her life now.

'OK. Fifteen seconds, studio. Quiet, please,' shouted Tim. He continued the countdown to zero, then the show's title music struck up.

As the cameras began to roll, they were all laughing. It was up to the four of them now. Christie heard a disembodied voice introducing Marina, Grace, Sharon, and then: '. . . and please welcome Christie Lynch, the merry widow, to ask her: is there dating after death?'

Oh, God! No! Why had no one briefed her that they weren't going to be taking the sensitive, dignified approach she had imagined? Because they realised she'd have shied away? Of course. She should have known better than to trust them not to trivialise the subject, but it was too late now. In front of the audience and her co-presenters, she had no choice but to keep smiling and try to think of something to say. Come on, Nick. Give me strength.

3

Before she knew where she was, the show was over. Mel had kissed her, said how brilliant she had been and disappeared off for a shoot with John Swannell, her favourite fashion photographer. Christie had climbed down from her stool and was taken to the green room, where she found all her belongings had been brought from the dressing room.

The entire programme team was there, enjoying sandwiches and a glass of wine. While Marina was sharing a joke with Sharon, Julia Keen discreetly engineered a conversation alone with Christie, lowering her voice almost to a whisper, as she said, 'You were good, darling. Much better than I expected. Now, do you have a good agent?'

Taken aback by Julia's directness as well as the apparent need for discretion, Christie, suddenly self-conscious, muttered, 'No. I've never really needed one.'

Julia's eyes seemed to light up from within. 'I think things are about to change for you. Perhaps we should have a little talk some time. Take my card.' She extracted one from a small silver holder and slipped it into Christie's hand. 'Just call me,' she said, giving Christie's arm a little squeeze just above the elbow. Then she turned to join the other women and, within moments, was laughing as if she'd been with them for the length of the joke.

Christie stared at her, watching how she stayed for just as long as was necessary before making her excuses. She realised this was her cue to leave too. She said her goodbyes, receiving polite and not unenthusiastic thanks from the producer. She left the building carrying a hand-tied bunch of Heavenly Scent flowers, a Diptyque candle and a card from the regular presenters thanking her. She had pretended not to see the producer hurriedly signing on their behalf when she'd thought no one was looking. The card that Julia Keen had given her was burning a hole in her pocket.

*

Not until Christie sank into the grey-leather back seat of her chauffeur-driven Mercedes and she was watching the black ribbon of the M40 disappear beneath them, did she stop to take stock. Only then did she realise that she had no idea what she'd said at any time over the past hour or so, or if any of it had made sense. Her brief conversation with Julia had taken on the quality of a dream. She dismissed it as an aberration. The woman had only said what she felt she had to. Hadn't she?

The driver had been asked to drop her off at her mother's where she'd left her car. There was just time to drop in before she went home to meet the children when they got back from school. The door chimes pealed, and through the dimpled glass, she saw the distorted silhouette of her most ferocious critic coming towards her. The door opened to reveal Maureen, slim, her streaked blonde bob as aspirationally gamine as ever, beady eyes darting this way and that, thin mouth stretched into a smile, a hand on the string of pearls that crowned her heather twinset.

'Christine! We *all* watched you, darling. You were surprisingly good, although I wasn't sure about your lipstick.' She held the door so Christie could just squeeze through. 'And the dress. A bit revealing but the colour wasn't bad.' She led the way into the sitting room where the only one of the 'all' who was left was Ted Brooks, Maureen's 'gentleman friend', whose right hand enveloped a sherry glass. Not the first of the day, if the colour of his cheeks was anything to judge by.

'Ah, Christie.' He glowed. 'Marvellous show.'

'Thanks, Ted. I was very nervous.' She waited, not wanting to have to prompt either of them to congratulate her on her contribution.

'I say, that Sharon is an attractive woman.' His watery blue eyes misted over, presumably in memory of that spectacular cleavage.

Maureen briskly changed the subject. 'I didn't expect you to know so much about alcohol or men, or to broadcast the fact to the entire nation. Are you looking for a new father for the children? It would have been nice if you'd at least told me first.'

'Oh, Mum, you know I'm not. That was just what they wanted me to talk about so I went along with it. But, anyway, why shouldn't I if the right person came along?' She ignored her mother's raised eyebrow.

23

'I'm not sure I liked everything else you talked about.' Maureen was lemon-lipped as she sat down, smoothing flat her tight catalogue yoga pants as she did so. 'Flatulence!' She could hardly say the word.

Ted laughed. 'Nothing wrong with the occasional farty wallah, Maureen.'

Maureen, pink, continued, 'Or S-E-X.'

'Nothing wrong with that either.'

'Ted, I think that's enough. It's only half past three.' Then she turned back to Christie. 'Alice and Joan left as soon as it had ended. I didn't really know what to say to them.'

'But did you think I was all right?' Christie could wait no longer, dying to hear that she had been, that her mother was proud of her. As the distance between her and the *Tart Talk* studio had grown, she had begun to piece together snippets of the show, remembering that, as the audience listened to her and laughed with her, her confidence had grown until she had become as opinionated and outspoken as the others. Being in front of a live audience was a quite different experience from recording her prepared or OB pieces for *MarketForce*. What was more, she had loved the whole experience of throwing round opinions with like-minded women and, for the first time in a long time, being herself. Not just mum, daughter, sister, widow.

'Well, yes. But you could do so much better.'

'For God's sake, Mum!' Christie experienced an overwhelming urge to smash one of her mother's precious collection of Lladro figurines into the immaculate tiled fireplace piled with artificial coal. 'What's happened to you? You've got so narrow-minded.

These are the sort of subjects that should be talked about openly. Mourning, dating, farting and drinking.'

Maureen visibly recoiled.

'Weird mix, I grant you. But we all do them.'

'I'm not sure everyone in the village would agree with you, dear.'

'Of course they wouldn't. They're stuck in the dark ages.'

'Will you be on again?' Ted asked, his eyes slightly unfocused as he lay back in the neat chintz-upholstered sofa that, like him, had seen better days.

'Oh, Ted! I think Christine's destined for higher things, don't you?'

'You're impossible, Mum. I came round hoping you'd have enjoyed the show – or that at least you'd say you had. And I've no idea whether I'll be asked on again. Probably not, if they felt the same about my lipstick as you did!' Christie stood up and crossed the room, dodging the occasional tables with their coasters and empty teacups, the only reminders of the disapproving audience of Alice and Joan.

'Now, Christine. Please don't show off in front of Ted.' Maureen's reprimand turned to alarm as she realised Christie was making for the door. 'Where are you going? Have you had anything to eat?'

Her mother always grabbed any opportunity to press food on her visitors. That was her *raison d'être*, and didn't Ted know it, Christie thought, glancing at the checked waistcoat that pulled across his rotund stomach – currently filled with Maureen's 'tiffin', as former ex-pat Ted liked to call it – then feeling ashamed of her lack of charity. They made each other happy in their own way and that was what mattered.

'Home. And I'm not hungry, thanks. I've got to get there before Fred and Libby get back from school. I'll let myself out. 'Bye.'

As she climbed into her car, Christie was fuming. However hard she tried to please Maureen, she never quite managed to reach the high standards expected of her, the elder child. But a word or two of encouragement wasn't asking much, was it? That was something her father had never failed to give either her or Mel. Maureen had always been harder to please. She must realise that being asked to appear on *Tart Talk* was a positive step forward from writing for the *Daily News*, a paper with a dwindling circulation and a new slash-and-burn editor. But Maureen's horizons had been limited by living in the sticks. Christie shuddered as she foresaw the same thing happening to her. Like mother, like daughter? Not if she could help it. She retuned the car radio to Radio 1.

As she turned into her driveway, singing loudly to the Kaiser Chiefs' 'Ruby' she stopped the car and looked at her home: a proper double-fronted house, its bricks a warm red in the spring sunshine, its windows glinting, especially the large ox-eye above the front door that let light flood onto the landing upstairs. She remembered the day they'd arrived, when she had felt so angry with Nick for not being alive to help her with the move, the fuse boxes, the over-excited children and the bloody DVD player. That night, after Libby and Fred had gone to bed, she had opened a bottle of wine, poured the first glass and sobbed. The next day, she had woken up, ignored the booze-induced headache and unpacked the silver frame with her favourite photo of Nick. In it, he stood squinting slightly into the sun, with the *campo* of Siena behind him. With the children to help, she had chosen to put him in pride of place on a side table in the sitting room where they would see him every day.

As she parked, she made a mental note to re-pot last year's pansies and geraniums that were straggly and half dead by the front door. Letting herself in, she dumped her bag on the hall chair and marched into the long kitchen. This was the one room on which she had splashed the money she'd had left over from buying the house, knowing it would be the heart of the home where the three of them would spend most time together. She'd had the grimy old kitchen units replaced with neat off-white cupboards, oak worktops, a heavy porcelain sink. The chimney-breast had been taken out to make space for the second-hand Aga, something Christie had always lusted after, its blue echoed in the check curtains. In the centre, an island provided an extra work area, with a two-ring gas hob for emergencies.

At the opposite end of the room a battered old sofa sat under an old school clock, but it was the long oak refectory table she had bought at auction that dominated. This was where every-thing and anything got done, be it eating, drinking, homework, painting, making things, chatting or good old family arguing. The windows and french windows on the long wall opposite the Aga gave onto the well-stocked if increasingly disordered garden. Whenever she came into the kitchen, looked at the kids' pictures framed on the walls, heard the thrum of the Aga and the hum of the large fridge (second-hand again), Christie always experienced a frisson of pleasure. This was home, and Nick would have loved it.

The clock told her she had half an hour before the kids were dropped by the school bus at the end of the drive: half an hour in which to put the kettle on for a cup of tea before getting supper on the go. Still infuriated by the way Maureen had managed to pour cold water on her mood and her achievement, she began to sort out the recyclable rubbish for collection. To hell with it! With a savage pleasure, she hurled the lot into one bag and dumped it outside the back door, delighting in the knowledge of how outraged Maureen would be if she found out. Going back inside, she sneaked a packet of blue Silk Cut from the glasses cupboard on the wall above the worktop, pulled one out and put it between her lips. Flicking the gas lighter for the hob, she lit it and took a drag. She opened the french windows and blew the smoke into the warm spring air. Loathing but relishing every last puff, her head swam as she pictured her mother's disgusted face. Tough shit. This is the new Christie Lynch: fearless, hard-working and top mum.

Expecting food, Mrs Harbord and Mrs Shrager, her two speckled Sussex chickens, ran to greet her. She had given in to the children's pleas and bought them as Easter presents. They watched her for a second, their busy button eyes reminding her of Maureen's. Disappointed when no grub was forthcoming, they walked very precisely over to the flowerbed, looking as if they were wearing new shoes and didn't want to get chewing gum stuck to the soles. They wiggled down into a dust bath, sending up a small cloud of dirt as they fussed and flurried their feathers. Leaving them to it, Christie stepped outside. Her garden had been tended lovingly by the previous owner but now Mother Nature had woven a natural magic all of her own.

As she wandered, she went through the pros and cons of work. Should she stay with the paper she'd come to hate? The list of pros was pitifully short. She liked the deputy features editor. That wasn't enough. Her days of investigating and exposing dodgy businessmen were long gone. The paper had been moving downmarket in a bid to increase its circulation and it was becoming clear that Christie's style and character were no longer such a close fit. As a result, the commissions were becoming less frequent as the younger freelancers were given the jobs.

In some respects, that had come as a relief. After all, there were only so many bread-makers, bicycles and dishwashers a woman could compare without going round the bend. Her last two budget assignments had been fish slices and cat food. She sighed. There must be more to life. Occasionally she got thrown the odd family piece, such as when she, Libby and Fred had trialled a low-cost holiday weekend in Llandudno (never the Maldives, of course) or a celebrity-oriented feature that no one else wanted, but her heart was never in them. They certainly didn't give her anything like the adrenalin high she had felt that morning on *Tart Talk*. They paid the bills but had no impact on the bank loan Nick had left her. Moreover, she still missed the headiness of the early days of *MarketForce* when she had worked in a more investigative arena and was able to exercise her brain. When she attempted to move into writing more meaty opinion pieces that would demand research, suggesting as possible topics the anonymity of rape victims or the future of inner-city children excluded from school, she had been told firmly that the *News* was no longer the paper for that sort of thing. She stopped to pull out a rogue sycamore seedling. Yes, the cons were far outweighing the pros.

If Nick were here, he'd say she had to follow her heart – but he wasn't. And because he wasn't, she had to earn some cash from somewhere so she could sort out her finances and begin to lavish much-needed attention on the house. Besides which, she knew she couldn't/shouldn't let life pass her by. What had happened to the girl who used to make Nick rock with laughter? It was definitely time to give her career a kick-start. If she could do that, everything might change. She thought of Julia's card in her pocket, took it out and read the details: 'White Management: Britain's Number One Talent Agency'. An agent of that calibre wouldn't give out her cards on a mere whim, surely.

She turned it over in her fingers and reached for her mobile. How strange that Fate should have led her to Julia just when she needed her, exactly as it had led her to that first chance encounter with Nick. Perhaps this was a sign. From him?

'Oh, God! I hate weddings.' Christie looked up at the stoic lines of the Victorian church, which sat on a grassy island in Ealing, surrounded by large, graceful Edwardian houses. Overhead, there was enough blue to 'make a pair of cat's pyjamas', as her mother was fond of saying, but the wind had got up, chasing white clouds across the sky. Christie was forced to hold on to her wide-brimmed hat as she progressed with the other guests through the churchyard and into St Stephen's.

As she stepped into the church, the organist was playing something she knew well but couldn't identify. Church music's a little like lift music, she thought, immediately familiar but impossible to name. She caught a whiff of incense, lavender and beeswax, none of them quite overwhelmed by the scent of the lilies that decorated the aisle and pew ends.

This was the third wedding she had been to in almost as many months. She had reached an age when all the girls she knew were getting married – except her, as her mother liked to point out with a sharp little glint. 'Darling Christine. You'll never meet a man unless you try harder. You career women will learn eventually that old age without a man is just . . . old age.'

Christie smiled as she accepted an order of service from a young boy swamped in his hired tailcoat, and went to find a seat. She spotted her sister about halfway down the aisle, sitting at the end of an almost full pew – Mel turned and called Christie's name, the single ostrich plume bouncing wildly in her hair as she waved. A flamboyant fashion-design student, she was everything that her shy, neutral-coloured sister was not.

'Christie, I've saved a seat for you.' She turned to the rest of the pew, encouraging them to shuffle along to make more room. 'Can you squish up? Sorry, what's your name?' she asked the slightly reserved man sitting on her left.

'Nick. Nick Lynch.'

Mel gave him a wide smile. 'Nick! Let me introduce my gorgeous, very single *big sister. If you're on your own, please chat her up and make me happy. If you're not on your own, then point her towards someone who is. It'll make my day! And our mother's, too, because she thinks Christie's destined for spinsterhood.' She stopped for a second to give Christie an encouraging grin. 'Don't look like that, Chris! I'm only trying to help.'*

Embarrassed, Christie smiled an apology at the amused-looking Nick before squeezing into the space that had been made for her. She was hoping Mel would shut up, but her sister was on a roll and there was no stopping her. Now her attention had turned from Christie to the groom, who was standing at his seat in front of the altar, talking to the best man, then turning towards the church door, expectant and nervous.

'I wish I could help him too,' Mel confided in a whisper. 'I wonder if he knows what he's letting himself in for. I was at the hen do

and there was no stone unturned . . . if you know what I mean! Here she comes. The blushing bride – with plenty to blush about.'

A shaft of sunlight suddenly lit the arched doorway and in stepped the bride on the arm of her proud father.

'Bet she's got no knickers on under that dress,' Mel whispered. 'It's her trademark.'

Nick caught Christie's eye over the trembling ostrich feather. He was smiling.

'Mel! Sssh.' Christie stifled the urge to gag her sister and burst out laughing.

'Another good man bites the dust,' Mel insisted. 'That's all I'm saying.'

And with that the organ went into a hosanna of tumbling chords. The groom turned for his first glimpse of his bride, and as their eyes locked, he blushed rather sweetly. She, on the other hand, was grinning like a Cheshire cat. She continued her journey down the aisle, and their mutual gaze never wavered until they were duly joined in holy matrimony.

The reception in a nearby hotel was long and dull. The photos had taken for ever and the food as long again to make an appearance. Christie's feet were aching. She sat in a quiet corner of the ballroom and looked at her watch. When would be the right moment to slip away without being rude? She hoped she could make her excuses before the disco hell began. She spotted Mel and beckoned her over. 'Mel, I've got to go in a minute. I have to make an early start on a piece I'm writing for the News. *It has to be in on Monday and—'*

'Oh, please stay a bit longer, you party pooper. You know Mum'll

grill me tomorrow. "Who did Christine talk to?" "Did she dance with anyone nice?" "What are we going to do with her?"' Mel impersonated her mother's elocuted voice perfectly. Christie giggled but still kissed her sister goodbye and, with promises of phone calls and a takeaway during the week, slipped into the gathering gloom of the car park.

As she fumbled for her keys, she dropped her new handbag, spilling its contents onto the tarmac. Crouching to pick them up, she was aware of another person bending to help her. She turned and looked straight into the eyes of the man she had met in the church: Nick Lynch.

'Hello, again. Your sister tried to introduce us before the service and I completely failed to chat you up. I'm Nick.'

'Thank God you didn't. I'd have been mortified. I'm so sorry.' She picked up her purse and her keys, while he grabbed her makeup bag. 'I'm Christie. Please ignore Mel. She's quite mad and the doctors don't often allow her out, but you know how lax security can be!'

They both laughed and then, in the silence that followed, Christie took in his face. Nice. Not too good-looking but pleasant with wide blue eyes, brown curly hair, broad cheeks and a slight dimple in his chin. He was a couple of inches taller than her and stockily built, but maybe that was his morning suit.

And he looked at her too. Later he would tell everyone it was love at first sight but in truth, even though he fought a strong compulsion to kiss her there and then, it took a few walks in the park, cups of coffee and dinners with friends for them to be absolutely certain that they were meant to be together.

4

'Julia's ready for you. Follow me.'

Christie stood up, straightened her jacket and followed Julia's PA, who had introduced herself as Lily Watson-Fellows – 'Call me Lily' – out of the plush reception area. They left behind the frenetic atmosphere created by two receptionists, who were buzzing about, answering phones and furiously typing, and entered the silence of a long corridor. The first door on the right was labelled 'Lenny Chow'. Inside the small, no-frills office, lined with shelves crowded with bulging files, a shirt-sleeved Chinese man of about forty was tapping at a calculator and making notes on his screen.

'That's Lenny, our accountant,' Lily said, in passing. 'He's indispensable and sorts out the money side of things for the agency.'

Lenny looked up and smiled at Christie through his wire-framed glasses. 'Hallo.'

'Hallo,' she replied, taking in his open, happy expression and his slicked-back black hair. This was a face that said integrity and duty, she thought. However, she couldn't but notice his nails were bitten to the quick.

'*Ciao*, Mr Chow.' Lily laughed.

Christie transferred her attention to the framed glossy photographs of White Management clients that hung on the walls. Most of them were household names, actors and presenters, often in the company of a perfectly groomed and always beaming Julia Keen – a hand on a shoulder, sharing a joke, deep in conversation – clearly a woman with a wardrobe, not to mention a roll-call of A-list talent. After passing Lily's cupboard of an office, Christie was shown into an elegant white room with a plush air-force-blue carpet and two walls of floor-to-ceiling windows that gave a spectacular view across the glittering Thames to beyond the London Eye. On the other two there were more photos, framed front covers of *Broadcast* and *Stage & TV Today* and an in-depth profile of Julia from the *Observer*.

'Sit down, darling.' Julia gestured at the black leather sofa opposite a low, round, glass coffee-table where one white orchid arched in solitary splendour. 'Coffee?'

When Lily had been dispatched to get *caffè latte* for Christie and water for Julia, the agent emerged from behind her preternaturally tidy desk. She was dressed as immaculately as the last time they had met, this time in a drop-waisted coffee-coloured jersey dress that spoke designer, though Christie had no idea which one. Her feet were encased in spike-heeled suede ankle boots and a short fur jacket was slung over her shoulders. Christie felt rather understated in her jeans with last year's black jacket over a plain white shirt. Julia brought with her the distinctive scent of Prada Cuir Ambre – smoky leather and scary.

'Now, what can we do with you, I wonder,' Julia spoke almost to herself.

'That's what I'm hoping you'll tell me.' Christie refused to let herself feel intimidated. Whatever Julia had to say to her, she would hold her own.

Julia gave a brusque laugh to show she'd heard, but she was obviously more preoccupied by her own thought processes. 'You know,' she began tentatively, 'I think you've got real potential as a live on-air presenter. Your appearance on *Tart Talk* was very well judged. As you gained confidence, the audience responded well to you. I liked that.' She was focused on the nail of her left index finger, which she was slowly stroking with her right thumb. 'You're intelligent and express yourself well. That's important.'

'Thank you.' High praise indeed.

Julia shifted her gaze to Christie. 'And you look good too. The camera likes you and that's crucial in this business. And you're not the average female presenter. A young widow. Two children. Juggling the work-life balance.'

Christie felt herself melting under the other woman's attention. Julia had the invaluable knack of making a person feel as if they were the only one in the world who mattered while they were with her.

'In the first place, let me see if we can get you more appearances on *Tart Talk* to help you find your feet. Then I'll put out some feelers. There's a couple of people I think you should meet.'

'That would be wonderful.' Christie couldn't believe this was happening. To be taken so seriously by such a big player in the entertainment industry was more than she had dared hope for. Several of Julia's clients had been quoted publicly, crediting her with their success. Just a little of that would be enough. Despite the speed with which Julia had agreed to see her, she had still half expected a polite brush-off.

Within a few minutes the meeting was over, bar a rapid summary of the formal terms of any agreement between them. Julia rapped them out too quickly for Christie to take in the minutiae but she did catch her commission rates: ten per cent on all of Christie's media work ('Your bread and butter, darling') and fifteen per cent on any commercial work, personal appearances, conferences, endorsements . . . that sort of thing ('The very welcome jam').

'Is there some kind of formal written contract between us?' Christie realised how naïve she must sound but wanted to be clear.

Julia gave a little laugh. 'No, no. Nothing like that. Just a simple gentleman's agreement based on trust. So much easier. My clients all have complete faith in me. The payment for any work I secure for you is sent to me and I take my percentage. The rest is paid directly into your bank and a remittance slip supplied for your accountant.' She looked up at Christie. 'Do you have any problems with that?'

Christie allowed a micro-second to elapse as she absorbed what had been said. 'No, of course not. But I'd appreciate you sending me a note confirming it, just in case I've missed anything.'

Julia gave her a wintry smile.

The following morning Julia phoned to say again how thrilled she was to be representing Christie and promised to get to work on her behalf immediately. Christie was stunned that Julia had taken time out of her busy schedule to call. This was it. Now it was up to her to be worthy of her new agent. If only Maureen could be as supportive. Had Nick sent Julia to be her champion? To do what he no longer could?

Their arrangement paid dividends immediately. *Tart Talk* wanted more of her, and within a couple of months, Christie was beginning to feel like an old hand at the presenting game. Even more reassuring, she was rediscovering a side of herself that had withdrawn from public since Nick's death. A Christie who was more confident, funny, unafraid to voice her opinions or even to shock her mother (which Mel found hysterical) was coming out of the shadows. She had begun to look forward to the mornings when she was picked up by a driver and whisked to the studio for eight thirty. In the production meeting, she swigged her Starbucks with the other presenters as they laughed and chatted their way towards an agenda for that day's show. As her confidence grew, she had established her own character within the group: potential best-friend material, who talked an edgy sort of sense. Sometimes the others ribbed her for being a bit old-fashioned, and she still regretted the day she had risen to the bait, announcing, 'I have *been* to Agent Provocateur, you know. There's more to me than meets the eye.' On air, too. The girls had never let her forget it.

The practical benefit was that her bank balance was healthier than it had been in months – well, years, if she was honest. Earning three hundred pounds an appearance meant she had been able to make small inroads into Nick's bank loan and, with

Julia's assurances of more work to come, had found a local builder to give a price for the collapsing conservatory, the leaking roof and the wonky chimney. When they were fixed, she would move on to the long-awaited overhaul of the plumbing and central-heating – last winter, scraping ice off the inside of the windows had been no fun – and finally she'd be able to get down to redecorating the rooms.

Maureen, meanwhile, had come to accept that this was the career path her daughter had adopted for now. She had even been known to accept the odd compliment on Christie's behalf in the village high street. Christie had once or twice noticed someone in the supermarket glance at her in recognition, and felt the satisfaction of doing a good job and knowing people liked her for it.

But at the beginning of July, *Tart Talk* was coming off air for eight weeks over the school holidays. Although not a proper regular on the show, Christie had come to look forward to her appearances, even to scything through Mel's wardrobe – and, of course, to the much-needed income. She was unsure what she was going to do, bereft of all three.

*

One morning, Christie was in the kitchen with her second cup of coffee. She had left the kids at school an hour earlier, Libby complaining that she needed a new pair of Ugg boots ('In the summer?' asked Christie) and arguing that she didn't want a haircut on Friday and, no, her skirt was not too short. Fred, in contrast, was itching to get stuck into the kick-about going on in the playground with his mates. How much less complicated a boy's childhood was, Christie reflected as she cleared the draining-board.

Of course, she ought to have been writing the piece she was compiling on celebrities who suffered from bipolar disorder – she'd put it off for so long that the deadline was in danger of whizzing by her – but every time she got a new commission from the *Daily News* these days, she found it harder to galvanise herself. Christie wasn't interested in bitching about the latest breed of female celebrities and the editor knew that. Her days at the *News* were definitely numbered. The only question was whether she or they would cut ties first. Her only regular income came from her new 'Straight from the Heart' column for *Woman & Family* magazine: a nice little earner, courtesy of Julia. But with *Tart Talk* off the air and no certainty that she'd be asked back, she prayed that Julia would get her something else. She needed the security of knowing she had more guaranteed TV work.

Still putting off going to her laptop, finding any displacement activity more appealing than writing the bipolar piece, she idly turned the pages of the *News*. Her attention was caught by the TV7 logo. The headline screamed 'NOT ONE, NOT TWO, BUT THREE FOR G'. Gilly Lancaster, the glamorous co-presenter of *Good Evening Britain*, the nightly news programme, was having triplets.

Her absence will be another blow for the popular programme, which was hit almost a year ago by the death of handsome anchorman Ben Chapman (34). He was found in the indoor

41

swimming-pool of über-agent Julia Keen's (49) luxury weekend hideaway. After the verdict of accidental death, Gilly was supported by TV bosses and viewers and has taken the show to the top of the ratings. When she'll start her maternity leave is to be announced, but TV7 will be looking for a replacement. Who will take over? Gilly says she will be back on the show as soon as possible and in the meantime is delighted and looking forward to giving her husband the family they have longed for. She is 35. (How dangerous is a multiple birth in elderly women? Pages 23 and 24.)

Christie remembered again the swimming-pool incident, which had been all over the papers. A tragedy for Ben's family, but it must have been very difficult for Julia, too. Not only the accident itself but the inevitable press speculation surrounding it must have damaged her reputation in some quarters. Despite her weepy denials, there had been definite suggestions that the client-agent relationship had developed into something less than professional. Having met Julia now, she had only admiration for the way her agent seemed to have weathered the storm and apparently not let the tragedy affect her, personally or professionally. What strength of character she must have. Christie shut the paper and went upstairs.

She opened the door to her study and, as always, felt a special calm overtake her. This was her sanctuary, her private room. The faded floral wallpaper was peeling from the cornices, one of the walls smudged brown by a large patch of damp. Nick's colleagues had given her the Edwardian mahogany desk at which he had worked. On either side of the knee-hole there were four pedestal drawers with brass handles, and on the rectangular moulded top there was a worn red-leather writing insert. She liked the idea of her elbows resting where his had, her knees filling his space. Above her lap there was a longer drawer that she filled with postcards and cards she thought might one day be useful. Behind her stood an old leather chair and a filing cabinet, its surface ringed with coffee-mug marks.

The July sun warmed her face as she sat down and looked across the garden to the fields beyond. She glanced up at the curtain-free metal rings on the brass rail above the window, then at the bookshelves to her left, which were filled with favourite novels, mostly by the crime-writers to whom she'd become addicted after Nick's death. She found that losing herself as she unravelled one plot-twisting mystery after another removed her from her grief. A couple of years on, she took as much if not more pleasure from them. In front of the books she had placed her treasures: the cribs from the tops of the children's christening cakes, a tiny toy cat in a basket given to her by Libby, a plastic Superman from Fred, and several Fimo figures they'd made together.

On the wall to her right hung a large picture that she and Nick had found when they were on holiday in the Limousin. Sunshine cut through two rows of sentinel-straight trees that flanked a country road, similar to so many they'd driven along. Beside it, there was a wedding photograph with a scribbled note from Nick stuck to the frame: *The happiest day of my life. Love you. N.*

She pulled out a tartan biscuit tin from the top left drawer of the desk. Inside were all the other love notes that Nick had written to her. When he was alive, she'd find them pinned to the back of a cushion, under her pillow, in her purse, among the cutlery in the kitchen drawer, fluttering from the pages of a book. Just a few words that often meant so much. She touched them, imagining his fingers on them once, as hers were now. She shut the lid, returned the box to the drawer and switched on her laptop.

Two hours later, having delved into the bipolar psyches of five lesser celebs, she was feeling rather manic-depressive herself. She'd made a passable stab at the feature but would polish it up the following morning – right now she wanted to get to school in time to talk to Fred's teacher about his total lack of interest in reading. Libby had rarely been seen without a book on the go when she was Fred's age but he was only happy with a football. Was that boys? Or did he have a problem she hadn't recognised?

Just as she was switching off her laptop, the phone rang. She didn't have a chance to say more than 'Hallo,' before she heard, 'Christie Lynch? Janey Smythe here. I'm Jack Bradbury's PA from TV7. He's asked me to arrange lunch with you at the Ivy on Thursday. I know it's short notice but could you manage that?'

Christie was astonished by the unlooked-for invitation. Why would TV7's director of programmes want to see her? She had only met Jack Bradbury once at *Tart Talk*'s wrap party, and was sure she hadn't made much of an impression. Presumably he wanted to talk about the show, but why? Julia hadn't mentioned anything and the producer, Helen, had always been the person who'd liaised directly with her. She thought quickly and decided it was politic to accept. 'Of course. That would be lovely. Thank you.'

Was she doing anything on Thursday? She couldn't remember. But, whatever, she'd cancel it. She didn't want to jeopardise any chance she had of returning to the new season of the show.

'One o'clock, then.' And Janey Smythe had gone.

Christie sat down at her desk again and stared out of the window, past the trampoline and the horse-chestnut trees to the field beyond, where sheep grazed contentedly in the sunshine. Why would Jack Bradbury want to see her? She was hardly more than an ant in his world. She picked up the phone again and dialled White Management. She was put straight through to Julia.

'Jack Bradbury's invited me to lunch at the Ivy.'

'Ah.' Christie detected a note of surprise that almost immediately vanished, as Julia continued, 'I've been telling him to call you for ages and at last my hard work's paying off. They all listen to their auntie Julia in the end. Would you like me to come for support? I can always get the best table.'

'His PA said she was making the booking.' Was that a snort of annoyance she heard? 'But I'll be fine on my own. I just wondered if you knew what was behind it.'

'I've got an inkling . . .' She clearly had no such thing and was as taken aback as Christie by the invitation. But she recovered herself quickly. 'If my plans come off this could be very good for you. Just make sure you look your best.' Christie didn't rise to the veiled insult about her dress sense. 'And don't talk too much about your dead husband. Jack likes people to be upbeat. Tell him how much you love *Tart Talk* and want to build your TV career, where you see yourself going. Be confident and positive and flirt with him – he'll respond to that. Of course, him being aware that you've already got me on side will help. He'll tell me how you did.'

Christie was beginning to feel like a five-year-old being prepped for an interview at a new school. However, she respected what Julia had to say, so heard her out without objecting. Eventually she hung up, none the wiser about the reason behind the invitation. She would have to wait until Thursday. But waiting didn't come easy to her. She had never managed to conquer that sense of nervous anticipation – especially before the more momentous events in her life. It was as if she had a sixth sense that something important was about to happen.

Waiting for the doorbell to ring, Christie's stomach was churning.
She remembered how, after dropping the entire contents of her
handbag at Nick's feet, he had produced his business card and
handed it to her with a smile.

'I owe your sister a chance to chat you up so if you feel like it
give me a ring.'

They shook hands and laughed again before getting into their
respective cars and driving off.

Mel was thrilled when Christie told her. 'God knows what he's
like, Chris, but he's a lawyer so Mum will love him. Serial killer
or not, go for it.'

Her sister stood over her while Christie dialled his number.
Expecting the voice of a secretary, she was surprised when Nick
answered. 'Christie, how good to hear from you. I was worried
you might think I was a serial killer or something.'

Mel, who was sharing the receiver, gave a thumbs-up. 'Sense
of humour! Good sign,' she whispered.

Nick continued, 'I don't want you to think I give my card to
every beautiful woman I meet.'

Mel pretended to swoon.

'In fact, you're the first. Was that very presumptuous of me?'

Christie wrenched the phone from Mel's grip, and sat on the sofa. 'Of course not. Do you think I'm too forward ringing you well before the designated "Thou shalt not ring back for seventy-two hours" rule?'

'Of course not! OK – so what are you doing tonight?'

'Play it cool. Play it cool,' mouthed Mel, who had picked up the cordless extension from her bedroom and was sitting next to Christie.

'Nothing. Free as a bird.'

Mel thumped her forehead with a palm, and Christie stuck out her tongue at her.

'Great. Where are you and what time shall I pick you up?' After he had written down her address and phone number they hung up.

Mel was bouncing up and down with excitement. 'You're going to have to tell me everything the minute you get home. I won't go to bed till you phone. Otherwise . . . I'll tell Mum.' The worst threat she could muster.

Christie laughed and swiped her sister with a cushion.

The rest of the day dragged. Christie should have written up an article about surfing the net, a fast-growing phenomenon that even Maureen was interested in. Instead she went shopping. There was a small second-hand dress exchange at the end of the road where she found the perfect Armani LBD. At a fraction of its original cost, it was still way over her budget but, how did you dress for a lawyer?

At last it was five to seven and the window of her top-floor flat was open so she could keep leaning out to see if he'd arrived. She'd shaved her legs, washed her hair and was just putting on the last coat of mascara when the doorbell rang. She jumped – and got mascara on her nose. 'Shit, shit, shit.' With a tissue covering the blot she hung out of the window and saw him standing on the steps. 'Coming,' she yelled, then leaped into the bathroom, cleaned herself up and ran downstairs.

They went to a small Greek restaurant off Charlotte Street. All rather clichéd – red and white check tablecloths, candles in retsina bottles and scarlet geraniums on the tables – but special all the same. He told her about his upbringing: only son of a now-retired lawyer and his wife, educated at a state grammar school with an ambition to follow in his father's footsteps. She told him about her darling father, a printer in Fleet Street for thirty-five years who had succumbed to a brain tumour four years earlier. As a little girl she would sometimes go with him to watch the Sunday edition go to press on Saturday night. Maybe those times with him had hooked her to journalism.

It was almost midnight when they got back to her flat. She invited him in for coffee but he declined. As he left he gave her the tenderest of kisses and promised to call in the morning. When she opened her flat door, the phone was ringing. She picked up, knowing exactly who it was.

'Well? Shall I buy a hat?' It was Mel.

5

'Perhaps he's going to offer you a permanent job on *Tart Talk*. Breathe in, for God's sake!' Mel pulled the zip of the dress between Christie's shoulder-blades and up to the top.

Christie had called in at her sister's tiny Chiswick flat on her way to the Ivy, only to be told that the black trouser suit she'd chosen for the occasion was all wrong, too severe.

'I wish. But none of the others have ever talked about leaving.' Christie turned to her, each breath a dangerous test of the seams. 'Is it meant to be this tight?'

'No, it's not. Get it off quick, before it rips. Here.'

As the zip was undone, oxygen flooded back into Christie's lungs and the dress fell to the floor among all the others Mel had suggested and Christie had discarded. Somewhere in the creative chaos of her bedroom Mel was sure she had the perfect outfit. It was just a question of laying her hands on it. Once again, the younger sister had taken charge and picked her way to the wardrobe, saying, 'You may be a brilliant wordsmith, but you have no style at all. You're so lucky I'm here. I finished the *Vogue* shoot yesterday and I'm off to Mauritius on Saturday.' Bags hung off the end of her bed; jewellery was scattered entangled across two bookshelves and the mantelpiece; scarves and belts were draped over the chair back and the open wardrobe door. Wherever a hanger could hang, it did, both inside and outside the wardrobe, off the back of the door and the window frames, all carrying the trophies that came with being a fashion stylist and victim. But Christie's mind wasn't on the mess.

'I only talked to the man for a couple of minutes at the end-of-term party and he didn't seem fabulously impressed by me. Why would he want to meet me again so soon?'

'Maybe so he can get to know you better. What about this glorious Vivienne Westwood? I got it for a shoot the other day and don't have to get it back to her till next week.'

'He's not that type. And that dress definitely isn't mine.' It was a blue and white floral shawl-sleeved wrap with a slightly asymmetrical bodice that would make her stand out far too far in a crowd. Perhaps she should have gone with Maureen's equally ridiculous suggestion of something from Country Casuals.

'Bollocks! Just get it on.'

Christie had always envied the way Mel was so sure of her opinions and never took no for an answer. She supposed that if anyone knew what she should wear to lunch with a head honcho at the Ivy, it ought to be her. She reached reluctantly for the dress.

'You've got to look the bloody part, woman. No one's going to laugh at you. There! It's absolutely perfect.'

'I don't know.' Christie turned in front of the mirror, uncertain. Mel stood behind her, dressed in tight blue jeans and a white T-shirt, assessing her.

'You look like a woman for once! Really great – honestly. I know what.' Mel picked up a large Stella McCartney handbag, dug out from its depths a lipstick and painted her sister's mouth a glossy pale orange. 'The perfect finishing touch. What do you think?'

'No. It is *so* not me.'

'Shut up. Yes, it is.'

Just at that moment the doorbell rang. It was the minicab.

'Get out of here, Cinders.' Mel kissed her cheek. 'And don't worry about the kids – I'll be there when they get home from school. See you later. Love you.'

Christie grabbed a white Joseph jacket that she'd tried on earlier, slipped on her new L. K. Bennett peep-toe wedge sandals and hobbled downstairs.

*

Sitting in the taxi, feeling sick at the driver's inability to brake gently and the prospect of her impending lunch, Christie remembered her first meeting with Jack Bradbury. The room had been packed with people – not because the wrap party was so enormous but because the green room they'd been allotted was so small. At least, it was compared to the one next door where there were huge celebratory shenanigans going on following the recording of an Elton John retrospective. After a couple of drinks, Grace and Sharon had persuaded her that, instead of the warm white wine and cold sausages provided for their party, they deserved something a little more A-list. Together, the three of them had sneaked to the kitchen of Studio One where, unnoticed in the hubbub, they liberated a couple of bottles of Krug and two glass plates of exquisite canapés – sage crostini with duck pâté, crab and asparagus tartlets, summer-vegetable roulades – destined for the dinner-jacketed liggers at Elton's bash. How much more appreciated they'd be by the people of *Tart Talk*.

Returning triumphant, half expecting to be cheered on for their efforts, they discovered the atmosphere in the room had changed during their brief absence. Raucous conversations had dropped to whispers, heads were turned towards the door. There was a definite sense of expectation in the air.

'Jack Bradbury's on his way down.'

Christie wasn't sure what the director of programmes for TV7 did exactly but, judging from everyone's consternation about his arrival, it was obviously not to be underestimated. Before she had time to find out, she caught sight of a newcomer in the room. Not tall, but slender, tanned, with the physique of a good amateur sportsman, Jack Bradbury cut an impressive dash in a superbly tailored Ozwald Boateng suit and, if Grace's whispered aside was right, a Paul Smith tie and shirt. He stood in the centre of the room and spoke: 'I would just like to thank the *Tart Talk* team for a really great run of shows this year. It's not easy to keep coming up with fresh ideas on a daily basis but, somehow, you keep doing it – and not too much over budget.' Light laughter permeated the party. 'So, congratulations, and see you all in the autumn.'

After the applause, he began to work the room, dispensing

charisma to the assembled crowd. As they got used to him being among them, the noise level gradually rose again until, by the time he'd reached Christie, the decibel level was humming.

'I don't think we've met? I'm Jack.' As he leaned forward to shake Christie's hand, he gave her an appraising glance. She caught a whiff of his perfect aftershave, neither too sweet nor overwhelming and certainly rather seductive. She noticed his perfectly squared-off nails and soft hands. His smile was an orthodontist's dream and his eyes were a sharp periwinkle blue. But, curiously, when she looked into them they lacked sex appeal. He might have no idea who she was, but she knew immediately who *he* was: a man who looked after himself, and a vain one.

'I'm Christie Lynch. I've been allowed to join the *Tart Talk* girls several times over the last couple of months as one of the guest presenters.'

'Of course you are. How are you liking it?' As she told him, he had taken a step forward with a gentle leer and placed his hand on the wall behind her, trapping her. She could see Grace and Sharon over his shoulder, laughing loudly, and wished she could be with them. She took a half-step forward in the hope that it would be enough to detach him from the wall, and offered him one of Sir Elton's canapés. The temperature between them dropped.

'No, thanks. Well, delighted to have met you at last. I've heard a lot about you. I'm sure we'll meet again.'

Her two minutes were up – but not before he had tried the Bradbury charm just once more: he held her free hand for a moment longer than necessary and looked her straight in the eye. Then he was off, working the rest of the room with equally meticulous timing.

'Look at him go.' Grace had stepped up beside her. 'There's a man who loves what God and TV7's given him.'

'What do you mean?'

'He makes George Clooney look like someone in need of a Gok Wan make-over, girl. Haven't you heard that he's got an ensuite bathroom in his office? They say it's so he can wash any part of himself if he happens to touch anyone lower than board level. All part of the deal. Just like the cream Daimler with the powder blue interior and Wilton carpet to match his eyes. And I saw you notice them!'

'Yes, in the way a mongoose notices a cobra. He's definitely not my type.'

'He's not anyone's type, darlin'. Nothin' and no one comes between Jack Bradbury and the business.'

'Well, I'm sure he won't notice if we have another drink, then. Let's see if we can persuade another bottle of Krug to find its way in here. Coming?' Putting Jack Bradbury firmly to the back of her memory bank, Christie had rejoined the party. And now, only days later, she was on her way to meet him again.

*

A baking July day and someone had sucked the air out of London. The traffic was crawling through the West End and she was going to be a few minutes late. The uniformed doorman at the Ivy greeted her, apparently oblivious to how hot and bothered she'd become on the way there. Her nerves about the impending lunch meant that she'd chewed off practically all Mel's lipstick. She surreptitiously applied some more in the cool of the lobby without the aid of a mirror and strode through the double doors into the restaurant, hoping she'd got it on straight.

Right, Christie Lynch. This is it, she told herself.

The charming *maître d'* asked her name. She replied, adding, 'I'm meeting Jack Bradbury. TV7?'

'Yes, of course. He's not here yet but let me show you to the table and perhaps you'd like a drink?'

What? Not here yet? She attempted to look her most casual as she walked between the tables, praying not to be shown to one in the middle of the room where everyone could see her. Joan Collins, Christopher Biggins and Peaches Geldof watched idly as she sat at the empty table laid for two just off-centre. They smiled then looked away. She had never felt more conspicuous.

She sat down, thanking God for Mel. The trouser suit would have been entirely inappropriate and far too hot. Toying with a breadstick, she ordered a Bloody Mary to steady her nerves, the perfect drink to disguise the fact that she needed Dutch courage.

As she took her first sip, she looked up at the sound of a familiar voice. Julia! Her agent was being seated – horror of horrors – only two tables away in pole position at the 'best' table in the room. From the back, her male lunch companion could have been any of those TV types – expensive, casual get-up, carefully gelled hair. From the sound of his frequent, eager-to-please laugh, he was young and anxious to impress. Over his shoulder, Julia caught Christie's eye, and inclined her head, giving a conspiratorial wink. Christie couldn't help but be impressed. Julia was clearly one smart woman who had organised her schedule to keep an eye on her new client. Christie welcomed the sense of security it gave her but felt even more on edge. Did Julia think she was incapable of managing this meeting on her own? If so, she was right to be insulted.

After twenty minutes, Christie knew the menu off by heart and was growing increasingly irritated and uncomfortable. Whenever she moved, she imagined Julia's eyes boring into her. When she'd tried to check if Jack had left a voicemail to explain his no-show, a waiter had rushed to her side, explaining no phones were allowed. She could have gone outside, of course, but she couldn't face running the gauntlet of stares again, least of all Julia's. Just as she was debating whether or not to leave, there was a flurry at the door and in stepped her host. He crossed the restaurant, stopping briefly to greet people at various tables, nodding, smiling and exchanging the odd word, then chatting to Julia for what seemed an age. He gave Christie time to assess him again, taking in his charcoal grey couture suit, the neat salt-and-pepper hair, the smugness of his flawless expression, the suspicion of an eyebrow wax. Finally he joined her, apologising for his lateness. Feeling more insignificant than she had thought possible, she tried to brush off his apology as if she hadn't even noticed the time.

He sat down and cut straight to the chase. 'Now, how long have you been with us?' He smiled, as if to encourage her.

'Only a couple of months or so.'

'Of course. I've been following your work for a while, you know, as well as watching you develop as a presenter.'

She had to hand it to him, he was as smooth as a snake. Did he really think she'd believe he'd ever watched *MarketForce*, let alone read her pieces in the *Daily News*? However, she couldn't help feeling intrigued and flattered by his attention. The waiter had materialised beside them, order pad in hand. Christie had decided to plump for the crispy duck and watercress salad then the halibut, but Jack surprised her by ordering for them both.

'I'll have my usual and my guest will have the same.'

She wasn't entirely sure that she was as impressed as he might have wanted her to be by this masterly approach that denied her what she wanted.

Within the snap of a finger, two flutes of perfectly chilled champagne were placed on the table. Another snap and there in front of them was a bowl of crushed ice with a tiny bowl of caviar on top, surrounded by blinis, sour cream, finely diced boiled egg, parsley and chopped shallots. Tiny mother-of-pearl spoons were placed on the table beside them. Christie tried to hide her surprise, having registered the price on the menu.

As they ate, Jack asked the questions, making her feel like the only woman in the restaurant as he focused entirely on her. His first was one Julia had warned he might ask: 'Where do you see yourself in five years?' He leaned forward, inviting her confidence.

Better bold than not, she decided. 'Oh, I've got my sights on the director-generalship.'

He smiled, and this time it did reach his eyes. He changed tack. 'Do you believe in heaven or hell?'

This is surreal, she thought, trying to find an answer that might appeal to him but only landing on, 'No.'

She didn't want to share with him the doubts she'd experienced after Nick's death that had forced her to question so many things in her life. As they continued, she remembered Julia's advice and remained positive and confident, aware that her agent's no doubt eagle ear might be trained on her. Jack went on to mention the features she'd presented on the show and how much he'd liked her contribution. 'You look the part and you've got an assurance that makes the viewers feel comfortable and included.' So he must have watched after all, even if it was only on DVD in preparation for this lunch. Either that, or Julia had done her job supremely well. Christie certainly wasn't going to admit to being anything other than the person he had seen or been told about.

As she began to relax, feeling she had got his measure at last, he said, 'Tell me, what do you think of TV7?'

That was fine: she'd rehearsed her answer the previous night in the bath. She was about to reply when he continued: 'Do you see the channel as a man or a woman? I mean . . . which characteristics do you think they share?'

My God! What was the man on? Julia was giving no sign of having heard a word of the conversation. Christie was on her own, all too aware she mustn't say the wrong thing. She thought for a split second, then looked deep into those blue eyes and said, 'Oh, a man, I think. It's smart, has achieved a lot in a short time and charms both men and women. A sort of male Marilyn Monroe, if you like.'

Jack beamed and nodded, clearly identifying himself with the channel. She refused the last blini and, while he ate it, indulged in guessing what the mystery second course would be. But instead, a moment after they'd emptied their plates, he called over the waiter and asked for the bill. So that was how he kept so trim. Bloody hell, she was starving! Hoping she still had the KitKat in the glove compartment of her car, she heard him say, 'I'd like you to come to the studio next week to see how *Good Evening Britain* is put together. I want to try a completely new face as a foil to Sam Abbott, who's taking over as main anchor while Gilly Lancaster's on maternity leave. I take it you've watched the show?'

Stunned into near silence, she hurriedly assured him she had. Who hadn't? *Good Evening Britain* was fast becoming a TV legend: a programme filled with warmth and humour while unafraid to tackle the big news agenda.

'Good, good. Gilly's leaving in a few weeks, so we need to see how you look on camera in the studio and whether you can read the autocue and manage the talkback. Quite simple. I'm sure you'll manage superbly. I'll ask Janey to call your agent with the details.'

She nodded her agreement. Just wait until Mel and Maureen heard about this. Julia too.

Jack leaned over the table and touched her hand with the

extreme tip of one finger. In a low, conspiratorial voice, he said, 'I've got to go, Christie. My car's waiting. We'll be in touch.' With that, he left.

Christie sat still in the centre of the room, feeling very alone and wondering what to do next. She reached for her handbag and was about to rise from her seat, when she froze at the sight of Julia steaming towards her. Julia's guest had dematerialised – they must have finished their meal already – and she was nodding right and left, ensuring that most eyes were on her. Her blouse was crisp and her figure-hugging Prada skirt had not one wrinkle. She settled herself at Christie's table, signalled to the waiter to clear away the remains of the lunch and ordered two double espressos. Then she smiled professionally at the speechless Christie.

'Now, Christie,' she asked, 'how did that go?'

6

Two hours later, Christie arrived home, starving and elated. Walking through the front door, she was overwhelmed by the unmistakable smell of over-fried onions and burning beef-burgers. Her appetite instantly became a thing of the past. There was only one person she knew who could cook something so simple so badly.

'Mel!'

Her sister was oblivious to everything as she jigged in front of the grill, a wooden spoon her microphone, swishing her apron can-can style over her jeans and wailing like a banshee. She had never let her family's frequent criticisms of her voice put her off belting out a good song.

'Mel!' Christie shouted again, this time grabbing the oven gloves from her sister's shoulder and swatting them at her waist.

Mel jumped round, the alarm on her face giving way to a grin. 'For God's sake, woman. Give me a heart attack, why don't you?' She turned to the iPod dock and lowered the volume, eager for Christie's news. 'What happened? Tell all. What did he want?'

'Hang on a minute.' Christie slowed her down. 'Where are

the kids? I asked you to give them a decent meal, not a few charred scraps.'

'They'll love it. It's not as bad as it looks. Really. Fred won't even notice because his mate Olly's here.' Mel flipped an unpleasantly blackened burger and thrust it back under the grill. 'They're outside on the trampoline and Libby's in her room, *comme toujours*.'

At that moment, Libby skulked into the kitchen and presented herself to Christie for a hallo kiss. She stared at the hamburgers and wrinkled her nose. 'Yeuch – what *is* that?'

'Libby!' Christie sympathised but had to draw the line at insolence. 'Don't be so rude. Mel's very kind to come over so that I could go out. Why don't you help by laying the table?'

Looking as if every movement was a huge effort, Libby took the knives and forks from the drawer and flung them in the direction of the mats before banging down four glasses.

'I'm sure it'll be delicious,' Christie said, as encouragement.

'Yeah, right.' Clearly sensing that her mother agreed with her, Libby added, 'Thanks, Auntie Mel. Laters.' Before anyone could say anything else, she slipped out of the room and upstairs.

Mel was unperturbed. 'What do you think of these?' She lifted a foot, rotating her ankle to show off a pair of pale grey ankle boots.

'Very practical,' Christie observed caustically, before pulling out a stool and settling herself in a position where she could supervise the last of Mel's culinary efforts, which was to open a tin of baked beans. But she couldn't contain herself any longer. 'Right. Want to hear my news?'

'Yes, yes, yes!' Mel sang, anticipation written across her face. 'Please. Every possible scenario has gone through my mind since you left this morning from the white slave trade to Jack Bradbury falling madly in love with you and proposing. I can't bear it another minute. Tell me!' She shouted the last two words.

'He only wants me to test as a replacement for Gilly Lancaster on *Good Evening Britain*.' Christie's voice rose to a shriek of excitement as Mel flung her arms round her, squeezing her till she could hardly breathe, the baked beans forgotten.

'I knew it! You'll be the best presenter ever and I'll make it as your brilliant personal stylist.' Mel was laughing. 'Let's celebrate. I snuck a little something into the fridge just in case.' She opened its door and pulled out a bottle. Christie watched her, touched by her sister's support. Then, while Christie went to the cupboard for two glasses, ignoring the temptation of her secret cigarette stash, Mel set about opening the *cava*. Just as the cork shot into the air, there was a tap at the door.

'Is this a private celebration? Or can anyone join in?'

Afterwards, Christie would remember the apparent dislocation of Mel's jaw as her eyes took in the outdoor type standing at the back door. He was wearing khaki fatigues topped by a checked shirt, open at the neck and with rolled-up sleeves. Tall with dark curly hair, square-jawed with high cheekbones and wide brown eyes, he was a dead ringer for one of those rugged models in the mail-order catalogues that kept dropping through the letterbox.

'Richard! Come in.' Christie waved a champagne glass at him. 'Meet Mel, my sister. We don't normally drink so early but this is special.'

'She's about to take the world of TV by storm.' Mel was exultant as she put her hand on Christie's shoulder.

'How exciting! Don't let me stop you.' Richard hesitated, then stepped into the kitchen. 'I've come for Olly. Sorry I'm early but I finished work so I thought I'd come straight over.'

'Mel, could you go and see what those boys are up to?' Christie asked, and Mel, giving her sister a knowing look, obligingly disappeared into the garden. 'Won't you have a drink while they have supper? It's just about ready.'

When he accepted, she led the way into the sitting room. The last thing she wanted was the embarrassment of him witnessing the burned offering that Mel was about to serve up to his son.

Olly and Fred had been number-one friends ever since Fred had come home from school and told her he had felt sorry for a new boy standing alone in the playground and had asked him to play. Her heart had swollen with pride at this evidence of her son's generous spirit. Since then, she had occasionally seen Richard at the school gates where she was aware he had set several mums' hearts beating faster. And with some reason, she thought, as he made himself comfortable on the sofa. A good-looking man with an air of mystery was bound to arouse interest. So far, school-gate gossip had it that he was divorced and had been in the army before recently setting up his own company, some sort of outward-bound executive-training business outside Aylesbury. Olly seemed to shuffle happily between Richard and his ex-wife, who also lived locally but was seen less often.

She caught him looking out of the window at the garden, still bright in the sunshine. For a moment he seemed lost in a daydream but, abruptly, he snapped back into the present. 'So, can I ask how you're planning to take the world of TV by storm? Sounds intriguing.' He put his glass on the coffee-table, before leaning back and waiting for her to speak.

Feeling self-conscious under his gaze, wishing she'd had time to change back into her usual uniform of jeans and top, she gave an awkward laugh. 'I'm afraid Mel was exaggerating. As usual. I've just been invited to try out for a presenting job. It probably won't come to anything.'

'Why on earth not? Be positive.' He lifted his drink and toasted her. 'Here's to your success.'

She smiled back. 'Thanks. To positivity!' And raised her glass.

At that moment there was a shout as two small boys raced into the room, skidding on the large rug. 'Dad, I'm Jenson Button and I've beaten Lewis Hamilton – that's Fred!' Olly squealed to a halt in front of his father, narrowly avoiding Richard's raised glass. His tow-coloured hair was threaded with leaves, his hands and flushed cheeks streaked with mud, his eyes bright with excitement. Bits of grass clung to his sweatshirt.

'No, you're not. My McLaren's much faster than yours.' Just as dishevelled, Fred ran a circuit of the room and disappeared again in the direction of Mel's shout of 'Supper!'

'Easy.' Richard ruffled his son's hair, sending a couple of leaves spiralling to the floor. 'I don't want you to break anything. Remember, this isn't our house where things aren't so precious.'

Looking round the room, Christie looked for something precious. Apart from Nick's photo, there was nothing except the pieces of wonky pottery that Libby had made at school and presented to her with such pride. Seeing it through Richard's eyes, she was suddenly aware of how makeshift the room looked. The furniture – the ancient three-piece, the coffee-table, two battered armchairs, the TV cabinet, a large free-standing bookcase – seemed small, worn and lost in this generous space.

'Is Mummy back yet?' Olly asked his father, with such hope that Christie had to fight the urge to hug him.

'Not yet.' Richard squeezed his son's shoulder. 'We'll ring her when we get home, though. Promise.'

Satisfied with the answer, Olly careered after Fred with a screech of brakes and a roar of engine noise.

'Caro's in Brussels,' Richard explained to Christie. 'She's a translator and is there more often than not these days.'

'Single-parenting's difficult, isn't it?' Christie sympathised.

'Actually, I don't find it that bad,' he contradicted her, with an apologetic smile. 'My work's pretty flexible.'

'I don't think I really know what you do.'

'I put overgrown schoolboys masquerading as company execs through team-building experiences. It's actually great fun and they really get something out of it. So do the women who, I'm happy to report, are very resilient. The farmland and woods we use are a paradise for kids. Fred must come over. In fact, Olly and I are camping out on Saturday night. Do you think Fred'd fancy that?'

'He'd love it. If you're sure.'

'Completely. Two boys are much easier than one. It'll be fun.'

Christie smiled. She'd welcome the opportunity for a bit of bonding time alone with Libby. Her daughter was busy embarking on the terrible teens with gusto and Christie wanted to narrow what sometimes seemed an ever-widening gap between them. Meanwhile, Fred would benefit from being with a substitute father-figure for once. The close adults in his life were all women, with the exception of Maureen's Ted – and he didn't really count. 'Yes, that would be great.'

'That's settled, then. Now tell me about your job.' He sat back again to concentrate on what she had to say.

Basking in his interest, Christie began to describe her lunch. The high that had accompanied her home from the Ivy returned and Richard was soon laughing with her, clearly astonished when she described Julia's presence. 'God! She sounds a bit full-on.'

'She probably goes there all the time.' But Christie felt less breezy than she sounded. 'But her being so near did make me feel a bit uncomfortable.'

'Isn't she the one who was all over the papers at the end of last year? I dimly remember reading about her.'

'That's her. One of her clients was staying with her and she found his body. He was on his own in her pool and must have slipped. A terrible thing.'

'Apart from that, how much do you know about her?' He seemed concerned.

'No more than necessary, and she's certainly not what I'm used to. But then again, everything I'm doing at the moment is not what I'm used to. I'm glad to have someone experienced on my side.'

'This might be teaching my grandmother to suck eggs, but wouldn't it be an idea to find out a little bit more?'

She was exasperated. 'If you met her, you'd see immediately what a shrewd woman she is. Whatever the press may have said about her doesn't make her a bad agent.'

'Well, do you trust her?' he asked, as if making a point.

'Oh, God, yes.' She thought about it, then said firmly, 'I would never have gone with her if I'd had any doubts.'

'I'm sorry. I shouldn't be saying any of this. Of course you wouldn't.'

She could see he thought he'd overstepped the mark. 'Oh, I don't blame you. Really. I know how crazy it sounds. She involves herself far more than I was expecting, but she's done some great things for me already so I can't complain. She'll probably lose interest eventually.'

But Julia's unexpected appearance in the restaurant had set one or two alarm bells ringing in her mind although she couldn't put her finger on why. Had it been coincidence? Or did Julia not trust her to do the right thing on her own? Christie was used to making her own decisions and didn't want to be manipulated or controlled by anyone.

'There you go again. What happened to positivity? She's lucky to have you.' Richard was smiling as he stood up. 'I'd better take that urchin home. But you must let me know what happens.'

'I will.' Christie took him back to the kitchen where Libby was scraping the food from her plate into the bin. Mel looked at Christie and shrugged. Not my fault.

Libby glanced up before putting her plate in the dishwasher. Then she planted a quick kiss on her mother's cheek. 'Got to phone Jasmine. I'll be down later.' Christie recognised the teen-speak for 'I'll be down in a couple of hours when I've rinsed the phone bill' but she didn't rise to it.

When Richard and Olly had left, and Fred had gone to watch a *Simpsons* DVD, Mel and Christie sat together at the kitchen table.

'You might have warned me,' Mel complained. 'I'd have dressed up if I'd known he was going to be here.'

'Who? Richard?'

'Yes!' Mel's voice was loud with disbelief. 'You know – the tall dark handsome apparently single bloke who has just left the house. Don't play the little innocent.'

Christie laughed. 'Oh, stop. It's only Richard. A really nice dad, that's all.' She paused, then said, 'And, anyway, I'm out of the habit of thinking like that about men. There isn't a switch I can just turn on when I want to.'

'Well, try harder. Tune your radar in. Or I'll have to come over more often and make a play for him myself.' Mel rubbed at a splodge of tomato ketchup on her T-shirt. 'I'm sorry about supper. Libby hated it.' She looked downcast, upset to think she might be falling out of favour with her adored niece. 'I'm worried she'll be hungry.'

'Don't. She'll be fine. You're fantastic to come and cover for me and that's all that matters. They like it so much better than when Mum comes.'

'Are you surprised? Elisabeth!' Mel mimicked Maureen exactly, brightening as she did so. 'Eat everything on your plate or you'll have it for lunch tomorrow and I'll keep on giving it to you for every meal until it's finished. For the rest of your life, if necessary.'

They both burst out laughing at their mother's renowned insistence on the proper way of doing things – it was often the butt of their jokes. Then, changing the subject, Christie told the story of her lunch for the second time.

'Wow!' said Mel, when she'd finished. 'That Jack sounds a complete prick. You must be starving. But I bet you get the job. How will you manage it with the kids, though?'

This was the one question Christie had been deliberately ignoring. Her children had always come first but this job would be an opportunity she couldn't pass up. Things would have to change. 'I am worried about that. No self-respecting nanny would want to look after a couple of kids for only a few hours a day and, anyway, that would be incredibly expensive. However nice the salary, I'm still paying off that enormous bloody bank loan.' She hesitated. 'You haven't told Mum, have you?'

'Of course not.' Mel was indignant.

'Thanks. Nick would kill me if he knew I'd even told you. It's sometimes so difficult having to cope with all the stuff that he dealt with. I so wish he was here to help. He'd know what was best for the kids.'

'Why don't you ask Mum?'

'To help out? Do you think she would? I could afford to pay her something. Or do you think she'd feel patronised?'

'Patronage or pin money – either way, you're in trouble. But . . .'

'That's Mum!' they shouted together, and laughed.

'Well, I'll be picked up by a driver every day . . .' she ignored her sister's whoop of glee '. . . about midday, so I could mostly get them up and to school. I'd be in the office at lunchtime and driven home about eight thirty so I'd only need her to be around for a few hours after school. The show goes off-air for most of the Christmas holidays and then my stint's almost over. I'll ring her, tell her about today and then drop a hint or two.'

'Well, you know you can count on me, if I'm not working.' Mel stretched across the table and grasped Christie's hand in a sudden burst of sisterliness.

'Thanks. I know.' Christie squeezed back, not wanting to admit how nervous she was feeling. If she got the job, what would she be letting herself in for? At the same time, she had to acknowledge that her overriding feeling was excitement, as if she was emerging from the shadows into a brave new world where she could be herself again, doing her very best for her family, and where absolutely anything could happen. What a long way she had come since Nick and she had first fallen in love. When he'd made his unexpected proposal of marriage, neither of them could have known what a difficult journey would lie ahead. Those heady days could never be repeated but at least they were safe in her memory for ever.

The drive to the Highlands took two days. They stopped off in the Lakes for a romantic night in Keswick before embarking on the final leg to Nick's parents' house. Ma and Pa. Ma was slim and upright, wearing a good tweed skirt, thick stockings and sensible shoes. She had a voice that was used to the draughts and space of old country houses and she could use her cut-glass tones to great effect when shouting for Pa in the garden. The two Labradors, Blackie and Scottie, adored her and never left her side. Pa was a gentler soul. He liked the garden and his greenhouse, and Antiques Roadshow.

The house was imposing from a distance: turreted and hewn from granite. But, close up, it was quietly falling into disrepair. Pa had bought it when he retired from his law firm in order to give his wife, who was rather further up the social scale than he was, the reward he felt she needed for marrying him in the first place. Nick's parents had done very well over the years with her inheritance and his hard graft, which had taken him from legal assistant to senior partner. He'd invested well but, in their final days, clearly didn't feel like spending anything on repair bills or heating. The house was as cold as the granite it was built from.

As they parked outside the front of the house, Ma and Pa, Blackie and Scottie came out to meet them.

'Nick, my boy. Good to see you, old chap.' Pa pumped Nick's arm. 'And this must be Christie. Welcome, welcome. Good of you to come.' He shook her hand too. 'This is my wife, Elisabeth.'

Christie's hand was taken in a firm but cold handshake. 'I'm so excited to be here,' she enthused. 'What a glorious spot.' Spot? What was she saying? Calling it a spot was like calling Balmoral a mobile home. She stood and took in the three-hundred-and-sixty-degree view. Only two houses, way in the distance, and the narrow potholed road on which they'd travelled. The rest she described later to Mel as 'Scenery! There's just loads and loads of scenery. And sheep. And that's it.'

'Thank you,' Elisabeth said, without apparently moving any part of her face. 'Do come in. I hope you'll be warm enough.'

'I'm sure I'll be fine.' Christie followed her, dying to see what was offered inside. But she wasn't fine. She was frozen. The fire lit in the library where they had tea and Dundee cake was barely glowing. She could almost see her breath on the air. No wonder Nick had packed for the Arctic. Later he showed her to her bedroom. It had a pretty view of the scenery, heather-sprigged wallpaper and a very high but single bed.

'Are we not allowed to sleep together?' she asked, taken aback.

'Ma doesn't approve. But it's much more fun this way. I can come and warm you up a bit later, if you like! Shall I run you a bath? Your lips are going blue.'

She punched his arm.

The bathroom was a perfect example of early-Victorian

plumbing. The enormous, stained bath stood on lion feet. Nick turned on the large brass taps only for there to be a time delay before icy water eventually came through. Ten minutes later, only a couple of inches covered the bottom but at least the water had got hotter and the steam seemed rather exotic so Christie did the best she could to enjoy it while Nick sat on the closed loo lid holding a big but balding bath towel for her. While she went to get dressed, Nick jumped into her water. As she put on as many layers as she'd brought with her, she wondered if anyone would notice that she was wearing two pairs of tights.

Supper was also in the library, where a small card table had been set up and laid by the fire. Elisabeth tottered in and out with bowls of cabbage, carrots and mash and finally a leg of lamb. Nick carved while Pa poured very generous glasses of Scotch for them all. The evening was memorable, and as Christie got to know Ma and Pa, she found them funny and kind. Elisabeth took a little time to weigh her up, but after a couple of hours she picked up her glass and made a toast: 'To Christie and Nicholas. We're happy to have you here with us.'

'What was that about?' whispered Christie, as Nick walked her up the stairs to her bedroom.

'I think it's her way of saying she likes you. Which is good because I like you too.' They stopped outside her bedroom door. 'And so does Pa. I can tell.' To her astonishment, he dropped on to one knee. 'Darling Christie, I like you so much I would like to marry you. Would that be all right? I love you.'

'Oh, my God. Yes! Yes, please!' Christie was giddy with happiness.

He stood up and just about managed to pick her up and carry her over the threshold of her room. And, funnily enough, she didn't feel the cold once that night.

7

The summer sun was slanting through the branches of the two magnificent chestnut trees in the south-west corner of the garden. Shadows danced on the grass where Christie had arranged the two deckchairs. She put down the mugs of tea, making sure they were steady before she let go. Between the two women, a plate of chocolate-chip cookies lay untouched. Maureen was watching her weight, as always, and had refused them with a small sniff. Christie took two, just for the hell of it, and balanced one on the arm of the chair as she took a bite out of the other. As the sweetness filled her mouth, she relaxed, but not completely. She had something to achieve first.

'I wouldn't ask you unless I had to.' As Maureen bristled, Christie realised how her words might have been interpreted. 'What I mean is,' she added hastily, 'no one could do the job as well as you and I wouldn't trust the children with anyone else, Mum. So, would you consider looking after them for me while I'm at work?'

Her ruffled feathers smoothed, Maureen brightened a little. 'I'd like to help but I need to check my diary.' Her involvement in local affairs was second to none. She organised local fêtes, coffee mornings, charity events, and was a stalwart of any adult-education opportunities on offer. And besides all that, there was Ted, her loyal companion. Her time was a precious commodity.

Christie relaxed a little bit more. This was to be expected. Maureen relished playing hard to get. That way, when she eventually agreed to a request, the gratitude she received was always the greater. After years of being irritated by the habit, Christie now accepted it as part of her mother's character. Her grandmother had died years ago, but Christie well remembered the straight back, the pinched face and the distressing lack of affection she showed to any of her family. Maureen had obviously paid the price for her upbringing and seemed to flourish with the reassurance she gained from being needed.

'It's not for ever,' Christie urged, 'just until Gilly returns to work full time. They're expecting that to be next spring or early summer. In the big scheme of things, that's no time at all. I should earn enough to keep us going for a while and do the house up a bit more. And I'll pay you for a proper job.'

'Let me think about it,' Maureen hedged. She raked a manicured hand through her artfully streaked hair. 'You know, I can't put my life on hold much longer. I've promised Ted that, one day, we'll go back to Rajasthan. He's desperate to see his parents' graves again. He had a happy time as a boy out there – "son of the Raj", as he calls himself – and *tempus fugit*, you know.'

'Yes, Mum, I do know, but right now I need you. *We* need you. Look at this place. There's so much crying out to be done. This is my chance to pay off my overdraft at last and put the house right. I've got to do something about the conservatory before it falls in and there's damp rot in my study and two of the bedrooms. Central-heating that worked would be a bonus. And I need a new washing-machine. I could go on and on.'

'I did warn you that it would be too much when you bought the place. But would you listen?'

Her knowing tone infuriated Christie, as it so often did. 'I'm glad I bought it, really glad. It's home – but the upkeep's a bit more than I'd imagined.'

Maureen sniffed again and arched her eyebrows.

'But now I've got a chance to begin to sort out the house and my financial problems.'

'Well, I'm not *not* helping. I'm just pointing out that it's not that straightforward.'

For that read, 'I want you know how much I'm sacrificing,' thought Christie. Instead, she said, 'It's not for long – not even a year – just to collect the kids from school or be here if they're getting a lift, give them supper, and then I'll be home.'

'Anything can happen in that time. Especially when you get to my age. Amy Stanbridge felt a bit strange . . .'

Christie gave an inner groan, knowing that one of her mother's stories about the Grim Reaper was coming up.

'. . . She told her husband she was going upstairs for a rest. Never came down again. He found her dead as a doornail on their bed. Hadn't even had time to take her shoes off. You see, when you get on a bit, you never know.'

'No, you don't. But I have to take this job for my sake and for the children's. If you want to go to India, fine. Just say so, and I'll find someone else.' But she knew that this trip was a pipe-dream – Maureen and Ted would never be able to afford it. And Maureen knew that too. Nonetheless, the look that said she was going to be as intransigent as she could be had crossed her face.

As her mother shut her eyes and angled her face to the sun, Christie resigned herself to the wait. She thought back to her screen test, which couldn't have gone more smoothly. She and Julia had been welcomed to the studio by the programme editor, who had explained that he wanted Christie to read the previous night's script from *Good Evening Britain*. She'd had to open the show, and then they had role-played a couple of short interviews. He helped her with the art of the four-minute live television interview. 'Ask daft lads' questions,' he explained. 'Who? What? Why? Where? When? And then a killer if you can.' Despite her nerves, she managed to read the autocue, simultaneously listening to the open talkback in her ear, through which she heard the comments, directions, cuts and ribald jokes from the producer and his team in the gallery.

Afterwards, Julia assured her that she had sounded quite natural. Her panic that the autocue would run too fast for her hadn't shown. She even enjoyed being 'interviewed' by Sam Abbott, who was very friendly, easy to talk to, and would be her co-host.

Thankfully, the doyenne of the show, Gilly, hadn't appeared, due to an appointment with her obstetrician, and Christie had left feeling confident that she had at least done the best she could. Two days later Julia phoned to say the job was hers. 'I've got the contract in front of me, all pretty standard stuff. Nothing we need to go through. Salary's agreed at five hundred pounds a show payable at the end of each month. I can get it biked round to TV7 this afternoon.'

'But don't I have to sign it?' Everything was happening so fast.

'With your permission, I can sign it as your representative. Then it's done and dusted. That's how I work with most of my clients. They're relieved not to be bothered with the detail.' Julia's brisk and businesslike attitude didn't invite argument.

'In which case, if you're happy with it . . . Better get it back to TV7 before anyone has second thoughts!' Christie laughed, glad not to have the responsibility of the paperwork.

'Mmm.' Julia didn't.

Now Christie had two weeks in which to put her ducks in a row before she made her début appearance on *Good Evening Britain*, when she would be introduced by . . . Gilly herself.

Terrified as she was about meeting the clever, witty, much-loved Gilly, her first priority was to appeal again to the more terrifying Maureen, whose eyes were still shut. 'I don't want to upset the kids' routine, if I can help it,' Christie began.

Her mother's eyes snapped open.

'I'll never get another chance like this.' Don't plead with her, she remonstrated with herself. That isn't the way.

She was interrupted by the sound of her mobile. She fished it out of her pocket.

It was Julia.

'Julia, hi.' She made a despairing face at her mother. Her family were already only too aware of the frequent phone calls she received from her agent at all times of the day. Didn't the woman have a life of her own? 'No, I haven't forgotten the photographer first thing tomorrow morning. No, don't worry, I'll be looking my best.' She became aware of Maureen gazing rather pointedly at the remaining biscuit on her chair arm. Defiant, Christie picked it up but hesitated as she remembered the slightly too-tight dress she was planning to wear in her publicity shot for the programme. 'No, Julia. I definitely won't be wearing trousers.'

A smile crossed Maureen's face as Christie hung up. 'I'm glad to hear that you've got somebody making sure you don't let the side down.' She paused. 'All right. I'll come over in the evenings from four till eight thirty and we'll see how it works out.' Overhearing the phone call had obviously tilted the balance.

'Will you really?' Christie put the biscuit down. 'Wait till I tell the children. They'll be so pleased.' No harm in bending the truth a little in the interest of family relations.

'Where are they, anyway?' Maureen turned towards the house. 'I thought they might at least come and say hallo to their granny.'

'Not here, Mum. In fact, I've got to go and pick them up in a minute. Libby's been over at Sophie's and Fred's been staying with Richard and Olly again. I can't tear him away from there. They have such a good time doing all those boy things that I've been so bad at.'

'You can't expect to be all things to them, you know,' said Maureen, sounding uncharacteristically wistful. 'You're not a bad mother, Christine. And perhaps this second chance is heaven sent. Nick and Daddy would be proud of you.'

Christie looked at her, surprised. This was rare praise indeed. A woman of few generous words, Maureen normally managed to convey a faint air of disapproval when confronted by the chaos her elder daughter generated. But occasionally Christie had to acknowledge that, deep down, her mother wasn't such a bad old stick. She had just become a creature of habit who controlled her life so that it ran with as few surprises and as much order as possible. They might not always see eye to eye but Christie knew her mother's heart was in the right place.

Having waved her off, she leapt into the car and drove to collect Libby. Her daughter was sitting on the doorstep of Sophie's house, swaying her head and mouthing the words to whatever was playing on her iPod Shuffle. As soon as she saw Christie, she got to her feet and ran down the garden path to the car.

'Where have you been? I told you Soph was going to London with her mum at five.' She wrenched open the car door and climbed into the passenger seat. 'I've been sitting there for hours.'

'It's only ten past!' Christie protested. 'I'm so sorry. I was sorting things out with Granny.'

'Tell me she isn't going to be over at ours every time you're at work. Please.' Libby cast her eyes heavenwards. 'We don't need anyone. I can look after us.'

'You're only twelve, sweetheart. I wouldn't put all that responsibility on your shoulders. Besides, it's illegal.' Christie wasn't entirely sure whether leaving a twelve-year-old home alone was or wasn't against the law, but grasped at the excuse, grateful that it had flashed into her mind.

'Who'd know?' Libby's reasoning was impeccable. Her father's daughter.

'Well . . .' Christie hesitated '. . . I would, and I wouldn't be happy. Look, it won't be for long.' She reached out to lay a consoling hand on her daughter's leg.

'But suppose they take you on for ever? People stay in those jobs for years, don't they?'

If Libby hadn't sounded so anxious, Christie would have laughed at the idea. Instead she reassured her: 'They won't. I'm only going to be there while Gilly Lancaster's on maternity leave. She'll be back.'

'But suppose you're better than her? Or suppose *she* wants to stay at home with *her* children?'

'Libby, don't. This will only be for a few months. Just understand that it's an opportunity for me that may work out well for us all.' She smoothed her daughter's hair. 'Look at me. I promise.' She leaned across and kissed her cheek. 'Let's go and get Fred.'

They drove in silence, Libby listening to her music, occasionally bursting into random snatches of song, while Christie thought about their future. The prospect of being beamed nightly into households all around the country was as daunting as it was exciting. However much she tried to reassure Libby, she knew at the back of her mind that her daughter was right. There was no doubt that their life was going to change, perhaps not altogether for the best, and there was nothing she could do to stop that.

This is what I wanted, she reminded herself. And, after all, it's only for a year tops, so I'd better make the most of it.

They turned down a long driveway, between two rows of rowan trees, the car crunching over deep gravel, and she stopped in the stable-yard at the back of a square, red-brick Victorian farmhouse. The door to the kitchen was open and Christie could see Olly and Fred's heads bent in concentration as they studied something on the kitchen table. They looked up when they heard the car door slam but immediately went back to the matter in hand.

Christie tapped at the door before she went in. Stepping over a pile of muddy boots and shoes, she found herself in a long wide room with a large pine table in the centre and wooden units along two of whitewashed walls, which were hung with rusty old farming tools at one end, cooking utensils at the other. Richard was standing with his back to her, intent on pouring a colourless liquid from a large brown bottle into a preserving pan.

'What *are* you all doing?'

'We found a bird's skull and some spine bones!' Fred gabbled. 'Olly and I are trying to work out what kind of bird from this book. You have to look at all the different shapes of beak. We think it might be a kestrel. See how hooked theirs are?'

'We're soaking them in hydrogen peroxide to sterilise them so they can take them into school,' Richard said, putting the pan safely at the back of the wooden draining-board and screwing the top back onto the bottle. 'Jigger, no!' Said too late as a black Labrador rushed through the door and jumped up at Christie, almost bowling her over. 'I'm so sorry. He's not meant to do that but he's young and very stupid.'

'Don't worry.' Christie was laughing as she took the cloth he offered and wiped at the paw prints on her jeans, turning away from the disobedient dog, which was now refusing to be shooed out by Olly.

'Mum, we've been learning to track in the woods too. And I know how to tell the time without a watch now.'

'Really? How can you do that?' she asked, giving the cue for a torrent of incoherent explanation from the two boys, who talked over each other as they described something involving the sun, a stick and some stones. 'Come and see.' They rushed out of a second door at the end of the room into the garden, Jigger chasing after them, jumping up and catching their sleeves with his teeth as they ran.

'I was going to offer you a cup of tea, but I guess we haven't got time.' Richard let her go out of the door first. 'Wouldn't Libby like to see too?'

'She's wrapped up in her music. Besides, anything Fred gets up to is way beneath her. She'll be fine provided we're not too long.'

They followed the boys across the garden to a stick that was standing with a circle of stones placed evenly around it.

'Go on, Mum. Ask me the time,' said Fred.

Christie obliged.

'Half past five,' he yelled, triumphant.

'That's amazing and completely right.' She knelt down to have the elementary sun-dial explained to her. When she looked up, Richard was gazing in her direction. She got to her feet. 'I can't thank you enough,' she said. 'This is just what Fred needs. He absolutely loves coming here.'

88

'And we love having him. Don't we, Jigger?' He bent to pat the dog that was wagging around his legs, shivering with delight at the attention. 'We were lucky today, not having any team-building groups in. Some companies want to come at the weekend – they simply can't waste a minute of the working week – and then it all gets a bit hectic on the childcare front.'

'Perhaps I could return the favour on those days,' Christie offered, as they began to head back to the car. 'Fred! Come on.'

'If Caro's away, I'll hold you to that.'

'Oh, sorry, how stupid of me.' She kicked herself for forgetting that his situation was not the same as hers.

'Nothing to be sorry about. But there is one thing I was wondering, which is . . .' He paused, as if nerving himself to say something. 'There's a pub quiz next Saturday and one of the regulars on our team can't make it. I don't suppose you'd like to come? Would you?'

Christie froze. Was he actually asking her on a date? She dismissed the idea as fast as it had entered her head. Of course he wasn't. They had the kids in common and he probably didn't have anyone else he could ask at such short notice. Mates, that's what they were. But then she remembered Mel's comment about tuning her radar. Perhaps they could be more. Perhaps she was failing to read the signs. 'I'd love to,' she answered. 'Provided I can find a babysitter.'

As they reached the car, Fred hurled himself onto the back seat while Jigger, having jumped in after him, was hauled out from the other side by Richard. 'Bloody animal! That's terrific. I'll pick you up at about six. We'll eat there.'

As they said their goodbyes and thank-yous and set off for home, Christie became aware that Libby had removed her headphones when Jigger made his unscheduled entrance and exit and was now staring at her with a look of disdain cut with horror. 'You're not going on a . . .' she could barely say the word '. . . *date* with *him*, are you?' She mustered all the scorn at her disposal. 'Aren't you a bit old? And, anyway, what about Dad?'

'You're never too old, Libby. Never.' Christie smiled at her daughter. 'And Dad would be proud that we're all getting on with our lives, you know. He really would.'

Her eyes on the road, she didn't see the two spots of colour that appeared on Libby's cheeks or the single tear she dashed away as she turned to stare out of the window.

8

Thirty minutes before her first programme, Christie was looking in her dressing-room mirror, studying the professional makeup on her face. Not bad. The photo-shoot (in a beautiful coral body-con dress that Mel had picked out for her) had been good, and the accompanying articles in the papers that day were positive.

There was a knock on the door of the tiny dressing room. It opened to reveal Gilly Lancaster, balancing a hand-tied posy on her pregnant stomach. In the flesh, she was smaller than she appeared on TV. A sleek mane of immaculately blow-dried blonde hair framed her face, and twinkling arrangements of gold and silver stars hung from her ears. Not a wrinkle showed above her neat, pointed nose or beside her wide mouth – all beaten into submission with Botox and filler, no doubt. For the umpteenth time, Christie swore she would stay out of the hands of cosmetic doctors and surgeons, whatever the cost to her new career. Gilly's welcoming smile revealed a mouthful of perfectly capped and whitened teeth. She was wearing an elegant dusty pink crêpe-de-Chine trouser suit with a jacket cut low enough to reveal a hint of pregnant cleavage, with a wide front bow, its ends long enough almost to disguise her bump. Looking long-ingly at Gilly's towering strappy shoes, Christie couldn't but remember her own pregnancies and her constant longing for comfortable slippers and tracksuits. She could no more have dressed like this than fly to the moon.

Today had been the first day they'd met and, following that encounter, Gilly was here with what must be a peace-offering. Earlier, Christie had walked into her first production meeting two minutes early to discover that everyone bar Vince, the programme editor, was already there. Gilly had been sitting on the far side of the large table strewn with newspapers, most of which were open at the page on which Christie's glamorous photo stood out beneath headlines such as 'NEW GIRL MAKES NEWS! LANCASTER LYNCHED', with flattering accounts of her suitability for the job and photos showing Gilly's burgeoning figure. There was an empty chair beside Gilly. She had put her hand on the back and nodded at Christie, saying, 'Come and sit here.' Grateful for the friendly gesture, Christie had sat down. Just then, the swing doors had banged open and Vince burst in. He took one look across the table, his face reddening. 'You're in my chair,' he said, with quiet menace. Mortified, Christie had moved to the other empty one at the end of the table. She had seen Gilly give Vince a look, as if to say, 'I warned you she was an idiot,' then glance at her with a one hundred per cent smirk.

Things had not improved when Vince then championed Christie and insisted she was given the second-lead interview with Jack Brown, one of the few firemen who had survived an oil-refinery blaze. Despite Gilly's furious objections, he was adamant that he wanted Christie to make a mark on her first show.

Christie remembered the glare Gilly had shot in her direction, yet now she was standing in front of her with a floral apology. The last thing Christie wanted to do was get off on the wrong foot with any of her new colleagues, especially on her first show.

'I didn't get a chance to give these to you before.' Gilly passed the flowers to Christie who thanked her and looked vainly for a vase in which to put them. The only one there held the wilting good-luck flowers that Libby and Fred had picked from the garden that morning. Defeated, she put the posy on her dressing-table.

Gilly was oblivious to the fate of her gift and carried on: 'Julia's told me so much about you. We talk all the time. Is she here yet?'

'Not yet. She called to say she was running late.' If Gilly wasn't going to refer to what had happened earlier, then Christie wouldn't either. Starting out with a confrontation or an apology would not make any kind of working relationship. She'd happily accept the olive branch and leave it at that.

'She's so amazing.' Gilly sat in the other chair, wincing as she slipped off a shoe and rubbed her slightly puffy feet. 'When I started, she made everything so easy. She knows everyone.' A burst of laughter escaped her lips. 'How are you feeling?'

'Excited, terrified and numb,' said Christie. 'I'll be glad when the first show's over.'

'You'll be absolutely fine. Sam's a poppet. He's learned so much since he's been working with me.'

Christie disliked the patronising note that had crept into Gilly's voice.

'What are you wearing?'

Julia had explained that she'd secured Gilly a clothes budget and a stylist who shopped with her, but the show didn't run to doing the same for the second-string presenters. Once Christie had proved herself, perhaps she'd be given a budget of her own. Until then, with Mel's help, Christie had vowed she wasn't going to be made to feel like Second-hand Rose.

'This dress?' She adopted a jokey pose. Mel had found a very simple figure-hugging bluey-purple shift with cap sleeves that seemed ideal for her first appearance.

'Fabulous.' Gilly's smile didn't quite reach her eyes this time. 'The perfect colour for you.' She was interrupted by another knock at the door, their call to go to the studio. 'Follow me. This place is such a warren. I don't want you to get lost.' She slipped her shoe back on and, limping, led the way.

Although she knew what to expect, Christie was always surprised by how small and intimate the studio was. The low, black ceiling was hung about with hundreds of studio lights that raised the temperature to Saharan heights. People were standing about, chatting quietly or listening to whoever in the gallery outside was talking to them via their earpiece. Across the smooth, shiny floor looped fat black cables attached to five cameras topped with autocue hoods that were focused on the brightly lit set, like monsters watching their prey. Against three of the walls were what looked like scuffed Ikea room sets. In the middle, two curved cream sofas sat empty in front of a softly lit orange backdrop. A carafe of water, two glasses and a box of Kleenex (for the more emotional interviews) were placed on two low tables. To the left was the demo area, the empty white corner that the designers could magic into anything: today, a kitchen set. On the right, in the hard-interview area, two uncomfortable-looking chairs faced each other across a coffee-table against a wide photographic backdrop: a collage of well-known buildings from around Britain.

As she waited for the floor manager to come over, Christie became aware that a couple of scene hands were staring at her, then looking away and smiling as if having a joke at her expense. Before she had time to ask them what was so funny, the director was talking in her earpiece.

'Christie, hi. Ian here. Just sit on the cream sofa and let Camera Two have a look at you.' As she sat down, his voice abruptly changed. 'What the fuck are you wearing?'

'I'm sorry? What's the matter?' Christie was completely thrown. She looked around for Gilly, who had admired her outfit, but she had vanished among the crew. If something was so obviously wrong, why on earth hadn't she said so when there had been a chance to put it right?

'The matter? No one wears blue on set. Surely you know that. You'll disappear into the chroma-key.'

'Chroma-key?'

'Oh, for God's sake. Someone tell her, for fuck's sake. And in the meantime – Lillybet!' he bellowed down the talkback to one of the runners, all of whom were pretending not to notice what was going on. 'Take her down to Wardrobe and see if they've got something suitable. Anything other than fucking blue!'

The entire studio had turned to look at her.

Wishing this was a nightmare from which she'd soon wake up, Christie was marched away through the maze of corridors. Lillybet quickly explained that chroma-key was a bit of TV magic that allowed all kinds of photos, films and weather maps to appear where they weren't. Some chroma-key screens were green. *Good Evening Britain*'s was blue. When they reached Wardrobe, she banged open the door, avoiding a giant pile of discarded shoes, and yelled, 'Quick. Emergency. Nell, we need something right now.' She grimaced apologetically at Christie, who was feeling so small she barely noticed.

Nell, a slight girl dressed in black with purple-and-black stripy tights, punky red-and-orange hair standing on end and a multi-ringed right ear and right nostril, emerged from behind a rail of clothes. Obviously peeved at being disturbed, she eyed Christie up and down. 'Haven't got much in at the moment,' she said grumpily.

'Doesn't matter. The show starts in fifteen,' said Lillybet.

'It does matter to me,' interrupted Christie, realising she didn't want to be remembered for making her first appearance on *Good Evening Britain* in a sack. Maureen and Mel would never let her live it down, never mind the press. And Julia! Oh, God. 'There must be something you've got that isn't too awful.'

'Just a minute.' Nell disappeared again and came back with a maroon skirt and a cream shirt with a semi-circular frilled arrangement across the bust. 'How about this? Right size. The best I can do.'

While Christie tried the outfit on, she could hear the director shouting through her earpiece and over Lillybet's walkie-talkie. She straightened up and looked in the mirror. As if making her look like a refugee from a seventies sit-com wasn't crime enough – the blouse put a good ten years on her. At least. 'I'm not sure about this. Isn't there something else I could try?'

'No time and you look fine. Really.' Lillybet didn't sound entirely convinced but another disembodied yell galvanised her. 'Come on. We'll be dead if we're not back in the studio in a couple of minutes.' She was already holding open the door.

Not wanting to make things worse, Christie had no choice but to follow her. As she approached the set where Gilly was waiting, seated on the sofa opposite Sam, she thought she saw a satisfied smile hovering on her co-presenter's lips. But, with only moments to go, there was no time to say anything. One of the makeup girls rushed up and neatened her hair, dabbing powder on her nose to deaden the perspiration. There was no point in worrying what she looked like now. She held her head high and went to sit beside Gilly, as instructed, listening to the familiar introductory music and waiting for the show to begin.

Gilly opened as usual, and led straight into Christie's introduction. With a saccharine smile, she addressed the nation, her fans. 'As you all know, I'll shortly be going on maternity leave to have my three little blessings so it gives me enormous pleasure to be able to introduce Caroline Lynch . . .' Christie and Sam looked at each other '. . . who'll be looking after things for me.'

Enough, thought Christie. Before Gilly could say any more, she cut in: 'I'm sorry to interrupt, Gilly, but those hormones must be getting to you. I'm Christie.'

Sam laughed to cover the awkwardness of the moment while an infuriated Gilly tinkled through her teeth, 'Of course. I'm so sorry.'

The next fifty-four minutes went smoothly enough, and Christie was relieved that her interview with the heroic fireman ran without a hitch.

When the show was over, the first person she saw coming towards her was Julia. Immaculate as ever in a sharp yellow swing coat, her face was thunderous. 'What were you thinking?' she hissed, clearly not wanting to be overheard.

'What do you mean?' Christie was genuinely confused. 'I thought it went well.' So well, in fact, that as soon as the cameras stopped rolling, Sam had got up and kissed her cheek. 'You were terrific,' he'd said. 'Especially the interview with Jack Brown – very emotional.' They'd both ignored Gilly's audible 'tsk'. 'We should give you a proper welcome,' Sam went on. 'Come down to the bar, when you're ready.'

'*You* went well – very well, in fact.' Julia softened slightly. 'But what on earth were you wearing?'

As Christie began to explain, she could see Julia's eyes glaze over. Her agent wasn't interested in excuses or explanations. She wanted results. She came to at the mention of Gilly and her apparent approval of the fated blue dress.

'You must have misunderstood her. She's a pro and would never have told you to wear blue. Never.'

'She didn't exactly tell . . .' But she had lost Julia's interest again. It was true that Gilly hadn't recommended she wear the dress, but she certainly hadn't advised her against it when there might have been time to salvage the situation. Perhaps their relationship was already more complicated than she'd realised. In future, perhaps she would be less trusting, more cautious. Christie said goodbye to Julia, who was dashing off to a first night in the West End, then hosting an after-show dinner at Sheekey's, so had no time to discuss anything more 'till the morning'.

With her heart in her high heels, Christie returned to her dressing room to change. Unable to face going home to listen to Maureen reiterate Julia's and probably the entire nation's view of her outfit, she tossed it into a corner and zipped herself into the offending blue dress, ready to face the music in the bar. Once she was on the outside of a glass of wine, surely her *faux pas* wouldn't seem to matter as much?

She pushed open the door to a crowd of staff, most of whom were completely unfamiliar to her. She spotted Sam near the bar and began to make her way to him. As soon as he felt her touch his arm, he turned and his face lit up. 'So you've escaped the wicked witch's clutches at last. Well done.'

For a moment, Christie thought he meant Gilly, but then he said, 'The Queen of Mean? Oops!' He winked. 'I mean Ms Julia Keen, of course.'

'She's not that bad.'

'No, she's a good agent, I'll give you that. But I'd keep her at arm's length, if I were you. She's scary. I know Ben was – well, perhaps, a little unhappy about her? And look what happened to him.'

'What are you saying? Whatever happened to Ben was an

accident. Julia was completely vindicated and you know it.' Christie automatically sprang to her agent's defence.

'OK, OK. I'm sorry. Just a joke.' He looked apologetic. 'Forget I said anything and let me get you a drink.'

Out of his regulation work suit, Sam looked younger than his forty-something years. He had changed into jeans, open-necked white shirt and dark blue jacket. His hair was gelled into its signature spiky disorder and his eyes, generously cornered by crow's feet, gave away a man with a good sense of humour. Within moments, Christie had a glass of white wine in her hand and was being introduced to the group that surrounded him. Caught up in the show gossip, she began to relax, watching Sam pull the crowd into his orbit. He was engaging, indiscreet without being scurrilous, and very funny indeed.

He was in the middle of a bawdy impersonation of Gilly and her husband, Derek: '"Oooh, Derek! However could you have defiled me so? Three babies! You must have drugged me."

'"More like the other way round, dear."' Sam put his hand on his hip, camp as anything.

'"Don't do that, Derek!"' he went on. '"My mother already thinks you're gay."

'"Well, she should know, the old fag bangle."'

Christie wasn't sure whether laughing was the right thing for her to do or not, so she tried to look pleasant but not too engaged.

The man beside her nodded at her. 'Hi, I'm Frank, the senior cameraman. I'm so sorry you had all that trouble with your dress tonight. Gilly's a cow. She loved how uncomfortable you were made to feel. I've worked on this show for years, love,' he patted the bar stool beside him, 'and I can tell you that you should be careful where Gilly's concerned. She won't like someone else treading on her patch, even if there's good reason. She'll be back as soon as those doctors let her, babies or no babies.'

'Well, that's fine by me,' Christie said, not wanting to give the impression that there were any difficulties between them. 'It's what I'm expecting. I'm covering two or three days a week until she's on leave and then again as she eases herself back into things.'

'Ease!' Frank laughed. 'Gilly doesn't do "ease". She'll be back as fast as a rat up a drainpipe. Mark my words. Did she tell you to wear that blue dress?'

Christie's face reddened. Then she caught herself. 'Well, not exactly.'

'I thought so. You're going to have to watch her like a hawk.' He paused to take a sip of his lager. 'Have you got a stylist?'

'My sister, Mel.'

'Do you have a gay best friend?'

She shook her head.

'Well, you do now. Why don't I come shopping with the two of you and help you with what looks good on camera?'

She'd never clothes-shopped with a man before. Nick would have peeled ten pounds of onions rather than go with her. He had left what she wore up to her, and was always gratifyingly appreciative of her choice, whatever Mel said. Why would she break the habit of a lifetime and go shopping with anyone, let alone a gay man she had only just met? She thought of Mel, her unofficial stylist, who was at that moment jetting her way to a fashion shoot in Hawaii, lucky sod. But, on the other hand, why not? She had warmed to Frank immediately and – who knew? – it might be fun. Besides, she obviously needed all the people she could get on her side after her inauspicious start. His was a hand of friendship being held out in unfamiliar shark-infested waters. She smiled and accepted his offer.

9

Two days later, Christie and Mel pushed behind Frank towards the corner table in the crowded wine bar. The place was swamped with Saturday shoppers, taking the weight off their credit cards while they had lunch. Insisting the two women took a seat, Frank dumped the couple of bags he was carrying for Christie, then fought his way back to the bar to order their drinks. They squeezed themselves behind the table, yanking the bags with them. Armed with her purchases, more than she had ever bought in one go, Christie felt like somebody out of *Sex and the City*. This must be what it was like to be a lady who lunched. She thanked the Lord for a brand new salary and a healthier bank balance.

While they waited she peered into one of the yellow Selfridges bags and pulled apart the tissue paper. A glimpse of the cream wool jacket made her wince with pleasure as she remembered the hit her bank account was about to take.

'Don't even go there, love,' Frank had said, when she questioned the expense. 'If you're going to start looking at the prices, I'm going straight home. Trust me. You need one or two designer pieces just to make the high street stuff sing. You've got to look good in this game. This is a necessary expense.' Mel applauded him and quickly absorbed his TV dress rules – no black (too dense), no red (the colour bleeds), no white (too dazzling), no stripes or checks (they strobe).

After that, Christie gave herself up to whatever would be, and shopping with Frank and Mel had turned out to be a joy: funny, inspired and inventive. He had a flair for seeing what teamed and toned, what mixed and matched, what would look good under studio lights in front of a camera and what would best hide the microphone and earpiece packs that got stuffed like two fag packets up her jumper. On top of that, he had oodles of patience that stood him in good stead while Christie made up her mind. Whenever she was losing the will to live, he'd appear at the cubicle door with exactly the right accessory to pull an outfit together: the wide woven belt, the heavy beaded necklace, the understated bracelet. Mel was the voice of reason if things got too camp and he took over when she got too *avant garde*.

Result? Two knock-'em-dead jackets, three dresses, a skirt and two pairs of trousers, plus various bits of cheap and cheerful jewellery.

Three and a half hours after they had first set foot in Selfridges, they had called a halt and repaired to the wine bar for lunch.

The sisters looked up to see him approaching, clutching three glasses of champagne. He squeezed in opposite them. 'Cheers,' he said, passing them round. 'Here's to Team Christie.' They clinked glasses and sipped. 'Why do we ever drink anything else?' he wondered, obviously not expecting an answer. 'Now. What I'm dying to know is, how did a nice girl like you get tied up with Julia? Tell all.'

Christie was exasperated by people's reaction to her agent. She was disappointed Frank thought the same as everyone else and gave her usual brisk answer. 'We met on the *Tart Talk* set. She invited me to see her and I was impressed. She's good. I don't understand why you've all got it in for her.'

'Well, I can't speak for the others, love, but I've known her a long time. Since drama school, in fact.'

'Drama school? Julia's an actress?'

'Yeah. I don't know why she didn't keep it up. She was very good at convincing everyone around her to give her the leading roles in the end-of-term productions. Several boys had their hearts broken because she persuaded them that they loved her. Funnily enough, she only ever made moves on the rich ones. Something to do with her upbringing, I guess. She ironed out her north-west accent very quickly, was always immaculately turned out and managed to get someone else to buy her supper. She must be struggling a bit at the moment, having lost a client in her swimming-pool last year. I know for a fact that one or two others have left her and, apart from you, she hasn't taken on anyone since he died. Mud sticks.'

'Poor Ben. She must have been so upset. What a thing for her to deal with.'

'Hmm.' He sounded doubtful. 'I once knew her quite well, but now she doesn't even acknowledge me. If you're in, you're in. But if you're out . . . Are you eating?' He passed across the long menu, just as one of the few waitresses stopped by their table.

As they waited for her noodle dish, Mel's salad and his steak *frites*, Christie regretted being so dismissive. 'Tell me more.'

He gave her a knowing look. 'Remember Max Keen? He came into the studio the other day with that actor . . . what's-'is-name.'

Christie nodded. Max Keen was Sam's agent and she remembered meeting him briefly when another of his clients, Clem Baker, was on the show. Max had accompanied him, keeping in the background, standing behind the cameras, quietly watching, while the Hollywood A-lister had talked to Sam and Christie about his latest Oscar-tipped performance. In contrast to the film-star good looks of his client, Max was a small, balding man, neatly but casually turned out. However, the two had a rapport, which was plain to anyone who watched them together and Max, however tough a negotiator he might be, had a transforming smile. She had seen that for herself when Sam had introduced her to him.

'Yes. Why?'

'He and Julia were married once. And he was the top talent agent in the country. He learned the business at Mellors and Crombie where his secretary was none other than guess who?' He left the gap, waiting for her to fill it in.

'Julia?'

'Got it in one. After two years, they got spliced despite, or perhaps because of, the ten-year age-gap.' His eyes lit up at the idea of a sexual shenanigan or two. 'They left M and C and set up their own artist-management company, Keen and Keen. Everybody wanted Max to take them on, but he was bloody choosy. As a result, he built up a bespoke client list that was second to none, sharing the responsibilities with his new wife.'

'So what happened? Why aren't they still together?'

'Two reasons, I guess. One: Julia's a ruthless, bitchy workaholic who takes all the credit she can – you must have picked up on that by now? And two: a leopard never changes its spots, so Max went off with his latest assistant. Lucy was young enough to give him the family he wanted. Such a scandal at the time.'

Christie could see how much Frank must have enjoyed it.

'They said Julia refused to have kids because they'd get in the way of her career.' He paused as their food was put in front of them, not wanting to the waitress to overhear. After he'd had a couple of mouthfuls, he continued, 'Against all expectations, instead of collapsing under the pressure of such a public divorce, Julia set up White Management in direct competition with Max. If it hadn't been too confusing I bet she'd have used his name. She hung on to it for herself, though. Nothing like success by association.'

'And then?'

'Only if we have another glass! Shiraz this time, I think. Your turn.'

Christie edged out and made her way round a group of shrieking women sporting sparkling antennae and pink T-shirts bearing the words 'Em's Hens On Tour'. But her mind stayed with what Frank had been telling her. Remembering Julia's elegance and style, it was impossible for Christie to imagine

Max and her as an item. He was so much shorter, so relaxed, and with more of the frog about him than the prince.

Suddenly one of the 'hens' grabbed her arm. 'Aren't you Christie Lynch?'

She shook her arm free, surprised. 'Yes, I am. I'm sorry, I don't think I know you.'

'I watch that news show every night.' Christie could smell the alcohol on her breath. 'Janey! Got your mobile? You don't mind, do you?'

Before Christie had a chance to answer, the woman had engineered herself so they were side by side and her friend was taking a picture of them together. 'Thanks ever so much. The kids'll be thrilled. They love Sam.' With that she turned back to her crew and left a disconcerted Christie to make her way to the bar. Although no one else approached her, she was aware that one or two people were staring at her. The unexpected attention had been quite harmless but made her feel uncomfortable. Recognition was one thing, being accosted quite another. But if the fans of the show were all like that, she had nothing too serious to worry about.

When she returned to the table, Frank and Mel were examining the two necklaces they had insisted she buy, one chunky, one sparkly. 'Now you're kitted out for every occasion,' Mel said. Christie popped them into their bag and, taking her glass, nodded for Frank to go on with his story.

'Julia was livid – there's no woman like Julia when she's scorned, I can tell you. She'd already built up a reputation that provoked envy, resentment, admiration, you name it. But without

Max's good influence, she lured clients from other agents – most often from him, of course – promising to double or treble their income. And, more often than not, she did. That's how to get an impressive list.'

'That's good, though, isn't it? All's fair in love and business?' Christie wasn't much enjoying the picture Frank was painting of her agent. If only she'd done some background research first, as Richard had suggested, like the well-trained journalist she was meant to be.

He took a sip and savoured the red wine. 'Well, her business tactics weren't exactly applauded but she got ten out of ten for chutzpah. What matters to her is where and how to get top dollar.'

'What about Ben Chapman?'

His face saddened. 'He was a mate of mine. Great guy. God only knows what happened to him that night or what he was doing in the pool.' He looked at his watch. 'That's for another time, though. Too depressing. Right now, I want to know more about you two girls.'

As they finished their meal, Christie told him about her career, Nick and the kids, then Mel talked about her glam but single life. Finally it was their turn to quiz him.

'There's not much to tell,' he said. 'I'm just an old queen who wanted a bit of glamour in his life. I was destined to be the next Tom Hanks, but a little smaller, fatter and gayer, and I ended up a cameraman at TV7.' He ran a hand over his tightly shaved head and Christie couldn't help thinking that he looked as if he'd polished himself before coming out. He was so shiny and smart, as if he'd just come out of the box – never mind the closet. For the next few minutes they encouraged him to tell them more about his life, but while he was happy to talk about others, he was surprisingly reticent about revealing too much about himself. Christie was content to wait until another time when she suspected he'd be more forthcoming. He needed to know that he could trust her. She loved his camp flamboyance, his outspokenness and, most of all, the generosity he'd shown her. She felt that of all the people she'd met on the show so far, he was the one she could trust: a brand new friend. She, Mel and Frank were like the Three Musketeers.

*

That night, with Maureen ensconced downstairs on babysitting duty, Christie showered, shaved her legs and painted her toenails, then pulled almost everything she owned out of her wardrobe to find something suitable for her date with Richard. She wanted to look her best but not as if she'd tried too hard. Whatever she wore had to be right. Her bedroom was more like Mel's by the time she had settled on her flounced long skirt, sleeveless T-shirt and tunic top, with the wide woven leather belt and chunky necklace she'd bought that morning. She knew Mel would have had a thousand fits over her boho sister, but she felt comfortable.

When she went downstairs, Maureen looked up from the magazine she was reading and gave her a long hard stare.

'What, Christine, is the point of asking me over so you can go shopping and then not wearing anything you bought?'

'Oh, Mum. That's different. I was shopping for work. I'd look a complete prat if I turned up in the pub dressed in that stuff. Trust me.'

But Maureen remained unconvinced, despite grudgingly admitting that she supposed what Christie had on was better than her usual jeans. She felt more confident when Fred and Libby gave her their half-hearted approval, tearing their attention from the TV for a nano-second. At least when Richard arrived, she thought she noticed his eyes widen with appreciation. As did hers. His checked Viyella working shirt had been replaced by a soft pink linen one that showed off his tan. She loved the fact that it wasn't perfectly ironed, although he'd obviously had a damned good go. His jeans were clean, and instead of his usual walking boots, he was wearing brogues, shiny with polish. She breathed in and caught the slight scent of aftershave

As he opened the door of the Land Rover, Richard apologised for its state, took out some muddy boots from the passenger side and flung them into the back. The smell of wet dog and dog blanket enveloped her as she climbed in. A lumberjack jacket lay on the back seat among sweet wrappers and Ordnance Survey maps; a compass jiggled on the dashboard. Her nerves settled as she sat beside him, hearing about Fred and Olly's frustrated attempts to train Jigger to climb a ladder. When they reached the pub, and were crunching over the gravel to the front door, Richard automatically put out his hand for her to hold. She took it, registering its roughness and strength, liking the unaffectedness of his gesture. Inside, the Oak and Archer had

111

been reinvented as a gastro-pub, with none of its more traditional clientele to be seen.

'Give me the old farmers and their three-legged dogs any day,' Richard joked. 'Nothing wrong with a bit of spit and sawdust.'

But Christie liked what she saw. A deep bar was surrounded by pine tables through which the serving staff threaded their way, carrying plates of steaming fresh food. Richard's friends were on the far side of the room. He introduced her to his business partner, Tom, Tom's girlfriend, Sally, and a couple staying with them, Helen and Robert. Richard encouraged Tom to move down the bench so Christie could sit between them.

As soon as she got the chance, Sally couldn't resist quizzing Christie. 'How long have you known Rich? Can't have been long. Or else he's kept very quiet about you.'

Richard overheard and answered for her: 'School-gate Mafia, Sal. That's all. Our sons are best mates and can't be separated.'

Christie shot him a look of gratitude. He winked at her as he moved the conversation smartly on to Tom and Sally's children, a subject on which Sally could hold forth for hours. Only being presented with the short but delicious-sounding menu made her break off mid-flow.

Having ordered, they began to talk again. Richard made sure that Christie was included in the conversation, taking time to explain when they wandered onto people or stories she didn't know. It was almost as if he sensed that this was the first date (if it could be called that) she'd been on since Nick died, and he was doing everything he could to make her feel comfortable. And his efforts were paying off. As she smiled and nodded, joining in when she could, her mind wandered to the real reason for her being there. Was she just a convenient walker for him, a stand-in for the team or, she caught her breath, might he be interested in her in another way?

Eventually, the meal over, the quizmaster emerged and propped himself by the long oak bar, waiting for the tables to charge their glasses before he began the questions. Their team soon discovered a shared competitive streak a mile wide as they urgently whispered their answers to one another and scribbled them down. When Christie confidently put forward a completely wrong answer, she was relieved that Richard just nudged her and smiled without making her feel any more stupid than she already did. Eventually joint highest scorers, no thanks to her sporadic contributions, they faced sudden death. Breath held, they listened intently for the final question. The quizmaster ramped up the tension with a long pause, then: 'What's the fewest number of moves with which a person can win a game of chess?' They turned to one another, each disappointed to realise that no one else knew the answer either. Richard and Tom started whispering and counting on their fingers. The other team were looking just as frantically ignorant.

'Never understood the game, myself,' said Sally, draining her gin and tonic, prepared for defeat.

'My husband played once.' As Christie envisaged the board permanently set up in their Chelsea living room for Nick's long-distance game with his father, she remembered his frustrated efforts to explain it to her. 'Fool's mate,' she said suddenly.

'Sorry?'

'It's just come to me. Fool's mate. Two moves. The answer's two, I'm sure.' She scribbled it on a piece of paper and dashed over to the quizmaster, who loudly declared them the winners. The rest of the evening was a blur of congratulation and laughter as they shared a celebratory round before saying their farewells and heading home.

Richard and Christie left the pub flushed with victory and, in her case, an extra glass of wine. To her consternation, an air of awkwardness settled over them in the Land Rover and they found themselves casting around for things to talk about.

'How's work?' Richard tried, opting for the safe ground.

Christie's relief was mixed with a touch of regret that he hadn't hit on something more personal. 'Actually, fine,' she said. 'I thought after that awful start that it was going to be a disaster, but there's a great team and I'm beginning to love it.'

'And Julia? Still happy with her?'

Her heart sank at the mention of her agent's name. 'Do we have to talk about her now? It's been such a great evening. I don't want to think about work at the moment.'

'Oh, OK.' Richard sounded surprised but seemed happy to listen to her talking about how much Fred had enjoyed camping with them and how she'd spent the time with Libby. As they neared Christie's house, Richard seemed to withdraw even more into himself. She felt as if she had babbled for the most of the way, cramming words into the silence as fast as she could while he slipped away from her, concentrating on the road ahead, nodding and smiling when he thought appropriate. But, if she was honest, there was only one thing on her mind: would he or would he not kiss her goodnight? And, if he did, should she invite him in? She ran her tongue round her teeth, regretting that last drink and wishing she had a peppermint.

When the car stopped, Richard kept the engine running. A sure sign he wouldn't be coming in. However, as he leaned towards her, she readied herself for the kiss goodbye, half closing her eyes in anticipation. She could feel the warmth of his skin as he came close, could smell his faint cologne. Just when she expected him to make contact, he swerved past her to wrestle with the door handle until he finally pushed open her door.

'Wretched thing often sticks,' he explained, as he sat back in his seat, putting both hands on the steering-wheel. He turned towards her, his features unreadable in the shadowy dark of the car. 'You were a star tonight. Thank you.'

Picking up her cue, she got out swiftly and said good night.

Later, sitting up alone and nursing a small, consoling glass of whisky, she had written off her disappointment in his evident lack of interest as an aberration brought about by the effects of alcohol and success. Her response moved from disappointed to pragmatic. If that was how he wanted things between them, fine. She counted herself lucky to have him as a friend. Thank God she hadn't embarrassed herself. She twisted her engagement ring round her finger. She had never doubted her feelings for Nick and she was sure he had felt the same for her. She still found it extraordinary how certain they had both been about each other from the beginning. Would she ever find someone like him again?

As soon as they were engaged, Nick wanted to make things official by asking Maureen for Christie's hand in marriage. He had spoken to her once or twice on the phone when she had rung to talk to Christie. She hadn't been impressed. 'Christine, why is your young man at your flat so early in the morning on a weekday? I hope you aren't living together. Your father would be so disappointed.'

'Mum, no, he's not living with me but he does stay the night sometimes. It's almost the year two thousand so, please, let me be.'

'Hmm. Well, I'd like to meet him, that's all. Just to make sure he's right for you. You've always been such a bad judge of character and could do with the benefit of my experience.'

'Mel likes him,' Christie protested.

'Well, I don't much approve of her lifestyle either. Fashion students don't live in the real world, do they?'

And now Nick and Christie were engaged. Mel knew and so did their friends. But they deliberately kept Maureen in the dark. As soon as Christie was wearing her rather large and sparkly engagement ring, she arranged to drive up to see her mother. 'Mum, is it OK if I come up for Sunday lunch?'

'Well, if it's nice I may be working in the garden and not want

to cook.' Maureen was justifiably proud of her small garden on which she lavished much care.

'That's all right. It's just that I was going to bring someone to meet you. Nick.' Christie held her breath, waiting for her mother's reaction.

'Why didn't you say so? You are silly and secretive sometimes. I'll do a coronation chicken salad with my new potatoes. Will he like that?'

As they pulled up at Maureen's, Christie couldn't help comparing this humble house to Nick's parental pile. Nick squeezed her hand. 'I'm a bit nervous. Do you think she'll like me?'

'Couldn't give a toss if she doesn't.' And she didn't. Nick was everything she had ever wanted in a man, and whatever her mother said wouldn't change her mind. As they clicked open the gate, the front door opened to reveal Maureen dressed in her best. She looked at Nick and almost fainted. As she was to tell her circle of church-flowers ladies later, 'He's like that Mr Darcy but with better manners. Christine's no Elizabeth Bennet but she's done very well for herself. I did think the ring was a little vulgar, though.'

Nick laid on all the charm he had for Maureen, and after lunch and the obligatory tour of her manicured back garden, he asked her if he could marry her daughter. Maureen couldn't get the sherry out fast enough. At last, a son-in-law. And a son-in-law who would inherit a highland castle at that.

10

'So what I'm saying is . . .' Julia seemed not to have drawn breath since they'd begun lunch. They were in Le Caprice, just around the corner from the Ritz, at her 'usual table'. Prominently positioned in the corner to the right of the bar, she could see everyone entering the restaurant and, more importantly, they could see her and her guest. From the moment Christie had sat down, Julia had taken control of the conversation. This was the first time since their working arrangement had been established that her agent had invited Christie to anything remotely social. Not that this was remotely social, as it turned out. They had discussed the minutiae of Christie's presenting style and one or two other media opportunities that Julia might pursue on her behalf.

Christie surreptitiously nudged at the sleeve of her cardigan so that she could see her watch. As she suspected, the time had whizzed by. If she didn't leave soon, she would never get to Libby's school in time for the meeting with Mrs Snell, the head teacher. Although she was listening to Julia, her mind was already on its way there. She had no idea why she had been asked to come in. It was still early in the new term and Libby hadn't mentioned any difficulties at school. Mrs Snell had been irritatingly circumspect, insisting that it was better they talked face to face. 'And perhaps it would be wise not to mention to Libby that you're coming to see me,' she'd added, as an after-thought, yet still wouldn't be drawn on the reason. Why not? Questions had been racing through Christie's mind since the call two days ago, but she had failed to come up with any answers.

'. . . you've got great on-screen chemistry with Sam,' Julia carried on. 'And you really do connect with the viewer. You're one of those presenters who can see right down the bottle of that camera lens to reach your audience. Your confidence is building and you're getting into your stride.' She leaned across the table. 'Your interview technique is interesting too. You make it all appear warm and friendly but, when need be, you're not afraid to ask the tough question. And . . .' she paused '. . . since the dress fiasco, you haven't looked too bad either.'

Christie was annoyed that her agent still insisted on referring to her first appearance in those terms. Julia had phoned her after each show during the subsequent two weeks, pronouncing herself satisfied or not with what she had seen. Meanwhile, Frank and Mel both took every comment personally until Christie stopped reporting back.

Having Julia's watchful eye had both reassured Christie and put her more on edge. She had breathed a huge sigh of relief when Julia had eventually pronounced herself satisfied. Her confidence had also grown because, since Gilly had introduced her to the nation, they hadn't crossed paths. Christie worked from Wednesday to Friday, happy in the knowledge that the other woman wouldn't be there to undermine her.

'There is one thing that I wanted to ask you about, Julia.' She twisted her wedding ring around her finger.

'Ask away.' Her agent gestured with a manicured hand that the floor was hers.

'I've just checked my bank account and I'm a bit concerned that I haven't been paid as much as we agreed. It's probably a mistake but I wanted to check.' Her shopping had made a nasty, guilt-inducing hole that hadn't been filled as promptly as she'd anticipated.

'Of course, darling. I quite understand. However, I think you'll find that Lenny, our accountant, doesn't make mistakes. We receive the payments from TV7, on the first of the month as usual, then deduct our fifteen per cent commission before forwarding the rest . . .'

'Fifteen per cent! But I thought you said you took ten, like most other agents.'

'But I'm not most other agents, darling.' Julia's smile definitely had something of the piranha about it. She ran her fingers over her hair, tucking the right side behind her ear. 'You've passed the probationary period, you see.'

'What probationary period?' Christie was mystified.

'Don't you remember, darling? We discussed it at our first meeting.' Julia looked straight across the table, almost challenging Christie to contradict her. 'You're paying for the best and that's what you're getting.'

Christie was almost certain they hadn't discussed any such

thing, but Julia seemed so sure. Perhaps she hadn't registered this detail in her excitement at being taken on. What was said at that meeting had become a bit of a blur as soon as she'd left the room, however hard she tried to piece it together. She snapped to. 'I don't doubt that and, of course, that's why I came to you, but I hadn't realised. You never did send me the letter detailing your terms.'

'I'm quite sure I did. I wouldn't forget something like that. I'll have a word with Lily. She must have missed it or it's got lost in the post.' She pulled out a wafer-thin leather-backed notepad and scribbled herself a reminder. 'Are you saying you want to go to someone else? You're quite free to. But, of course, they won't have my contacts and they won't work so hard on your behalf.' Julia remained quite cool, unperturbed by Christie's reaction, and sailed on. 'I was going to save this till I had definite news, but since we're talking frankly . . . This morning I had a breakfast meeting with the marketing team from Drink-a-Vit.'

Christie looked blank.

'The vitamin drink for women,' Julia explained. 'Gilly's the new face of the brand but, for obvious reasons, she couldn't complete their nationwide advertising campaign. She did all the filmed ads before she got too big but now we don't think she can do the press campaign. She must look after herself and rest as much as possible. So I suggested they use you instead. You're ideal. To be honest, you're not a big enough name to stand a chance of getting such a high-profile gig on your own. So this would be a huge break for you. They're paying the earth too.' Julia studied the nails of her left hand, running the pad of her right thumb along the top of them. 'Now *that's* what you're paying me for. The "jam" – remember? If it's not what you want, then by all means go elsewhere.' She looked up at Christie, her gaze completely steady. 'My ex-husband, Max Keen, might even take you on. In the past he's done a reasonable job with one or two people I've let go. At the percentage you want.'

Christie was appalled by the unintended turn the conversation had taken and hurried to get it back on track. 'You know that's not what I want. You're marvellous, Julia. I just hadn't fully understood your commission rates.' She knew that leaving Julia now would be a mistake. A big mistake. Others might easily misinterpret such a rapid falling out between them to mean that she was a difficult or underperforming client. That was not the reputation she wanted. 'So how much will you be deducting for the commercial work now?' she asked, as the fifteen per cent she remembered vanished in a puff of smoke.

'Twenty per cent. I did explain to you, darling, when I took you on.' Julia was calmness itself. 'At the time I did wonder whether you'd taken all our terms on board, but you assured me you had.'

'I'm sorry. I misunderstood, that's all. But if you could put it all in that letter . . .' Christie let the sentence hang in the air. She was stunned by this hike in Julia's charges but thought it better to remain calm rather than make a fool of herself by overreacting. Maybe this was the way it worked, the price she had to pay for being with the best.

Julia waved away the waiter who had arrived with the dessert menu and smiled. 'Well, that's sorted out, then. Coffee?'

Christie glanced at her watch again. If she left in the next fifteen minutes, she would just get to the school on time. 'Yes,' she said. 'Coffee. Thank you.'

After Julia had paid the bill, the two women got to their feet, Christie trying not to look as if she was hurrying to get away. She put the jacket she had bought with Frank and Mel over her arm as Julia shrugged into an expensive cheetah-print coat. On the pavement, they air-kissed.

Christie hailed a cab to rush her to the station but, as it pulled up, Julia edged in front of her and took the door handle. She climbed in, rolled down the window and leaned out. 'Lovely to see you, darling,' she said. 'I'll be in touch as soon as I hear from Drink-a-Vit.' With that, and a barked instruction to the cabbie, she had gone, leaving Christie open-mouthed on the pavement. There wasn't another empty cab for five minutes by which time she knew she had definitely missed the three o'clock train.

Sitting at Marylebone station, watching the 'delayed' signs on the departures board, she had plenty of time to think. She had unintentionally put herself in the position of having to make up ground in her relationship with Julia. If only she had paid closer attention when they first met, she would have known about the percentages. So, fifteen per cent went to Julia and forty per cent to the taxman. Suddenly her excitingly vast salary had been decimated. Everything she had been planning to spend it on was almost as far away as ever. Her face burned as she thought how stupid she had been. She had been too insecure and easily flattered when they had met, but Julia's reputation made her a formidable person to have on-side – whatever Frank said. However, she was beginning to recognise her agent for who she was: a woman who cared about her clients but for her own reasons. Their relationship existed on a purely professional footing for what Julia could get out of it. Nothing more. This was business. The reverence, admiration and respect that Julia received from her clients was her life blood. The deal was everything to her. Her cut was everything else. She was supportive, generous when necessary, there when required, but she wasn't and would never be a mate. Christie felt a pang of anxiety and loneliness.

Right now, she would have given anything to be able to share all this with Nick. He would have known the best way to handle Julia. When he was alive, they would sit up long after the children had gone to bed and chew the fat together, catching each other up on their separate days. Even though they'd only met one or two of each other's colleagues, they both felt as if they knew them all intimately. No detail was spared as they discussed their problems and tried to help each other solve them, commiserating when things went wrong and celebrating their successes. They delighted in hating each other's enemies and toasting each other's small victories. They could boast to each other about their triumphs at work in a way they couldn't and wouldn't to colleagues and friends. How she still missed that togetherness. Nick would have been able to help her see what she wanted from the new life she had chosen. Their marriage had been a gift.

Their wedding day was perfect. Christie refused all Mel's fashion ideas, along with all Maureen's catering ones. She went for a simple cream hip-skimming sheath of duchess satin that flattered her shape, and lunch for twelve at their favourite understated Italian restaurant. The day was exactly how she and Nick wanted it. The only person missing was her beloved dad.

After their three-week honeymoon, driving Nick's old MGB through France, then down the Adriatic coast to Portofino and back, they took up residence in a small Victorian two-up two-down terraced cottage in Acton. Nick's career as a solicitor and Christie's as a consumer journalist on the Daily News, *and occasionally on TV as a consumer pundit, kept them in a peaceful comfort. The following year little Libby was born, and three years later, Fred. Nick and Christie revelled in their family life. Of course there were rows, especially when the children were small and sleep deficit kicked in, but life was good. And it got better. In his mid-thirties, Nick was given a senior partnership in his law firm and the big salary increase bought them a mews house in Chelsea, closer to Nick's central London office.*

Maureen often came up to town from her house in

Buckinghamshire. She enjoyed showing off to her bridge friends about the brilliant marriage her daughter had made. Of course, she never told Christie this. She only tutted about how untidy the children's bedrooms were and why there wasn't a three-course, home-cooked meal on the table for Nick when he came home. 'Men like to be fed, darling. It makes them feel loved. I'm quite surprised you've hung on to him for so long.'

Christie would smile at her mother but shed tears of frustration in private. Nick held her and advised her to 'take no notice of the old bat'.

One night when Fred was coming up for six and they were lying in bed in each other's arms, having just made love, Nick murmured, 'Chris, I'd love us to have another baby. Shall we give it a go?'

'I thought we just had!' Then, seeing his expression so serious, she asked, 'Are you sure? It'll put us right back to square one in terms of sleep, potty training and everything else.'

'But in another few years we might regret it if we don't at least try. I promise I'll massage your back and brush your hair whenever you want.' He put his lips on her neck and started to kiss her.

'Mmm.' She wriggled appreciatively. 'Can I have that in writing?'

'I'll get a contract ready to sign in the morning.'

'In that case, Mr Lynch, you have a deal. Shall we get on with the preliminary negotiations?'

11

Running from the train to the car park and battling through the local traffic, Christie finally pulled up outside the school at five o'clock. She had tried to phone to say she was running late, but no one was answering the main switchboard. The tall wrought-iron gates were padlocked. Lights shone through the windows of the gym and along the corridor that led to the classrooms. She rang the bell, hoping that Mrs Snell might have waited.

'Hello?' She recognised the voice of the school caretaker quavering through the loudspeaker.

'It's Mrs Lynch. I'm afraid I'm late for an appointment with Mrs Snell. Is she there?'

'Gone home fifteen minutes ago. Sorry.' There was a click as the phone was hung up.

Oh, shit, shit, shit. What would Mrs Snell think of her? She would never understand how impossible it had been to make a getaway from lunch. In the head teacher's eyes, the welfare of the school's pupils took precedence over everything. She was right, of course. Why hadn't Christie made her excuses and left on time? Despite her initial determination not to, she had allowed Julia to take full control of their relationship. Feeling the guilt of being the least responsible mother in the world, Christie rammed the key into the ignition and drove home very slowly indeed.

*

Maureen was waiting for her. As soon as she could, she took Christie into the sitting room where she could talk to her without Libby overhearing. 'Well? What did Mrs Snell have to say?' She'd never had much time for the head teacher who, she felt, had risen too far above her station. Something to do with her broad northern accent and her generous waistline, and nothing to do with the praise Christie often gave her for being so good at her job.

'Nothing. I got there too late and she'd gone.' Christie sank into a chair as if all the strength had gone from her legs.

'Gone? She should have waited. Why didn't she wait?'

'Because I was nearly an hour late. Don't say a thing,' Christie warned, aware that she might say something she'd regret in response.

But Maureen couldn't stop herself. 'An hour!' she gasped, disbelieving that anyone could be so tardy. 'Oh, Christine, really.'

'Yes, an hour. And before you say any more, I know I should have made my excuses and left lunch earlier but it was impossible. Julia wouldn't understand and I don't want to get on the wrong side of her. Not when things are going so well. I left as quickly as I could. There were no taxis and then the trains were delayed.' Despairing, she leaned forward, resting her elbows on her knees and her head in her hands.

Maureen put a hand on her daughter's shoulder. 'But it was for Libby,' she said quietly.

'I know it was for Libby!' Christie exploded. 'Why do you think I rushed there as quickly as I could? There must be a problem and I've no idea what it is so I can't even begin to try to put it right. How do you think that makes me feel?'

Affronted by her daughter's outburst, Maureen took a step back. 'Feeling sorry for yourself isn't going to make things better.'

'I should never have taken the bloody job,' Christie muttered, ignoring her mother. She glanced at the photo of Nick. Seeing him strengthened her resolve. 'But I did, so I'm just going to have to make the best of it. I'll go into school in the morning and see if I can catch her then.'

'I think you should,' Maureen agreed. 'Actually, have *you* noticed something's not quite right with Libby?'

'If there *was* something wrong, I'd know.' Of that Christie was absolutely certain.

'Would you? You've been so preoccupied for the last few months. I know this "new career",' Maureen rolled her tongue around the words, 'means a lot to you, but you mustn't forget your family.'

'Forget? What do you mean? How dare you insinuate that I've forgotten the kids? I'm not just doing this for me. I'm doing it for us. Remember that, Mum. For all of us.' Christie banged her fist on the arm of the chair, simultaneously freeing a little cloud of dust that rose up between them.

'If you say so, dear.' Maureen pursed her lips. 'Just don't say I didn't mention anything.' She walked to the door and turned as she opened it. 'I'll see you tomorrow when you get home. I've left supper in the fridge for you.'

Christie didn't try to stop her leaving although she was ashamed of her loss of control. Maureen was doing her best to help her and all she'd done was shout. This was not how it was meant to be. She unclenched her fists, noticing that the pressure of her nails had left little half-moon prints in her palm. Why is life so bloody difficult? she wondered. I'm just trying to have a life and a family. Is that too much to ask?

She felt guilty for not being at home by the end of Libby and Fred's school day when they emerged full of stories about what they'd been up to and what their friends and teachers had said or done; guilty that by the time she got home, they'd moved on to other things and barely responded to her questions about their day; guilty that, if she was honest, when she was in the studio, she didn't have a second to think about them. Being there took up all her energy and concentration. A live daily news show was exhilarating, like riding a tiger, and it made her feel alive again. The print journalism she'd done since Nick had died now seemed like coasting. At last she was doing something that stimulated and fulfilled her.

She loved her growing friendship with Frank, as well as the working relationship she was developing with Sam. They didn't criticise her views or what she looked like but accepted her for who she was and respected how she approached her work. There must be a way to marry her two lives without sacrificing either. All she had to do was find the key. She sighed.

'What's the matter, Mum?'

The small voice from the doorway almost made her jump out of her skin. She turned to see Libby standing there. Her hair had grown over the summer and she wore it with a side parting so the way it fell hid much of her face. Standing there in her loose tracksuit bottoms and a baggy long-sleeved top, shoulders hunched and hands hidden by her cuffs, she looked like a waif who'd strayed in from the cold. Christie held out her arms.

'Come here, Libs.'

Libby crossed the room and sat on her mother's knee, resting her head in the dip under her collarbone. For a moment, they were silent, taking comfort from their closeness. Times like this had become increasingly rare and correspondingly valuable.

'Nothing, darling. I was later than I meant to be and then Granny and I disagreed over something. The usual stupid grown-up bickering. That's all.'

'I heard her say something about me.' Libby shifted her position slightly so that Christie became aware of her bony bum digging into her thigh. 'You weren't arguing about me, were you?'

'Of course not.' Mrs Snell had asked for her silence and Christie would respect that until she had heard what she had to say. As for Maureen, her child-rearing techniques had gone out with the Ark, so she wasn't going to be fazed by her views.

'I don't want you to argue. I don't like it.'

How small she felt, how vulnerable. Christie stroked her daughter's hair back from her face, as she had done since she was a toddler. 'I'm just tired, darling. Nothing more than that.'

'Will you phone her and make up? Please. I don't want her to be cross when she comes tomorrow.'

'I'm sure she won't be but, yes, if you want me to, I will. Pass me the phone.' Libby straightened to reach for it, then snuggled up while Christie punched in Maureen's number. After a couple of rings, the answerphone kicked in. Maureen must have called in on Ted on the way home, wanting to let off steam, no doubt.

'Mum? Hi. Just to say I'm sorry for shouting. No excuses, just tired. And I will think about what you said. Thanks for everything. You know how much I appreciate it, really. See you tomorrow.' She hung up and gave Libby a squeeze. 'There. Happy?'

'What *did* she say?' Libby wasn't going to let it rest.

'Supper's in the fridge. That was all. Come and help me put it on the table.' Christie changed the subject. Although she wanted to be able to talk to Libby openly about anything, she didn't want the moment spoiled. Libby had become so mercurial and her reactions so unpredictable that she didn't want to say something that would trigger a change in her mood. So what if they didn't talk tonight? Doing something together was definitely a step in the right direction. When Fred was next at Olly's, they would have more time to discuss whatever the problem was. Tomorrow she would learn what Mrs Snell had to say and then she would decide how to play it. She followed Libby into the kitchen and slipped *Queen's Greatest Hits* into the CD player. Ever since the children were babies, Nick and she had played this on car journeys, singing along at full volume, and most of the songs had become family anthems. She opened a drawer, passed a handful of knives and forks to Libby, and they began laying the table, screaming out the words to 'Bohemian Rhapsody'. And as they sang in and out of tune, Christie gave herself up completely to the pleasure she took from their togetherness. Her own anxieties about her work, the house and their future almost receded into the distance – even those concerning the loan with which Nick had saddled her.

Nick was a good man but no saint. The small things that drive husbands and wives to rows flourished in their house too. The loo seat being left up and his clothes draped around the house were high on Christie's list of annoyances. Nick's greatest grievances were continually being asked to take the rubbish out, and the smell of fake tan when she came to bed. The row about the fake tan was the worst they had ever had until the Big One.

One morning, Christie opened a letter from the bank addressed to them both. It was confirming a bank loan of £500,000 that had been requested earlier that week. The interest rate and final amount to be paid off after twenty-five years was very high. The letter went on to add that the equity in their house and its current market value were sufficient collateral.

She phoned Nick at work. 'Darling, I've got a letter from the bank here about a half-million pound loan. Do you want me to ring and say they've got the wrong people or will you drop in there this afternoon?'

'No, no. Don't do anything.' Nick sounded unusually flustered. 'It's nothing to worry about. I'll explain when I get home.'

That night, supper was washed up and put away and the

children in bed before the two of them had a chance to sit down and talk. Christie's mind had been in overdrive all afternoon.

Handing him a glass of wine she said, 'What's going on? You can tell me anything, you know. Why do you need all that money? Are you in trouble? In debt? Ill? What is it?'

He explained, and the subsequent row was nuclear. They didn't speak, touch or share a bed for days. Gradually she understood his reasons but neither of them could have foreseen how far the ripples of one small pebble tossed into the pool of their lives would spread.

12

The café tables were busy with yummy mummies chatting and laughing, their attention only half on the toddlers who were playing loudly among the tables that were scattered with half-empty baby bottles, bibs, rattles, toys and teacups. One small boy who was clearly just learning to walk wobbled slightly, then, with bent knees, dropped onto his very full nappy. A smelly miasma of poo escaped. Christie groaned inwardly. Ramsay's Tea Rooms was her favourite place for coffee but not when it was overrun like this. She checked herself. How mean-spirited she was being. She remembered how stir-crazy she had felt trapped in the house when the children were small, as well as the fantastic relief she had gained from being among like-minded women who understood exactly what she was going through. She ordered an Americano and an almond croissant and went to sit at a small table for two in an out-of-the-way corner by the window where she could think about what Mrs Snell had had to say an hour earlier.

She had arrived at the school with Libby and Fred at eight thirty. To her relief Miss Whittle, the deputy head, was already in so Christie had been able to nab her in the main corridor and give her lame excuse for her previous afternoon's no-show.

She knew no one would be really convinced by a delayed train out of Marylebone, even though it was almost the truth, but equally she didn't want to reveal herself as someone too weak to extricate herself from a lunch. Miss Whittle's disapproval was almost palpable but she had said nothing and checked the head's diary to find there was a slot free at nine fifteen, after assembly.

Sitting on the second chair in a regimented line along the corridor outside Mrs Snell's office, Christie had felt as if she was queuing for a punishment, having been disobedient in class. By the time Mrs Snell ushered her in, she was feeling quite repentant.

'Come in, Mrs Lynch. I did wait yesterday but I gather from Jenny that your train was delayed.'

Christie was almost sure she could see a curl in the head's lip marking her disbelief.

'Such a nuisance,' she went on, brusque and businesslike as she always was when dealing with parents. 'But never mind, you're here now. Can I offer you a cup of tea?'

Tea? That must mean she was about to say something upsetting or at least something that merited more than a couple of minutes of her time. Anxious to get on with the conversation, Christie refused. Mrs Snell ushered her into the room that always surprised her: its apparent disorganisation was so at odds with its occupant. She moved a pile of fancy-dress costumes from a chair so that Christie could sit down, then piled them onto the top of a filing cabinet already occupied by a set of dusty NatWest piggybanks. The rest of the room was crowded with the paraphernalia accumulated from years spent in the same school. Personal mementoes kept company with photos of sports days and fancy-dress parades, childish drawings, tea-towels printed with images of children's self-portraits, boxes of Christmas decorations, books, a map of the world and various unidentifiable clay models. Every surface was crammed with stuff. A sharp growl announced the presence of Meryl, a tiny Chihuahua, tethered by a long lead to a leg of the desk. Both women ignored her.

'Right, let me tell you of my concerns.' Mrs Snell walked round her desk to sit so that she was half obscured by a vase containing five burnt-orange chrysanthemums. Christie edged her chair across so that she could see the head teacher over the piles of paper and books.

'First of all, I wondered if there was anything in Libby's behaviour that was concerning *you*?' Mrs Snell put her elbows on the desk and leaned forward to concentrate on Christie's reply, her eyes like polished agates.

'No. Nothing more than what usually comes with being a teenager. You know, a bit moody, difficult. Though my mother . . .' She stopped, not wanting Maureen's observation to be part of this conversation. At least, not yet. She didn't want her to have noticed something that had escaped her. If Maureen was proved right, she'd never hear the end of it.

'But she's not a teenager yet, is she?' Mrs Snell reproved her. 'And that's what's worrying us. She used to be such a happy little girl, but her class teacher has told me that she's becoming increasingly withdrawn. Instead of being one of the main contributors to class discussions, she now rarely speaks. I wondered if she'd said anything to you.'

'Nothing. But we haven't been able to spend quite so much

time together recently. I've got a new job that's been quite demanding.'

'Yes, I heard. Congratulations.' Never had the word sounded so hollow.

Christie was racking her brains, turning over Libby's recent behaviour in her mind, searching for clues that might explain her apparent change of personality at school. Certainly she had withdrawn at home too, but not so much as to cause any real worry. When Christie had been that age, she had liked nothing more than retreating to her bedroom where she could curl up on her bed with a good book, a secret stash of biscuits and a couple of parentally approved oranges. Once she'd been given a stereo, she'd hidden away practising her dance moves and singing in front of the mirror, experimenting with the makeup that Mel had shop-lifted from Boots. Was Libby doing anything different from her? She'd felt she was doing the right thing as a mother by respecting her daughter's privacy, but perhaps she was wrong. Had she missed any signs that were more disturbing?

'Is something wrong here in school? Is she being bullied?' Suddenly panic possessed her. Not her beautiful daughter – she had always had such a strong personality. 'A force of nature', Nick had called her. Why would anyone dislike or want to hurt her?

'I don't think so. We've kept a careful watch in the playground and at lunchtime and there's no evidence of that.' Mrs Snell sat up straight in her chair. 'We have a strict anti-bullying policy here. She isn't the most popular girl in her class – that's usually reserved for the sporty or naughty ones – but she has friends she's very close to.'

'Aren't anger and introspection normal for girls her age? What else could it be?'

'That's why I wanted to see you, Mrs Lynch. I'd like you to go home and talk to her, try to draw her out and find out what's bothering her, if anything, so that you and I and my staff can help her. She doesn't appear to be thriving. Is she eating enough?' She paused as if to give Christie time to think before continuing. 'I don't like to let anybody slip through the net. It may just be that she's missing you being at home most of the time. And children don't like their parents to stand out from the other parents, you know. To have a celebrity as a parent can, I imagine, be mortifying. I'm very proud of Libby and I can see you've got your work cut out as a single working mum but I'm sure that together we can get the old Libby back again. After all, she has to start her GCSE preliminaries next year.'

Christie felt as if her guts were twisted in a vice. A dead father, a minor-celebrity mother and a prickly grandmother to greet her after school. Poor, poor Libby. At that moment Christie had felt like the worst parent in the world.

A loud crash brought her back to the present. Another stray toddler had tripped and fallen against a chair leg. The crash was followed by a long silence before a deafening yell pierced the air, alerting a mother who came hurtling to the rescue. Watching her made Christie think. She was just as guilty of taking her eye off the ball as this woman. Nick had always had such a close relationship with Libby. When he came home from work, he'd sit on her bed every night and read a story, working his way through the childhood classics. At first he had done the reading, but then, bit by bit, he had begun to share it with Libby. When he came downstairs afterwards, he would tell her the funny things Libby had said to him, and they would laugh together. Tears pricked at her eyes.

Don't do this. Do not cry.

'Excuse me.'

Christie blew her nose and looked up to see a middle-aged woman, quite oblivious to her distress, holding out an open magazine, a napkin and a pen. 'We watch *Good Evening Britain* every night. We think you're so good. Would you mind signing these?'

Not now, please. Go away. But Christie smiled. 'Of course not. I'm glad you enjoy the show.' She signed her name quickly, desperate to be alone with her thoughts again. After a couple of minutes, the woman shuffled off to rejoin her companion at a nearby table. A couple of the mothers were staring at Christie now, obviously discussing her. She acknowledged them with a nod of awareness that made them turn away. Fixing her gaze on the table, she felt horribly exposed as they, no doubt, picked her to pieces. But she wasn't going to be driven out of her favourite café, whatever was being said about her. She sipped her Americano and slipped back into her memories.

It had been so easy to let Libby's bedtime story go after Nick's death. Her own grief had knocked her sideways for so many months, and trying to cope with Fred's demands had meant that Libby was forgotten and had stopped being in the centre of the family. Well, no longer. Bedtime stories might be a thing of the past but on the nights she was home Christie would make the effort to be more interested in Libby's schoolwork and try to inveigle her downstairs so they could do something together. A direct conversation would be too confrontational. Instead, she would find out what was troubling her daughter by using more circumspect methods. She had agreed to meet Mrs Snell again in six weeks, assuming nothing more significant happened meanwhile. By then, she would be on top of the situation. And in the first place, she would go to the library and see if she could find any books that might help with Libby's term project on the Romans. That was something they could look at together tonight.

*

The library was almost empty. The ripple of a gentle snore barely disturbed the hush. The only other sounds were the gurgling of the old-fashioned radiators and the rustle of newspaper pages being turned. Christie inhaled the comforting musty smell of used books that never failed to bring back childhood Friday evenings when her father would take her and Mel to their local library after school. She walked through the adult section into the children's, where she had to be reminded of the way to the reference section. Working her way through the history books, she became aware of someone standing right behind her. One step too close. Anxious, she turned, only to find Richard reaching for a book over her head.

'Oh, it's you. Hello.' She felt a sudden pleasure in seeing him, having him stand so near to her.

'None other.' He pulled the book towards him. 'Not working today?'

'Yes, but trying to be a good parent as well.'

'Snap.' He looked at the book Christie had open in her hand. 'What have you got there?'

'Roman myths and legends. I used to love them. It's such a shame that kids don't read them any more. I thought Libby might be interested for her school project.' She said it like a question, not absolutely certain that Libby would show any interest at all. 'What are you after?'

'Dinosaurs. What else? But then I saw you. Got time for a coffee?'

'I wish I had.' She lowered her voice in response to a loud 'Sssh' from the librarian. 'But I've got to dash home.' She didn't want to explain that she had to be there for a short phone interview that Julia had set up with one of the women's magazines about what was in her fridge. How was she going to make that even remotely interesting or out of the ordinary? Perhaps she should stop at the supermarket on the way home. Yes, the two sides of her life were better kept separate if possible.

'Shame,' he whispered, as they walked towards the exit. 'But we'll see you at the weekend? Olly's got his heart set on making a Fimo version of Jurassic Park so we need Fred.'

She laughed. 'Well, we can't let him down, then.' She watched as he crossed the road, turning to wave before he rounded the corner. This was the first time she'd seen him alone since the pub quiz. Since then they had met only when they'd ferried the boys between houses. Without saying anything, he had made it clear that he didn't want more from her. He was happy with their friendship as it was.

146

13

'So, what do you want to tell me?' Frank could hardly contain his excitement. He was almost bouncing on the edge of his seat with glee. There was nothing he liked more than to be first with a piece of decent gossip. He had eagerly responded to Christie's call, asking him to join her for coffee in TV7's canteen.

'I'll tell you when you take your eyes off Jeremy.'

Frank's eyes were fixed on one of the young sparks who was chatting by the coffee machine. Butch, like something out of the old Levi's ad, but with short, streaked hair, he wore low-slung jeans, a large-buckled belt and a T-shirt so tight that every honed muscle was visible. Christie blinked. Was that the hint of a nipple ring?

'Mmm. Sorry, love. An old gayer like me can look, can't he? Oh, to be young again.' He sighed.

'Come off it. You don't look bad.'

'Not like the old days, though,' Frank patted his stomach, which was just inching over his belt, before turning to his bacon and eggs. 'Now! Could this little chat have anything to do with Gilly's enforced bed rest?'

'You know?'

147

'Darling, the entire studio's been rejoicing since the news hit the wires last night. How did you hear?'

'A phone call first thing this morning telling me to meet a film crew at her home this afternoon.'

His expression said this was news. So she still had the ace up her sleeve.

'And I'm to be the sympathetic female interviewer!'

For a moment she thought Frank might choke. A dis-believing snort developed into a crumb-spraying belly laugh that ensured he had the attention of the entire canteen. And not in a good way. He stared at her. 'Darling! You? A minnow to interrogate a Great White? She'll eat you for breakfast.'

'Thanks so much for the vote of confidence! But this time I'll be ready for her, I promise.'

Frank rearranged his face. 'Of course you will. You'll do brilliantly. Just make sure you tell me every single detail! What colour carpet, how many photos of her are on display – and check out the downstairs loo. What's her bedroom like and is there any sign of Derek sharing it with her? Derek's definitely on the lavender bus, dear. If he hasn't got on it yet, he's definitely got a ticket.'

*

The car drew up outside Gilly's Twickenham address. A small crowd of paparazzi was gathered in front of the high wooden gates. A single policeman moved them to one side as the driver leaned out to press the button on the entryphone. The car moved forward as the gates pulled back to reveal a brand new

Georgian-style mansion backing onto the Thames. To one side of it, in front of the garage, was parked the family fleet of cars: a top of the range Range Rover, registration DL1 and a custom-painted gold Aston Martin DB9, registration G1 LLY. As they parked outside the building, the gates closed behind them and the front door opened. Welcome to Gilly Central, Christie said to herself, as she climbed out of the car.

A tall, perma-tanned man dressed in black jeans and a crease-free black and white striped shirt with a pink cashmere jumper hung about his shoulders stood waiting to greet them. A weak mouth widened into an insincere smile that was reflected in his pale blue eyes. 'Hello, I'm Derek. Gilly's husband.' He offered his hand to be shaken. Christie grasped it, surprised at its almost feminine softness. Could Frank's jokes about Derek's sexuality be nearer the mark than she'd given him credit for?

'Hi. I'm Christie and you probably know the others.' She turned so that he could see the cameraman, sound recordist, lighting man, makeup girl and Jeremy, the muscly sparks who'd come along as the cable basher, all standing behind her.

Derek's eyes locked on Jeremy's for the briefest of seconds. Jeremy smirked at him. Derek looked away and gave a cursory nod before gesturing them inside. Only Christie registered their silent exchange. She knew how interested Frank would be. As soon as they were through the door into a large, enclosed porch, they were quietly requested to take off their shoes before going any further. Another door opened and they were toe-deep in ivory Axminster that stretched across the vast, double-height hallway to the twin staircases that curved in almost a heart shape to join the first floor. On the back wall between them a life-size portrait of Gilly, dressed in a long, white, Grecian-style gown, gazed benignly at all comers. On a table at its foot, a single candle burned beside a large bunch of white lilies that filled the air with their heavy scent. That and the huge domed atrium way above their heads contributed to the inappropriate religious atmosphere. As the crew stood staring, Christie drank in every detail to repeat to Frank later.

The silence was shattered by a loud and recognisable voice that reverberated down the stairs. 'Derek!'

'Coming, my love,' he shouted back, then wearily turned to the crew, catching Jeremy's eye again as he did so. 'Gilly's expecting you.'

At the top of the stairs, he knocked on and pushed open a polished wooden door, then stood to one side. As she stepped through, Christie had to check that her jaw was still in place. They had been shown into the largest bedroom she could remember being in. More extraordinary still was that there was not a splash of colour to be seen – just acres of whiteness, accessorised with gold, nothing else. To her left, there was a white velvet three-piece suite, the sofa occupied by a white Persian cat that lay stretched on its back in front of a *faux* coal fire. By the arm of one of the chairs, a glass occasional table held an arrangement of ten gleaming gold-dipped white roses, a gift tag propped against the vase. The walls were hung with an impressive collection of Venetian mirrors, the light from the recessed ceiling bulbs and artfully placed floor lamps playing off the intricacies of the cut glass. Above the white marble mantelpiece was a vast canvas that was – well, white. Christie had to suppress an urgent desire to laugh.

A cough took her attention to the other end of the room where Gilly sat, like a glorious ad for the White Company, propped with pillows on an enormous bed, its height exaggerated by being raised on a platform with three shallow steps that ran all the way round. Behind her, from a gold tiara fixed high on the wall, two sheer cotton voile drapes swept down to either side of the bed where they were held in place by gold tie-backs. Beside them were two enormous arrangements of white roses. Near the right-hand foot of the bed, a large cheval mirror was angled so that Gilly could catch her own reflection. She checked herself as she greeted them weakly, forgetting that they must have heard how loudly she could still shout.

'Gilly! How are you feeling?' Christie took a step forward, determined to meet her on the common ground of motherhood. One mum to a mum-to-be.

'Furious at having to let everyone down. Nothing could be more inconvenient.' So bed-rest had yet to bring out the hidden mother in her – if there was one. 'Shall we get on? The doctor's called to say he'll be here shortly. Bloody nuisance. How I hate being a burden.' She adopted a theatrical wan face again, checking it in the cheval mirror.

'Sure.' Christie dropped back into professional mode. 'Shall we go through some questions while the boys set up?'

'I don't think we need to do that, do you? I know exactly what I want to say. I don't know why they bothered sending you, really. I could just do a straightforward personal piece to camera.' She smoothed the highly threaded, satinised duvet cover in front of her. 'Is Marie there?'

The makeup girl stepped forward, clutching her box of tricks.

'Thank God it's you, Marie. I wouldn't have wanted anyone else. No rouge today. I'm a little pale, I know, but I want the viewers to see the real me.' She pulled her white marabou-feather-edged bed-jacket closer round her shoulders and flopped back, as if exhausted by the effort.

While Gilly lay beached on her bed, Christie walked around the bedroom (note to Frank: no obvious sign of Derek's sharing it), and managed to sneak a look at the card with the vase of gold roses. 'To darling Gilly,' she read. 'My number one golden girl. Hurry back. The nation and I are waiting for you. Your devoted agent, Julia.' She fought down what she was appalled to admit to herself was resentment – quite unjustified resentment at that.

'Christie. We're ready for you.'

She turned and caught a vicious glint of satisfaction in Gilly's eyes as she went over to sit on the edge of the bed.

'Camera running, speed and action,' called the director.

She began gently, asking nothing controversial, letting Gilly relax. 'Tell me, Gilly, how excited are you and Derek now your instant family is imminent?' As the interview progressed, they touched on the design of the nursery that was being finished off down the corridor, the thrill of buying three sets of baby clothes and the difficulties of choosing names for the little darlings. Then they alighted on Gilly, the mother herself, and that was where they stayed as Gilly talked enthusiastically about her favourite subject until Christie, tired of hearing about exercise (body and facial) and beauty products, decided it was time to up the pace.

'Now, Gilly, so many women see you as their friend.' Gilly looked her most demure as Christie continued, 'Having triplets at your age is quite something. What advice have you for any woman pregnant for the first time so late in life?'

There was a shocked silence. All that could be heard was the faint hiss of the fake fire and the clatter of Marie dropping a hairbrush onto her makeup box. Gilly pulled back a little, her eyes blazing. 'Well, I . . .' She hesitated.

'There must be something.' Christie smiled her most encouraging smile.

'Well, women may have weak and feeble bodies but I have the heart and mind of a man.'

Christie was slightly taken aback by this unexpected non-sequitur. Was Gilly channelling Elizabeth I, the Virgin Queen? That seemed unlikely, not to say inapt. She pressed on regardless: 'What about practical advice? You're a role model for so many older women, they'll want to hear from you.' She ignored the basilisk glare.

'I'm not sure I . . .'

The shrill jangle of her mobile prevented Gilly going on. She seemed relieved. 'Can we break for a moment? I'm so sorry. Julia! Hi. Yes, utterly beautiful. I'm looking at them now. Christie's just been admiring them.' This time there was no mistaking the little look of malicious pleasure directed at Christie. As Gilly turned away to continue her conversation, Christie exchanged glances with the crew who were regarding her with new-found admiration. Everyone in the studio knew that Gilly's age was off-limits. Once the interview resumed, Gilly switched the conversation to life as a working mother and avoided any further discussion of her age.

After the interview was over, Christie had raced back to the studio where she edited the tape for that night's programme, making sure her question and Gilly's bizarre answer remained intact. When it was done, and before she went into the studio, she called Julia.

'Christie, darling. How did the interview with Gilly go?' she purred.

'Very good, I think. Viewers will definitely see another side to her.'

'Oh?' A note of alarm sounded. 'I'd better ring her.'

'Before you do, I need to remind you about next week. It's half-term, remember?' Christie tried to sound as reasonable as possible.

'I think you may have mentioned it.' She sounded as if it was the last thing on earth to be of interest to her. 'Why?'

Christie cursed the stagey other-worldliness of the woman. 'If you remember, you said you'd squared it with Jack that Gilly would cover four days next week, so that I could be at home and spend some proper time with the children. So, if Gilly isn't able to work, who'll cover for me?'

'Oh, yes, Jack's already been on the phone. I've said you'll stand in, of course.'

'You've done what?'

'You heard. Don't tell me you're going to be difficult.' A steeliness had entered her voice that warned Christie not to be.

'But who's going to look after Libby and Fred? I've promised them I'll be at home. You can't agree something like that without discussing it with me.'

'Of course I can, darling. That's my job. As far as I'm concerned, I have a star performer whose life may be at risk, not to mention the lives of her three babies. None of us can afford to be selfish. This is a great opportunity for you. I'm sure you can find someone to help out.'

'It won't be that easy at such short notice, Julia.' A flame of anger licked through her. 'Look, I've got ten minutes before I go on air so we'll have to discuss this later. I'll speak to you after the show.'

Julia had made it quite clear with which of her clients her loyalties lay. Christie hung up, furious but with no time to think about what she should do. She had only ten minutes in which to run to the green room to meet the guests on that night's show before they went on air. Her childcare problems would have to wait.

*

Going home that evening was like walking back into normality. The hallway was strewn with Fred's football kit. Children's fingerprints had marked a grimy line at hip height down the stairs and along the corridor. Coats were hanging off the end of the banister. The sound of the TV blared from the living room where she found Maureen lying on the sofa, eyes half shut, and Fred engrossed in some gory science-fiction serial. She tiptoed out and went upstairs to Libby, who was curled up on her bed texting. The carpet was invisible under the clothes, clean and dirty, that were dumped there. Grungy boy bands stared down from the posters that now almost completely covered the horse pictures that had once held pride of place. Just the head of one grey stallion emerged from behind the latest, which featured Cheryl Cole. Among the magazines on the desk, Libby's laptop was open and switched on. Along the window-sill stood a row of discarded My Little Ponies, collected when Libby was much younger. The small selection of soft toys that were still her friends lay on her bed between the pillow and the wall.

She looked up as Christie tapped on the door.

'Mum! At last! I saw the show where you interviewed Gilly. That house was so gross.' She flipped shut her phone and sat up.

'It wasn't that bad. Not everyone wants to live in a pigsty like us, you know.'

'Maybe.' Libby fished out a copy of *Time Out* from under the magazines on her bed. 'I've been looking at what's on next week. Which day are we going to town together?'

Christie's heart sank. She had promised Libby they would have a girly day's shopping with a film thrown in while Fred was at Olly's and now she would have to disappoint her. 'Well, Libs, the thing is . . .'

'What?' Her daughter's excitement turned immediately to accusation.

'I'm going to have to work next week after all.'

'I thought you said you were going to spend it with us? You promised.'

'I was. I want to. But the doctors have told Gilly to stop work

156

so I've got to step in. I'm sorry. You could come to work with me, though. Might be fun.' She didn't sound convinced, even to herself.

'Whatever.' Libby flipped open her phone again and returned to texting.

'Libby, please – I've got a blinding headache and I've got to talk to Julia again in a minute. I know I can't get out of this one. Sometimes in life we have to do things we don't want to. This is one of them.'

'Yeah, right.' Libby didn't look up.

'Don't be like that.' Christie was torn between wanting to strangle her or to scoop her up and cuddle her but, anticipating Libby's reaction, she did neither. 'I'll make it up to you, I promise. What about this weekend?'

'You always say that. Forget it. Sophie's asked me for a sleep-over tomorrow. Remember? Jess is going too.'

Of course Christie didn't remember. Libby must have thrown the information into another conversation when her mind was elsewhere. That was her tried-and-tested method for getting what she wanted. Get a yes when her mother was preoccupied with something else. Then wait until the maternal guilt factor was sky high to bring the request up again as a *fait accompli* so Christie couldn't refuse. Always worked. Crushed by her daughter's rejection, racked by her failings as a mother, frustrated by the demands made on her by Julia and TV7, ashamed of her pointless feelings of rivalry with Gilly, Christie retreated downstairs. She opened the fridge, poured herself a large glass of Sauvignon, sat down and sent up an accusatory message to Nick ('This is all your fault!'), made a mental note to stop drinking and picked up the phone.

'Julia? Sorry to call so late, but I wanted to wait until I was at home.' She ignored her agent's attempt to cut in. 'I will work next week, but please don't agree to anything like this again without asking me first. My family's going to suffer and I don't know how I'm going to persuade my mother to pitch in. She's bound to have her own plans.'

'I'm sorry, darling.'

Christie double-took. Was that contrition she heard in Julia's voice? Surely not.

'I should have asked you, I know. But I was forced to make a quick decision on your behalf. I thought I was acting in your best interest.'

'Next time, you must remember that there's my family to think about too,' said Christie, taken aback by Julia's apparent change in attitude.

'I will. I promise. Now, I must fly, darling. Dinner with the director of programmes at Space TV.'

There was nothing left to be said, except goodbye. Christie hung up, feeling much better about the balance of their relationship. Julia couldn't walk all over her whenever she wanted. She wouldn't let her. After all, who was working for whom here? She knew what her agent's answer would be.

She looked ahead to the following week with foreboding. Julia was driving her up the wall, exactly where Maureen would go when she heard the news, while Libby was already up there. She took a sip of wine and closed her eyes. How would Nick have advised her to deal with their prickly young daughter? He would be so surprised if he knew how much their adorable baby had changed.

'You're going to be fine, dear. Keep breathing and push when I tell you and Baby will be here soon.'

But the soothing voice of the West Indian midwife was getting on Christie's wick. 'I don't want to be here. I want to be on the beach reading a book,' she moaned.

Nick picked up the damp, lavender-scented flannel and patted her forehead with it.

'Don't do that. Don't touch me. This hurts and I'm tired.' Another contraction swept through her. She felt nauseous. 'I'm going to be sick.'

'Pass me a paper bowl, please.' The midwife pointed with her eyes to where they were piled up. 'Come on, dear. One more big push, I can see Baby's head. There.'

Libby slithered into the world and Nick and Christie fell in love. She was called Libby after her paternal grandmother and she smelt like sheets that had dried in the sun. Eventually, she latched on to Christie's swollen breast. Then, when she'd fallen asleep, she was passed to Nick. He carried her to the window, like a precious parcel, speaking quietly to her: 'I don't mind what you do in life, Libby my love, as long as you respect yourself.'

'I'll remind you of that when she's thirteen with dreadlocks and an unsuitable boyfriend.'

'No chance. I'm not letting her out till she's thirty-five.'

14

The weekend seemed never-ending. On Saturday morning, Libby punished Christie by behaving as if she weren't there. She answered questions, but as tersely as possible, and otherwise refused to talk at all. As soon as she could escape to Sophie's, she did. Fred went to stay with Olly and Caro, who was briefly back from Brussels. Maureen agreed to help out during the following week but made it clear that she didn't approve of arrangements being changed at such short notice and that no amount of gratitude would be enough. By Monday, Christie had never been so glad to get into the car and be driven up to TV7 for her first full week.

Over the weekend, the feedback from her interview with Gilly had been better than good. The tabloids had responded with features on the older mother accompanied by quotes from and pictures of Gilly. Christie enjoyed a certain delight when she thought of how furious Gilly would have been when she saw them.

But on Thursday she took greater pleasure in an interview with Josh Spurrier, a comedian at the top of his game who had recently suffered a breakdown. The previous week she had written a personal note to him inviting him to be a guest on *Good Evening Britain*, guaranteeing an interview that would be compassionate but honest. The tabloids were full of the news that he had been seen leaving the Priory, but rumours as to why he had taken a near-fatal overdose were all unsubstantiated. Knowing the truth, Frank had suggested to Christie that Josh might want to put the facts straight: that he had gone into freefall following the death of his gay lover – a lover who had been kept secret from the public for years. Following his advice, Christie had written with all the understanding of a bereaved partner, offering a sympathetic platform on which Josh could come out publicly, before the press started digging and drawing their own conclusions. Josh's agent had emailed agreeing to Christie's suggestion, asking if they could run the interview on Thursday evening and that she be the sole interviewer. At least she'd get something out of working over half-term.

*

'Chris, you were brilliant,' said Mel, as she ripped the covers off their Indian takeaway. Christie swept the pieces of costume jewellery strewn over the table into a box and got some forks out of the drawer.

'Josh was brilliant, not me.' She remembered the quietly spoken comedian who had outed himself with dignity, then had the generosity to go on record admitting he had never been so open and honest in public. He had ended by saying, 'I must thank you and TV7 for handling me so fairly.' There were few celebrities who would stop to acknowledge that an interviewer had done a decent job for them, and Christie was touched that he had bothered.

'Did anyone else notice?'

'My God, yes. The great god Jack himself came down and said, "Not many others could have done it so well. Not even Gilly." Then the press office went mad and put the press release on the wires, along with a quote from Josh about how relieved he was to be able to grieve openly at last. Poor man. I so feel for him.'

'It'll make the papers tomorrow. Bound to.' Mel tore off a bit of kitchen roll to mop up the dhal she'd spilled during her frenzied opening of the cartons.

Christie sipped her wine. As the sisters began to talk, time was forgotten. Relaxing with Mel, Christie thought, was the best treat in an otherwise difficult week. Her sister's flat was like a safe haven where no demands were made on her. She loved being in the small kitchen with its bright red walls covered with photos of the places where Mel had travelled: clichéd palm-fringed beaches; an African village; a Mexican church; grinning Asian children. Her sister definitely had a photographer's eye. One row of stainless steel units was home to odd souvenirs from her travels: the dark wood fruit bowl from Botswana and the wooden carving of the Indian god, Ganesh to bring luck. On a swing over the table just big enough for two hung a bright green papier-mâché parrot from Brazil. Whenever she was here, she felt as if the two competing sides of her life were put on hold for a few hours, and for that time, she was answerable to no one. She had switched her mobile off, the better to enjoy their time together, so when Mel's landline rang she knew it wasn't for her. While Mel answered it, Christie helped herself to another spoonful of chicken korma.

Mel held out the phone. 'Chris, it's for you. It's Mum.'

Christie made a throat-slitting gesture. 'Mum, hi. Is everything OK? I'm running a bit late. Do you mind staying on for an hour or so? I was just about to call.' She closed her eyes and prayed for forgiveness for the lie.

'You said you'd be home at eight thirty.' Her voice was clipped. 'More importantly, you told Libby that. Fred's in bed but I've got Libby here. She wants to have a word with you.'

'Didn't I say I was having a quick supper with Mel?' Christie defended herself.

'Not in my hearing,' snapped her mother. 'Sometimes you take me too much for granted.'

Christie grimaced as Maureen put Libby on the phone.

'When are you coming home, Mum? You said we'd do the pumpkins. And Fred wanted you to help him with his costume.'

Shit. She'd forgotten all about the Hallowe'en preparations she'd promised she'd do for the weekend's fun.

'I'm so sorry, Libs. I stopped at Auntie Mel's but I'm on my way now.' Her eye fell on a new addition to Mel's collection of kitsch: a smiling Hawaiian hula doll complete with green grass skirt, white and yellow *lei* and a strategically placed ukulele. Right at that moment, she envied her sister's freedom.

'Well, I'm not going to bed till you get back. You promised.'

Having pressed every single guilt button in Christie's battery, Libby passed the phone back to Maureen.

When Christie hung up, Mel put an arm around her. 'Everything OK?'

'I'm the worst mother, that's all. I've let Mum and the kids down and now I've let you down as well, because I've got to go. I'm not sure I can manage juggling family and work. The magazines have got it wrong. You can't have it all.'

'It's early days, Chris. Everyone's happy to rally round and we know it's not for ever. Mum's enjoying being needed and I had a great time taking Libby to see that ghastly vampire movie yesterday. Even though I hated it.'

'I know. And I'm incredibly grateful to both of you. But whatever I do isn't right by Libby. Why can't she be just a tiny bit pleased for me? Instead, she's as difficult and uncommunicative as possible. Sometimes I feel as if I don't know her at all. I need to be around her more.'

'Being around isn't always the best thing. You've been putting every hour God sends into the job, you're exhausted and it's good for you to have a bit of time out. Mum loves being with them, whatever she says. Anyway, look on the bright side. Your kids are terrific . . .'

Christie shook her head.

'Yes, they are. I won't hear a word against my nephew and niece. You've got a great job. Shame about the agent – but you can't have everything. And you've got Richard in tow. What more do you want?'

'In tow? I have not!' Christie felt herself getting hot.

'Christine Lynch! You're blushing. You do fancy him, don't you? I knew it.'

Christie knew that if she even half admitted that she found him slightly attractive, Mel would never let her hear the end of it. In truth, she still wasn't sure what she felt. All she knew was that her feelings hadn't subsided into the friendship that was expected of her. 'Actually, I don't,' she said, pouring cold water on Mel's ideas before they took root.

But at home later that night, when everyone else was in bed, Christie lay alone in hers watching the green figures on her alarm clock flick away the time as she listened to the sounds of the night, thinking of her and Mel's conversation, unable to sleep.

*

The following morning, relieved to be at the end of a difficult week, she picked up the papers that Tony, her driver, always left on the back seat of the car for her with a Starbucks. The front page of the *News* showed Gilly being rushed to hospital, then waving as she was returned home in an ambulance after a scare. Trust Gilly to steal the limelight from Christie's interview with Josh Spurrier. Truth to tell, she was more than a little relieved to be buried on pages eight and nine, but her professional side knew that more exposure would have pleased Julia. She read on to find out what Gilly had had to say. As Tony turned into the busy traffic on the M40, her mobile rang. Julia.

'Darling. Just to let you know that Gilly and I watched your interview with Josh. You did a good job.'

'Thanks. How is Gilly?'

'Behaving like the little trouper she is, though sickened not to have been able to do the interview with Josh herself, of course.'

'Of course.' She didn't bother explaining her own responsibility for the interview, knowing it would be ignored.

'She won't be back at work now until after the babies are born – so you're full-time from now on.' She sailed on. 'But I'm calling for three reasons. One, I'm sending over another batch of publicity shots for you to sign and send back, and two, I've fixed an interview for you with the *Daily Telegraph*. Sarah Sterling will be at your house by ten next Monday. With a photographer. Your first big profile. OK?'

'Er, yes. OK. What do they want to interview me about?'

'Oh, Christie, just be creative and dazzling. They'll love you. And wear something *pretty*. And, three . . .' Julia paused for effect. 'The boys from Drink-a-Vit have come back to me. You *are* going to be the face of their press campaign. I've just got to negotiate the fee. Isn't that wonderful?'

'Yes, fantastic. Actually, Julia, how much do you think—'

'No need to thank me. Must dash. Taxi waiting. 'Bye, darling.'

'—you'll get for me?'

The only answer was the dialling tone.

*

After the show that evening, Christie refused Sam and Frank's offer of a drink in the bar. Sitting in the back seat of the Mercedes on the way home, she had the thinking time she needed. Half-term

167

was over, so work would be more manageable from now on and she would devote what time she could to Libby and Fred. At least they'd all have a proper routine for the few months she had left with the show.

Lights were blazing from the house when she finally arrived home. The rich smell of baking potatoes and chicken stew filled the kitchen. Maureen was washing up and smiling at something Richard was saying. In front of him sat four large orange pumpkins, their chopped flesh scattered on the newspaper that covered the table. Fred and Olly were concentrating on cutting ghoulish faces into the hollowed-out skins. Next to them, Libby and a girl Christie didn't recognise were cutting cats and broomsticks out of black paper. Dressed in uniform black, their nails painted green (Libby) and black (friend), they made a witchy pair, bent over with their hair shielding their faces as they concentrated on the task in hand.

'Welcome home.' Richard was the first to notice her. 'Maureen asked me if I'd help with the lanterns. So here I am.'

Christie bit back her surprise that Maureen had involved Richard, a man she didn't know, before she registered that of course she did know him. They often helped one another out in the week. She could see from the beam that lit up Maureen's face that Richard had made a hit.

'Mum!' Libby looked up, pleasure on her face for once. 'Come and see what Chloë and me are making. We're going to stick them on the windows for tomorrow night.'

'They'll look great.' Christie was relieved that the Libby she knew and loved was back. 'Can I help?'

'We need some witches' hats. Could you cut those?' She passed over a spare pair of scissors and a sheet of black sugar paper.

'But I need you to help me with these teeth,' Fred wailed. Before an argument began, Richard grabbed the knife and began chipping away at a gaping pumpkin mouth.

'Christine, before you do anything, could we have a quick word?' Maureen nudged her towards the sitting room. Christie could see that she was burning to get something off her chest.

Her mother was brisk. 'Look, Christine. As you weren't here, I've booked an appointment at the doctor's for Libby.'

'Why?' Christie's maternal hackles rose. 'What's wrong?'

'She's very pale, she didn't touch her packed lunches last week and she's only been picking at her meals over half-term.' Maureen softened with concern before becoming more definite again. 'She's going first thing next Monday morning. With you.' She ran her hands over her hips to straighten her skirt and mark the end of what she had to say. 'And I'm going home now to try and catch up with my own life.'

'Yes, Mum, and thank you, but on Monday morning I've got a *Daily Telegraph* interview at ten o'clock.'

Maureen looked straight into her daughter's eyes. 'Then it's a good job that the appointment's for ten to nine. You'll have plenty of time to do both. I've seen these.' She picked up a women's magazine and one of the TV listing guides that Christie had left on the floor. Each ran a story on her, celebrating that she was a new face on a popular show and was rapidly establishing a strong and positive rapport with the viewers. 'I hope you won't be getting above yourself.' Before Christie could reply, she had turned back to the kitchen, said her goodbyes and left the six of them busy finishing their preparations.

Christie felt the familiar guilty twist in her stomach. ''Bye, Mum. And thanks,' she called after her.

Eventually the children drifted off to their own devices, leaving Christie and Richard to pour themselves a glass of wine while they tidied up. Then they lit the lanterns and put them in the sitting-room windows before settling themselves in front of the fire.

'Busy week?' As she asked, Christie noticed for the first time the razor-thin scar to the right of his upper lip and wondered how he'd got it.

'Not bad. We had three companies in this week so it's been quite full on. Luckily Caro was around so it didn't affect Olly. He was thrilled she was back and loved taking Fred over there to show off his other bedroom and his other lot of games and toys. How was yours?'

'Mmm, OK. I can't thank you enough for helping out. I've been worried about Libby. Mum's just said something too, but she doesn't seem too bad tonight. Hormones, I hope.'

They let the conversation take them round their children, school (she didn't mention Mrs Snell), TV7, the new assault course Richard was designing. Lulled by the warmth, the wine and the easy sense of companionship, Christie found herself relaxing, comfortable in his company. It was only when they sat down that she realised just how much she was enjoying being with him. She looked at his face, seeing what Mel must have noticed on their first meeting. But he had more than just good looks. She saw a vulnerability in his face that intrigued her. There was definitely more to him than met the eye. Realising how little she knew about him, she wanted to ask about his background but at the same time she didn't want to intrude on his privacy. Did she fancy him? And, more pertinently, did he fancy her? Just a bit?

When he eventually got up to go, she followed him to the door. He called to Olly and stood in the hall, waiting for his son to appear. They were standing so close she could smell the faint scent of him.

She leaned towards him to kiss his cheek. As she did so, he turned and, unintentionally, her lips met his. He tasted of red wine with the slightest hint of cinnamon. She suddenly felt an intense longing for her past life. For Nick. For someone. Forgetting herself, she leaned into him and closed her eyes for just a second. He jerked back as if he'd been stung. When she looked up she saw panic in his face.

'Ooops,' she said. 'Sorry.'

'It's fine,' he said awkwardly, holding the pumpkin lantern between them. At that moment, Olly and Fred tore down the stairs, Fred bumping into Christie and almost knocking her off balance. Richard reached out to steady her but she stepped back from his hand, not wanting to make the situation worse.

'Come on, boy. Let's get you home.' He put his hand on his son's head and shepherded him out of the house. 'I'm sure we'll see you soon. Thanks for the wine,' he said, sounding horribly formal all of a sudden.

Christie watched the tail-lights of the battered Land Rover

disappear down the drive. What had she done? How could she have misread the signs so badly? She might be out of practice but she was sure he'd felt as comfortable with her as she had with him. She'd obviously been quite wrong. The kiss had been just an accident, she told herself. Or had it? She shut the door behind them. Well done, Mrs Lynch, she congratulated herself. Another bloody cock-up. She walked into the sitting room where the candle-lit pumpkins flickered in the window, sat down and looked at Nick's photo. He was laughing at her. Picking it up, she spoke aloud: 'I don't know, Nick. Have I lost my touch? You'd have kissed me, wouldn't you?' She touched the glass. 'I loved you so much but I've got to move on now. I need more than your memory to keep me going. He's a nice guy, you know. I think you'd like him. And I thought he liked me. Oh, well, I guess I was wrong. No accounting for taste, eh?' She gave a sad little laugh. 'Still, you know me. I'll live to fight another day. And at least I've got the kids.' She put the photo down, gave her husband a last look, and went to round up Libby and Fred for bed. Who knew what was going on in Richard's mind, what he was keeping hidden? Men were strange creatures. After all, even Nick hadn't been entirely straight with her until she had prised the information about the loan from him and promised to keep its existence secret.

'I'm doing this for Ma and Pa, OK? Ma knows nothing about it and must never know. Promise you'll never tell her, or anyone else for that matter. Pa is a proud man and I can't let him go under. I just can't. I'm his only son and it's taken him seven years to tell me the truth. Please understand. I need your support more than ever.'

He explained that Pa had invested heavily in Lloyd's and the returns on his investment had bought the highlands house and a decent income. However, at the tail end of the eighties the dividends were drying up, and by the nineties, Lloyds were asking their backers to pay back huge sums in order to get them out of the red. Pa expected the market to pick up so hung in there. He cashed in some insurance plans and other savings, but by 1999 he was in hock to his bank for half a million pounds and they were threatening to take the house. Eventually, with his pride round his ankles, he had told Nick the truth. He had tears in his eyes at the thought of bringing such a loss to Elisabeth. 'I'd blow my brains out if I hadn't already cashed in the life insurance policy.'

'Pa, don't say things like that. I'll do anything I can,' Nick had promised.

173

Christie had never seen him so out of his depth. 'Were you hoping I wouldn't find out? Is that why you went to the bank on your own? Would you have told me if I hadn't opened the letter?'

'I don't know. Probably not.'

That was what had lit the fuse to Christie's temper. 'You weren't going to tell me? I'm not your mother living in a dream world of times past. I'm your wife. *I'm not an idiot and I never expected that you, of all people, would treat me like one. Oh, my God, Nick – you, of all people. You're not the man I thought you were.'*

And so sensible Nick Lynch put everything he had, including his young daughter and pregnant wife's security, on the line – and the millstone of a debt of half a million pounds was born.

15

Libby was furious. Her face was pale, her mouth a thin, stubborn line, her eyes dark and sparking with anger. Her school shirt bagged over her navy-blue skirt, the skinniness of her beanpole legs accentuated by her black tights and heavy black shoes. She'd paused to eat a mouthful of porridge before filling her book bag, cramming in everything she needed any old way. Christie's insistence that she removed her green nail varnish before school meant that the edges of her nails were marked with colour that she hadn't managed (or bothered) to get off. Her school jacket and the oversize navy-blue jumper in which she insisted on drowning herself every day hung on the back of a chair.

'I don't need to see the doctor and I'm going to miss English. The only lesson I like,' she said, taking a quick slurp of tea. She made a face at the sweetness. 'Unlike sugar, which, if you ever bothered to listen to me, I've given up.'

'Well, if you get a move on and stop being beastly, you won't miss English,' said Christie, through gritted teeth. 'Fred's been sitting in the car for the last five minutes. Do hurry up.'

'Oh-kay-er.' She managed to drag the simple phrase into three syllables. 'I'm ready.' Libby threw on her jumper and jacket before grabbing her bag, which was now so heavy that she stomped outside with one shoulder higher than the other.

Christie sighed as she locked the house behind them. They had argued over the visit to the doctor last night but she had stood firm. Neither had she gone into the reason for the appointment, masking it as a routine check-up. If Libby got wind of Maureen's anxieties, she would refuse point-blank to go. To be truthful, Christie was sure Maureen was making a fuss where none was needed. But if this kept her quiet . . .

Having dropped Fred at school, they drove to the surgery on the edge of town where they sat on sticky plastic seats surrounded by posters offering help to smokers, drinkers and the overweight, advertising clinics for sexual health, diabetes, babies, and advising flu jabs, regular smears and breast checks. After twenty minutes, regularly punctuated by Libby's sighs and irritated tuts, Dr Collier put his head round his surgery door and invited them in. He was a gruff, kindly man who had been at the practice for years and had helped Christie start to find a way through her grief and depression when she had first arrived in the area. He had listened to her and she trusted him implicitly. More twinkly Dr Finlay than *ER*'s smooth Doug Ross, he was tweed-suited and waistcoated, a stethoscope around his neck, rimless half-specs sitting low on his nose. He gestured them to the two chairs beside his desk, catching Christie's eye and nodding to reassure her, before directing his attention to Libby.

'Now, Libby. Can I ask you to hop on the scales?'

Without saying a word, she kicked off her shoes and obliged. He played around with the weights until he was satisfied, then asked her to stand where he could measure her height. He raised one bushy grey eyebrow as he made a brief note. 'Are you eating enough, my dear? You really need to put some meat on those bones.'

Libby returned to her seat without answering, earning herself a nudge in the ribs from Christie. 'I'm fine,' she muttered.

'Let me check your blood pressure too. Roll up your sleeve.' He turned away and started unfolding a dark grey cuff attached to a monitor. Libby sat there, not moving, picking at a cuticle.

Christie nudged her again. 'Come on, Libs. The sooner Dr Collier's done, the sooner we can get you to English.' She wished her daughter would behave as well in public as other people's children seemed to. Why had she been blessed with a small thundercloud?

'Your sleeve?' Dr Collier held out the cuff.

Impatient, Christie tried to help her. Libby pushed her away and defiantly pulled up her shirt-sleeve. Between her left wrist and elbow there was a row of four parallel angry scratch marks. They were quite distinct. Christie could tell from the doctor's expression that he was as taken aback as she was. 'Libby!' she gasped. 'What happened?'

'Nothing.' Libby wrenched her sleeve down again. 'I haven't done anything. I was just playing with Sophie's kitten.'

Dr Collier peered sagely at her over his glasses. 'I'd stop playing with it, if I were you, my dear. You might do yourself some lasting damage.' He shook his head at Christie, advising her not to say any more. They would speak later. 'Now, if I can just do this . . .'

Libby reluctantly bared her arm again and let him tighten the cuff above her elbow while Christie sat, her eyes fixed on the marks, far too regular to be cat scratches. They could only have been made deliberately, but with what? And why? Could Libby be self-harming? She was only too aware that countless young girls did, but had never knowingly come across one. But why would Libby want to do such a thing? If only she could get inside her daughter's head and find out what was going on in there.

Before they left, the doctor cleared his throat but Libby kept staring at her lap. 'Look at me, Libby.'

She did so, her eyes large and insolent in her pale face.

'I think you should come back to see me in a week's time. If you've lost any more weight, I might need to run some blood tests. And stay clear of that kitten.'

*

Christie parked outside the empty playground. On the drive back to school, she had been running through what she *wanted* to say to Libby and what she *should* say. Three people – Mrs Snell, her mother and Dr Collier – had noticed something was wrong with her daughter, but not her. She ached with the knowledge that she had let her daughter down. She longed for the help and advice of Nick who had loved and known Libby so well. He would have have had an idea what to do, who might help them. But . . . she stopped herself . . . was this the same girl he had understood and loved? Libby seemed to have changed in so many ways since he had died. This was something Christie had to deal with alone.

'Libs. I don't know why you don't want to talk to me at the moment,' she began gently. 'I miss you and our little chats. I love you very much, you know.'

Libby turned to her and Christie could see the tears welling in her eyes.

'Oh, come here.' She held out her arms and they hugged awkwardly as the gearstick dug into her hip. 'I know things aren't easy with my long hours and your schoolwork. Is that what's upsetting you?' She rested her cheek on the top of her daughter's head, inhaling her familiar smell, never wanting to let her go. There was a small sniff. 'Whatever is it? Libby, tell me.'

Libby's voice was so muffled, Christie could only just make out what she was saying. 'Why do you have to be on TV?'

Her heart sank as she judged her reply, but Libby carried on.

'You're not ours any more,' she gulped. 'You're everyone else's too. Everyone at school talks about you. I liked it better when you were ordinary and no one knew you, and when Dad was here.' She pulled away from Christie's arms and sat hunched in her seat, picking at another cuticle.

Christie so longed to come up with a quick-fix for her daughter's pain. If only life were that easy. So her mother and Mrs Snell had been right. 'Believe me, Libs, I wish Daddy were here every minute of every day. I miss him so much – we all do. But he's left me in charge, so this job is just to help me fill the coffers and then I can go back to peace and obscurity. You've changed too, my darling. You're growing up and I have to let go of my baby Libby, don't I?'

'I know. But that's different.'

'It's not really, you know.'

They sat in silence, each considering what the other had said. Unable to bear the sight of her daughter's red-raw fingertips, Christie took her hand, stroking it with her thumb. 'Libby. If something else was wrong, you would tell me, wouldn't you?'

Libby leaned her head against the window. The first spots of rain began to run down the glass behind her.

'Why've you given up sugar in your tea? Are you trying to be . . . healthy?'

'Ye-es . . . and Sophie says I need to lose weight.'

Christie opened her mouth to speak but Libby got there first. 'And before you say anything, I do. I need to get rid of my fat thighs and hips.'

Christie hugged her. 'And were those scratches really from Sophie's cat?'

Her daughter's face crumpled as the tears began to fall. She tried to wipe them away with her free hand.

'What happened?' Christie pressed her, then waited.

'You won't tell Sophie's mum?' Libby begged.

'Promise.' Christie dreaded what she was about to hear.

'When I went to Sophie's, she showed me her arms. She's been cutting herself for ages, ever since her dad left them. She said it made her feel better. So I thought I'd try. But it didn't make me feel better.'

Christie thanked God.

'It hurt and I didn't go anything like as deep as Soph.'

'So you won't be doing it again?' She had never felt so out of her depth.

'No.' Libby sniffed, while Christie fumbled in her pocket for a grubby Kleenex to share with her. 'It didn't stop me thinking about Dad, except for a second.'

Christie hugged her again. 'Libby, we must sort this out.' An extraordinary sense of calm came over her as she took control. 'I had no idea you felt so bad. I think perhaps we should try to get some help. No, wait . . .'

Libby was shaking her head as she tried to open the car door. But Christie kept a firm hold of her other hand so she wouldn't be able to escape.

'We aren't in the right place to talk about this but I will find someone who'll help us both understand what's happening here. Perhaps I should have done that when Dad died.' Her words provoked another outburst of sobs. 'But I didn't. It's not too late, though. We'll get through this together, and you will feel better.'

Libby's tears slowed and she blew her nose. Her body visibly relaxed and her face showed the relief she felt. 'D'you promise?'

'I promise.' Christie drew her child to her again, feeling how the tension had left her. Libby was relying on her and she wouldn't let her down. 'Now, you'd better go. Or you'll miss English altogether. Splash some cold water on your eyes in the cloakroom and no one will notice anything. We'll talk more tonight.'

A kiss on the cheek and Libby was gone, leaving Christie staring after her, wondering what the hell she should do next. Remembering the *Telegraph* interview, she checked the time on the dashboard. Oh, fuck! Ten minutes to get home and do her hair and makeup. As she drove, she considered to whom she should turn: Mrs Snell or Dr Collier? She decided the sympathetic doctor was the more attractive of the two. She would call him as soon as the interview was over.

*

Sarah Sterling was charming. If anything, slightly too charming. In her forties, smart in black, with straight, streaked hair and an inquisitive gaze, she arrived with a photographer. They decided to photograph Christie in the kitchen, even though she had tidied the sitting room specially. Sarah helped clear the breakfast things into the dishwasher, chatting all the while. I know the routine, Christie reminded herself. Get the interviewee to relax, make sure you've got enough material for the piece then, when they're off their guard, go in with the killer question. She held herself ready. When the table was clear, she followed the photographer's directions and posed, smiling, until he was satisfied he'd got the shot he wanted. Only then, she realised her coffee mug had been in every shot – the one Mel had given her with 'SEX BOMB' in large letters on its side. When she had finally succeeded in persuading them that this was not the image she wanted to convey to *Telegraph* readers and he had agreed to airbrush the words out, she was left alone with Sarah.

They quickly covered the obvious subjects of her growing up and her early career, peppered with a few throw-ins about her philosophy of life (make the most of what you've got), her favourite possessions (my photo of Nick and the pottery pig made by Libby), greatest weakness (my quick temper), what she hated and liked most about herself (I try not to hate anything, and my optimism), then her thoughts on town (negative) and country (positive) living. That led inexorably to her marriage and Nick's death, which had so radically changed her life. Sarah was pleasant, interested, and Christie found herself warming to her as they chatted. She had no problem with talking about Nick. Writing about their marriage and about him had rehearsed her in what she did and didn't want to say. Thinking about him for the second time that morning she wondered again how he'd advise her to deal with Libby.

'How do you find Julia?' A question from left-field.

'Great. She's a fantastic agent and person to have on-side.' Christie was not going to let Sarah trip her up.

'Not too domineering? One or two of her ex-clients have complained that she can be too pushy. That children's presenter, Katie Belstead, swears she lost the children's Saturday show job thanks to Julia demanding too high a fee even though she'd asked her not to.'

Neither was she going to be tempted into indiscretion. 'I don't know anything about that. Certainly hasn't happened to me.'

Realising she was getting nowhere, Sarah changed the subject. 'Being left with two young children must have been hard?' She helped herself to another Jammie Dodger from the tin.

If only you knew, thought Christie, but instead gave her stock reply: 'To begin with it was, but I've had amazing support from my mother and sister.'

'How have the children – Libby and Fred, isn't it? – managed? It must have been hard for them too.' Sarah had eaten the top of her biscuit and was now nibbling at the filling, leaving the jam button till last.

'They've been fine.' Christie studied the pointed toes of Sarah's black knee-high boots as she closed the subject. Her children were a no-go area.

Sarah looked thoughtful. 'I only ask because a friend of mine was in a similar position – well, divorced, not widowed – and although her daughter seemed to be coping at first, my friend's just realised that she's being bullied at school and has started self-harming. She doesn't know what to do.' She took her last bite of biscuit.

Suddenly she had Christie's full attention.

'It's so difficult for kids these days,' Sarah went on, helping herself to another. 'They have so much to cope with at that age that we didn't. I watch Milly, my thirteen-year-old, like a hawk to make sure she's eating enough. I worry she's too thin. A couple of my friends' daughters are anorexic,' she went on anxiously, no longer the journalist but a mother. 'It's been incredibly difficult for them. But cutting themselves – I don't understand why they do that or how one wouldn't notice.'

'Oh, I can.' The words slipped out almost without Christie noticing. To her horror, she felt her chin wobble.

'Can you?' Sarah leaned forward, concerned, her eyes intent on Christie.

'I've just come back from the doctor with Libby. I'm so worried about her.' Immediately she knew she'd said too much. She drew back, appalled that she'd fallen straight into the journalist's trap. 'That's off the record.'

'Of course.' Sarah clicked off her tape-recorder, but looked as though she wanted to carry on talking.

'I think we've finished, haven't we?' Christie stood up and took the mugs to the sink.

Sarah nodded, glancing at her watch. She had all she needed. 'God! Is that the time? I've got to be in Covent Garden for two thirty and you've got to get to the studios. I must go. I'm sorry, but good luck with your daughter. Who said being a mother was easy?' She laughed, the professional again, before letting Christie see her out. She'd got her story and was leaving her interviewee in a blind panic.

*

In the chauffeured car to the studio, Christie spoke to Mrs Snell, assuring her that Libby's problems were being looked after. After that, she had a long reassuring conversation with Dr Collier, who said he'd refer them to a family therapist. Christie had one more call to make.

'How did it go, darling? Sarah's good, isn't she?'

'Very,' she replied, looking out of the car window. 'Julia, I need you to do something for me. I stupidly fell into the trap of saying something about my daughter that absolutely must not be made public. I need you to make sure she doesn't use it.'

'I'm sure whatever it was can't have been that bad.' Julia had switched into soothing-client mode.

'It was, trust me.'

Silence fell between them.

'You're going to have to tell me, darling. Otherwise I'm not going to be able to help.'

Christie knew she was right, yet she held back. Sarah had caught her at a vulnerable moment and had known just how to exploit it. But if she told Julia, that would be two people too many who knew what was going on within her family. Once the secret was out, she would have no control over it any more. But she desperately needed Julia to do a damage-limitation exercise so she had to trust her.

'Whatever you tell me won't go any further. You have my word.'

She had no alternative. She repeated the conversation she had had with Sarah Sterling. She heard Julia's surprised intake of breath. 'If it gets into the papers, Libby'll never trust me again and I'll never get her better.' Christie could hear the pitch of her voice rising. 'It mustn't.' She groaned.

'Calm down. This isn't the first time something like this has happened. I'm almost certain children under sixteen are protected by law. They'd need your permission to print anything about her.' The cogs whirring in Julia's brain were almost audible. 'But better safe than sorry. I've got an exclusive up my sleeve that I can trade with Sarah. Don't worry. Leave it with me. She'll understand.'

'Julia. You must not share this with anyone else. Promise me.'

'Don't insult me, darling. I'm your agent. It won't go further.'

Christie clicked off her mobile with a sinking heart, praying that Julia would keep her word.

Christie's relationship with Libby sometimes seemed so tenuous. Always had been. Usually they overcame whatever tested them, but public exposure of Libby's problems was something from which they might never recover. Nick's close relationship with his daughter had seemed so different. Even in the short time they had had together, an unbreakable bond had formed between father and daughter that, right now, Christie envied.

Nick had always understood Libby's moods. If ever there was a daddy's girl, she was it. And he was helplessly wrapped round her little finger. On her fifth birthday, the little family went to stay with Granny Maureen, whose house was a short drive from the Secret Town, a model village so realistic that it even had miniature trains running round it. Freddie was beside himself with excitement as he squatted down at each station to see them arrive and depart. Libby was following the printed treasure hunt given to visitors so they would spot the smallest things. She loved the prisoner escaping from the police station, and the bride coming out of the church. But most exciting of all, for her, were the large koi carp swimming in the pond.

Nobody saw what happened, but they heard the splash. Somehow Libby had climbed over the barrier, walked across the train track and past a small boathouse and was now floating face down in the water, her hair streaming out behind her.

Christie stood there, paralysed by shock, for a moment unable to speak. Then she yelled, 'Niiiiiiick!' as loudly as she could. But he was already in mid-air leaping the barrier, track and boathouse to get to his daughter. His splash drenched Fred, who began to scream hysterically. Within seconds, Nick had Libby in his arms and didn't let her go until they reached the first-aid room where she was pronounced fine but shocked. Back home, that night, Nick slept with his daughter in her tiny bed. He couldn't bear to let go of her. And for her part no one but her daddy would ever do.

16

The night sky was clear and the temperature had dropped well into single figures, bringing the first real intimation of winter. Sam, Christie and the crew had spent the day in Rillingham, filming and broadcasting a *Good Evening Britain* special almost entirely devoted to the key by-election that was so significant to the Lib Dems. It seemed certain that Labour weren't going to retain the seat but there was a chance that the overweening confidence of the Conservatives was not going to pay dividends. The Lib Dems had run a very efficient and effective campaign but opinion was divided as to who would win.

Christie was wrapped up in her red winter coat with the fur (*faux*, of course) collar, complete with gloves and hat. She had been standing outside the polling station for what felt like hours, warm when the OB lights were on but freezing when they were turned off. Her feet were blocks of ice. She and Sam had been interviewing all day, trying to get a fix on whether or not the Lib Dems were going to clean up on this highly contested seat. They'd been to the constituency offices of the main parties before catching up with some of the more extreme candidates. The weather had meant that there had been a decent voter turn-out so they'd got some good varied vox-pops. She thanked God the live broadcast was over at last so they could all retreat to the warmth of their hotels. Once the results were announced in the morning, they'd be on the spot to re-interview the candidates and canvass public opinion for that evening's show.

Never had Christie been so happy to see a hotel. An old timbered coaching inn, it radiated history and charm. Through the mullioned windows, she could see the lights of the crowded restaurant, and heavy oak beams. She imagined the buzz of conversation, the warmth of a blazing log fire, and shivered in the night cold. They were crossing the road towards it when a youngish man, protected against the cold by a tartan scarf and grubby dark overcoat, stepped out from the shadows in front of Christie, making her stop dead. Behind him stood another man with a professional-looking camera. 'Could we have just one photo with you?' he said. 'Just one. Please.'

'Sorry, mate,' Sam intervened. 'We've all had a long day. We're dying to get inside. No photos.' He took Christie's arm and tried to guide her past him, Frank closing ranks on her other side.

The man took no notice, trying to insert himself beside Christie while his friend ran in front, camera at the ready. 'Please,' he begged, reaching towards her sleeve. She recoiled, bumping into Frank.

As Frank drew Christie closer to him, the man darted behind them. By now she was really alarmed, quickening her pace to keep up with Sam and Frank, who were trying to hurry her into the hotel. The man gave Frank a shove that almost sent him flying. At that moment, Sam dodged in front of him.

'That's enough. OK? We don't want any trouble but you're frightening the lady. Go home, or I'll call the police. Now.' He stretched out his arm, allowing Christie to make a dash for the door.

Her heart was pounding as she collected her key from the small reception desk and excused herself to go upstairs to change. Her room was on the first floor down a crooked corridor lined with hunting prints. She let herself in and collapsed onto the heavily draped four-poster bed. She was unsure which she was most surprised by – her unwanted fan or Sam's transformation into her saviour. She shivered as she thought of the guy – sad, really. He hadn't seemed dangerous but his assault was an eye-opener. She'd discovered a big downside to becoming public property. There was little she could do except try to put the encounter out of her mind and be more watchful in future.

As the feeling gradually returned to her fingers and toes, she sat up and removed her coat and jacket. That only left the overwashed M&S thermals hidden beneath the thin terracotta-coloured cashmere jumper and dark-green skirt. She swore that never again in the middle of winter would she wear a skirt and high heels when reporting on the road. Big mistake! She went into the bathroom where she brushed her hair and repaired her lipstick. Then she rang home to make sure all was well. Since Hallowe'en, things had been on a better footing with her family. Libby seemed happier and had agreed to see Angela Taylor, the family therapist that Dr Collier recommended. Julia had worked whatever magic she needed with Sarah and nothing had appeared in print. Nonetheless, she was still running close to her credit limit with Maureen so it was important to try to do everything right and not upset her. Finally ready, she went downstairs to meet Frank and Sam.

Frank had booked a table in the bar for a late supper. The dark panelled room was busy for a weekday, full of news hounds gathered there for the by-election. Christie caught sight of the two men deep in conversation at the back of the room. She made her way through the tables to join them and caught the last of what Frank was saying: 'She's out for number one.'

'Who are you talking about?'

Frank pulled out the chair beside him. 'There you are. Are you OK?'

She sat down. 'Yes, thanks to you two. Thank God you were there.'

Sam reached for the bottle of white Rioja and filled their glasses. 'What a creep. Forget about him.'

'Nothing else I can do, is there? So who were you talking about?'

'You weren't meant to hear, but . . .' Frank's embarrassment didn't last for long. 'We're just talking about Julia.'

Sam glared at him as if to say, 'Why can't you keep your mouth shut?'

'It's OK.' Christie picked up the menu and began to read. 'What were you criticising her for this time?' She decided on the salmon fishcakes and sorrel sauce, with spinach.

The two men looked sheepish, neither volunteering anything, both concentrating hard on the menu.

'Oh, come on. You can say. Frank, I know *you* can't keep a secret.'

'All right,' he said, tugged between the pleasures of indiscretion and the near impossibility of tact. 'But I know you won't like it.'

'Try me,' said Christie, intrigued.

Sam beckoned the black-uniformed waitress over to give their orders. Once she'd taken and double-checked them, they were left to their conversation.

'There's been more about Julia in the papers,' Sam explained.

'Why? Why can't they leave her alone?'

'Laura, Ben's partner, has been papped out in public for the first time with her new fella so the journalists have dug up the case again and added some new stories that put your agent in a worse light than ever.'

'What are they saying now?' Christie felt weariness descend on her. She could see Frank was enjoying himself.

'You've heard the rumours that the director of programmes at Space TV won't deal with her?'

She shook her head.

'Great story,' Frank sat back. 'An ex-client of hers claims he took the idea for *Dead Cert* to her, she pooh-poohed it and then, according to him, went straight to Space and sold the format for a fortune.'

Christie knew the hit programme: it was an unlikely cross between *I'm a Celebrity* and *Midsomer Murders*. She listened, disliking what she was hearing. At the same time she reminded herself of how positive Marina had been about Julia when

195

introducing her on the *Tart Talk* set. Clearly, not everyone had their knives out for her.

But Frank hadn't finished. 'Anyway, when her ex-client produced evidence that the idea was originally his, Space had no choice but to pay him off. They said they'd never work with Herself again.'

'What's her side of the story?' Christie asked, curious.

'Usual face-saving guff. Dismisses it as a misunderstanding and that her heart's broken not to be able to do business with such decent people. And there's more.' He rubbed his hands together. When they didn't stop him, he went on, 'And Franny Gallagher has come out saying she moved back to Max from Julia – silly girl should never have left him in the first place – because Julia promised her a big contract with *Morning TV* and big bucks to move to her, and then Jackie Love, a higher-profile client of Julia's no less, got the job instead. That woman's not good news.' He gave Christie a meaningful look. 'Have you double-checked your contracts to make sure everything's above board?'

'I don't need to. I've got complete faith in her. No, honestly,' she added, when she saw the way they were looking at her. 'We've got a watertight arrangement.'

'Well, don't say you weren't warned.'

'You say that, and of course I've heard all the stories. But, if she's on your side . . . We've had one or two little misunderstandings, true, but nothing that outweighs all the good work she's done for me. I wouldn't be sitting here now if it weren't for her.'

'That may be true, but I still think there's something fishy. I was just telling Sam that I can't help feeling it was odd, Ben dying at her house.'

'Not this again.' Christie sighed, but Frank continued, undeterred.

'Ben told me the week before he died that he had money worries, and he was planning to discuss them with Julia. Thought she might have been dipping her fingers into the till to fund that lavish lifestyle. Then he dies in her house. Doesn't that seem odd to you?'

'What are you saying exactly? Are you accusing her of murder, Frank? Is that what you're getting at?'

'No, not exactly.' He screwed up his face as he thought.

'Then what? What are you trying to say?'

'I'm not sure but it never felt quite right.'

'Frank, stop it!' She looked at him over her glass. 'I know you and Julia go way back and that you don't like her, but Ben's death was an accident. He somehow slipped, banged his head and drowned. Julia was in bed, asleep. What you're saying is slander. She may be a shrewd operator but there's no way she's a murderer.' Christie glared at him, daring him to say more. He didn't. 'Now, you silly old poof, have another glass of wine.'

Frank smiled. 'Fair enough, you frustrated old fag hag. Just don't go anywhere near her pool.'

He saw from Christie's expression that he'd gone too far so confined himself to a grimace, then shook his head. 'It's Ben and his family I feel sorry for. They haven't had a chance to stand up for him. Remember that awful third-rate soap star who kissed and told in the *News* after his death? She totally assassinated Ben, making out he was a party-loving, drug-crazed sex fiend but I'm certain drugs weren't his scene.' He sounded puzzled. 'And he hadn't looked at another woman since he met Laura. None of it rang true.'

'Perhaps you didn't know him quite as well as you thought,' Christie conjectured. 'Who knows what goes on in anybody else's private life?' But although she dismissed the subject, she had to admit that a little bit of her was as intrigued as the others were about what had happened that night. She didn't want to disbelieve Julia's account, but she couldn't help wondering if it was the whole truth.

'But the press have their own agenda,' said Sam, indignantly. 'Or someone does. Come on. We know how much of that stuff is ill-informed guesswork or pure fiction – but they've got to fill the space somehow. Just because the Wednesday witches haven't sharpened their pencils for you yet.' He leaned back so the waitress could put his rack of lamb in front of him. 'Mmm. Smells good.'

'Oh, I'm very dull,' said Christie, dismissing the female columnists who gave nothing for anyone's reputation.

'You must have *some* secrets.' Frank leaned across the table, his eyes wide with interest. 'Aren't you going to share them with your two favourite boys?'

'Don't be ridiculous. I wish I had one to share.' She thought of Richard. Since the kiss, they had maintained the same polite distance, made easier by the fact she was at work every weekday evening. Their arrangements for the kids were made between him and Maureen, who wouldn't hear a bad word against him.

'He's perfect for you, Christine,' she'd said one night, unaware of the uncharted waters she was entering. 'But I expect he's already spoken for.'

Christie had ignored her. She still didn't get it, though. She was a reasonably attractive woman, wasn't she? Why would he react so strongly against her? He'd told her that he'd been divorced for a couple of years from Caro, who was spending more and more time in Brussels with her work and her lover. There was nothing standing in his way of a relationship as far as she knew. Unless he was gay, of course. The idea slipped into her mind from left-field. She caught her breath then concentrated on her meal, annoyed that she might have given too much away.

'Don't believe you.' Frank was obviously delighted to have caught a whiff of a secret. He wiped his mouth with his napkin. Sam smiled at the cameraman's lack of subtlety and winked at Christie.

'Oh, all right, then.' She gave in. Why shouldn't she confide in them? They had become such a tight threesome over the months they'd been working together that she wanted to share with them. Frank had opened up to her after their shopping expedition and she knew that all he wanted was a good man to love and be loved by in return. He so often disguised the loneliness he felt with lusty innuendoes about the muscle-bound studio scene-hands: men who laughed with him and teased that maybe he could 'turn' them before they went home to their wives and girlfriends. He never put his gaydar to the test, too fearful of middle-aged rejection. Sam was less of an open book but she got the impression

199

that he had had his fair share of success with the ladies without committing himself to anyone in particular. She'd heard him out when one woman had taken him too seriously and he was running scared, seeking sane advice. Both men had trusted her with their confidences so perhaps it was about time she let herself go and trusted them. They might even be able to help her. A different point of view from Mel's – her sister was her only confidante – might give her a new take on things. Besides, she wanted to steer the conversation away from Julia.

When he heard her story about Richard, Frank's reaction was instant. 'Turning you down? Obviously mad or gay, darling.'

Sam was more considered. His brow furrowed as he thought, his eyes serious. 'Perhaps he's more damaged by his divorce than you realise. He might not be ready. Maybe your vibe says you're not ready either.'

'But it's been two years since the divorce,' she protested.

'Yes. And it's over two since Nick died and look where you've got to.' He was cutting his lamb slowly then arranging it on his fork with a piece of potato dauphinois and some broccoli. Before he put it into his mouth, he said, 'You're an attractive woman, Chris.'

Christie was suddenly aware of the pressure of his knee under the table. She looked up sharply. The expression on Sam's face hadn't changed one iota, but his eyes met hers before he glanced away.

His attention on his plate, he said, 'You're out of practice, that's all. You know what they say. Use it or lose it. You've just got find it again.'

'Easier said than done. And I should know,' said Frank, ruefully, placing his napkin on the table. 'Anyone for a nightcap?'

They moved through into the snug where they continued their conversation, sitting in comfortable green and rose chintz-covered armchairs in front of the inglenook fireplace. At one side of the blazing fire there was a large reed basket of logs and at the other a set of shining brass fire-dogs. The low ceiling gave the room a cosy intimacy that encouraged the three of them to talk until they agreed they wouldn't be fit to work in the morning if they didn't go up. They kissed each other good night and went to their separate rooms.

As Christie changed for bed, she thought about what the boys had said. They had laughed together about finding ways to get her mojo back in working order but in the end had agreed that practice was the only way.

She was startled by a quiet rap at the door. Grabbing her coat as a dressing-gown, she went to open it. Sam was standing in the corridor, holding two glasses of brandy and smiling in a boyish way that lit up his whole face.

'I've been thinking.' He offered her a glass. 'Seems to me that I might be the ideal person for you to practise your romantic techniques on. No strings attached. Just a bit of fun to get you started.'

'Are you kidding?' That last glass of wine had definitely gone to her head, making her feel pleasantly tipsy. She pulled her coat tighter round her, wishing that she had packed something other than Nick's old pyjamas.

'No, I'm serious. But if you don't fancy it, well, have the brandy anyway.' He held out one of the glasses.

'Er . . . thank you. But . . .'

Go on, she imagined Mel's voice in her ear. Who needs to know? He's good-looking, you trust him, and he's saying he won't come back for more. Look at it as the first hurdle. Once you're over it, the next one will be much easier. And, you never know, it might even be quite nice.

She laughed as her inhibitions took flight. What the hell? 'Why are you standing out there?' She stepped back, pulling the door open.

'Really? Are you sure?' His confidence deserted him. She liked him for that.

'Let's have the brandy and see. But if we do, no strings. And no telling Frank. We'd never hear the end of it.'

'None and absolutely not.' He came into the room and raised his glass in a toast. 'Dutch courage.'

*

The next morning Christie woke up alone. Sam had left after they'd had a really very enjoyable time together, giving her a chance to catch some sleep and to get ready for the day ahead. He had been right, she thought, as she took her shower. Some skills don't go away. They just need a bit of a polish. She had always imagined that she would feel guilty and terribly disloyal to Nick if she slept with someone else. At last she had realised that enjoying herself with another man didn't mean she would forget him. No one was going to replace him in her heart, but that didn't mean she had to sign up to the nearest convent. Mel was right. Of course. One slightly drunken night had shown her that she could enjoy herself without being racked with remorse. Before he left her room, Sam had emphasised once again that he didn't want any ties and she was more than happy with that.

She was second down to breakfast. Frank was already in the dining room, with a cup of coffee and a half-eaten plate of scrambled egg. On her way to the table, she stopped to pour herself some orange juice.

'Well, look at you!' The light reflected off the top of his head as he gazed at her over his reading glasses, assessing what he saw.

'What d'you mean?' All innocent.

'Doesn't take Einstein to work out what happened to you last night. You look as if you've had your flue well and truly swept!'

Christie blushed. 'Frank! For God's sake, shut up!'

'You're glowing, darling. Well, it couldn't happen to a nicer couple is all I can say.'

'Get one thing straight, Frank Bolton. We're not a couple. It was a one-off no-strings number.'

'No need to bite my head off.' He squeezed her arm. 'Your secret's safe with me.'

Christie hoped so.

Sam was looking at his watch as he came over. He was slim in a pale grey suit that gave a pleasant hint of what was underneath. He gave her a friendly kiss on the cheek. She blushed, remembering the pleasure she'd experienced the night before when those lips had been so very intimate, and earned herself another sly squeeze from Frank.

Without bothering to sit down, Sam poured and slugged back a half-cup of black coffee, then grabbed a piece of toast before turning to go. 'Come on, guys. We've got to get down to the town hall for the results. They're posting them at eight thirty.'

'I'm ready. Just let me get my things and check out.' She drank the last of her coffee and stood up. She felt better than she had for ages. Sam had done her a favour and she understood the deal between them. Her radar was being cranked back into working order. She hurried upstairs, feeling quite ready for whatever the day would throw at her.

17

Julia was late. Very late. Christie had asked for this meeting and had arrived promptly, just as Julia expected her to when she called a meeting. She was naturally aware that she was one among many on her agent's long list of priorities, but even so, to be kept waiting for almost an hour (so far) bordered on rude. The time had been punctuated with messages saying she was on her way, unavoidably delayed. If it hadn't been for those, Christie would have left ages ago, happy to arrange another appointment. As it was, the continuing promise of her agent's imminent arrival had kept her there. A deliberate and well-practised power ploy, she suspected. She sat in Julia's office, comfy on the black leather sofa, having been shown in by her assistant, Lily. After she'd flicked through the copies of *Harper's*, *Vogue* and *Broadcast*, Christie fell to wondering what conversations these walls must have heard, how many careers had been made and bank balances improved in this room.

She got up and went to the window behind Julia's desk. The street below was glistening wet, with the rain bouncing off the roof of a passing bus. She watched a young woman attempt to hail a cab, then shake her feet as a car ran through a puddle and splashed her. Christie turned and looked at Julia's desk: immaculate, with neither a coffee stain nor an ink smear on the caramel leather. She jumped as Lily put her head round the door with another message.

'I'm sorry, Christie.' They had dispensed with the formalities half an hour ago. 'Julia's rung in again. She's ten minutes away. She really won't be long. Can I get you another tea?' She crossed the room to take away Christie's cup.

She was an attractive girl with an unusual face: full lips, quite a large but well-shaped nose, wide-apart eyes that registered interest in everything she heard, and the sort of pale skin that burned with the first hint of sunshine. She wore little makeup apart from a dash of mascara and a pale lip-gloss that she had obviously reapplied since she'd last appeared. Her dark hair was cut short in a funky asymmetric design. An extremely short tartan skirt exposed most of her very long legs down to her flat leopard-print pumps. A variety of droopy Top-Shop-style layers covered her upper half and a silver locket hung next to a cross on a thin chain around her neck. Nothing could be further from the studied and expensive elegance of her employer.

'I won't, thanks.' Christie's eyes travelled to a photo on the wall of Julia with Ben Chapman, laughing together at some awards ceremony. In one corner was scrawled, '*To the best agent in the world. The best is yet to come. Love Ben xx.*' She'd studied it on and off during the times she'd been there and now remembered Frank and Sam's disbelief over the way their friend had died. She stared idly at the presenter's face, open, friendly, conventionally handsome. 'I suppose you must have known Ben?'

'Yes. He was one of Julia's top clients.' The cup she was carrying rattled against the saucer as she straightened up.

'He must have been. I've heard so much about him. Whatever happened that night? Do you know?'

'I only know what we all read in the papers,' Lily replied, her eyes not meeting Christie's. 'You can imagine how devastated Julia was by his death.'

'Mmm, I can. Someone I know mentioned he had money troubles.' She said this thoughtfully, surprising herself that she dared to mention it out loud, given where she was sitting. 'But that couldn't be true, could it?'

'I honestly wouldn't know.' Lily headed for the door, avoiding catching Christie's eye again. 'You'd have to ask Julia.'

She was reaching for the handle when the door opened and in swept Julia, looking abnormally ruffled. She dropped her leather attaché case by the side of her desk. 'This bloody weather. The moment it rains in London, the traffic's impossible. I'm so sorry to have kept you waiting. My breakfast meeting was interminable and I couldn't get away. Then when I did, it took an age to cross town.' She handed her fur coat and dripping umbrella to Lily without thanking her, stripped off her gloves and tucked them into her Chloé bag before crossing the room to a round mirror on the wall. She touched her hair, coaxing every flyaway strand into its right place, then smoothed her lips together to even out her deep red lipstick. Happy with what she saw, she turned to Christie, who blushed at being caught behind her desk.

'But I'm here now. What was it that you wanted to see me

about?' No pleasantries, just straight to the point as she shouldered past Christie and inserted herself behind her desk, straightening her shoulders as she sat down.

As she was obviously in no mood for small-talk, Christie moved to the smaller chair opposite and attempted to be equally direct. 'I'm a little anxious about money, Julia. We're coming up to Christmas, and although I did the Drink-a-Vit campaign weeks ago now, I've only received the first payment. I'm still owed a second for completing the job.'

Julia's attention was on her computer screen as she moved the mouse across its mat. 'Oh dear, Christie. Not this again. You're money mad at best, greedy at worst. Paranoid.' She laughed. 'I explained last time that you shouldn't worry about it. Lenny, our accountant, is on top of everything. You'll still have good meat to eat, as my ancestors would have said.'

'Julia! I'm not mad, greedy or paranoid. And I'm grateful to you for negotiating such a good deal for me. But I'd like to give my family the best Christmas possible since they've put up with me being away so much.'

Julia flicked a button on her phone. 'Lily! Could you bring in Christie's file? Right away.'

Within seconds, Lily came through the door, clutching a green folder. She put it in front of Julia and left the room again. At the same time, Julia got something up on screen, concentrating as she scrolled down the page.

'Now, let me see what Lenny's done. Here we are. Yes. They should have paid you a further twelve and a half thousand pounds. We'll chase it up right away.' She smoothed down the sides of her fitted dress, pushing out her bosom as she stretched her back.

'But that's only twenty-five thousand altogether! Didn't you tell me you were trying for thirty-five?'

'Darling! I don't know why you pulled that figure out of the air. Wishful thinking, I suppose. I'd never have got that for you. Now, some companies are much slower to pay than others. There's not much I can do about that but, if we ever do work for Drink-a-Vit again, I shall make sure I send a dispatch rider round for a cheque for the full amount before you even do the job. It's dreadful how some people do business. I had hoped to get the last payment out before Christmas, but I agree it's looking tight now.' She studied her left hand, adjusting the large gold-and-diamond dress ring with her thumb. 'If things are really tight for you, I'll ask Lenny if he could advance you two and a half thousand on account. Would that be enough? Maybe you need some advice on how to manage your money. You're obviously very good at spending it.'

Christie sat still, smarting at the suggestion that she couldn't handle her finances and angry that she had made herself open to ridicule. She thought for a moment. 'Julia, I've got two kids, a house with emergency repairs being made and bills to pay. I'm not a spendthrift but I am very grateful for your offer. I'll take the advance on account of the money White Management owes me.'

'Less twenty per cent, darling.'

'What?'

'You really are in a muddle, aren't you? I did tell you that was the percentage I took for corporate work. If there's nothing else, I think we're done.' Julia pressed a button on her intercom. 'Christie's just leaving, Lily. Sorry, darling, but this morning's a nightmare so I really have to get on. And I know you've got to get to the studios.' They shook hands, air-kissed as usual, and before she knew it, Christie was standing outside under her umbrella, looking for her waiting car.

Through the passenger window, she could see people hurrying along the rain-soaked streets huddled under their umbrellas, while others stood in doorways gazing skyward, hoping for a break in the downpour. The flat grey light made everything look miserable – even the shop windows stuffed with Christmas decorations. But Christie didn't notice. She picked up the *Guardian* that Tony, her driver, always left with the other papers on the seat, horribly aware that she hadn't done as much preparation for that night's show as she might have. Sitting in Julia's office had taken care of that. But she couldn't concentrate. She'd obviously made a mistake over the Drink-a-Vit fee and, after all, she was still being paid an embarrassingly large sum of money for posing with the small bottle and smiling inanely.

She decided to be sensible and put some of the money towards the loan repayments, then began to calculate whose bill to pay first and what to treat the kids to for Christmas. Perhaps she would get Freddie the Wii he wanted so much if he didn't get the iTouch. And for Libby? One of the silver tabby kittens she had seen advertised in the local paper just days ago. She would phone as soon as she got to the office. For the first time since Nick had died, she had a chance of giving them a Christmas to remember. This year, 25 December was on a Sunday so the timing of everything was perfect. The show would be off air from Friday the twenty-third, and they didn't go back until ten days later on Tuesday, 4 January: the first proper holiday they'd had since she started. She couldn't wait. She was going to do her utmost to recapture the magic of those family Christmases, especially the last one they'd shared with Nick, which she still remembered so clearly.

Christmas at the Lynches' with Maureen and Mel became a tradition. Ma and Pa never left Scotland now. Ma was getting increasingly forgetful and confused and Pa preferred to stay with her.

If Christie had known it was to be their last, would she have spent a bit more on Nick and the children? They were certainly rich in love and Christmas fun, and when she looked back at her own childhood Christmases, it wasn't the presents she remembered but the games she'd played with her father and the fights she'd shared with her sister. That last Christmas morning, Nick had brought her tea in bed, and in the mug, right at the bottom, there had been a simple diamond eternity ring.

'We can't afford this!' She sucked the tea off it then held it out to look at it properly.

'Charming! And happy Christmas to you too, my darling.'

'Nick, it's wonderful and special and I love it but . . .' She slipped it onto her finger and stretched out her hand to show it off.

'If it makes you feel better, I could tell you it's paste.'

'Is it?'

'No.' He laughed.

'I love it! Thank you.' She reached up and pulled him down onto the bed to kiss him.

'Bundle!' shouted a small voice from the door and Fred jumped on top of them, followed close behind by Libby. She couldn't have asked for a more loving start to their last Christmas together.

After Nick's death, Christie had considered selling her engagement and eternity rings, but she couldn't. She had some vague idea that the bank loan Nick had taken out to help his father might have died with him. In fact, because it was in their joint names, she was now held responsible. The bank manager was very clear about her financial situation. The mews house in Chelsea was her only asset, and even if she sold it, she wouldn't have enough to pay off the loan, and certainly not enough to buy another house.

Nick's partner in the law firm where he'd worked was more helpful. Nick had taken out a life-insurance policy, which would pay out three hundred and fifty thousand pounds. Might she consider selling the mews house, paying off a bit of the loan and using the insurance money and what was left to downsize and move out of London? Good advice. But she had blown it by falling for the draughty money-pit she now called home – and she still had to pay off the loan.

18

Mel's flight had been due in at five that afternoon, the day before Christmas Eve. A taxi would have dropped her at the house a couple of hours ago, so Christie was rushing home to see her. Because Mel had changed her plans at the last minute and extended her latest exotic shoot into a Caribbean holiday, the sisters hadn't spoken to each other for weeks. And before that, work, the children and the builders had overshadowed everything else in Christie's life as she journeyed back and forth between them, always preoccupied by one or another.

They had occasionally emailed each other, Mel waxing lyrical about the delights of St Lucia and about the photographer on the shoot, Jean-Pierre, who, at equally short notice, had taken the same two weeks as holiday. Funny, that. They had been holed up in Rodney Bay, having a high old time. In return, Christie's replies had been brief, only hinting at the events in Rillingham. She was dying to tell Mel all about what had happened with Sam, but she deleted the message time and again because she couldn't manage to convey the exact mood of the evening. What she didn't want was Mel to misinterpret it and to cast Sam as a chancer (which he was, of course, but in the most charming way) and her as pathetically desperate (which she absolutely wasn't). Instead she resorted to teasing her sister with veiled suggestions about a mystery man, which she knew would have her fizzing with desperation to know what had really gone on.

Neither had she told her about Libby, about their visit to Dr Collier and the subsequent appointments with Angela Taylor, the private family therapist he had recommended. Despite her initial reservations about sharing her family's intimate problems with a complete stranger, she had been impressed by the way Angela had encouraged Libby to open up, even at their first meeting. She had also found some release herself by talking things through on her own. Angela said little but what she did say was perceptive and cut to the heart of a concern, pointing her towards new ways of looking at her own and Libby's reaction to Nick's death. Angela was quiet, non-judgemental and, after only three appointments, had given Christie hope. But these were stories best saved for a long evening with a bottle of wine, when she could explain everything going on in her head without Mel drawing the wrong conclusions. And, at last, this might be the evening. She hoped it would be the first of many, as they all hunkered down for a fabulous Christmas together at home. No work. No Julia. No worries.

Approaching the house, Christie could see the Christmas-tree lights, a blaze of colour in the sitting-room window. To the left of the door, the kitchen window was almost obliterated by Fred's cotton-wool snowscape where an unevenly plump Father

Christmas and his sleigh descended to the chimney of a house that, with a bit of imagination, was something like theirs. Brightly coloured squares of presents flew off into the sky behind him. He had no means of steering since her and Libby's scissor skills had stopped short when it came to the reindeers' legs and harnesses. The faded red paper lantern, bought on honeymoon in a strange Christmas shop she and Nick had found in the backstreets of Naples and brought out at Christmas every year since, hung in the ox-eye window above the front door.

She took the presents that she'd been storing in her studio dressing room out of the boot of the car and rushed them upstairs to be hidden in her study without anyone catching her. The smell of burning cheese confirmed Mel's presence in the kitchen. She tiptoed downstairs, wanting to surprise everyone. Just as she turned at the bottom of the stairwell, something lurched at her out of the darkness. She grabbed at the end of the banister to steady herself.

'Gotcha!' Fred clung to her like a monkey, his lips pressed to her cheek. She hoicked him up to her hip – before he broke her neck – and, breathless with surprise, kissed him back.

'Look up, Mum. Auntie Mel and me put it up there.' He pointed an ink-stained finger towards a bunch of mistletoe tied to the light fitting. 'She's been here for hours and hours. And she put some presents under the tree. Can I . . . ?'

'No, no, no.' She unhooked his arms and lowered him to the floor. 'You've got to wait until Christmas Day.'

'But . . .' He was fidgeting with excitement, pulling at her hand.

'No.' She knew exactly what he was going to say. 'Not even one. Come on, let's see what's for supper.'

To her surprise, she heard a man's voice in the kitchen – Richard. What was he doing there? Then she heard Libby laugh, followed a second later by Mel.

'God, I'm hopeless. Rich! I thought you said if I kept stirring it wouldn't go lumpy.'

Rich! Since when had the two of them been on such close terms?

'For God's sake, woman! Pass me the pan and I'll do it.' Christie could hear the amusement in his voice.

'Not only is he handsome, he can cook as well. What do you think of that, Libs?'

'P'raps he could teach you.' Libby laughed again.

'I'm trying. I'm trying.' Richard groaned before the sound of whisking took over.

Standing in the chilly corridor, Christie was suddenly overwhelmed by a horrible sense of exclusion from what was going on in her own kitchen. Mel had been back for five minutes and already everything was happier families than it was when Christie was around. The thought was fleeting but it hurt. She told herself not to be so bloody stupid, took a breath and walked in to see the three of them busy making supper. Libby was watching the chops under the grill, Richard was rapidly stirring something on the Aga while Mel was checking a pan of boiling water.

'Chris!' As soon as she saw her, Mel replaced the saucepan lid and rushed over to hug her. She was looking fabulous, sun-kissed and, despite the December temperatures, wearing a floaty aquamarine dress that did everything for her tan. Her hair had lightened by several shades and was cut to frame her face, accentuating her high cheekbones. 'You're back already. I wanted to have this cauliflower cheese done for you, but Libby and I got into such a muddle.'

Christie looked over at Libby, her face pale but happy as she smiled at them both and gestured with despair towards the table where a casserole dish sitting next to a wire-rack of mince pies contained what was obviously their incinerated first attempt.

'So that's the smell?' Christie hugged her sister back and planted a big kiss on her cheek.

''Fraid so. Luckily I asked Richard in for a coffee when he gave me a lift from the airport so help was at hand. What a man!'

Richard had turned so he was standing with his back to the Aga, holding on to its rail. Christie looked at him, liking how the corners of his eyes creased when he smiled, how the ends of his mouth slightly turned up even when he didn't. She experienced a sinking sensation that came with the realisation that something she thought she didn't much want was no longer available to her. Suddenly she wanted him more than anything.

'Gave you a lift from the airport,' she echoed.

'Yes, Maureen mentioned Mel was getting an expensive taxi and, as I was in town at a business lunch, it was easy to reroute via Heathrow.' Richard picked some dog hairs off his beige sweater and smiled as her sister nudged him aside so she could return to the cooking. Mel had been right. He was gorgeous.

Christie thought fleetingly of Sam. She felt no flip of the stomach when she saw him. And now I fancy Richard, she thought. Oh, Christie, get over yourself. Why does it matter to me that he and Mel click? I should be pleased.

She didn't need long to work out the answer. Of course he isn't gay. You never really thought he was. He just doesn't fancy you. He fancies your sister. Get over it.

'Anyway, I've asked him to supper since he's virtually cooking it. That's OK, isn't it?' Mel took the pan off the Aga and crossed the room to drain the cauliflower.

'Yes, yes, of course.' No, no. Actually, it's not. I want you on your own to find out exactly what's been going on.

'Do you know what?' Mel looked as if she was receiving divine inspiration. 'I've had an even better idea. Why don't you come to Christmas lunch?' She didn't notice either Christie's or Richard's look of alarm, or she ignored it. 'He was just saying, it's him and Olly on their own before they go to his mum's on Boxing Day. They aren't even having a turkey or Christmas pudding. It's a brilliant idea, isn't it, Chris?'

'It's rather short notice for you, though?' Richard sounded unsure.

'Come! Come!' shouted Fred, thrilled with the idea. 'Say they can, Mum. Go on.'

Christie pulled out a chair from the table and sat down, feeling as if her world was spinning off its axis. How could Mel be so insensitive? Then she remembered how she had denied all interest in Richard. She had no one to blame but herself. At the same time, she had imagined that she might still be in there with a chance. She was willing to square up to opposition – but unknown rivals for love were one thing. Her own sister was quite another. The last thing she wanted was to spend Christmas Day with them cosying up to each other, leaving her in the cold. She was aware that all eyes were on her, waiting for her decision: Mel and Fred's demanded she say yes; Richard's were questioning, and Libby's dark and unreadable.

'There's always way too much food and Mum adores him,' Mel urged, as if he wasn't there. 'And it would make such a change.' She spun round, almost knocking Libby off her chair. 'What d'you think, Libs?'

'Whatever.' Libby's demeanour had inexplicably changed. She got up and disappeared through the door, leaving the chops to Mel. They heard the sound of the TV switched on in the sitting room. Mel shrugged in a that's-teenagers-for-you way. Christie desperately wanted to go after her daughter but knew the mood meant she'd be cold-shouldered. Now was not the moment. What would Angela advise her to do?

'Why don't you ask the mystery man you hinted about in your email?' Mel was bubbling with enthusiasm. 'Then it would be a real party.'

'Don't be ridiculous,' she said sharply, aware of Richard studying her with new interest. 'I haven't got a mystery man.'

Mel looked confused. 'But you said . . .'

'Mel!' She stopped her in her tracks, saying firmly, 'No, I didn't. You must have misunderstood. Too much sun and too many rum daiquiris, I bet.'

'Probably.' Mel deflated, then recovered herself quickly. 'But I thought . . . Well, what about Rich and Olly, then?'

'Of course,' said Christie, making sure she sounded more welcoming than she felt. 'If you're not doing anything else, we'd love it.'

*

The next morning, Christie lay in bed, half dozing while a cup of tea grew cold on her bedside table. Mel had put it there, then given her a chance to have a much-needed lie-in by taking the children into town to get some last-minute bits and pieces. She went over the previous evening. Richard hadn't hung around, saying he was sure they had plenty to catch up on without needing him there. But when she finally had Mel to herself, Christie couldn't bring herself to ask her what was going on between them. Apart from not wanting to spoil the mood, she found she didn't want to know the answer. Instead she listened to Mel's adventures in the Caribbean, which mostly revolved around her affair with the photographer, and in turn regaled her with stories from work, interviews she'd done, her growing friendship with Frank and Sam and, of course, the night in Rillingham. Mel had listened with a mixture of astonishment and delight on her face. When Christie finished, she put her arms round her and nearly squeezed her to death. 'What an amazing guy! It's the best thing you could have done. You don't really fancy him, though, do you?'

'No,' she said decisively, not even having to think about her answer.

'Pity,' Mel murmured. 'Imagine the headlines.' She dodged, laughing, as her sister had tried to push her off the sofa.

Christie stretched, revelling in the warmth of the duvet but bracing herself for the moment when she would have to get up. She pushed herself up against the pillows, keeping the duvet as close to her chin as she could, then inched her left arm out into the cold to pick up the mug. She'd hoped to have the central-heating in by now, courtesy of Drink-a-Vit, but thanks to the delay in payment, she'd only been able to afford to get the conservatory windows and the chimney done. The up-side of that was that the sitting-room fire drew beautifully now, no longer smoking and exacerbating her mother's theatrical cough. The down-side was that, although she was hardly skint, she still didn't have money to burn – at least, not until she'd paid off more of Nick's bloody loan. Around her, the house was silent. She sighed, contented. No one was there to demand anything of her. The mile-long list of self-inflicted Christmas chores could wait for another couple of minutes, she told herself, screwing up her nose at the taste of the tea. No sugar. Downstairs, the phone was ringing. She ignored it. The only reason she had to leave the house today was to collect the silver tabby kitten she was giving Libby. She hugged herself with pleasure, imagining Libby's face when she saw it. With that, and everything else she had in store, this Christmas would be perfect.

Mel had left *The Times* and the *News* on the bed beside her.

She idly opened the *News*, thanking God she no longer had to write for them. Of course, the editor's dismissive attitude to her had changed the moment she'd landed the *Good Evening Britain* job. What a pleasure it had been to be able to refuse his entreaties to stay on. On page three there was a picture of Gilly and Derek celebrating the birth of their triplets and a short feature taken from the huge photo-shoot, which occupied at least ten pages of the Christmas edition of *OK!* 'CHRISTMAS BRINGS THREE CHEERS FOR GILLY'. The babies, Aphrodite, Melissa and Oscar, born on 13 December, lay on a white fur blanket: tiny things dressed in baggy red Babygros, their faces scrunched and pink, their fingers curling and uncurling. Gilly, dressed in a white silk robe, with flawless hair and makeup, was gazing out at the camera wreathed in a beatific smile, while Derek, his arm around her shoulder, looked down at his children, totally focused and adoring. And the babies, for all their newness, were sweet. Rather her than me, though, thought Christie. One baby at a time was exhausting enough. But those early days would be different for Gilly, who would be nannied, spoiled and supported to the hilt, unlike most new mothers who braved that precious time alone with their partners.

Christie flicked over the page and stopped dead. There was no mistaking the next photograph either. The photographer had caught her at her worst. Little makeup didn't help but the angle at which she was holding her head made her face look pinched and anxious, her hair lank and unbrushed. She was clutching her coat collar tight against the freezing weather with her shoulders hunched up around her ears. Worse still, as she studied the photo with mounting horror, she realised she was walking out of Angela Taylor's consulting room. Appalled, she read the accompanying text.

CHRISTIE IN CHRISTMAS CRISIS?

Exhausted Christie Lynch (42) emerges from a session with a family counsellor near her Buckinghamshire home. Has being thrust into the public spotlight become too much to bear? A friend says that Christie, whose husband Nick died over two years ago, is concerned that her family aren't taking easily to her new-found stardom. Other friends are also concerned that TV7's new star presenter may not be coping with the additional pressure as well as television executives hoped.

The piece went on to use quotes from 'close friends' and 'programme sources' to hint that Christie wasn't exactly popular at the studio and was becoming a tearful foot-stamping diva. Who hated her enough to make this stuff up? Downstairs the phone was ringing again. She took no notice, re-reading the piece, thanking God there was no direct mention of Libby, although the reference to 'her family' could mean only one thing. Who the hell were these so-called 'friends' who apparently knew her so well? Only Maureen, Julia and Frank (he'd winkled the truth out of her one evening, intuiting that she needed a friendly ear to confide in) knew the full story and she was certain that none of them would break their silence. Would they? Beyond that, Julia had assured her of Sarah Sterling's discretion.

Shortly after their conversation, Christie had seen an exclusive with Sarah's byline on *Tart Talk*'s Marina French and her clandestine affair with co-presenter Grace Benjamin. At the time, Christie had been as astonished as the rest of the British public and wondered whether the claims were true, given the vehemency of Marina's denial. Unable to bear the idea that her stupid slip of the tongue was responsible for this and the subsequent feeding frenzy in the other red tops, she had phoned Julia to ask if this was the story she had traded for Sarah's silence. Her agent's curt, 'What you don't know won't harm you,' was enough to confirm her suspicions. She had been both ashamed and horrified. Still was. Although Libby's privacy was vital, this dog-eat-dog method of survival was completely alien to her and she didn't like it one bit. She looked at the snapshot on her bedside table of Nick and the smiling children building sandcastles on Constantine Bay and sighed. Oh, Nick, why did you have to die? Come back to me, please. She closed her eyes, willing him to walk up the stairs. Nothing.

She examined the newspaper photograph again. Caught by a paparazzo she hadn't even noticed. The clinic was on a busy road and he must have been sitting in one of the cars parked opposite, waiting, having followed her there. Could the paper, despite her previous relationship with them, have put a reporter on her tail who had just got lucky? Her next thought was for the children. They mustn't see this, especially not Libby. Their Christmas mustn't be spoiled. Afterwards, Christie would sit her daughter down and try to explain what might have happened and how no one would know Libby was involved.

Oblivious to the cold now, she leaned out of bed, fished her mobile from her bag and switched it on. As she dialled Mel, a sequence of buzzes alerted her to a number of missed calls.

'Mel. It's me. I'll explain later but whatever you do, don't let Libby see a copy of the *News*. Yes, I know it's unlikely but just don't. I'll explain when you get back. No, I'm fine.'

She checked the missed calls. All from Maureen. Shit! She'd obviously seen the paper and reacted like an Exocet missile, immediately homing in on her reprobate daughter. Christie decided to call her after she'd spoken to Julia. By this time, her fury had been replaced by an icy calm. She would sort this out and she and Libby would weather the fallout – if there had to be one.

Julia picked up immediately. 'Have you seen the piece in the *News*, darling? Not looking your best but all publicity is good publicity.'

Christie took no notice. 'Nobody is supposed to know that we're seeing Angela. How the hell did they find out?'

'I've no idea. The press have their methods. But look on the bright side. We know you're fine, really; Libby's not mentioned and the speculation will you keep you in the public eye while *Good Evening Britain*'s off air. Glass half full, darling. Remember?'

Christie felt like throttling her. Julia had never expressed any genuine interest in Christie's life outside her work unless it impinged on some arrangement she had made. Whatever she said, she would never understand the potential internal damage a story like this might do to her family. There was no point in arguing. Christie would just have to keep a wary eye open for photographers in future and continue to keep her children out of the limelight. She cut the conversation short, suddenly desperate to be up and dressed, ready for the children when they got back. No newspaper was going to spoil the weekend ahead of them, and neither would the togetherness of Mel and Richard.

She went downstairs and relaid the big open fire with each scrumpled page of the day's *News* but, at the last moment, kept the page with her photo and took it up to her study. She made two more calls, one to her mother to reassure her that the story was a vindictive fiction, that she was fine and that, no, Libby would not find out about it. The second call was to Angela who listened and asked, in time-honoured therapist manner, what Christie was going to do. They discussed the pros and cons of telling Libby. Angela was all for telling her immediately, but Christie didn't want to risk ruining Christmas. They compromised by agreeing that she should be told before New Year, and keep an appointment with Angela, who would catch the fallout. Finally, Angela asked how Christie was.

'Please don't be nice to me. I'll cry,' Christie muttered. Then amid tears and nose-blowing, she poured out her upset and hurt over the article, her fears for Libby, for the security of her family, and for her financial mess. After about fifteen minutes, she felt a lot better and thanked Angela, whose last suggestion was for her to have a shower, put on some makeup and enjoy Christmas with her loving family.

19

By that evening, everything was as perfect as Christie had hoped. She, Mel and the kids had spent the afternoon in the kitchen, singing along to Christmas carols from King's College, Cambridge, and getting ready for Christmas Day. Mel struggled with the instructions on the packet of instant stuffing while Libby and Fred (briefly, in his case) helped peel the veg. Christie decanted the M&S pudding into a white mixing bowl and, with string, secured some greaseproof paper over the top – to howls of derision from the others who swore they would tell Maureen that it wasn't homemade. Finally, the turkey was taken out of the fridge and put in the cool of the newly repaired conservatory so the space could be filled with everything they'd prepared. There, done.

At last, they all dispersed to wrap the remainder of their presents, Libby and Fred giggling and whispering together. Christie went to her study to find the kitten curled up asleep on her favourite cardigan. She'd kept the radio on to drown the sound of any miaowing that might spoil the surprise, but the little thing seemed blissfully content, his black and grey tiger-stripes rising and falling with his rhythmic breathing. Christie sat in the old leather armchair that had once belonged to her father, heaving a sigh of satisfaction. She half tucked the offending page of the *News* down the side of the cushion, wishing she could forget its contents while telling herself to dismiss them as just a hiccup in proceedings. Maybe, just maybe, this evening was going to be all right after all.

Half an hour later, she was woken by Mel tapping on the door.

'Chris! Can I come in?' She twisted round the door, careful that the kitten shouldn't escape, holding a blue and grey silk head square. 'Do you think Mum will like this?' She flicked it in half, put it over her head and tied it under her chin.

'I shouldn't think so for a moment.' Christie yawned, stretching her arms above her head. 'But it is lovely. Beautiful colours. What about this?' She pointed towards a pot containing a few apparently moribund stems.

Mel pulled out the label and read aloud, '"Sweet Dream, a small apricot-coloured rose bush, double bloomed and lightly scented, perfect for the patio".' A pause, then: 'Christine! It's very pretty,' she mimicked, snorting with laughter, 'but I've decided that all the flowers on the patio this year are going to be white. Ted might like it, though.'

'You're joking?' Christie sat up. 'She hasn't?'

'No, not really. But I wouldn't put it past her.' She picked up a pencil and began waving it in front of the kitten, which stretched out a lazy paw to trap it. 'Libby's *so* going to love you, though.'

Every year, Christie and Mel went through the same ritual

230

of trying to second-guess their mother but, however hard they tried, they never got her quite the present she wanted. Brooches were the wrong shape, gloves not the right colour, clothes inevitably the wrong size, Champagne too extravagant, chocolates too fattening, and candles smelt too strong, too sweet, too flowery. They both knew that the scarf would somehow fail to meet her expectations, as would the rose Christie had once been so sure was the perfect gift.

They heard Fred shout from downstairs. Carefully shutting the study door behind them, they barged each other out of the way, like schoolgirls, racing along the corridor and down the stairs to find him in the sitting room, trying to attach an old rugby sock of Nick's to the mantelpiece with Sellotape. 'Every time I put it up, it just falls off,' he complained.

'I've got a better idea.' Mel took the sock and hung it over the fifties wooden clothes horse that Libby had pulled out of the loft to hang her Christmas cards on. 'That way, Father Christmas can't miss it. Suppose he comes down the chimney and forgets to look up. He might not see it on there.'

'S'pose not.' Fred looked doubtful.

After supper they sat together watching *Home Alone* (yet again). Fred lay sprawled across Christie's lap, helpless with laughter, while Libby sat by Mel's feet, casting the odd withering glance at him and smiling when she thought no one was watching. But Christie was. They were surrounded by their usual Christmas decorations: the over-decorated tree in the window; cards pegged unevenly to red ribbons pinned across the two alcoves on either side of the fireplace; pieces of holly just beginning to dry out and curl over the picture frames; paper chains made by Maureen and the kids criss-crossing the ceiling in two vast swags, held up in the centre by a rainbow-coloured tissue-paper ball. On top of the bookcase stood a green fabric wind-up Christmas tree that sported pink high-heeled button boots and wriggled and sang 'Santa Baby' on demand. Abandon taste, all ye who enter here, thought Christie wryly. But she wouldn't have had it any other way. This was what family life should be: togetherness and time-honoured pleasures. If only she could maintain the status quo through the next ten years. She caught Fred's hand sneaking towards the Christmas tin of Celebrations. 'Enough, Freddie. You'll be sick.'

At last the film was over, the brandy, carrot and mince pie left out for Father Christmas and Rudolph, an over-excited Fred had been packed off to bed and Libby, playing it cool this year, had followed soon after. Mel and Christie quietly filled Fred's sock and Libby's fishnet stocking, then made a pile of presents under the tree before turning the lights out, checking the kitten for the last time, then kissing one another good night.

*

A grey dawn was stealing through the gap in her curtains when Christie was suddenly woken by the icy touch of Fred's feet on her leg.

'Mum!' he hissed, his mouth over her ear. 'Can I go downstairs?'

She groaned, rolled towards him and reached out an arm for him to snuggle under. 'Stay here and let's wait for Libby.'

With a sigh of disappointment, he curled into her but for the next half-hour wriggled and fidgeted so much that by the time Libby came in Christie was well and truly awake. As dictated by family tradition, the kids fetched their stockings, and when the bed was buried under a mound of ripped wrapping paper and presents, it was time to get up.

They found Mel already in the kitchen making coffee. Christie pulled out a chair, wishing she'd had another hour's sleep. 'Oh, Libs, I've just remembered. I think I left the radio on in my study last night. You wouldn't switch it off for me?' She kissed the top of her daughter's head. 'I'm dying for this coffee.'

'If I must.' They heard her tramping upstairs and, as her footsteps sounded down the corridor, they tiptoed after her, shushing a puzzled Fred. The study door clicked open, and then they heard Libby's huge gasp. 'Mum!'

Christie took the remainder of the stairs two at a time to find Libby walking towards her, cradling the kitten, her face alight with joy and disbelief. 'Is he really for me?'

'He really is.' Christie put her arm around her shoulders. 'Now all you have to do is think of a name – oh, and bring the litter tray down with you.'

'What about me?' piped up Fred, engulfed by a sense of unfairness.

'Don't worry, Fred. It's your turn now.' She took him by the hand leaving Libby to debate names with Mel. From under the tree she pulled out a box and watched the excitement in his face fade. He picked at the paper, his eye on the other presents as if hoping another pet was going to materialise from one of them. Then his eyes widened and he gave Christie a grin that almost split his face in half.

'A Wii! That's wicked, Mum. Can I phone Olly and tell him now?'

'No, he can see it later. Let's have some breakfast, then Mel can help you set it up while I get lunch on the go so we're ready when everyone arrives.'

'Gee, thanks, sis.' Mel laughed.

The rest of the morning sped by, Fred and Libby occupied with their presents while she laid the table and got on with lunch, and Mel zipped back and forth between the three of them. As Christie prepared the meal, she couldn't stop her thoughts circling round as she anticipated everyone's arrival. She was still annoyed with herself for feeling jealous over Mel and Richard's new friendship and for being miffed that Mel hadn't said anything even though she hadn't exactly been upfront herself. Still disheartened over his reaction to her kiss, she reassured herself again that they could at least be good friends if nothing else.

'Anyone in?' The sound of her mother's voice brought her back to the here and now. Christie glanced up at the old station clock at the far end of the kitchen. One thirty already. The smell of the roasting turkey, sausages and bacon, potatoes and parsnips filled the kitchen. On the Aga, the pans of water were coming to the boil, steaming up the window over the sink. At the other end of the room, the table was looking its best, dressed in a red cloth with crackers at every place. The glasses glittered and the silver gleamed, while the centrepiece of holly and gold balls that Christie and Libby had made together looked as if it might even stay the course of the day without collapsing.

As soon as she saw Maureen, Christie knew they were in for a bumpy ride. In her mother sailed, looking ever so slightly tiddly, with Ted a few paces behind, carrying two hessian bags of presents. Her mauve beret had slipped to one side, giving her an unusually jaunty look that sat well with the belted mac (more Parisian prostitute than country chic, as Mel would later point out), which was removed to reveal a tweedy suit. They had obviously been down to the Legion for Maureen's favourite tipple on high days and holidays: a large schooner (or two, by the look of things) of Harvey's Bristol Cream.

'Happy Christmas, Mum.' Christie embraced her. 'Why don't you go through to the sitting room?'

Mel took a bottle of Champagne from the fridge. 'Shall I open this now?'

'Perhaps we should wait until—' Christie began, but Maureen interrupted her.

'That would be lovely, Melanie. So extravagant.' She led the way through and stood by the roaring fire, her sharp eyes checking the signatures in the Christmas cards while she waited to be given a drink. Ted plumped himself on the sofa, undoing the gold buttons on his blazer and releasing his paunch. He loosened his tie, presumably to clear a passage for some oxygen to get through to his disconcertingly puce face, and scratched about what hair he had left before reaching towards the glass Mel was offering.

'So Richard's coming, a little bird tells me.' Maureen looked her most mischievous. 'Such a charming man. I really thought he'd be perfect for you, Christine, but am I to gather that Melanie's got there first?'

Both her daughters stared at her, speechless. Mel was looking uncomfortable, fiddling with the row of tiny buttons that ran down the front of her dress. Christie couldn't move, knowing that if she did, she'd take a swing at her mother. Both Libby and Fred stared at their grandmother, shocked.

'I thought a little match-making was all that was required.' She smiled, all innocence but clearly aware of the effect she was having. 'That's why I asked him to pick you up from the airport, dear.'

Christie banged down the plate of smoked salmon and brown bread on the side table, making Maureen jump. 'Have I said something to upset you, Christine?'

'Mum! Please don't make silly, embarrassing assumptions. Richard's a friend. Of all of us,' interrupted Mel. 'Yes, I like the man. So does Chris. But it's not a competition. And I think we'd both prefer it if you didn't get involved with our love lives. We're grown women and quite capable of managing them on our own.'

Ted shuffled uneasily on his seat and sank half of his Champagne in one. Libby and Fred left the room to look for the kitten, which had taken advantage of the situation and skittered out of the door when no one was watching.

'But you're not, dear, are you? Or, at least, neither of you are making a very good job of it.' She nodded knowingly, so the beret slipped a little further over her left ear, and settled herself into a chair. 'A mother often knows her daughters better than they know themselves.'

Christie instantly thought of Libby. As the two of them struggled to come to terms with Libby's growing up, neither of them seemed to know her better than the other. But that was not something to dwell on today. Nothing and no one, not even Maureen, was going to spoil this Christmas. She forced a smile and, to everyone's obvious relief, changed the subject as Libby returned with her kitten.

'Have you met Smudge yet, Mum?'

With Maureen's attention distracted, Christie excused herself to finish off the lunch. She took the turkey from the oven and set the roasting tin on the worktop with a crash. Peeling away the tinfoil, she stabbed the skewer into the turkey, checking it was cooked through. Shaking the pan of roast potatoes vigorously to make sure they were evenly cooked before they went back into the oven, she imagined Maureen's neck between her hands.

Mel joined her. 'Take no notice. You know what she's like.'

'Do you know what?' Christie said, through gritted teeth. 'I really don't care. Who you do or don't see has nothing to do with me.'

'Don't be like that.' Mel was taken aback by Christie's sudden hostility. 'You know I'd tell you if anything was going on. Here, let me help with the veg.' She was about to tip the carrots and peas from the chopping board into a pan but Christie took the board from her.

'Do I?' Christie challenged, surprising herself. Then,

remembering her resolution, she changed her tone. 'Actually, I'd rather you entertained the old bag. I'm fine in here on my own. Really.'

They stood, staring at one another, uncertain what to say next. Mel looked anxious as if she still wanted to defuse the situation while Christie tried to control the resentment, envy and guilt that were warring for first place. The moment had come when she could ask the questions she'd held back over the last couple of days. At the same time, she knew that the timing couldn't have been worse. She rarely fell out with Mel but when she did it was never pretty. They hadn't spoken for days after one Fireworks Night, years ago, when, without asking, Christie had borrowed a necklace given to Mel by her then boyfriend and lost it during some vigorous snogging in the back of a taxi.

'I don't know what you're thinking,' Mel broke the silence, 'but don't let Mum ruin everything. It's just not worth it.'

Before Christie had a chance to say anything, there was a knock and in walked a well-muffled Richard and Olly.

20

'Happy Christmas! We let ourselves in. Hope that's all right?' Mel and Christie turned together to see Richard already unwinding his scarf and shedding his thick blue coat. Beside him stood a pink-cheeked Olly, clutching a shiny red remote-controlled car to his chest.

'Of course it is. Come on in. Happy Christmas.' Mel flung her arms round a somewhat startled Richard before she turned to Olly, admired the car and demanded to see it in action immediately.

Christie hung back, unsure whether to follow suit, but Richard solved the problem for her by stepping forwards, simultaneously spiriting a bunch of red gerberas and white roses from behind his son's back. 'Happy Christmas. I wasn't sure what to get you.'

'They're beautiful. Thank you.' She took the flowers, ran some water into a large ribbed blue jug, put them into it and stood it beside the draining-board. 'I'll arrange them in a second.'

'And there's this.' Smiling, he held out a small flat parcel. 'Caro thought you might like them. And one for you too, Mel.'

'Let's put them under the tree and open them after lunch

with the others.' Mel took Christie's present, apparently quite unperturbed that his ex-wife should have been involved in his choice. 'Come in and have a drink.'

They followed her through while Christie stood there, watching them together, struggling with another unpleasant rush of envy. This wasn't the time for that, especially when she was facing the last-minute dash to get all the various bits of Christmas lunch ready at the same time. She turned, quietly relieved to be working to her own (well, Delia's) timetable, with no one else in the way.

Twenty minutes later, she was ready and the others crowded into the room at her shout, waiting to be told where to sit.

'Mel! Could you finish off the gravy while I carve?' Suggesting they work together was her attempt at a truce, but Mel didn't hear. She was too busy fascinating the boys with the story of a haunted cave high on a St Lucian mountain.

'I don't think you need do that, Christine. Here's Richard. I'm sure he'll help,' Maureen purred, obviously having already succumbed to his attention.

'I can manage, thanks,' she said, rebuffing his attempt to take the carving knife. 'Why don't you sit down? You go between me and Mum, with Ted on my other side, and, Fred, you can sit at the other end of the table opposite me with Libby between you and Mel, and Olly next to Mum.' She felt bad about putting Olly beside her mother but told herself that being next to Fred would be all that really mattered to him. But should she have put Mel next to Richard? No. How much did being apart for a couple of hours matter?

'Can't I help at all?' Richard interrupted her thoughts.

'Really not.' She paused, then relented. 'Unless you want to take charge of the drinks.'

'I'd love to.' He ushered Maureen and Ted to their places, pulling back Maureen's chair so she could sit down. Then, with obvious relief at having a job to do, he set about opening and pouring either Burgundy or Chablis, taking Cokes from the fridge for the kids. Mel nudged Christie to share her glee at the undisguised approval Maureen bestowed on their guest as he moved around the table. Christie managed a smile in return. There was a 'Snap!' as Fred and Olly pulled the first cracker, Fred hesitantly reading out the appalling joke before they put on their paper hats. Everything was going to be all right.

Even Maureen couldn't find fault with the lunch: the turkey moist under its crisped skin; the sprouts and carrots with just enough bite; the delicate dusting of Parmesan on the parsnips; the potatoes crunchy on the outside, soft within; the hint of onion and cloves in the bread sauce; the citrus tang of the relish. Richard kept the wine circulating, admirably circumspect when it came to filling Maureen's glass. He hadn't needed to be told.

Once the table was cleared, the flaming pudding was produced to rowdy whoops and the bangs of party poppers. Finally, unable to eat another mouthful, they returned contented to the sitting room where, among cups of coffee, glasses of wine and chocolates, they collapsed in front of the fire to unwrap their presents. The sisters' predictions had been, of course, right. The scarf was 'Lovely, but just the wrong shade of blue, darling.' As for the rose: 'Beautiful, I'm sure, but it won't really go with my pink

Gertrude Jekylls.' Christie rose above her growing exasperation with her mother's ingratitude and carried on smiling, covering the sound of Mel's amused snort by loudly offering Ted a brandy. He accepted while making appreciative grunts over the socks and scarf he'd been given.

But all Christie really cared about was Fred and Libby. She watched as Libby screamed with delight over her longed-for grey-knit Ugg boots and a skimpy Zara dress, while Fred immediately tried on his combat trousers and climbed into his sleeping bag, before they both crossed the room to hug her. She shut her eyes tight with pleasure.

The smoothie-maker she had given Mel was a wild success (not a surprise, given the heavy pre-Christmas hints) while Mel had presented her with a painted tin kitchen-roll holder in the shape of a crowded yellow St Lucian bus and something flat and floppy. She unwrapped it slowly, rolling up the ribbon then carefully unfolding the paper (ingrained habits instilled by Maureen), aware of Mel itching for her to hurry up. She tore the sticker off the tissue paper and pulled it apart. Oyster silk, black lace. As she touched it, the fabric slid open across her lap, revealing itself as a sexy strappy chemise and matching thong. She snatched at it, not wanting the others to see something quite so personal. Too late. Ted sat forward; Maureen tensed; Richard busied himself with the battery for Fred's new torch.

'There! I thought you needed something to spice up your love life. Aren't they gorgeous?' Mel was unabashed, oblivious to anyone else's reaction, least of all her sister's. 'I hope you'll put them to good use.'

242

'Melanie, really!' Maureen's voice cut through the embarrassed silence. 'Hardly appropriate in front of the children.'

'They're lovely,' Christie whispered, her cheeks flaming, hurriedly folding her presents any which way back into their tissue. Her sister was several glasses of wine the worse for wear and meant no harm, and any other time Christie would have laughed off the innuendo but today she couldn't – especially not in front of Richard. Mel subsided into an uncharacteristic silence, a sure sign that she'd been hurt by Christie's apparent dismissal of her gift.

Richard swiftly crossed to the tree and picked up his and Olly's present to Fred, deflecting everyone's attention as Fred tore the wrapping off a metal detector and let out a long gasp of excitement. Between him and Libby, Smudge was pogoing in and out of the discarded paper, ears pricked, tail upright, spooking at invisible shadows, making them all laugh again.

At last there were only two presents left: the small packages from Richard. Mel ripped hers open to reveal a pair of sassy tangerine-coloured gloves made of the softest leather. While she tried them on, thrilled, turning her hands this way and that, Christie carefully unwrapped hers, looking forward to a matching pair (though perhaps in a more muted colour). But instead she found herself staring at two sturdy sheepskin gloves. She did her best not to show her disappointment. Was that how Richard really saw them? She a dowdy country cousin to Mel's funky city girl?

'Thank you,' she said, forcing herself to smile. 'They'll be incredibly useful.'

'I noticed that the fingers on your others had come unstitched,' he explained, obviously anxious for her to understand his choice. 'That's what gave me the idea and Caro approved.'

'Well, I love them,' she said firmly, taking a swig of wine, before putting them on the pile of three weighty Swedish crime novels that, to her delight, Ted had given her. 'More coffee, anyone?' A moment alone in the kitchen was all she needed.

Five minutes later, coming into the hall with the tray of mugs and Christmas cake, she almost bumped into Richard, who was heading towards the loo. At the same time, Mel came down from upstairs. For a moment, the three of them paused, each waiting for the others to move first, when Mel suddenly stood on tiptoe, put her hands on Richard's shoulders and kissed him smack on the lips. He didn't pull away. A punch in Christie's stomach would have been kinder.

'There,' Mel announced, satisfied. 'I knew that mistletoe would come in handy.'

'For God's sake!' Christie muttered under her breath, but loud enough for them all to hear quite clearly. Immediately she regretted it.

'What?' Mel demanded, her mood changing. 'For God's sake, what?'

Richard edged past the sisters, mumbling something about the loo being free at last. Mel didn't try to stop him. She was concentrating too hard on her sister.

'Nothing. Forget it.' Christie was aware that she'd gone too far. She turned to the sanctuary of her kitchen, wanting to wind back the clock five minutes. But Mel followed her.

'What the hell's wrong with you?' she demanded. 'It's Christmas Day and suddenly we're all treading on eggshells round you.'

'That's unfair and you know it.' Christie leaped to her own defence. She was not going to be put in her place by anyone, least of all by her little sister.

'One Christmas kiss and you go all prim and proper. What's your problem?' Mel picked up an abandoned wineglass from the table and slugged back its contents.

'*I* don't have a problem.' Christie could see that Mel was slightly drunker than she was but she wasn't going to allow her the upper hand. She would keep calm but fight her corner. 'Look, I'm sorry if I've annoyed you but I've had a lot of stuff on my plate recently, not to mention putting all this together.'

'Oh, get a grip.' Mel had never sounded so unforgiving. 'Loads of women run jobs, families and Christmas. And they do it without the help of their mother and sister. Mum's bending over backwards for you to make everything work. Me too, for that matter.'

'They don't do it without the help of their husband, though.' How pathetic she sounded, but it was true.

'Oh, put the self-pity away or I'll get out the violin. Please.'

Christie stared at her sister as if she'd been slapped but Mel hadn't finished. 'Look, I couldn't be more sorry that Nick died and nor could Mum. He was a lovely, lovely man. But you can't keep bringing him out as an excuse whenever things go wrong. He'd hate it and you know he would.'

'How dare you speak to me like that? How dare you?'

Suddenly the anger she'd been suppressing since the morning took over, making her grip the back of a chair for support. 'You've no idea what it's like. Libby's not well, I'm having to treat Mum with kid gloves, Julia's on my tail and I've had a letter from the bank saying I'm reneging on the loan repayments. On top of that, I'm trying to handle being recognised in the street and written about in the papers. You haven't a clue about the pressure I'm under.'

'Oh, poor old you. And who chose the fucking job? Not us. Not Libby or Fred. Not me or Mum. You did. You wanted it and all the crap that comes with it. And we were all thrilled for you because you wanted it. But now you're turning into a selfish, thankless cow because of it.' Mel's eyes glittered with fury.

'If we're talking thankless cows,' snapped Christie, 'look at yourself for a moment. With you, it's number one all the way and nobody else to think about. Any man you want, no kids, just a stupid self-indulgent worthless job as a fashion guru.'

Standing in the doorway, Richard gave a quiet cough. Christie whipped round, her eyes stinging with tears, her head spinning, horribly conscious that their argument had spiralled way out of control and that the others must have heard everything.

'Erm . . . I think it's probably time for us to go,' he said quietly. 'Ted and Maureen have asked me to give them a lift home. Ted'll collect the car tomorrow.'

'But don't you want coffee?' They couldn't leave now – the day wasn't over.

'I don't think we should. Maureen says she's very tired.'

'Perhaps you could take me too,' Mel demanded.

'Mel! You can't go yet.' Both of them had spoken out of turn and they needed time to straighten all this out.

'Think not? Watch me!'

Before Richard had time to agree to her request, Mel had dashed upstairs, taking them two at a time, and returned with her case. Within what seemed like moments, awkward goodbyes and thank-yous had been exchanged, and the Land Rover carrying half her Christmas party was turning from the drive onto the road as the first flakes of snow began to fall. Christie stared after them, not quite able to believe what had just happened, feeling as if she had walked onto the set of some excruciating Mike Leigh film. She snatched up Smudge, who was making his own small bid for freedom, and shut the front door, but not before a blast of freezing air had entered the house.

Behind her stood Libby, her kohl-rimmed eyes making her face look even paler than usual. In her hand was the single sheet torn from the *News*. 'Satisfied?'

'Where did you get that?' Christie tried to take it from her. 'I told you never to go into my office without asking first.'

'I was looking for Smudge and the door was open.' Libby stood her ground. 'So, are you? Are you satisfied with what you've done? Everyone's gone home and now I've found this.' She threw the paper onto the hall floor. 'You promised me. You promised me no one would know and now everyone does. I hate you.'

Christie grabbed her arm. 'Libby, darling. It's not like that. I don't know how they got the story but there's nothing there to suggest that me seeing Angela has anything to do with you.'

Ignoring her, Libby pulled out of her grip. 'This is all your fault. If you hadn't taken that job, none of this would have happened. And we'd still be having Christmas.'

'Libs, don't do this. It's not my fault. You know I love you more than anything.'

'No, you don't. If you did, you'd be at home with us like before. You've ruined everything.' With that, she seized Smudge from Christie's grasp and ran upstairs. A moment later, her bedroom door slammed. The only noise in the house was the murmur of voices from the TV. Fred had sensibly chosen to tune out of the domestic mayhem and immerse himself in whatever was on the box.

Christie went into the kitchen and poured herself an enormous glass of wine – right up to the brim – took a huge gulp and sat with it at the table, her head in her hands. As she wondered whether she should go to Libby or leave her to calm down before trying to talk to her, the phone rang. Mel! It must be Mel wanting to make up. She ran into the sitting room, anxious to answer before her sister hung up. As she reached for the phone, she knocked into the side table, sending Nick's photo flying towards the fireplace where it smashed against the grate. Cursing, she put the phone to her ear, at the same time crouching down to pick up the pieces. 'Mel?'

'Darling! Happy Christmas.' Julia. Of course, Mel would be far too stubborn to call so soon. What had she been thinking? She tuned back into Julia's voice.

'I'm having a marvelloushly relaxed time all on my own but I couldn't get through the day without wishing all my clients the compliments of the sheason.'

'Sheason'? Had she been drinking? Cristal Champagne probably, accompanied by a suspicion of calorie-free caviar, thought Christie, crossly, but managed, 'That's so sweet of you, Julia. Thank you. And thank you too for the glorious McCartney bag.' She began clearing the shards of glass into a piece of wrapping paper.

'My pleasure, darling. Just keep up the good work into the New Year.'

'I'll try.' And she would.

''Bye, then. Hippy Chrishmas.' And Julia had gone.

Whatever anyone said, Christie determined to stick to her guns and do her best to prove the others wrong. She had to, to show herself and them that she had it in her to achieve something of her own. That this was all worth-while. Nick's death didn't mean she had no place in the wider world. She picked up the broken frame, unpinning the back so she could take out the photo. As she removed the backboard, a piece of paper fluttered to the floor. Curious, she picked it up. Her stomach lurched as she recognised Nick's handwriting. It was one of the messages he used to leave hidden around the house for her. She'd thought she'd found them all. Sometimes they were little expressions of love, sometimes just an observation. This was both.

If you've found this one, don't forget: the best bit about fighting is the making up afterwards. I'll always love you. xx

She was overwhelmed by a sense of loss so extreme that she struggled to catch her breath. He must have written this after they'd disagreed about something but she had no memory of what. She sat down, bending over her knees until her head cleared. What had she just done? Not only had she lost him but her stupid, selfish behaviour had driven her family away too. Mel had never spoken to her like that before. Maureen had never looked so disappointed – and that was saying something. After what Christie had said, Mel had every right never to speak to her again. Who would blame her? Somehow she had to put matters right, although she knew Mel could be so intractable if she set her mind to it. She might not be able to bring back Nick, but she had to make amends with the others, Richard included. If she could. Watching the embers of the fire, she suddenly felt horribly alone.

She sat for a little longer before picking up her mobile again. She ran down her contacts list, watched as the numbers appeared on the screen, then dialled. After a few rings, someone answered.

'Frank?' As she said his name, she began to cry. 'Could you come over? Please.'

21

When Christie had called Frank, he had just got back from Christmas lunch with his aged mother and was only too willing to abandon his evening alone with a DVD of *It's a Wonderful Life* and a bottle of whisky. By the time he reached Christie's, both Libby and Fred had gone to bed, upset by the way the day had ended, an exhausted Smudge was curled up asleep by the Aga and Christie was finishing the clearing up, mascara-smudged streaks of tears on her cheeks. Frank took one look, led her into the sitting room and sat her down, gave them both a large brandy and revived the dying embers of the fire, making the sparks fly as he tossed on another log. In return, Christie poured out the whole story exactly as it had happened. He didn't interrupt, just occasionally shook his head or tutted, sometimes in sympathy, sometimes not. When she finished, he knelt in front of her, taking both her hands in his.

'You poor old thing. But you know what?'

Miserable, she shook her head.

'Whatever the rights and wrongs, you've got to apologise. As far as I can see, you've alienated almost everyone close to you, apart from my good self. It's no use waiting for one of them to make the first move.'

'Apologise?' She was aghast at the idea.

'If you're going to be that difficult, you'll end up like Julia,' he warned.

She managed a feeble grin. 'Oh, God! Not really?' She tried to pull her hands from his grip but he held tight.

'Yes, really. Do you want to become an embittered old bitch with nothing but her work to keep her going?'

'Don't be so silly. They'll come round.' But she didn't sound convinced, even to herself.

'Why should they? Sounds to me as if you managed a five-star demolition job. And on Christmas Day too. What timing.' He sat back on his heels, letting go her hands.

'You don't really think I'm getting like Julia?' Even though she didn't truly believe he meant it, she didn't like the idea one bit. 'Do you?

He laughed. 'Get over yourself, will you? I was joking.' He stood up, brushed the knees of his trousers and took the brandy bottle from the mantelpiece. 'Another?'

She nodded.

'Listen. Nobody's like Julia. I told you I knew her at drama school, way back in the seventies.' He sat down beside Christie, swirling the brandy in his glass. 'By the time I met her, she'd lost almost all trace of her Scouse accent and was busy re-inventing herself as an actress, getting a few bit parts here and there, and temping to keep the wolf from the door. Well, we all did waitering, bar work, all that stuff, until it dawned on us that we hadn't a cat's chance of making it. But she met Max.'

Christie was intrigued to have the story she'd already heard fleshed out.

Frank smiled, stretching his legs in front of him and staring into his glass before he took another sip. 'Now her knickers are welded on, but back in those days, she'd drop them for anyone who might help her climb the slippery pole to success. And legend has it, she climbed many slippery poles, dear! Anyway, poor old Max didn't stand a chance. For years, he was a means to an end for her, though I doubt he ever saw it like that. And don't forget they never had the children he really wanted – they would have held her back.'

'Don't be so mean. Maybe they just couldn't.' Christie couldn't believe that anyone would be capable of sacrificing the most precious thing that could happen to them to the hard-nosed world of work.

'Listen to you. Always Little Miss Loyalty.' Frank looked amused as he poked at the fire. 'And ever since, brilliant and successful agent she may be, but if Julia has any friends, she keeps them well hidden. That woman's on one long power trip – and if you're not careful, you'll be on it with her!'

'Stop it!' Christie leaned across and smacked his arm. 'I'm not anything like that bad.'

'If you were, I wouldn't be sitting here, love,' Frank reassured her, dodging her hand. 'But I'm serious about putting things right. These are the people who love you.'

'And one who doesn't!' Christie reminded him.

'Granted, that's unfortunate. But don't ditch the others because of him.'

They talked and drank on into the night, he gently persuasive, then increasingly impatient at Christie's drunken reluctance to make the first move. 'After all, I'm not the one who nicked my sister's bloke from under her nose.'

Frank listened to everything she had to say, but eventually he glanced at his watch. 'Time for bed, sweetheart. If you're going to insist on being so bloody-minded, let's sleep on it and see how it all looks in the morning.' He got to his feet. 'Don't worry about me, I'll slum it in your sister's sheets . . .'

But sleep didn't come easily to Christie that night. Every time she was about to drift off, her conversations with Libby, Maureen and, most often, Mel spun through her head, giving her ample opportunity to ratchet up her guilt by thinking of everything else she could have said or done that would have avoided confrontation. She was sure she'd only slept a couple of hours when the doorbell woke her: Sophie and her mother to take Libby to the Boxing Day sales. Libby was out of the house like a greyhound out of a trap, leaving her mother to nurse her thumping hangover.

'Nothing like a brisk walk to blow away the cobwebs,' pronounced Frank, after they'd shared something like a gallon of black coffee over breakfast and their heads were a little clearer. 'Let's go, before the snow comes.' They dragged Fred away from his Wii, wrapped up and headed out.

The earth was frozen hard underfoot as they trudged along the bridle path, hands stuffed into pockets, hats pulled down over ears, noses and cheeks pink with cold. For as far as the eye could see, a winter wonderland stretched away from them: woods and ploughed fields powdered with snow, trees and hedges rimed with frost, patches of ice that cracked under their weight. To the south, the featureless grey sky was relieved by a hazy washed-out sun that was failing to break through. Fred dawdled behind them, poking sticks into frozen puddles.

'You're a bloody idiot, you know,' said Frank, his breath visible in the air ahead of them. 'Stop feeling sorry for yourself and think about what Mel said. Is there any truth in it?'

'Of course not,' she objected. 'I'm exactly the same person I ever was.'

'Are you sure?' He wedged himself through a kissing gate, swinging it back for Christie. 'Think Julia.'

'Positive.'

He looked at her sceptically as she zigzagged through, obviously suggesting she might think again.

'Well, -ish,' she qualified. They walked on for a while without speaking, both thinking about the ongoing conversation they'd been having ever since Frank arrived the night before, Fred still bringing up the rear.

As they walked, Christie had grudgingly to admit that, in the sober light of day, Frank was probably right. She should say sorry. Perhaps she had changed – but not all for the bad, she rapidly justified herself. The time was definitely right for her to emerge from the paralysis of her grief, and Mel had encouraged her. Everyone had. She just hadn't foreseen all that her new job or, for that matter, being managed by Julia would involve. She'd had more to deal with than she'd anticipated, including the impact on her children, especially Libby. But that wasn't an excuse to take it out on everyone else. Despite her unwillingness to admit she was in the wrong, someone had to take responsibility and square things. That much she knew.

'OK. I give in.' She broke the silence. 'I'll phone her. Though God knows what she'll say.'

Frank slipped his arm through hers. 'Right decision. At last. Can we go home now? I'm freezing my butt off out here.'

Christie laughed, letting him turn them round. 'And I'll take a long hard look at myself, provided you promise to keep me on the straight and narrow.'

'Why do you think I came?' He tightened his grip to stop her falling as her foot slid on a patch of ice while Fred ran ahead, delighted to be heading home at last.

*

After a scratch lunch of Christmas leftovers and baked potatoes, Frank left, confident he had done all he could for her. Christie kissed him goodbye, thanked him for being a true friend, and promised that as soon as she and Fred had tested the new metal detector in the garden, she would phone Mel.

An hour later, with freezing fingers and gutted at not having discovered a horde of Viking treasure, Fred climbed into his sleeping bag with a rebellious Smudge and returned to his Wii. With him torn between his game and coaxing the kitten

256

back into the bag, Christie at last had the chance to make herself a strong coffee and head upstairs to call Mel undisturbed.

Her sister picked up immediately. Christie went in at full throttle, having decided not to give her a chance to get a word in edgeways. She didn't want the argument to kick off again, making matters worse with their recriminations. 'Before you say anything, I'm so sorry. I've been a complete cow. I needed you to point it out and I didn't mean what I said yesterday. Not any of it. I feel dreadful. Can we kiss and make up? Please. As for Richard, I'm cool with you seeing him. Really. I was just being unbelievably selfish.' She paused for breath, having meant every word.

To her astonishment, Mel started laughing – the one reaction she hadn't expected. 'Stop! Stop! I was going to phone you this evening when I thought you might have calmed down. I was just as bad. Jet lag and drink – killer combo. I only got up a couple of hours ago and feel awful about what I said.'

'But it's true,' Christie insisted. 'I *have* been horribly demanding and critical, wanting everything to go my way. I wasn't thinking about you and Mum. I see that now, thanks to Frank, who's talked yet more sense into me. I guess I was starting to believe my own publicity. Well, the good bits anyway.'

'Well, maybe you were, a bit,' Mel conceded, adding hastily, 'but I don't really blame you.'

'Friends?' Christie said anxiously.

'Friends.' There was no doubt in her sister's voice. 'Can I come over tomorrow instead?'

'Of course.' She felt the weight fly from her shoulders. She had been so scared that Mel would be much harder to pull round than this.

'As for Richard . . .'

Christie froze, bracing herself for what was about to come.

'I'm not having and I'm not about to have a fling with him. I like him a lot, but my heart's set on Jean-Pierre, my St Lucian photographer. Not that I'd ever tell him. Not yet, anyway.'

'You're not?' Had she misheard?

'Absolutely not. Besides, if Richard likes anyone, it's you.'

'He does?' Surely Mel was mistaken. 'But how do you know? I . . . I never said anything.'

'You didn't need to, you idiot. But he's terrified of you because you seem so in control.'

'If only,' she whispered.

'Why do think he's always showing up at your house or thinking of another reason for Fred to go over to theirs?'

'Because two boys together are easier than one. He said so.'

'"He said so,"' Mel mimicked, frustrated by how dense her sister could be sometimes. 'Chris, he likes you. Believe it. When I hinted about the money problems you've been having, he was so concerned for you.'

'But what about when he wouldn't kiss me?'

'I don't know about that, but he certainly ain't interested in me. He's a decent man and a good dad who's had his problems. Has he ever talked to you about what's happened to him since his time in Iraq? Sounds more than anyone could bear. Seeing your friends blown to pieces, finding a local family you'd become close to lying dead by the road. How do you recover from something like that?'

'I didn't even know he'd been to Iraq! He's talked to you about it?'

'A little. There's nothing like a car journey or two to break the ice. You know me.'

Bloody hell! Mel would have made a better journalist than *she* was. Christie could imagine only too well how her sister's curiosity wouldn't have let Richard get away with the dismissive replies he'd given the couple of times she'd asked about his army days. With him captive in the car, Mel would have taken the opportunity to grill him about everything she could. Christie was shocked to hear what he had experienced. Like most people, she only had the vaguest idea of what an active soldier's life involved. She saw the news, was momentarily affected by the announcement of another young serviceman's death, but then she went back to her own life, to her own comparatively trivial concerns.

After they'd finished talking, she walked downstairs with some hope back in her step. As she reached the bottom, the front door opened and in walked Libby, armed with three shopping bags. Behind her, Christie saw Sophie waving from the car. Anxious to smooth her way back into Libby's good books, she dashed out to ask Sophie and her mum in for a cup of tea, but they were hurrying home. By the time she was back inside, Libby had disappeared upstairs. She went into the kitchen to get out the Christmas cake and make some tea. A few minutes later, she heard a shout. 'Mum!'

Surprised even to be spoken to, she went to the foot of the stairs and looked up to see Libby standing at the top wearing a floaty, sleeveless long black dress, low cut with three buttons down to the empire line. Round her neck glittered a necklace of silver rings and white beads. Gone was her Goth daughter, replaced by a coltish beauty who was quite unaware of how lovely she was.

'What do you think?' Libby sounded nervous, apparently having forgotten their last disagreement.

'Wow! You look sensational.' Her voice cracked as she caught a glimpse of the young woman Libby was becoming. She noticed that the marks on her arms had almost disappeared. If you didn't know . . .

'Really? Sophie's mum said it was perfect for their New Year party.'

'Yes, really.' Christie took a step up towards her. This was the moment. If she'd apologised to Mel, she certainly should to Libby. 'Libs, I'm sorry about last night.' She saw her daughter stiffen. 'Really sorry. I found one of Dad's notes after you'd gone to bed. It must be the last one. It said, "The best bit about fighting is the making up."'

Libby let go her grip on the banister and brushed the hair back from her face as she gazed down at her mother. 'Where did you find it?'

'Tucked behind our favourite photo of him. The glass broke. He's right, though, isn't he?'

Libby inclined her head as she took in what Christie said. 'I s'pose so. What about Auntie Mel, though? She ought to be here now, like she is every Christmas.'

'I know. I've said I'm sorry to her too and she's coming down tomorrow. She'll love that dress.' Libby gave a glimmer of a smile as she heard her mother out. 'We didn't really mean all the stuff we said, although I know she was right.'

'Mmm. Whatever.' Libby turned back to her room, not wanting to be involved in their row.

'Love you, Libs. Daddy and I are so proud of you,' Christie called after her. She knew that melting her daughter's heart always took time, but the thaw had begun and she was prepared to wait.

*

Fred and she were in the middle of a game of Super Mario, shrieking at each other above the noise with every point lost and gained, when she heard a car pull up outside the house. To her annoyance, she lost a barrage of points as her concentration wavered. 'Fred, pause the thing while I get the door, will you?' She caught sight of her score plummeting as she stood up.

The bell rang as she walked down the hall. 'Coming,' she yelled, as she yanked open the door – and stopped dead. Standing in front of her, Richard was stamping his feet and rubbing his hands against the cold. She stared at him as he looked up, clearly apprehensive of the greeting he was about to receive.

'Mel called me,' he began uncertainly. 'She said she thought it would be all right for me to collect Olly's scarf and hat. We left them . . .'

'I know. In your hurry to escape! Come in.' She held the door open and he stepped past her into the warmth, saying he couldn't stay long. 'I'm so, so sorry you had to hear us arguing like a couple of crazed cats. We don't do it often, but when we do . . .'

'You really go for it. She said that too.' They stood looking at each other, Christie all too aware that his opinion of her must be at rock bottom.

'She did?' She could almost hear her sister blurting out whatever came into her head and cringed. It wouldn't be the first time. 'And anything else?'

He hesitated then took a big breath as if steeling himself. 'She said something about a massive misunderstanding, and that if I were to ask you for a drink, you might not say no?'

Christie gave a half-smile. 'My sister is such a meddler. I might have known she'd phone you right away. She's done something like this to me once before.'

'Is that a no, then?' He looked so deflated, but she couldn't stop herself smiling.

'No. It certainly is not.' This, after all, was what she'd been waiting for, been longing for, even if she had needed Mel's interference to achieve it. 'I'd love to.' She picked up Olly's hat and scarf from the end of the banister and passed them over. Christmas was definitely taking a turn for the better.

'Then why don't I bring Olly over tomorrow and we can all go to the pub?'

'I've got an even better idea. Mel's going to be here then, and since she's all but set us up, I'm sure she won't mind staying in with the kids for a couple of hours.'

Memories of their last kiss vanished as he lifted one hand to her face, the back of his fingers brushing her cheek before he cupped the side of her head. He leaned forward and kissed her. His lips were soft and warm against hers. This time she abandoned herself to her feelings, knowing that this was what he wanted too. He held her close before they broke away from one another.

'I've been longing to do that,' he murmured. 'That first time I wasn't sure you were ready or that you even wanted me to kiss you back.'

'Oh, I did,' she whispered back. 'And I definitely do now.'

*

Nick often came to her in her sleep. In the early days she had woken up shocked that the empty side of the bed next to her was not warm from his body. She often dreamed of him walking up the drive to the new house.

'How did you know where to find me?' she'd ask.

'I always know where you are. I'll never leave you,' was his reply.

In the last few months he'd been appearing to her less frequently, and when he did, he was hard to reach. Something was holding him back, taking him from her. She could see him talking to her but she could no longer hear his words.

The night she kissed Richard, she did not dream of Nick.

22

The arrivals hall of Terminal 2 was busy with February half-term travellers. Those newly arrived passengers who weren't keeping an eye on their children stood focused on the conveyor-belt as the cases thudded down the ramp, one after another – but almost never theirs. Libby's was one of the last off. Grabbing it, she hoisted it onto their trolley, almost knocking Fred over as he climbed aboard.

'Hurry! We've got to catch them up,' he yelled, bouncing up and down, watching Olly being pushed towards the exit by Richard.

'Get off!' insisted Libby, giving him a shove. 'I can't get this one on if you're sitting there.'

'Leave it out, kids.' Christie put out a hand to steady their bags. 'We've managed a week without a row. Do you have to start the minute we're back in England?'

Libby actually apologised and put her hand beside her mother's, helping to steady the trolley, which seemed to have grown wheels with a mind of their own. They yanked it towards the exit. As the boys argued about whether they were riding horses or motorbikes, Libby glared at them with contempt. Richard and Christie exchanged a private smile, sharing their amusement over the squabble. They pushed out into the terminal building, looking for the directions to the car-park bus. Suddenly, as they skirted the edge of a WHSmith, Fred let out a bellow and pointed. 'Hey! Look, Mum. Isn't that you?'

Christie turned towards the direction in which he was pointing. She stopped, letting her trolley skid into the back of Richard's legs. A stack of *OK!* magazines was staring face out towards them with the words 'LYNCH IN A CLINCH' so bold and such a bilious yellow they couldn't be missed. Above them was a photo of Richard and her smooching on the snowy chalet balcony. She remembered exactly the moment on their first night away when they'd stepped outside to escape the kids, but someone must have been waiting with a long-distance lens. Worse still, overlapping the picture was another of Sam looking unusually dishevelled, his body half hidden by the question 'BROKEN-HEARTED?' The implication was obvious.

'Oh, my God.' She felt as if all the breath had left her body.

Fred and Olly had made a beeline for a rack of sweets and were already arguing over the choice of two jumbo Haribo packs. Libby, cheeks burning, was looking anywhere but at her mother.

'Whatever's the matter?' Richard was rubbing his calf. His gaze followed Christie's. 'My God! What's that about?'

'Would you mind buying a copy?' she asked him.

'Er . . . yeah . . . if you really want to read it.' He sounded uncertain.

'I do.'

266

He went over to the stand, picked up a copy, then paid for it and the boys' sweets.

Christie pulled her woolly hat a little further down in a fruitless attempt to disguise herself from the other customers in the shop – she was sure they must have read every word and were staring at her.

Richard gave the boys their sweets, tucked the magazine into his shoulder-bag and put his arm round Christie. 'Come on, gorgeous. Let's get you to the car.' He whistled up a barely responsive Libby and the five made their way to the bus stop.

On the bus, Christie sat next to Libby and took her hand. 'Darling, I'm so sorry to be such an embarrassing mum. It's terrible for me too.'

Libby snatched her hand away and turned up her iPod Shuffle.

While they were driving home, Christie read the magazine piece, which said little but implied that she and Sam had been seen having cosy dinners together. Apparently he had hopes for more than a professional relationship with her. Richard was portrayed as a handsome single father whom she'd homed in on at the school gates. There were 'quotes' from a so-called 'mum at the school', who claimed that no dad was safe from the attractive, well-paid widow and TV broadcaster who was beginning to believe she was better than Gilly Lancaster. She was even accused of attempting to push Gilly out of *Good Evening Britain* altogether. The piece was full of lies, peppered with the odd grain of truth to make it convincing.

Richard kept quiet, merely asking if she was all right.

Later that night after supper, Christie and Richard sat together on the sofa with the boys sprawled on the floor, gripped by *Harry Potter and the Half-Blood Prince*. Richard dozed, making little sputtering noises whenever he exhaled, while Christie lay back, her eyes half shut, reliving the past weeks.

How thrilled she had been when Richard had suggested they all went skiing at half-term, but she had vetoed the idea immediately. The job came first and she knew it was out of the question to ask Julia to wangle any time off for her. She could imagine the response. 'More time off? You've just had Christmas. Out of the question.' But then the news came through that Gilly was desperate to get back on air. Two months at home with the triplets was driving her crazy, so she had begged Jack to let her return, just for a week. Her doting parents were thrilled to be grandparents at last and allowed to look after the babies.

In the end, it was Julia who asked Christie to take the week off. She'd be doing them all a huge favour if she agreed to step aside, even though they were all aware this would be a breach of her contract. 'And I know how keen you are on money,' Julia had added, quite unnecessarily. 'So I'd better tell you now that you won't be paid. They can't afford two salaries. I don't want you to think that I've taken it out of your pay packet.'

Christie assumed this was a poor attempt at a joke after she had pursued her yet again about the cheque that still hadn't come through from Drink-a-Vit. A louder snore from Richard reminded her that she didn't want to think about all that now. She'd have plenty of time to sort out her finances after she was back at work the next day. Instead, she transported herself back to the Alps.

With only three weeks to go, Richard had managed to find a last-minute booking in the ski resort of Les Gets. For the first couple of days there, he had spent his time alone, high on the black runs, while Christie humiliated herself on the nursery slopes with the kids. Despite the undoubted attractions of Gustave, their hunky instructor, she was constantly debating the pleasure of sliding down a hill, falling over, and then climbing back up just to repeat the experience. Her thighs, knees, calves and feet screamed for mercy at every step. The idea of hot chocolate and a good whodunit seemed infinitely preferable. Then, at the end of the third day, she actually began to stay upright more than not and to enjoy the sensation of speed (however slowly she was moving, it felt fast!), as well as the cold air in her face, the majesty of the snow-covered mountains. By day four Fred and Olly, whose daring knew no bounds, were practised enough to go off on the red runs with Richard in the afternoons, leaving Christie and Libby to their lessons.

Libby was a changed girl. She laughed with Christie, flirted with Gustave and even played snowballs with the boys and Richard, laughing when Richard pushed one down her neck but always pulling away when, unthinking, he kissed her good night. She blossomed into an attractive young woman with clear, tanned skin and a smattering of freckles. Christie was so proud of her, wishing she could bottle each moment they spent together.

For the last two days, they had all been able to ski together, if cautiously. The evenings were filled with hot baths, mulled wine, good food, plenty of laughter and the best nights' sleep she could remember.

Christie had to pinch herself when she thought how much their lives had changed in such a short space of time. And it all seemed completely right. Since Boxing Day, her relationship with Richard had moved effortlessly forward. A drink in the pub had progressed to dinner out, to evenings spent comfortably together in one another's homes – although they had yet to spend a whole night in the same bed. To her disappointment, Richard had insisted on not sharing a bedroom, even in France. He argued that they had plenty of time, and that the most important thing was for the children to adjust to the idea of them being together. So although she was dying to get him between the sheets for more than a delicious snatched hour or less in an empty house, she was happy to bide her time. But not for too much longer.

The boys hardly noticed how close their parents had grown, and certainly seemed not to care. The more time they could spend together, the happier they were. The only obstacle in the way of Christie and Richard's happiness was Libby, who was beadily aware of what was going on. Richard had been at pains to show her he wasn't trying to replace Nick, that her father was not to be forgotten. He asked her about him, what they had done together, trying to draw her out, but she held herself back, never hostile but always wary. 'All she needs is time,' he'd say, watching her run after Smudge or stomp up to her room.

Christie became aware of the music swelling into a finale: a sure sign that Harry had failed to conquer Voldemort yet again. She opened her eyes, just as Olly leaped on his father yelling, 'I'm a death-eater!'

Richard woke with a start, rolling Olly onto the arm of the sofa. 'No, you're not. But you are a monstrous pain in the neck.' He ran his hand along Christie's thigh as he sat up. 'We're going to have to go.'

'I don't want half-term to finish,' said Fred, turning his mouth down at the corners, pretending to cry. He jabbed the poker into the fire. Christie removed it from his hand and put it back on its stand before he set the house ablaze.

'I know, but there's nothing we can do about it. Work and school tomorrow.' Richard stood, raising his arms above his head and stretching. Christie thought how fit and well he looked, helped by the skiers' suntan, even though she knew it went no further than his collar line.

'Why don't you just stay?' asked Fred. 'You might as well.'

Olly took his father's hand and looked up at him, hopeful.

'Think so?' He grinned at Christie over the boys' heads. 'We'd both love that but everything we need's at home. So, no choice. Perhaps next time.'

'Yes, perhaps,' she agreed, grinning back.

*

'Thank God you're here again.' Sam kissed Christie's cheek as soon as she walked into the green room the next day. 'I'd forgotten how grim working could be. Never ever take another holiday. Please.'

'Gilly's been so bloody difficult,' Frank kissed her other cheek. 'Fussing about camera angles and lighting. Thank God for Tim, who somehow managed to calm her down. Having babies has done nothing whatsoever for her.'

Christie laughed. 'She can't have been that bad.'

'Believe us, she was. I even heard her giving Julia an earful. They were in this very room and I just happened to be passing . . . quite slowly.'

'Go on, tell. You know you want to.' Christie smiled, thinking how much she'd miss all this when the time came to leave.

'Well!' Frank put his hands on his hips with the campest of movements. 'I couldn't help overhearing.' He ignored their joint, 'Yeah, right,' and carried on regardless: 'Derek wants a Rolex Daytona Cosmograph, white gold with diamonds. No change from sixty K, retail. As God is my witness.' He paused for effect. 'And Gilly doesn't have the spare cash. Can't understand why not.' His voice rose to a falsetto as he mimicked her. '"I thought I had plenty after that Drink-a-Vit ad campaign, Julia. I promised him. What can you do about it?" On and on she went.'

'So what happened?' Christie was fascinated by this nugget of information, which suggested Gilly's problems might not be so far from her own.

'Julia calmed her down and promised everything would be fine, of course. She's not going to upset one of her highest earners, is she?' He looked at Christie as if she was stupid, then grinned. 'We longed for the day when you'd be back.'

'Come off it. It was only a week, and she'll be back for good soon. Nothing I can do about that.' Christie hung up her cream jacket, then picked up the half-empty bottle of milk that was on the coffee-table and put it back in the fridge Not surprisingly, nothing had changed in her short absence. The unforgiving neon lights still flickered on the ceiling and the coffee stains on the carpet were still there. The worktop was crowded with open biscuit packets, boxes of tea and coffee, used scripts and unwashed cups and plates.

'And what about you two? Splashed all over the front of *OK!* – that really got Gilly going.' Frank changed the subject, unable to resist the lure of scandal.

'What can you do but laugh? It's so pathetic.' Sam stepped in a little too swiftly. 'Anyone want a biscuit?'

'I think I might just have been insulted.' Christie tried to look indignant as she piled up the newspapers to make space for the plate of chocolate digestives that Sam brought over.

'You know I don't mean it like that. I'm honoured to be associated with you,' he teased. 'But who on earth dreams up these stories?'

'Someone who was at the same hotel in Rillingham?' Frank suggested mischievously. He brushed the crumbs from a chair and sat down, resting his Hugo Boss trainers on the table edge, then removing them as he became aware of Sam's and Christie's disapproving looks. 'Not me.'

'Frank! You promised,' hissed Christie, gesturing towards Jeremy, the handsome young sparks who had made such an impression on Gilly's Derek. He was hunting for a clean mug as the kettle boiled in the corner, steaming up the one and only mirror.

'I certainly did. And not a word has crossed my lips. But hotel corridors have ears and eyes, you know.' He pulled down the front of his Merc jersey and slightly hitched up the legs of his Gap jeans, revealing an inch of stripy Paul Smith sock.

'Shut up!' She glared at him, zipping her mouth, although aware they probably couldn't be heard over the three TV screens on the wall that were blaring out *Bargains in the Basement*, the show ahead of them in the schedule. 'We've all moved on.'

'So we see,' Frank said enthusiastically, his face glowing. 'He's quite a dish, your Richard. When do we get to meet him, then?'

'I'm keeping him to myself for as long as I can.' Christie watched as their first guest, the mother of a reality-TV star, was escorted down the corridor to the studio. 'That's the last time we're being papped, if I have anything to do with it. So keep your indecent ideas to yourself.'

'As if. And after all I've done for you.'

'Well, you know what it's like.' Christie couldn't keep the smile from her face as she thought of Richard.

'If only I could remember!'

Lillybet put her head round the door. 'Fifteen minutes.'

'Show time!' Frank sashayed out of the room without waiting for them.

'He wouldn't have said anything, would he?' Sam asked. 'After all, he's the only one who knows.'

'Nah. Not a chance. It's some journalist doing guesswork that got a bit near the knuckle. You're not broken-hearted, are you?' She retrieved her jacket and slipped it over her blouse, doing up the buttons as she made the adjustment into her role of TV presenter.

'No way. Oh, sorry. That came out wrong.' Christie laughed

so he didn't need to justify himself. 'No, but when we're done, I've got to tell you about Melissa. She's gorgeous. Met her at Mahiki's a week ago. And this time it really is different.'

'Yeah, yeah.' Sceptical but amused that he hadn't changed any more than their surroundings had, Christie led the way out of the green room. As she turned into the corridor towards the studio, she was almost sent flying by none other than Jack Bradbury, who was hurrying towards the lift. He stopped to check she was all right before he recognised her.

'Well, well. Christie "Lynch in a clinch". Looked like a good holiday – and all paid for too. Thanks for stepping down for a week. I appreciate it.'

She was taken aback by his unexpected concern, never mind his thanks. 'No problem. It tied in well with everything at home.'

'So we saw.' He gave a pearly smile and slipped between the lift doors, clearly anxious to escape the grotty nether regions of his empire.

It wasn't until she was sitting on the sofa with Sam, interviewing a woman who was starting a campaign for better road signs at accident black spots, when Jack's words came back to her. 'And all paid for.' What had he meant? Julia's attempt at humour over what she saw as Christie's penny-pinching meant that she remembered quite clearly she wasn't being paid for her week off. Sam's thumb dug hard into the underside of her thigh. The interview! To drift off was a cardinal broadcasting sin. She recovered herself immediately, hoping the viewers would have interpreted her lapse in concentration as a moment when she was considering her next question. She rejoined the conversation as though nothing had happened and was careful to complete the show without another slip.

However, in the car home that night, she returned to Jack's comment and to her relationship with Julia. Whatever reservations she might feel, she owed Julia everything. If it weren't for her, she would probably be out of work, sweating over some freelance writing commission, worrying about where the next cheque was coming from. Equally, if it weren't for her, they wouldn't have the new washing-machine, the conservatory; the roof wouldn't have been mended, they wouldn't have gone to France and she'd still be getting unpleasant letters from the bank. Next on her list of must-dos when she could afford them was to get the central-heating sorted, decorate downstairs and – this was what really pleased her – buy two business-class tickets to Delhi for her mother and Ted. They had been so happy for Christie and Richard, and at least she could give them the treat Ted longed for as a thank-you to them both.

However, Julia and money were awkward subjects. The second Drink-a-Vit payment had yet to appear and she still had no idea what Jack had meant about being paid for half-term. Was he mistaken? Julia would know. After Christie had been taken on by *Good Evening Britain*, she had continued to allow her agent to sign her contracts on her behalf – once they'd gone through any unfamiliar or unusual clauses over the phone together – persuaded that this was an efficient business method Julia used with all her clients. Christie was embarrassed by her lack of financial savvy and the panic she felt when faced with a page of accounts. Nick had always looked after that side of things and she had passed on the responsibility to Julia with huge relief. Having someone you trusted to look after the money made life ten times easier, even if it meant she was more ignorant than perhaps she should be about the finer detail.

She thought of Gilly, who, she had imagined, would be completely on top of what she was earning, what she had and hadn't been paid and what she lost in commission. She wasn't the type to risk anything to anyone else. Yet the conversation between her and Julia that Frank had overheard suggested otherwise. So, what was going on?

'And paid for too.' That was definitely what Jack had said. As the car turned off the M40 she resolved to have another conversation with Julia. There was no question that it was time to sharpen up her own act. This time she was not going to be flannelled into accepting the first thing she was told. She wanted answers and she would get them.

23

As Christie walked into Julia's office, ready for battle, her agent picked up a thin yellow plastic folder off her desk and came to sit next to her on the sofa – unprecedented in their relationship so far. Usually she kept the table or the desk between them. Lily provided coffee and water, then, at a sharp command from Julia, pulled over a hard upright chair and sat opposite them in silence, poised with pen and paper to take notes. Christie noticed that she'd smartened herself up since last time. Wearing a tailored short-sleeved black pencil dress with heels, she'd morphed from casual to chic in one swoop.

Leaning forward, Julia patted Christie's knee. 'I don't need to ask whether you had a good holiday.'

'No, you don't.' For a moment, Christie was put off guard by this sudden unlooked-for familiarity. She shifted her position so her legs were just out of Julia's reach. 'But how did anyone know where we were?'

'Well, I might have mentioned it.' Julia made a face that said she knew she shouldn't have but, equally, it didn't really matter, did it? 'Everyone's so hungry for material after Christmas and I didn't think it would do any harm.'

'But you're supposed to be on my side,' Christie protested. She looked briefly away from Julia through the wall of glass on the other side of the office. In the distance, a flash of lightning lit up a bank of thundercloud that was rolling slowly towards them over the London roofscape.

'Darling, of course I am.' Julia's expression, reasonable and controlled, asked how Christie could possibly think otherwise. 'All I'm doing is keeping up your profile so that I can find you your next job after *Good Evening Britain*. You haven't got all that long to go till Gilly comes back. In fact, I think I've already got something that you're going to jump at.' She took a piece of paper out of the folder. Christie could make out a few indecipherable squiggles in Julia's writing.

'I don't see how my being photographed with Richard with a snide implication that I was having an affair with Sam and that I'm some sort of prima donna is going to help get me any kind of work.' Christie wasn't going to let her get away with this. 'I'd rather get by on my presenting skills not on my private life. And if I can't, too bad. So, if possible, I'd prefer you not to mention what I'm doing to the press.'

'Calm down, do.' A phrase guaranteed always to wind Christie up to snapping point. She bit the inside of her lip hard to stop herself saying anything she might regret while Julia drew back from her and sat upright, indignant. 'I certainly didn't say anything about Sam. However, methinks you do protest too much. It's not true, is it?' She leaned towards her again. 'Darling, you're blushing!'

'Of course it isn't.' Christie took a couple of deep breaths, hoping to stop the rush of heat to her face. Too late. She cleared her throat. 'Before we talk about anything new, can we clear up a couple of things?' That's right. Take control of the conversation. She was aware of Lily's head moving as she watched one, then the other of them speak. Through the window, thunder rumbled as the storm moved closer.

A knowing smile had been playing on Julia's frosted pink lips but, seeing Christie wasn't going to give away anything more promotable about her personal life, she arranged her features into a more businesslike expression. 'Not the Drink-a-Vit money again? Darling, we've been chasing them, but no joy. I'm afraid you're going to have to leave it with us for a little longer. There seems to be a glitch in their accounts department but we should have it sorted by the end of the month.' She looked at Lily and barked, 'Remind Lenny, will you?' then recovered herself and patted the folder on her lap. 'Now, can I tell you about this?'

'Not yet. There's one more thing. I bumped into Jack Bradbury the other day. Why did he say that my holiday was all paid for? What did he mean?'

Julia bent down to rifle in her bag for something. When she straightened up, she had a spectacle case in her hand. Opening it, she took out a pair of rectangular glasses and put them on her nose. In the bright light of the office, the photochromic lenses darkened so her eyes were almost hidden. Christie noticed the word 'Versace' winking at her from one of the arms.

By the time Christie had asked her questions, Julia was sitting still, quite composed. She waited, then removed her glasses and said, 'Yes. And?'

'You were quite clear that I was doing the decent thing in stepping aside for Gilly but TV7 wouldn't run to paying us both. I went along with that because having half-term off was important to me.'

'How on earth did you get that impression?' Julia shook her head, as if despairing. 'You must have misunderstood me. Again!'

'Julia, you said you knew how keen I was on money and so you were telling me that I wasn't being paid. "They can't afford two salaries," you said, "but I don't want you to think that I've taken it out of your pay packet." Those were your exact words.'

Julia stared at her, twirling her glasses between her fingers, then threw back her head and laughed. 'I was joking, darling. My client's livelihood is *my* livelihood. I'd never have let that happen. You know me.'

As the steeliness with which Julia had begun the meeting returned, Christie wondered how well she did know her agent. She remembered the stories about her shadier business dealings that had reached the press, the suggestions that Ben had been broke when he died, that Julia might have had some responsibility for his death, that their relationship had been closer than they had wanted people to know. Perhaps she should quit while she was ahead – she still was, wasn't she? – and find another agent, after all. Except she needed what was owed to her and she was curious to know what the new job that Julia had lined up for her was. This wasn't the moment to cut loose. Their relationship might be difficult, but as long as it was working to her advantage, she shouldn't complain. However, something had just happened between them – of that she was sure. She didn't know exactly what it was, beyond a feeling of having caught Julia on the back foot. Unless, of course, she really had misinterpreted what Julia had originally said, but she didn't believe she had. The sound of rain spattering against the windows made them both look away.

'No.' Julia was back in her stride. 'The money will be in your account as usual by the end of the month. I know how much money means to you and I won't joke about it again.' As far as she was concerned there was obviously nothing left to say on the subject. She swept on without giving Christie a chance to interrupt. 'Now, let me tell you about this new project. You've been such a hit with TV7 that they want you to present *Top of the Class*, a new quiz show for secondary schools – a sort of *University Challenge* for kids. This is ideal for you. Sixteen schools in a knock-out competition that'll go out once a week over fifteen weeks, straight after the *Good Evening Britain* slot. But – before you say anything – the recordings will take place over three or four non-consecutive weekends, four or five half-hour shows a weekend, so short bursts of hard work that will barely affect your *very* full private life.'

You really have no idea, have you? Christie thought, torn between excitement at the idea of being the sole presenter of a show with credibility and kids, and dismay at not being home for weekends, however few.

'You need a continuing series to help you through after Gilly comes back. This is perfect. And the other reason for doing it? It's a "bank raid", pure and simple.'

'A what?'

'Eighty thousand pounds for four weekends' work – five K a programme. If that's not a steal, I don't know what is.' Julia sat back, evidently pleased with herself. She put the glasses back in their case and undid her black wool jacket so the Lurex lining glittered in the light. She crossed her legs with the faintest swish of silk, swinging out the top one and rotating her ankle to admire her nude patent-leather Jimmy Choos.

Christie found herself looking towards the photo of Ben Chapman, as if he would help her come to a decision. But he kept smiling at Julia, locked for eternity in her gaze. She thought of the money – eighty thousand pounds. She had never come anywhere close to earning such an incredible amount. She thought fast. Yes, it would be hard work but the reward would make such a difference to their lives. She could pay for Maureen and Ted's trip to India, finish the work on the house, give the kids a fab summer holiday, make further inroads into the loan *and* have some savings at last. So tempting. Four non-consecutive weekends. Now Libby was out so often with Sophie, and Fred with Olly, would they really notice if she wasn't there?

'Christie!' Julia clicked her manicured fingers in front of Christie's face. 'Did you hear anything I just said?'

Christie came to. 'Of course. I was just thinking about the implications, whether it would fit in.'

'Fit in? What do you mean? You must make it fit in! It's perfect for your profile as a thinking family woman. And the pay is very generous indeed.'

Christie looked at her agent, so poised and calculating, but with eyes that flashed anger at the possibility of not getting her way. For a second, Christie felt something like fear. Her conversations with Frank and Sam whirled back into her mind. Did Julia really have so little loyalty to her clients that she'd steal their money, their ideas, their lives in the interest of safeguarding her agency and her reputation? Was she looking at a woman capable of murder? Christie gave a slight shake of her head to pull herself together. The worst was just hearsay and gossip, while the rest came from competitor resentment or from clients who'd had a bad experience. Every agent had one or two of those.

'You're right,' she said, almost decided. 'I think I should do it but let me discuss it with my family first. Give me all the details and I'll get back to you first thing tomorrow.'

Julia nodded, obviously irritated by Christie's refusal to commit herself immediately. 'Now, why don't you let Lily take you for lunch? On me! So there's another saving you can make, Ms Getty.' Julia laughed unpleasantly. 'She can give you the dates involved.' She looked at her watch and stood up to signal the end of their meeting, straightening her pleated black skirt. 'I've got be at the BBC at two o'clock so I can't join you, I'm afraid. But I want my clients to get to know Lily better so that you're comfortable dealing with her whenever I'm unavailable.'

Christie had almost forgotten that Lily was still there. And the way Julia was talking, she might as well not have been. However, remembering how much she had liked her last time she was in the office, Christie was happy to go along with the plan, although she wondered whether she was being fobbed off because she'd dared to speak out of turn.

*

Their lunch had to be quick since Christie was due at the studios by two but it was none the less pleasant. Because it was early, Uncle Mac's Diner, right around the corner from the office, was quiet. The two women were directed to the last in the long line of booths. They slid across the red leatherette banquettes to sit opposite one another by the dark brick wall. If they leaned forward, they could see each other beneath the large metallic shade of the low-hanging light. After studying the menu – salads or burgers and fries – they ordered tuna niçoise and began to talk, Christie drawing Lily out by asking her about life in the office. Without the shadow of Julia hanging over her, Lily's confidence had returned.

'I love it and I'm learning so much. My dream job, really.' She sounded enthusiastic but, as she picked up her pistachio milk shake (off the children's menu), her frown suggested another story.

They talked a little about what she did, and her ambition to become an agent in her own right one day, until Christie moved the conversation on. 'Julia's wonderful but she strikes me as quite a demanding boss.' She was itching to know more about what made her agent tick, what she was like behind the scenes, what the truth was behind the stories.

'She's a perfectionist,' Lily admitted, concentrating on her plate as she organised some salad onto her fork. 'But I can put up with her fault-finding for the start in the business she's given me.' She paused. 'She's got a very short fuse sometimes.'

Christie nodded at the waitress who hovered beside them, waiting to know if they wanted more water, then returned her attention to Lily. So she wasn't as happy as she made out (no surprise, given what she'd seen for herself). Julia seemed to have everything anyone could possibly want in her life, yet still wasn't satisfied and thought nothing of taking it out on her staff. What drove her to want more? Christie remembered the pictures she'd seen of her house after Ben's death: they gave the impression of a luxurious and desirable Cotswold country retreat. She was prompted to ask whether Lily had seen it.

'I once had to drive down in a hurry to collect a pair of shoes she needed for a gala evening at the Ritz. There was no one else to go and she doesn't trust anyone she doesn't know.' A note of pride crept into her voice.

'Is it as amazing as it looks in the photos?' Christie knew the answer she was about to hear.

'More. I've never seen anything like it. There's a cinema and a gym in the basement, the biggest kitchen I've ever seen. The gardener's just done the most fantastic job with the re-landscaping. There's even a tennis court. And she's talking about getting another interior designer to redo the five guest suites – but they're perfect already.' Lily's face showed exactly how impressed she was.

They paused as a group of young office workers crowded

into the booth behind them. The place was filling up as it reached one o'clock, the noise level increasing around them.

'How often does she manage to go there?' Christie raised her voice so she'd be heard.

'Most weekends. She invites people down there – usually the ones she wants to impress or do a deal with.' She covered her mouth with her hand. 'Sorry. I shouldn't have said that.'

The nails on her long fingers were bitten to the quick. They reminded Christie of someone else. Then it came to her: Lenny the accountant. Both he and Lily were young and smart but both had chewed nails. What was it about working for Julia? Surprised, Christie tried to sound reassuring. 'Who am I going to tell? So, her life's all tied up with work, then? No significant others?'

Lily looked as if her eyes would pop out of her head, then she started giggling. 'Can you imagine? Who would dare? She—' Again, she cut herself short.

Christie gave her a complicit smile. 'Now you say it, I can't imagine either. I did wonder about Ben Chapman . . .'

'No way! He was much too nice and, anyway, he had a girl-friend. That evening was a business . . .' She stopped, as if aware that this time she really was about to say too much. She rubbed the side of her nose as an odd look came into her eyes.

'Don't worry. I'm not asking you to break confidences,' Christie said, wanting to put her at ease again. 'I'm just curious about the woman who's done so much for me, that's all.' More curious than you could know.

Lily pushed her plate away, salad eaten, tuna steak left on

the side, her composure recovered. 'But I'd like to know more about you: what you want to do. With the business expanding, Julia's asked me to get to know all the clients better.'

'That's a difficult one,' Christie finished her last mouthful of fish. 'Too long for the time we've got left, really, but I'll have a go.'

Over coffee, she amused Lily with stories about her family, including the one about Smudge weeing in Mel's Stella McCartney handbag so that she spent an entire day wondering where the terrible smell was coming from. Lily laughed too, relaxed and obviously interested as Christie described how much she enjoyed working with the *Good Evening Britain* mob and how important it was to her to have a part of her life that was hers alone, separate from the family.

Eventually, having noted down the recording dates for *Top of the Class*, she thanked Lily and suggested they had lunch together again some time. On the way to the studio, she leaned back in the taxi, pleased that she had at least one friend in White Management.

*

After supper, Christie took herself to her study so she could speak uninterrupted to Maureen, Mel and Richard – in that order. Armed with a cup of coffee and a bar of her favourite Green & Black's cherry chocolate, she turned on the desk light, then the fan heater, aiming it at her feet. When she finally got the bloody money from Drink-a-Vit or *Top of the Class*, whichever came first, she'd have the bloody central-heating fixed and would keep it on full blast – even in August. As she sat in the old leather armchair, she felt her body relax into its familiar contours as she picked up the phone. Two hours later, having gone through the details of the new TV7 show with them all, as well as the possible child-care implications, she eventually hung up after finally talking to Richard, her mind made up. The fact that they had all supported her gave her a warm glow as she thought again how fortunate she was to have them. After Maureen had agreed to help when necessary, liking the sound of a show that was more the sort of thing she had in mind for her daughter, Christie broke the news about her gift of the trip to India that Maureen and Ted had often talked about.

Her mother was quick to rebuff the idea. 'We can't accept that, Christine.' But Christie could hear that she was only saying what she thought she should. 'This is your money. I don't want you to waste it on us.'

'Too bad.' Christie broke off another square of chocolate and slipped it into her mouth to melt next to her left cheek. 'I'm afraid it's up to me what I do with it. You both deserve a holiday and I really want to give you this in return for everything you've done for me.'

'Well, if you put it like that . . .' Maureen sounded excited and relieved that Christie had made the right decision. 'Ted will be thrilled.'

Mel was over the moon for her, as Christie had known she would be, while Richard thought through the implications and quickly came to the conclusion that *Top of the Class* was too good an offer to refuse. Decision made, he changed the subject to when they would next see each other and what they might do. He wasn't one for doing a discussion to death – just one of the many things she liked about him. Listen, weigh up the pros and cons, and decide: that was his method.

*

The next morning, after getting the children off to school, Christie called Julia and agreed to take the new job, thanking her for having secured it (hoping this would put her back in her agent's good books). With time to spare before she had to head for the studio, she decided to tackle the mountain of emails accumulating on her laptop. Deleting the junk, highlighting the messages she'd deal with when she had more time, she came across a reminder from her accountant that her end-of-year accounts were due in a few weeks. This in turn reminded her of the Drink-a-Vit problem. She knew she should leave matters in Julia's hands but now she had a legitimate reason for needing to know when to expect the money. Angered by Julia's casual attitude towards it but simultaneously not wanting to irritate her by asking again, she made a snap decision to take the matter into her own hands: she would ring the Drink-a-Vit people herself. Why not? She might not be observing normal protocol but maybe, just maybe, she would get a result.

She was put straight through to the finance department, to a young man who was as helpful as she could have wished. He didn't seem to mind her calling direct and quickly pulled up her account. Vivaldi's *Four Seasons* flooded her ear as she waited for him to check the figures. After a minute or two, he came back and said, 'Good news. The full amount has gone through to White Management.'

'Can you tell me when? I just need to know when the money might reach my account,' she explained, relieved.

'No problem. Hang on.' More tinny Vivaldi. Christie held the phone away from her ear until she heard his voice in the distance. 'There may have been a slight hold-up because we moved office just before Christmas, but, er . . . no. You were lucky. The full amount of thirty-five thousand was paid in your name to White Management on 12 November, last year.'

'Thirty-five thousand pounds,' Christie repeated slowly as the implication of his words sank in. 'November? In one chunk? Not twenty-five thousand? Are you sure?'

'Completely. I can send the paying-in slip, if that would help.'

'I think it might,' she replied, uncertain. What the hell was going on? Julia had definitely said she was due twenty-five thousand pounds. That she'd failed to negotiate the larger sum. In fact, Christie had made a note of it in her diary, as she always did when payments were mentioned. And why had Julia told her part of the payment hadn't come through? She wouldn't deliberately withhold money from her, would she? Obviously not. There must be a reason – or was she simply unaware of what was going on in her agency? Was Lenny up to something Julia didn't know about? This and the half-term 'misunder-standing' over her pay didn't add up.

She hung up, having dictated her address. She stared at her

bookshelf, absent-mindedly thinking that a bit of straightening and dusting wouldn't go amiss as she wondered what to do next. Her first instinct was to call Richard. Her second was that she had to deal with this on her own. Abandoning her independence as soon as a man came into her life was little short of pathetic. She picked up the phone again and dialled. She was put straight through to Lily, who agreed immediately to send her a copy of the Drink-a-Vit contract.

'Don't bother Julia with this, will you?' asked Christie, as an afterthought. For the time being, the less Julia knew about what she had found out, the better.

24

The next morning, from the kitchen, Christie heard the snap of the letterbox and the muffled thud of the post hitting the mat. She put down the cafetière and went into the hall. Among the usual bills and uninteresting junk mail, a large manila envelope was addressed to her in a childish round copperplate. She pounced on it, then picked up the rest of the mail and ditched it on the bottom stair to be taken up to her study later. Back in the kitchen, with her waiting mug of coffee, she slit open the envelope, tipping it up to let a photocopied document slide onto the table-top. At last, the copy of the contract she'd been waiting for. There was no accompanying note.

Sitting down, she began to read it. Impatient with the legalese that made all the terms unnecessarily difficult to grasp, she flicked to the second page. There, written numerically, so leaving no room for doubt, was the sum she was to be paid for her work: £35,000 in a single payment. She sipped her coffee, staring into the middle distance as she thought. Julia was not the sort of person who made mistakes, particularly not where money was concerned. But there was no doubting the figure on the contract. She turned back to the first page and took her time, reading every clause to make sure there wasn't some hidden penalty that would deduct ten thousand pounds from the total sum agreed. By the time she reached the last page, she was certain that she was not the one making the mistake. But when she reached the end, there was another surprise in store. At the bottom of the contract was a date and a signature: hers.

She double-checked. Definitely her signature. But if she had never seen this contract before, how could she have signed it? According to their arrangement, Julia should be the signatory. But if neither of them had signed, someone else must have forged her signature. She remembered the batches of publicity photos she had signed and sent back to Julia's office. The only explanation could be that someone had copied from those. But who?

*

She sat in the back of the car on the way to TV7, thoughts buzzing round her head. Unable to concentrate on the newspapers that, as usual, Tony had provided, she parked her Starbucks latte in the armrest and took out the contract from her bag to read again. She stared at her signature – admiring, despite herself, the accuracy with which it had been copied. Initially she had been uncertain how to investigate this new development but, by the time she arrived at the studio, she had come up with a plan.

Confronting Julia was not an idea she relished. Before subjecting herself to another barrage of self-justification and belittlement, she needed to be absolutely sure of her ground. She sat through the pre-show briefing almost on auto-pilot.

As soon as it was over, having reassured Sam that, no, there was nothing the matter with her, she rushed back to the newsroom and started work on her evening's script. Beside her, Gilly's desk remained empty. In her absence no one had dared to usurp the comfort-giving super-ergonomic chair. The last of the helium Congratulations balloons sagged above it, the scented candle sat unlit, the phone-sanitising spray was unused. Christie refused to let herself be distracted by any of the banter tossed around between the other journos, the crack of empty coffee cups hitting the waste-bins or the constant comings and goings as the diehards went outside for a smoke. Above her desk a row of TV screens soundlessly displayed the terrestrial and satellite channels. She didn't lift her head until she had finished. She checked her mobile – half an hour until she was due in Makeup. Perfect.

She left the open-plan office and followed the corridor to her dressing room, where she could use her phone without being overheard. Everything told her she was taking a colossal risk, but her memory of what Frank had told her about Gilly's apparent cash-flow crisis and lack of Drink-a-Vit payment spurred her on. If Gilly was having similar problems with Julia, then perhaps she was the one to shed some light on their agent's methods of working. Given that Gilly had exchanged barely one friendly word with her, Christie was aware that she was embarking on a high-risk strategy but there was an outside chance she might be about to find an ally.

Gilly answered immediately. When she heard who was calling, her manner turned from politely distant to brusque. Her terse replies to interested questions about the triplets reinforced all

Christie's doubts about what she was doing. Nonetheless she nerved herself to continue and changed the subject to the real reason for her call, hoping the deference she put into her voice would persuade Gilly to talk.

'Gilly, the thing is . . . I've got a bit of a problem and I'm wondering if you can help me.'

'Yes?' Abrupt, but there was definitely a smidgeon of interest.

Christie looked down at the lines she'd written for herself earlier. 'It's just that I'm preparing my end-of-year accounts and I wondered whether you were aware of any irregularities in White Management's accounting methods that I might not have completely understood. In particular Drink-a-Vit. Julia hasn't received my money yet. Have you got yours? I can't ask Julia because she already thinks I'm such an idiot.' She gave a self-deprecating laugh. This was a really dumb idea. Whatever had made her think Gilly would help her?

Silence echoed along the phone line, then, 'No, I haven't noticed anything unusual.' Gilly was short, dismissive. 'Why don't you get yourself a decent accountant?'

'Actually, I've got one.' Christie's hackles rose at being spoken to so rudely. 'But accountants don't always understand the ins and outs of talent contracts so I wanted to be sure I did.' For God's sake, get off the line before you say something you'll regret, she warned herself. 'So you haven't noticed any discrepancies in your invoicing, then?' She could happily have bitten out her tongue.

'None at all. As long as cash comes out of the wall, all must be well.' Gilly's voice was shrill with dislike and disapproval. 'If there's something you don't understand, you should talk to Julia. Is that all?'

Why was it that whenever they spoke Christie ended up feeling furious and about two feet tall? 'Yes, I'll do that. Thanks for all your help,' she snapped back, wishing she'd never picked the phone up in the first place.

As she walked along the corridor to Makeup, she told herself to calm down for the sake of the show she was about to present, if nothing else. She was about to enter the cramped room with its familiar bulb-framed mirrors, the counters spread with boxes spilling over with makeup, brushes and hair spray, when her phone rang. She smiled at Marie and Rose, gesturing that she'd be back in a minute. Stepping back into the corridor, she answered without checking who was calling.

'How dare you?' The voice was tight, controlled and venomous.

'Julia? Hallo. How are you?' Christie tried to make herself sound as breezy as possible. She concentrated on her foot as it traced the outline of a stain in the grubby grey carpet tile.

Julia ignored her. 'I've just heard from Gilly . . .'

Christie's foot stopped moving as she waited for the tirade that would follow.

'Going behind my back to another client is something I will not tolerate. If you have doubts about the way I run my business, then I suggest you either ask me about them or find representation elsewhere.'

'Julia, hang on. I don't know what Gilly's said to you but it wasn't like that.' Christie immediately took up the line of most resistance. 'I thought she might be able to clear up a couple of queries I had, and I didn't want to disturb you.'

'"Discrepancies in your invoicing" sounds like a pretty big doubt to me. Before you deny it, Gilly told me everything. This isn't the first time you've come close to accusing me of malpractice,' Julia continued, 'and in my books you're beginning to sound like a spiky paranoid fantasist.' Each word was pronounced with crystal clarity. 'If you try anything like this again, anything, you will be hearing from my solicitor. Understood?'

'Completely.' Christie was experiencing everything she remembered feeling when she left the headmistress's office after being punished for some minor misdemeanour: a bitter-sweet mixture of shame, guilt, relief and fury at the injustice of the world.

'This time, I'm prepared to give you the benefit of the doubt. I believe you and I have a lot more to achieve together. But if you question the way I run the business again, our relationship is over.'

'I quite understand how it must seem to you – and forgive me for being naïve – but my accountant needed some figures clarifying and also asked who signed my contracts for me. By the way, who does sign them?'

Julia, taken by surprise, answered quickly. 'I do. Who else?'

'That's fine, then. So they're signed by you, Julia Keen?'

'Of course they are. Really, Christie. What's wrong with you?'

'Nothing. I needed to clear that up. Thank you. And forgive me for upsetting you.'

'You have to trust me.' Julia sounded slightly less aggrieved.

'And I have to trust you. I don't want to work with anyone who's not happy with White Management.'

After she'd hung up, Christie leaned back against the wall. Well, well. If Julia was signing the contracts, who was forging Christie's signature? Julia? Lenny? The watchdog journalist in her had emerged, hungry to unpick what was really going on at White Management, but to do that, she needed to remain on Julia's books. She'd been party to the investigations of enough crooked businesses in her days on *MarketForce* to know that if you're on the inside the chances of finding out the truth are significantly higher.

*

After the show, she stopped Sam on the way out of the studio. 'Can we talk? I've got a bit of a problem and you're the only person I can ask.'

A look of alarm flashed across his face, quickly replaced by concern. 'Sure. Let's go down to the bar.'

'If you don't mind, I'd rather go somewhere private.' She pointed down the corridor to her dressing room.

To Christie's amusement, the look of alarm returned. 'Don't worry, I'm not pregnant or dying of unrequited love,' she re-assured him. 'I just need your professional advice.'

'Well, thank God for that. Oh . . .' He groaned and thumped his forehead with the heel of his hand. 'You know what I mean.'

'Don't worry. I'm immune to your insults by now.' Smiling, she led the way and held the door open for him. 'Glass of wine?'

She took a bottle from the mini-fridge, unscrewed the top and poured them both a glass. Aware that Tony was outside, waiting to drive her home where Maureen would be waiting, impatient, she wanted to be as quick as she could. Pulling shut the vertical blind, she offered Sam the one comfortable chair while she perched on the edge of the chest of drawers and came straight to the point. 'What do you know about talent contracts?'

His face said it all, but in case she was in any doubt, he added, 'Not a lot. Why? Max looks after that side of things.'

'Max Keen? Julia's ex?'

He nodded.

'Of course. I'd forgotten you were with him.' This bit of information disturbed her, making her feel uncomfortably as if they were on opposing teams without her having realised it.

He checked his watch. 'I've got to be quick. Melissa's meeting me.'

'OK. Look at this.' She pulled the Drink-a-Vit contract out of her bag and showed it to him, explaining the discrepancy between the figure on the contract and the figure Julia claimed was due to her, plus the fact that the full amount had been paid more than two months earlier but she had yet to see it all. Then she showed him the signature. 'Looks like my signature, but it isn't. I've never seen the contract until now.'

'And?' He began to knead his shoulders with both hands, stretching his neck forward and twisting it to the side. 'Melissa's wearing me out,' he explained, with a wink.

'And is this what happens with Max?' she asked, impatient. 'Does he forge your signature on your contracts?' Christie wanted Sam's full attention but he didn't seem the slightest bit interested

302

in the nuts and bolts of their employment contracts. His mind had obviously moved on to the evening ahead with his latest squeeze.

'No, of course not.' He gave his head a final shake and rolled his shoulders. 'I sign my own. Look, Chris, I don't like her but Julia's a player. She's not going to mess you around. Too much to lose. I'd leave it to her. That's what agents are for.' He stood up, tucking the side of his shirt back into his jeans, then leaned towards the mirror to check his hair.

'Even though my signature's been forged? Surely that's fraud.' Christie was amazed that he could be so dismissive of something so serious.

Content with his reflection, he turned back to her. 'Yeah, but you got the gig, didn't you? And she's going to have to give you the money some time. You must have made a mistake over some extra commission she rakes off the top, that's all.' He drained his glass, stood up and took a step towards the door, signalling a halt to their conversation.

Perhaps he was right. Perhaps she was making too much of a fuss. Or was it that he was just young, single and had other more pressing things – such as Melissa – on his mind? He clearly thought there was nothing to worry about. Perhaps this *was* just the way things were done in this business and she had to get used to it, however much it went against her sense of right and wrong.

As they headed out of the building, he took her arm and squeezed it. 'Don't worry so much. I'll ask Max's advice, if you like.'

'No!' She stopped dead. 'Sam, you mustn't mention this to anyone else. Promise me. You're probably right and Julia will have her reasons for doing things the way she does. I just don't get them yet.'

'You will, my love, you will. And if you don't, just enjoy the profits of all she does for you. That's my advice. She might not endear herself to everyone but she sure knows how to advance her clients. Look at you and Gilly.' With that, he kissed her cheek, stepped into the revolving door and disappeared in the direction of a Saab sports convertible where a woman's hand waved from the driver's window.

And look what happened to Ben. The words rose from nowhere to the front of her mind. Doing up her coat, Christie walked over to where Tony was waiting. She disliked being bracketed so glibly with Gilly, and felt cross with herself for failing to get any closer to understanding how this business worked.

*

After Christie had overseen the end of Libby and Fred's supper, struggled with Libby's maths homework and read Fred the next adventure of *Swallows and Amazons*, with Libby curled up beside them, the children had finally given in and gone to sleep. With time to herself at last, Christie sat on the floor of the sitting room with a mug of hot chocolate, leaning back against a chair and warming herself by the fire. She lifted up Smudge, who was kneading her legs with needle-sharp claws, and put him on her lap, stroking him until he stopped fidgeting. With no more distractions, she had time, at last, to think.

All the call to Gilly had done was confirm her colleague's quite unreasonable hostility towards her, and that she was lying about the Drink-a-Vit money. What puzzled Christie was why such hostility existed when, as far as she was aware, she had done nothing to provoke it. Going behind Julia's back had definitely been a bad plan. As a result, she'd been labelled a 'spiky paranoid fantasist'. Although Christie was undoubtedly in the wrong, this was going too far. Was that really what people thought of her? 'Spiky'? Perhaps occasionally, when things got on top of her or someone crossed her and she reacted badly, but no more than anyone else. 'Paranoid'? No. She didn't believe that anyone was really out to get her. The way Gilly snubbed her friendly overtures had been witnessed by plenty of other people. And 'fantasist'? That wasn't true either. Something fishy was going on at White Management. She had some proof of that now and was going to get to the bottom of things. She picked up the latest detective novel she was reading, opened it, then put it on the chair behind her. She had her own mystery to solve.

Shutting her eyes, she let her thoughts drift freely in and out of her consciousness. But always they arrived back at the same person. Julia. Who was the woman to whom she'd entrusted her livelihood and who wielded such power in the entertainment world? Where had she come from? All Christie knew was her business reputation and what Frank had told her. She eased the purring Smudge onto a cushion and went upstairs to fetch her laptop. Settling back by the fire, she began to Google. After an hour, she had found out nothing more about Julia than she already knew. Various press interviews revealed her as a subject who guarded her own privacy but who would speak readily on behalf of her clients. Most of the photographs Christie clicked on she had already seen on the walls of the White Management office. Julia's Wikipedia entry held nothing about her early life until she attended drama school, bar a birth date of 11 March 1961 – and who was to say whether or not that was correct, apart from Julia herself? Beyond that, her biography was short, noting her marriage and divorce from Max Keen, and her involvement and absolution from blame in the death of Ben Chapman.

Yawning, Christie tried a different tack and Googled Ben Chapman. One last shot before she went to bed. Perhaps somewhere in the flash-flood of features run after his death she would find something more revelatory about Julia. She scrolled down the entries, many of them inevitably the same as those Google had thrown up about Julia. She was just about to shut the laptop down when her eye caught something new: *Gone Too Soon, a biography of Ben Chapman*. She clicked the link to Amazon. Months after Ben's death, a scissors-and-paste account of his life had evidently been whacked together to satisfy the public appetite for information about him. It was already out of print but a couple of used copies were available. Why not? At the least, it might give her a fuller picture of Julia's involvement with Ben. She ordered a copy and snapped her laptop shut with new resolve.

25

A week later, Tony had just turned out of the TV7 car park and was heading towards the M40 when Christie was surprised to see Maureen's number come up on her mobile. Her mother never rang unless there was something urgent to discuss. What could be so important that it couldn't wait for her to get home? Alarmed that something might have happened to one of the children, she picked up immediately.

'Christine? Is that you?' Maureen said in a loud whisper, as if anxious she might be overheard.

'Yes, of course. What's wrong?'

'It's Libby. She's very upset.' The words 'Libby' and 'upset' came through loud and clear.

Christie's heart sank. Everything had been going so well recently. Mrs Snell was happy with Libby's progress and Libby herself seemed to be enjoying school again. She'd chosen to have her hair cut back into a bob, had put on a little weight and had even been seen with her sleeves pulled up. 'Upset?' she repeated. 'Why?' She turned her head away from the dazzle of the oncoming headlights. 'Couldn't this wait till I get home and we can talk properly? I'll be back in about half an hour.'

'I thought I should prepare you.' Maureen raised her voice, though Christie still had to strain to hear her over the traffic noise outside. 'Some girls at school have told her you're bankrupt and that you're going to have to sell the house and move. She's terrified they're telling the truth and you haven't dared break it to us yet.'

'What? That's nonsense. Wherever did they get hold of that?' Christie almost laughed aloud.

'I told her that's what you'd say,' Maureen said, audibly relieved. 'That you'd have told me.'

In fact, her mother was probably one of the last people she would have told had she been in such trouble, Christie thought, imagining the reactions she'd get: the disappointment; the 'I told you so'; the 'What about the children?'; the 'What will the bridge circle say?' And not necessarily in that order.

'But it's all over one of those magazines.' Distaste for them dripped from every syllable. 'And that's not all they say.'

Christie's heart began to race. Since Christmas, she had gradually resigned herself to being a target for journalists and paparazzi. She had come to accept that this was what went with her job. As a result, she made a concerted effort not to look at the magazines devoted to celebrity gossip unless she absolutely had to, which she rarely did. But, however resigned she might be on her own account, she couldn't bear the idea that any stories, particularly ones that weren't true, should upset her family. Maureen was saying something else but, unable to hear clearly, Christie cut in: 'OK, Mum. Thanks for the warning. I'll see if we can pick them up on the way. Back soon.'

They stopped off at a twenty-four-hour garage where Tony insisted he should be the one to get out and buy whichever of the offending magazines he could find, leaving Christie fretting in the back of the car. When he returned, he was shaking his head as he passed her two of the celebrity-obsessed weeklies. Turning on the reading light, she saw that she featured on both covers. One screeched, 'DEPRESSED?' across a shot of her all togged up at a lunchtime event she'd attended recently, while the other offered, 'DOWN AND OUT?' with a picture of her looking tired and harassed arriving *sans* makeup at the studio. Inside, the articles expanded on the theme. Poor widowed Christie, the new darling of TV7, was struggling with depression that was disrupting her family life and threatened to ruin her relationship with her new man (insert photo of Richard and her walking down the high street). Financial worries, which stemmed from being without any prospect of work after Gilly's imminent return, apparently meant she might have 'to abandon her idyllic country lifestyle' (where did they dream that up?) for a more modest existence elsewhere, which, in turn, meant her long-suffering children would have to change schools and friends.

She leaned her forehead against the cool window, looking out into the darkness. Tony kept a tactful silence. There was nothing she could do about the journalists who had made up these stories. She had put herself in the firing line – she had no one but herself to blame for that – and she appreciated they had a job to do (God knows, she'd come close to doing it herself), but the way their editors blithely ignored the collateral damage that might be caused by their failure to check facts and their obsession with circulation were beyond her. No wonder Libby was upset. Some parent or pupil at the school must have seen and believed what was written and passed it on, leaving Christie to pick up the pieces. They may not have meant any harm but they were ignorant of Libby's fragile state of mind and couldn't have taken it into account. Until now, the sessions with Angela Taylor had seemed to be paying off, with Libby returning to her old self. She still had her moods – not to have them at all would be asking too much of a girl her age, reflected Christie with a wry smile – but at least she seemed much more settled, happier in herself.

But this would almost certainly get worse before it got better. Christie had seen how one story could spread through the media like a firestorm, being embellished and altered as it went, heedless of the truth. Look what had happened to Marina and Grace, outed by a broadsheet only to have the history of their private lives dissected for weeks in the tabloids and gossip columns. Her stomach tightened whenever she thought about her unwitting role in that – as well, of course, as Julia's. She had sold her own client down the river for the sake of another. Suddenly exhausted, Christie closed her eyes and visualised Angela Taylor's consulting room: pale lemon walls with a couple of framed Monet posters, stripped-pine floor, chest of drawers with potted palm beside it, cool calico curtains and two comfortable red chairs opposite one another, a low table with a potted African violet and a box of Kleenex. Imagining herself in the chair nearest the window, conjuring up the measured rhythms of Angela's voice, she tried to recapture the soothing effect of their sessions, which helped clear her mind and sharpen her thoughts: preparation for dealing with the raging teenager who was waiting at home.

*

Contrary to her expectations, the house was deathly quiet when she walked through the front door. She went along the dark hall towards the light in the kitchen to find her mother washing up. Ted had come to give her a lift home and was sitting at the table with a paper and a cup of tea. Maureen turned when she heard footsteps, sloshing water onto the quarry tiles. A too large red and white stripy apron protected her mail-order beige trousers and brown tunic top. Her face was pale and tired. For the first time in longer than she could remember, Christie registered that Maureen looked her age at last, and felt sorry for her. No amount of Pilates, diet and wishful thinking could hold back the advancing years for ever.

Wiping her forehead with the back of her Marigolds, Maureen abandoned the sink and flumped down onto one of the kitchen chairs. Christie hated seeing her mother so weary, especially when she felt so responsible.

'You've seen them, then?' Maureen nodded towards the magazines in Christie's hand.

'Yes.' She tossed them onto the table. 'But I promise you that there isn't a grain of truth in these stories.'

Ted picked one up and began leafing through it, his eyes round with appreciation of the paraded female celebrities.

Maureen took it from him and slapped it shut, giving him a warning glare as she slid it out of his reach. Obviously not *that* exhausted, then.

'Look, Mum. Please believe me. I know that people think there's no smoke without fire, but these stories are just malicious shit.' Maureen winced. 'More tea?' Although her mother and Ted shook their heads, Christie ran some water into the kettle and banged it onto the Aga. 'Let me spell it out for you. Remember *Top of the Class*? I do have work in the pipeline. I am not going broke. Would the central heating be going in at last in a couple of weeks if I were? And Richard and I couldn't be happier.' She sat down, feeling as if every ounce of her energy had drained away.

'I'm sorry, Christine.' Her mother leaned towards her, both hands flat on the table. 'Of course I believe you. What with Libby tonight, everything got on top of me. We're not used to your new world, that's all.'

'I know that, Mum. I'm sorry too. It all gets too much sometimes.' Christie reached across the table for her mother's hand, feeling bad for having been so snippy. If she was finding it hard to adapt to becoming public property then how much harder must it be for her mother?

'Is there anything we can do? You can talk to us, you know.' This was a rare offer but there was no doubt that it came from Maureen's heart.

Christie shook her head. Then, when she saw the genuine concern in her mother's eyes, she changed her mind. She remembered how Maureen had patiently listened to her pour her heart out after Nick died. Day to day, that compassion was disguised by her mother's brisk, no-nonsense façade. Christie longed to find that part of her mother again so she started to tell them about her problems with Julia. When she'd finished, Maureen thought for a moment and said, 'I've always thought there was something suspicious about that woman. I know you can't believe everything you read, but she didn't come out well when Ben Chapman died. All that talk of an affair – and all those news reports. Nobody had one good word to say about her.'

'Mum!' Christie said it as a warning not to say more.

'All right, all right. I didn't say anything at the time because she seemed to be sorting you out. But this just goes to show. Don't you think, Ted?'

He nodded, his eyes still on the magazines across the table.

'This isn't helping,' Christie said. 'I need advice on how to sort things out.'

'Sorry, Christine. But if you can't speak to Julia, clearly you should talk to someone else there. Doesn't she have an assistant who can explain how things work?' She looked at Ted, who nodded in agreement.

Before Christie had time to reply, Ted chipped in: 'It certainly sounds as if there's something funny going on. Couldn't you ask to see your accounts? I haven't forgotten everything from my days as an accountant. Maybe if I took a look I might be able to help.'

'Yes – Ted used to be a partner in FDCK, you know,' Maureen added, proud to be mentioning him in connection with such a prestigious firm.

'Really? I'd no idea.' Christie was stunned. The idea of Ted ever having done anything that didn't involve him sitting in the bar at the Legion was completely new to her. In fact, the thought of Ted ever having had a life before Maureen had never entered her head. She rebuked herself for always having taken him at face value. She had obviously underestimated him. 'Thanks, Ted,' she added. 'You know what? I think I could. I'll ask Lily.'

Maureen was beaming at Ted. 'I'm sure all this can be sorted out. You see, as I always say, a problem shared is a problem halved.'

Christie couldn't remember her mother ever saying that, but she felt a surge of affection for her all the same. Perhaps she had been wrong to leave her out of the loop so often. If she hadn't, they might have got on better. Note to self: make more effort but don't be disheartened if it doesn't work!

As the kettle began to boil, Maureen got up to take it off the Aga, then put it down when Christie shook her head, nixing the idea of tea. She turned back to the sink.

'No, Mum,' said Christie. 'Why don't you both go home and leave the rest of the tidying up to me? I'll finish it off when I've talked to the kids. You've both been amazing.'

'If you don't mind, Christine, I think we will.' Looking pleased with the compliment, Maureen peeled off the rubber gloves and hung them over a tap. 'The children are upstairs somewhere. I'll be back tomorrow. Usual time.'

Shutting the front door behind them, hearing the crunch of gravel as they drove off, Christie longed more than anything for a restorative glass of wine and something to eat. But before she could look after herself, she had something more important to do. Instead, she turned her back on the kitchen and, with a heavy heart, began to climb the stairs.

*

The next morning, she watched Fred and Libby trudge through the school gate. With their eyes fixed on the tarmac of the playground, they looked as if they were moving in slow motion, immune to the hubbub around them. Even Fred had lost the usual spring in his step. They parted to go into the separate first and upper school buildings without saying a word to each other.

Christie rested her forehead on the steering-wheel. When she shut her eyes, she could still see Libby's tight, angry little face staring at her as she explained how the stories written about her were untrue. Libby had heard her out, then thrown back all the familiar accusations she had used in the past.

'You love your job more than us,' she'd shouted, banging her fist on her bed. When she'd finally simmered down, the last thing she'd said was, 'I wish Dad was here. He'd know what to do.'

Christie had sat beside her, putting her arm round her shoulders, feeling the tension still bottled up in her daughter. 'But we've got Richard now,' she said. 'He can help us.'

That provoked the worst outburst of all. 'I hate Richard! He's not our dad and never will be. It's all right for you and Fred when he and Olly come over, but it's not all right for me. I hate them coming here.' She had edged out of Christie's protective embrace and turned to face her. Christie couldn't remember ever having seen her so fierce and unforgiving. That look had stayed with her ever since. All the time, Fred sat on the bed beside her, listening quietly to Christie's reassurances, pressing himself against her side, as if that would be enough to rescue him from the confusion he was feeling. When Libby had weighed in against Richard and Olly, he had still said nothing. Usually, Christie would have expected him to defend the two people who had become so important in his life. Instead, ashen-faced, he stood up, retrieved the worn Spiderman slipper that had fallen from his right foot and left the room. A second later, they heard his bedroom door click shut.

'Good riddance,' yelled Libby. 'Don't come back!'

When eventually Christie was convinced that Libby half believed her, she went down the corridor to Fred. His light was off and all she could see was the dark silhouette of his body in bed. There was no response to her whispered, 'Good night.'

She'd gone downstairs feeling more despondent than ever. How could children of their ages be expected to understand how all this worked? How hard it must be to imagine why people would go to such lengths to include their mother – of all people – in a magazine, especially at the expense of the truth.

That morning, the three of them had rushed through breakfast saying as little as possible to one another. Christie hadn't needed to hurry either child. They couldn't wait to be out of the house. Yet school didn't seem a very happy alternative. She sighed and wished for an easier life. At the same time she was certain that this storm would eventually blow over. They always did.

There was a tap on the passenger side of the car. Richard's smiling face was framed in the window. She felt a familiar flutter in the pit of her stomach. He opened the door. 'What's up with you? You look as if the world's about to end.' He slipped into the seat beside her and took her hand.

'No, not really. Just recovering from another jolly evening with the Lynch mob.' She made a face. 'Have you seen the latest gossip mags?'

'No. Let's go for a coffee and you can tell me all about it.'

In her wing mirror, she saw a dark-haired middle-aged man in a brown fleece standing in the shadows of the school hedge. He was holding a long-lens camera and now slid into a white van. Behind him, a red Nissan Micra was pulling out and Christie recognised the driver's woolly hat as belonging to one of the most persistent of the paparazzi she'd seen. Should she get out and say something, appeal to them to keep out of her children's life? What was the point? They no doubt had their snaps of her with her head on the steering-wheel, of Richard. Nothing she said to them would make a difference. And they weren't the ones going to write the words. She glared at the man who had been by the hedge. He gave her a cheery wave.

She didn't mention to Richard that she'd seen them.

*

Fifteen minutes later they were sitting at a quietish table in Ramsay's Tea Rooms. By getting there so early in the morning, they had stolen a march on the mid-morning descent of the

Nappy Valley mothers and tots. While Richard spooned sugar into his coffee, stirring it noisily in the large white mug, Christie related everything that had happened since Maureen's call to her the night before.

He listened as she told him the stories that were now doing the rounds at school. With his sympathy and support, she could at last laugh at how ridiculous they were. When she got to Libby's response, she didn't stop short of telling him everything that had been said. As she felt the release of talking about it, the words flooded out without her thinking about what she was saying. She didn't even leave out her daughter's reaction to the mention of him. When she saw his eyebrows tighten, she immediately wished she'd been more careful. The news of Libby's hostility was poor reward for all the effort he had made with her. A shadow crossed his face as he leaned back in his chair, folding his arms over his chest. He looked at Christie thoughtfully, drumming his fingers against his upper arm. Unable to tell from his expression where his thoughts were taking him, Christie suddenly felt uneasy.

'Penny for them?' she asked, picking up her mug and gazing at him over its rim.

'I'm worried about Libby, that's all. A child of her age shouldn't have to deal with all this crap. And I'm including me and Olly in that.'

Christie should have known that Richard's first consideration would be for Libby and not for himself. At the same time she wasn't sure she liked the direction in which he was going. She hurried to reassure him. 'Libby'll be fine. Really. I shouldn't have said anything. She's a drama queen, always has been. We've weathered much worse than this. She'll come round as soon as her friends get it into their heads that they can't believe all they read.'

'Mmm . . . but obviously me being around so much isn't making it any easier.'

She could almost hear his thought processes ticking over. No, this was definitely not going the way she wanted. 'That's not true. Remember France?'

'Of course I do.' His eyes lit up as he smiled at her.

That was more like it. Christie relaxed.

But the smile only lasted a second. 'I didn't tell you what she said to me that evening when you took Olly and Fred down to buy their beanies, did I?'

Christie felt as though her heart might stop beating. 'No?' She remembered their last night in France when she had taken the boys off, leaving Libby absorbed in reading *Twilight*, while Richard made them all some supper. She had been in her room when Christie and the boys came back.

'I wasn't going to mention it because I didn't want to upset you and, anyway, I thought it would blow over but now . . .'

'What did she say? Tell me.'

'I simply asked her to lay the table and she exploded, screaming about how I couldn't tell her what to do, I wasn't her dad, all that stuff.'

'Oh, God! I know it's hard.' Christie put down her mug and looked into his eyes. 'And there are bound to be setbacks.'

'Of course. And perhaps it would be easier if she only had

me to get used to. But I suspect I'm just a small part of her problems.'

Christie didn't need him to remind her. Thanks to Angela's sympathetic probing, she had only recently realised that Libby had always blamed herself for not saying goodbye to Nick on the last morning of his life. There were one or two ghosts that the two of them had only just started laying to rest.

But Richard hadn't finished. 'Having lost Nick, I think she's frightened of losing you too. I know,' he said, responding to her faint grimace, 'cod psychology! But I kind of understand where she's coming from. After Iraq, I saw an army shrink about the guilt I felt for surviving when friends hadn't.' He carried on talking: 'But if I were her, I'd feel I was already sharing you with everyone who watches the show and reads these magazines. I wouldn't want to share the little bit that was left with anyone else.'

Christie felt tears prick her eyes as she heard him echo Libby's words. She concentrated on her next mouthful of coffee, dreading whatever he was about to say next.

'Don't take this the wrong way but I think we should have a break from each other. I can't do this . . . to Libby, or to you.'

Outside, the traffic roared by, pedestrians walked past purposefully, the sun shone. Yet in their dimly lit corner of the café everything stood still. The two of them sat motionless, mugs raised, neither wanting to acknowledge what had just been said.

'What?' Christie was first to break the silence.

Unable to look at her any more, he lowered his gaze. 'I don't want to be responsible for tearing your family in two. Libby needs more time.' The sound of his mug hitting the table was loud in the small space.

'And I need *you*.' Christie felt as if she'd been cast adrift at sea, with the one remaining life-jacket caught in the swell and floating away from her.

'Darling Chris. It's not a question of your needs. Libby has problems. I don't want to be the cause of another. This is really for the best.' He stood up, looking miserable.

This was what he'd been trained to do, she reminded herself. Listen, weigh up the pros and cons, decide and act without further ado.

'But you can't say that,' she appealed, even though she suspected it was pointless. 'We just need to get through it. And we will.'

'I'm not saying "for ever". I'm just saying "for now". Perhaps when Libby has grown up a bit, we might try again.' He smiled a small, sad smile. 'Come on. We should go.'

'You can't just go. Not like that. We should talk.'

'There's nothing more to say. Trust me. It's for the best.' He stood up and turned towards the door.

Christie got to her feet, grabbing her coat, then bending over to pick up the sheepskin glove that had fallen to the floor. She caught him up at the counter where he was paying. As they emerged into the street, they had to screw up their eyes against the sudden brilliance of the sunshine.

'Will I see you again?' Christie asked, horribly conscious of sounding like a Z-list actress in a B-movie.

'Of course you will.' He took a step back to hold open the

tea-room door for a woman attempting to manoeuvre a twin buggy inside. 'I don't want to spoil Olly and Fred's friendship. We can still be friends too, can't we?'

'Of course,' she said quietly, as she asked herself how he could take a step back from their relationship so effortlessly. How could he give up like that? Wasn't what they had worth fighting for? Christie was far from sure that being friends was going to be straightforward – for her, anyway. His sensitivity towards Libby was one of the things she loved about him but now she hated him for it too. Did he expect her to switch off her feelings for him just like that? Was that what he had just done? Did that ability come from his army training too?

With nothing left to say, he walked her to her car and watched as she climbed in. Then he kissed the tips of his fingers, pressed them against her window so they left a little steamy mark, and walked off to his Land Rover. Christie watched him in her mirror, then banged her fist hard against the steering-wheel. She was not going to give up so easily. She'd expected so much from him. Perhaps too much. But this was not over yet.

26

Ten days later, Christie and Mel were sitting in the kitchen with Saturday lunch on the table between them. Mel poured them some of the Macon Lugny she'd brought with her and put the half-empty bottle back in the fridge. Two days earlier she had returned from Wales where she'd spent six days on a blowy, wet beach, waiting for the sun to make an appearance so they could complete a beachwear shoot. 'It would have been cheaper to fly us all somewhere warm for a couple of days,' she moaned, reaching for another Kleenex to blow her nose. 'Prestigious brand they may be, but so tight on the budget.'

With the side of her hand, Christie swept the breadcrumbs scattered over the chequered tablecloth into a neat pile to the right of her plate and began to talk. The children were out so the sisters were making the most of the opportunity to catch up on the events of the previous week. They'd last seen each other two weekends ago when Christie had picked Libby up from Mel's when the first *Top of the Class* weekend was over. Since then there had been the predicted blizzard of articles in the press and online about Christie's personal and financial crises. They'd raked through her dress sense, her haircut, and whether she was a suitable presenter (given her mental instability) for a prestigious children's programme. Every one of them had been written by a woman. Whatever happened to the sisterhood? she wondered. Was there anything left for them to fork over and find wanting? Women will never bust through the glass ceiling if they continue to feast on each other like piranhas.

'Look at this.' She pushed the previous Monday's *Post* under her sister's nose. 'This was meant to be the piece that set the record straight, that told my side of the story. Julia set it up especially. I should have followed all my instincts and said no.' She knew the piece off by heart, not least the bold header 'LYNCH CHRISTIE'. Beneath it, the journalist, Hannah de Manner, looking sultry in her accompanying publicity shot, had managed a spectacular hatchet job. Phrases kept coming back to Christie: '. . . aiming to be the new Gilly Lancaster but misses woefully . . . too nice, too mumsy, too plain dull . . . does the chemistry with the divine Sam Abbott extend beyond their working hours . . . as it is rumoured Christie would like . . .' and on it went, accompanied by photos of her with her head on the steering-wheel and looking distraught as Richard walked away from the car.

Mel read it, then picked it up, tore it to pieces and got up to put them in the bin. 'That's all it deserves. What did Julia have to say?'

'Not her fault. I must have antagonised Hannah, who had agreed to be nothing but positive. In fact we got on like a house on fire and I opened up too much – again! Why can't I learn

my lesson? I said in January that I wouldn't do any more interviews but Julia convinced me that this was the right thing to
do. I should have asked for copy approval but completely forgot,
like an idiot. So Libs has spent the entire week in a gloom,'
Christie concluded, absent-mindedly putting a finger into the
crumbs and remoulding the shape of the pile. 'Whatever I say
won't jog her out of it. She refuses to go to Angela's in case we're
followed. I can't very well drag her there, screaming and kicking.
Imagine the stories if I did!'

'Who's going to follow you, for heaven's sake?' Mel cut herself
a sliver of cheese, which immediately fell to pieces. She pulled
the board towards her and concentrated on trying again.

'Mel, it's been really awful. You can't imagine. The paparazzi
have been following us to school.'

Mel looked up in open-mouthed disbelief, her knife halted
halfway through the wedge of cheese.

'Honestly, that's what's been happening. I can hardly believe
it myself. I've been on telly for almost a year, that's all, and the
whole thing's gone mad. Sometimes I wonder whether someone
isn't feeding this nonsense to the press and telling the paps
where I'll be.'

That earned her a stern look from her younger sister before
she went back to the cheese. 'That's a bit paranoid, isn't it?'

'Probably,' Christie conceded, with a shrug. 'But Libby's
worked herself into such a state about them. She's even been
worried that something's going to happen to me.'

'Like what?'

'I don't know. But look what happened to Princess Di. I'm

not saying I'm like her – of course not – but these guys can be dangerous.' She helped herself to some quiche. 'If there was someone to blame for all this, then I think I'd find it easier.'

'Can't you haul in Richard as a bodyguard – in more ways than one?' Mel winked as she fingered the silver feather pendant at her throat.

'Mmm . . .' Christie hesitated. 'That's something else I haven't told you . . .' She pushed the quiche away, took a mouthful of wine and got up to refill her glass from the bottle in the fridge.

'No, Chris!' Mel looked towards the ceiling. 'Tell me you haven't fallen out with him. Not after all we went through at Christmas.'

'Not fallen out exactly.' She had another swig of wine, then went on to tell Mel, word for word, about the conversation in the tea room.

'Friends! He's got to be kidding!' Mel burst out, as Christie drew the story to a close.

'So I haven't seen him since. Actually, I thought I'd deliberately avoid him for a bit while I work out what to do. Anyway, absence makes the heart . . . and all that. At the same time, I'm determined not to let him go without a fight.'

'You go, girl!' Mel punched the air. 'That's what I like to hear. But don't leave it too late before you take action. Men don't hang around single for long at our age. Olly hasn't taken the same tack, I assume?'

'God, no. But Mum's nobly agreed to do the ferrying backwards and forwards between us. She's even picking him up this afternoon on her way back from her bridge morning. But there's a definite whiff of burning martyr about her.'

'We all know where she thinks the sun shines from.'

'Tell me about it. She obviously feels I've let her down badly by allowing him to slip through my fingers.' Christie laughed ruefully, knowing that Mel would understand.

Mel cut another piece of cheese and piled it with some ham onto a piece of bread. 'This is crazy. You're obviously made for one another. How can we get him to see sense? Couldn't you – I don't know – couldn't you find a reason to ask his advice, like dealing with your feckless plumber who still hasn't turned up?'

For the next hour, they tossed the various possibilities around. But Christie rejected every one. She knew Richard too well, she insisted. Once he'd made a decision, that decision was final. Seeing her or talking to her wouldn't be enough to change his mind. Something else would have to change. She didn't want to use the boys' friendship as an excuse to see him. And Libby was hardly in the right frame of mind to be approached with a conversation about her mother's love life.

Mel was tossing up the difference between a cup of coffee and opening a second bottle of wine – the wine won – when Fred ran into the room. 'Where's my metal detector?'

'By the back door, as usual,' Christie said. 'Why? Come here and give me a kiss first.'

'Mu-um!' he objected, giving her the briefest possible peck on the cheek as he raced past on the way to the door. 'We found a Roman ploughshare buried in the wood this morning. At least, that's what Richard thinks it is. When I go back, we're going to clean it up. I'm going to have another look in the field.'

Just envisaging Richard with the boys was enough to make Christie's insides tip. She gratefully accepted Mel's offer of another slug of wine as Fred rummaged around in the accumulated clutter of boots, sports gear and an old sledge. They heard footsteps in the passage.

'Can I come and see?' Mel asked Fred, grabbing her glass and disappearing out of the door after him, with peerless timing, just as Maureen came in from the hall.

'All well, dear?' She eyed the wine bottle with a sniff and the familiar lift of an eyebrow. 'You're not taking to drink, are you? It won't help.'

'Of course I'm not. Mel and I are just catching up. Do you want some?' She got up to get her mother a glass from the cupboard, anticipating the answer.

'Well, perhaps just a small one,' her mother relented. 'But I am driving.' She removed her sheepskin coat and hung it on the back of her chair, then sat down, straightening the knife-like creases in her trouser-legs as she did so.

'Have some bread and cheese to soak it up.' Christie half filled the glass and passed it across the table, then took a plate from the dresser for her. 'How were things at the farm?'

'Farm?' Maureen seemed confused for a second, then light dawned. 'Oh, you mean Richard's? I only stopped there for a minute. He introduced me to Marianne. Charming woman.' A wily expression crossed her face. 'Do you know her?'

'No. Never heard of her.' Christie had started clearing the

table, deliberately avoiding her mother's eye. 'But he's got loads of friends I haven't met.' Shielded from Maureen's gaze by the door of the fridge as she put the pickles away, she checked herself from rising to anything her mother said. But she was shocked by how shaken she felt at the news. There was probably a perfectly innocent explanation. Richard would hardly have started seeing someone else so soon – would he? Then another thought occurred to her – could he have been looking for an excuse to break up with her, when she had obligingly presented him with one on a plate? Surely not. Now *that* was paranoia.

But Maureen hadn't finished. 'She looked a bit more than a friend to me. *Very* at home, she was.' She left no doubt about the implication. 'If you're going to get him back, Christine, I suggest you get on with it.'

'Mum, you know I can't.' Christie spoke slowly, willing herself to be patient. She scraped the Brie back into its paper and wrapped it up. 'He's made up his mind. Until Libby is better, my hands are tied.'

'She's only a child, Christine,' Maureen objected. 'Surely what you say goes.'

'Doesn't seem to work the way it did in your day, Mum.' Christie could remember how she and Mel had jumped into line without question at the slightest word from their mother or father. Discipline had been their watchword. If only life could be as easy now, she reflected, longing for children who leaped to her bidding. 'She wants things back the way they were before. But that's not going to happen. Nick's dead, and I'm not going to give up my new life, however much she may want me to.

Apart from repairing the roof over our head, the show's given me a kind of escape route. When I'm there, I become the capable, intelligent – well, reasonably – and amusing woman that I'd almost forgotten existed.' She could see that Maureen was fidgeting, uncomfortable hearing views with which she found it hard to sympathise. 'Don't get me wrong, Mum. Of course family comes first – but being my own person, insulated from all this for a few hours every day, has been a revelation. Just as being with Richard was. I hoped I could have both but it's not going to happen. I'm stuck with Libby, and I guess she's made the choice for me, whether I like it or not.'

A small cough in the doorway made them whip round. Neither woman had heard the noise of the front door or of Libby coming in. The three stared at each other until, with a whimper of distress, Libby rushed towards the stairs.

'Libby, come back,' Christie shouted after her. 'I didn't mean that the way it sounded.'

A door upstairs slammed.

Maureen got up to follow her, but Christie grabbed her arm. 'Leave her, Mum.'

'But can't you see how much she's hurting?'

'Yes, of course I can. I see it every bloody day. But I know that whatever we say doesn't get through to her. Especially not when she's feeling angry. God knows, I've tried. And, actually, she's hurt me too.'

'But, Christine, you have to keep on trying. You know that. You must never give up on your children.'

Christie sat down, putting her head in her hands. She felt

terrible that Libby should have overheard what she had said, but it was the truth. She had meant it exactly the way it sounded. Oh, why was this all so impossible? What was she doing wrong? She felt Maureen's hand on her back, moving in circles, soothing her as if she was a child again. She heard her quietly humming 'Greensleeves', just as she had done when something went wrong in her childhood. All her mother wanted was to see her broken family mended. Once again she wished for the key that, if turned, would make everything better. If only one of them could find it.

*

She didn't get a chance to speak to Libby. An impromptu sleep-over at Sophie's had been arranged. Fred was staying with Olly, and Maureen had taken Mel to the station so she could get home in time for a hot date with Jean-Pierre, so Christie had the evening to herself. With a nagging headache, courtesy of too much lunchtime wine, she made herself a coffee. Then she went through to the sitting room and curled up in a chair with *Gone Too Soon*, glad of the chance to see what, if anything, she would learn about Ben Chapman and Julia. She quickly became absorbed in what was a surprisingly thorough and well-written account of Ben's rise to TV stardom.

Although she was most interested in the later years when Ben was involved with Julia, she flicked through the early chapters and learned that he had come from a modest northern background. After getting his 2:1 in classical civilisation and politics at Leeds University, he had moved to London where he was one of the lucky few accepted onto TV7's graduate training scheme. Given the chance to work in various departments, he had eventually settled in News until he was given his break: presenting *Good Evening Britain*. Christie was just about to settle into the chapter about how he had hooked up with Julia when the phone rang. She put the book and her mug on the floor, noticing how threadbare the rug had become – another thing to attend to once the room had been painted – then picked up.

'Hi, my love. Frank here. I'm at a loose end and thought I'd call.' He sounded extremely chirpy for a lonely Saturday night. 'Haven't seen much of you this week – except in the press. Are you OK?'

What a friend he was, Christie thought. He knew just the moment to call and offer support. 'I'm doing my best to keep a low profile, that's why,' she explained. 'God knows who's coming up with them but those stories are causing havoc here.'

'I'm all ears.' The sympathetic sound of his voice was all Christie needed, and for the second time that day, she found herself pouring out her heart about Richard and Libby. When she'd finished, Frank gave a long sigh.

'As soon as I sort you out, you mess up again. Phone the man, for God's sake.'

'Frank, you don't know him. It won't make any difference.' She rearranged herself so that she sat sideways with her legs hanging over the side of the chair.

He tutted. 'Sounds as if he's just as stubborn as you.'

'Perhaps you're right – perhaps I don't know him as well as I think. That's what Mum and Mel think I should do too.'

'Well, get on and do it, then. I was right last time, wasn't I?'

Like Mel, Frank was always so confident, so sure that his advice was on the money.

'OK, OK. I give in.' Perhaps she should be more proactive and not assume Richard's mind was as closed as she thought. Waiting for the situation to change was hardly putting up a fight. By the time she hung up, she was convinced. She would phone him, persuade him to come over and they would sort out their relationship once and for all. However hurt Libby was, she couldn't be allowed to ruin what they had. One day she would leave home, her life ahead of her, and Christie didn't want to be left alone having missed her second chance. Besides, if she didn't make a move now, she might be giving Marianne, whoever she was, a welcome opportunity to make herself even more at home. And Christie would never hear the end of it from Maureen.

Excited at having made up her mind to act, she got up and walked into the kitchen and back, silently rehearsing what she would say. She had to be careful not to plead or coerce but to be reasonable and to remind him of what he was missing. Failure to convince him that she was right was not an option. Finally, clear in her mind about how she would persuade him that Libby should not be the reason for him to back off, she sat back in her chair and lifted the phone again. She listened to the purr of the dialling tone for a moment, then held the receiver away from her ear and pressed the numbers that she knew by heart, each beep breaking the night silence. She closed her eyes, aware of her chest rising and falling with each deliberately deep, calming breath, and waited for Richard to pick up. She imagined the phone on the wall in his kitchen, the sound bringing him from wherever he was in the house, his footsteps on the stone flags. He would get there in a moment. She waited for his voice.

But the phone rang and rang. No one picked up, not even the voicemail system.

27

Christie was running late. She had kept Tony waiting as she delayed in her study, making some last-minute notes, and then they had sat in the slow-moving motorway traffic unable to make up the lost time. She ignored the newspapers on the seat beside her and stared out of the window, sipping her coffee, thinking not of the lunch she was going to be late for but of the interview lined up for that evening's show.

Three days earlier, at an editorial meeting, the producer and programme editor had announced that, from today and for the next three days, they would all be expected to have their security passes ready for inspection at all times. No personal guests would be allowed into the studio and the information they were about to receive was to be kept embargoed. The prime minister, the Right Honourable Teresa Billington, had agreed to an exclusive half-hour interview on the Thursday show – a huge broadcasting coup. That was the day she was due to give a speech in the House concerning the latest government review of the NHS. She was expected to announce the planned withdrawal of government funding. 'Abuse' of the system had gone on long enough. In future, the public would be expected to take out private medical insurance in the same way they did for their cars or their cats. The airwaves were already fizzing in anticipation. But it would be *Good Evening Britain* that aired the only live one-to-one interview the PM was prepared to give on the subject.

'This, darling, is a career-maker,' pronounced Julia, when she heard. She had called Christie from LA, late on Monday night. 'Get it right, and you're made. It's obvious that you've been chosen because her advisers see you and Sam as being the sort of soft interviewers who won't dislodge her from her comfort zone.' Christie had bristled at the insult, but let Julia carry on. 'You have to prove them wrong. She might expect to bamboozle you and the audience, but you've got to surprise her. Do your research. Get the figures.'

Since that conversation, Christie had been in a state of barely controlled panic. She had done as much research as she could, read the relevant chapters in a recent joint biography of the PM and her husband, trying to establish her weak spots and the best way to manoeuvre her into a position where she would have to answer key questions without being able to fall back on the usual political flannel. She and Sam were both chuffed to have the chance to show their mettle and, between them, had gathered the statistics they needed, plus a surprise guest: a former NHS manager who was more than ready to argue against the PM's new strategy.

Christie had thought of nothing else for the past three days, ever since the PM's appearance in the TV7 studio had been confirmed. The prospect of the interview had focused her thoughts and occupied what little spare time she had, so – despite Frank's nagging – she had yet to try calling Richard again. She hadn't dared confess that, after her first attempt, she had lost her nerve and was relieved to have something else to occupy her, something that she could use as an excuse.

Right now, she'd rather be in the studio, preparing for the show, instead of heading towards a restaurant to have lunch with Lily. But, she reminded herself, she mustn't forget the reason for their meeting. This was important to her too. She could have talked to Lily over the phone but had decided that face-to-face was more likely to get results. She mustn't leave without having persuaded Lily to help her.

At last, Tony pulled up in front of Gianni's. Christie hopped out of the car and rushed through the door of the restaurant into the warmth, checking her watch at the same time – twenty minutes late. She looked for Lily among the row of tables for two on her right. She was nowhere to be seen. Greeted by the *maître d'*, Christie was shown past the long bar into a large airy room at the back of the restaurant, safe from the eyes of curious passers-by. Lily was sitting at a table in the corner, beside a large window that overlooked an outside courtyard, tapping rapidly on her BlackBerry. She looked up as Christie approached. Her face broke into a wide smile, and she stood up to greet her.

'I'm so sorry I'm late,' Christie apologised, handing her coat to the *maître d'* before sitting down.

'No problem.' Lily poured them both some water. 'It gave me a chance to catch up with my emails. Everything's manic with Julia in LA. She emails every day with a long list of things that need doing and then phones in to check that I've done them all.'

Now she was sitting opposite her, Christie could see what she hadn't from a distance. Lily was pale and there were dark smudges under her eyes. That and the way she kept glancing downwards was enough to suggest that she was both anxious and exhausted. 'What's she up to out there, anyway?' she asked. 'I hadn't even realised she was going until she called me at the weekend.'

'Just her annual trip to see Nathan Brookstein. He's the talent agent who looks after our clients out there. She catches up with him and with her contacts at the TV and film studios too.' Lily's gaze flicked towards a man laughing loudly at a nearby table.

'Leaving you in charge?' Christie hadn't meant to sound quite so surprised, although Lily appeared not to notice.

'Yup. Well, with Lenny, of course. We manage together.' She beamed, delighted to be trusted with the added responsibility.

When the food arrived, Christie changed the subject and began to ask Lily about herself. She guessed that working with Julia was Lily's way of saying to the world, 'Hey, look at me. I'm going to make it on my own.' Otherwise, why would a bright girl, who could probably do well in anything else she chose, want to throw herself into what was such a cut-throat business? She couldn't help wondering where Libby's choices would take her and whether she'd object when the time came.

They were reaching the end of their meal when Lily looked down at her coffee cup, and began to fiddle with a teaspoon, clearly uncomfortable with what she was about to say. 'I've seen the magazines,' she began, 'and I'm sorry you're being treated so unfairly. I know half of it's untrue, but I don't believe—'

'Half of it?' Christie groaned. 'All of it, you mean. Thank God no one at TV7 seems to be taking any of the reports about my "depression" seriously. I wish Julia could talk to the editors and get them to lay off.'

'But she talks to them all the time,' protested Lily. 'Half my day's spent fielding calls from the press, putting through the right editor at the right time so Julia can play both ends against the middle.'

'But I thought she only spoke to them when she had to, especially after Ben's death.'

'No,' Lily said, adamant. 'After all, that's her job, publicising and protecting her clients. Her contacts are amazing.'

'How odd.' Of course, what Lily had said made sense, but if Julia was that well connected, why hadn't she used her influence to protect her? 'I wouldn't mind so much for myself,' Christie continued. 'It all goes with the territory, I understand that – but no one takes into account how it affects the children.'

'The children?' Her puzzled expression suggested that Lily had never made the leap from reading whatever was reported about a client to thinking of how might affect anyone close to them.

'It's hard enough having your mum become a public figure,' explained Christie, 'but to have your friends at school gossiping in the playground about her sex life, her fashion sense or her boob job – or whatever else they dream up – is hellish for them. Imagine.'

'God, yes. I'd never thought.' Lily looked dismayed.

'Yeah, well, it's not much fun dealing with the fallout, I can tell you. I guess the answer is that I shouldn't have taken the job in the first place if I can't stand the heat. But getting offered *Good Evening Britain* seemed such a break that I didn't think about the long-term. And now it's too late. But I haven't dragged you here to talk about that.' She smiled as Lily began to protest that she'd wanted to come, no question of being dragged. 'I want to ask you a favour.'

Lily looked pleased to be asked. 'I'll help if I can.'

'It's nothing much, just that I haven't kept thorough enough records for my new accountant.' How odd to be referring to Ted like that. 'I know Julia doesn't like being bothered with this sort of stuff, so I wondered if you'd send me a record of what I've earned to date. It would make my life so much easier.'

'Well . . . I don't know.' Lily looked dubious. 'Lenny keeps a very tight grip on finance. I suppose I could ask him, though.'

'I'd rather you didn't,' Christie entreated. 'I'd prefer neither of them knew how really hopeless I am. That's why I'm asking you.'

Flattered at being taken into Christie's confidence, Lily thought for a moment. 'All right. Leave it with me and I'll see what I can do.'

*

By the time Christie reached the studio, she had put all thoughts of her lunch and Lily to the back of her mind. The pre-briefing meeting went quickly since the main item on the programme was the interview with the PM. Apart from a brief look at the main headlines of the day, the entire show was to be dedicated to her interview, although at the end they would bring in the NHS manager and open up the phone lines and emails for the viewers to put their questions. The PM would have the final word after a cracking call from a GP with a terminally ill wife during which she was expected to be sympathetic but to hold the party line: 'The nanny state is dead.'

Christie had just settled down to concentrate on the notes for her final script when her mobile rang. She fished it out of her bag, irritated to see that Maureen was calling. Her mother knew how important it was to her that today went without interruption. Her finger hovered over the 'reject' button, but she thought better of it and took the call.

'Thank goodness you're there, Christine. I was so worried you wouldn't pick up.'

The panic in her mother's voice set off a clarion call of alarm bells in Christie's head. 'What is it, Mum?'

'Libby hasn't come home. She wasn't on the school bus.'

That's all she was phoning for? Christie tried to keep her temper as she calmed her mother down. 'I'm sure it's OK. Remember she did this once before? I was frantic until I discovered she'd gone to the nail bar with Chloë and "forgotten" to tell me. I thought I'd drummed into her head that she shouldn't do it again – I obviously didn't.'

'I've tried to call her but her mobile's off and I've phoned all the mothers and friends whose numbers I've got. None of them have seen her. As far as they know, she was coming straight home.' Fear was making Maureen gabble.

The room around Christie blurred and seemed to tilt away from her. She closed her eyes to steady herself. When she opened them, everything around her seemed to be going in slow motion as she forced her thoughts back into order. Thought number one: there must be a simple explanation.

'Christine! Are you still there?' Maureen's voice made her jump.

'Keep calm, Mum. I'm sure she's fine. Have you phoned Sophie's mum? She's probably there.'

'She was the first I tried. Sophie's no idea where she is.'

'She can't have disappeared. You must have forgotten someone.' Of course that's what must have happened, she told herself, keeping her own panic in check.

'No, I've tried everyone. I'm sure something's wrong. You've got to come home.'

This was the mother she knew of old: decisive, controlling. And Christie's instinctive reaction, born long ago, was to resist.

'Mum, I really have to be here for the PM's interview,' she said firmly. 'It's important.'

'Yes, I know that. I'm sorry. But, Christine, sometimes you have to put family first, whatever the sacrifice. I can't deal with this on my own.'

Don't guilt-trip me now, thought Christie. It's not fair. She had been looking forward to getting her teeth into a more serious piece of TV journalism. Trust Libby to pull a stunt like this today of all days.

'You'll be letting Libby down if you stay,' Maureen protested.

Christie knew that she was right. In a crisis, her place had to be at home. If anything had happened to Libby and she wasn't there to do everything she could, she would never forgive herself. Libby was her priority. There was no alternative but to abandon ship and go.

Dreading the reaction from Vince, the programme editor – what Jack Bradbury and Julia would have to say didn't bear thinking about – Christie first looked around for Sam. He'd know how best to break the news to Vince. And he was bound to welcome the challenge of carrying the interview on his own. It would be a great break for him. But he wasn't at the shambles that passed for his desk, two down from her, so she had to go straight to Vince.

She found him in the gallery, having a quiet moment in front of the rows of screens, chatting to members of the PM's security team who had been checking the building entrances and exits. At her request, he stepped out into the corridor to talk. As she explained what had happened, her scant hope for a sympathetic reception dwindled. He stared at her, his eyes unblinking, his face turning a gentle scarlet, until he exploded.

'No fucking way! You can't waltz off and leave us two hours before we go on fucking air!'

She flinched as a spot of saliva landed on her lapel. 'I know. I'm sorry, but my daughter's missing. I *have* to go. Sam'll do a good job on his own.'

'Sam!' His face grew more purple than she'd imagined possible, the tendons in his throat standing out like ropes. 'Sam's too much of a lightweight for a solo interview like this. He needs to be paired with someone who's not afraid to cut through the crap. Someone who can pull a bit of gravitas out of the bag. Woman to woman. What the fuck am I supposed to do now?'

She might have taken this as a compliment if she hadn't been too busy concentrating on the way his face was changing by the second. Then, something seemed to switch on in his brain, and a look of relief was paired with the beginning of a smile. 'Of course!' he pronounced. 'Gilly!'

'What?' Christie felt sick. This wasn't the solution she had envisaged at all. 'She'll never get here in time.'

'But she's already here, sweetheart.' The smile spread across Vince's face as it resumed its normal colour. 'She's brought the triplets in today to meet everyone. And, even better, she's got Derek and a battleaxe of a nanny with her. Lillybet!'

The runner materialised at his side.

'Find Gilly and bring her here right now. She's got to be somewhere in the fucking building.'

As the runner disappeared, every fibre of Christie's being was screaming, 'No!' The last thing she wanted was for Gilly to benefit from her misfortune. She stood by Vince, trying to look as if she shared his pleasure at coming up with such a programme-saving solution, but it was hard.

'Look, I must go,' she said, suddenly aware of time passing and Maureen's growing concern. 'I'm sorry.'

'Wait right where you are. We'll sort this in a couple of minutes.'

Not wanting to cause any further ructions, she waited. After what seemed like an age, Gilly's voice could be heard demanding

344

Lillybet slow down. Then she swept round the corner, almost knocking the runner out of the way. She looked as groomed as ever, and improbably squeezed into a gorgeous red stretch cotton dress: far more mannequin than mother. She gave Christie a cursory nod but turned the full beam of her attention on Vince.

'What's so urgent? I've really got to see to the triplets.' She put both hands on her hips, and stood, jutting her chin towards him, challenging.

'One great big crisis, that's all. The PM's coming in and Christie has to go home. I need you to step in.'

'Me?' All innocent. 'But what about the babies? Besides, I'm not prepared.' She straightened the neckline of her dress.

Christie could see that Gilly was going to milk this one as much as she could.

'Gilly, you're a pro,' Vince wheedled. 'I know I can rely on you to do a top-class incisive interview. Aren't I right, Christie?'

Although it almost stuck in her throat, Christie managed a strangled 'Yes.'

'Well, put like that . . .' Gilly ran a hand through her hair, pushing it up at the back. 'I'll have to tell Derek and Eunice to take my babies home without me.'

I should think that'll be a blessing for them, at least, Christie thought.

Gilly pursed her heavily glossed lips as she thought through any other implications, although all three knew it was only a matter of time before she agreed. 'OK. I'll have to go to Wardrobe and see what they've got. Nell may have to get something in specially.'

'I knew I could rely on *you*,' said Vince, a little too pointedly for Christie's liking. 'Right! Christie, if you give Gilly your research notes and whatever you've done on the interview script, that should make Gilly's life easier.'

'Sweet of you, Vince, darling. But I don't think I'll be needing those.' Scorn rippled through the last word. 'I've been following the news and you know I always prefer to do my own script, however last minute.' She turned to Christie, with the look of a cat that had snaffled all the cream. 'Isn't it lucky that Julia mentioned to me the PM was coming in today? I hoped I might get a chance to meet her . . . again. I've a very good sense of what's needed.'

*

When she left the TV7 studios, all Christie felt was the crushing disappointment of having had such a major opportunity snatched away from her, as well as real sympathy for Sam. All their preparation had gone up in smoke. She hadn't managed to find him before she left the building but could imagine his horrified reaction when he heard their interview had been hijacked by Gilly. Nor could she help asking why Julia had broken confidence and alerted Gilly to the PM's appearance in the studio. What were the two of them playing at? By the time the car approached the M4, she was no nearer to finding an answer.

As they left London, her thoughts turned to what would be waiting for her at home. Until this moment, she had successfully convinced herself that a load of fuss was almost certainly being made over nothing. Then an awful thought occurred to her. What if it wasn't nothing? Suppose something had happened to Libby? Pulling her phone from her bag, she checked to see if there was a message from Maureen. No. She started to dial her mother's number, then stopped. She didn't want to stoke up more alarm by communicating her own panic. If there was any news, Maureen would have let her know. But if Libby wasn't with one of her friends, where on earth could she have got to? The thought of losing her was unbearable. Christie shut her eyes and took a few deep breaths to steady herself. If she didn't master her worst fears, she'd be in no shape to help Libby, wherever she was. What about Fred and Maureen? They needed her to be calm and to take control. She looked down to see her fists clenched tight on her lap, the knuckles white.

By the time they turned off the motorway, she was praying that by the time she reached home, Libby would be there or at least on her way.

But that wasn't how it was at all.

28

As soon as Christie shut the front door, Fred ran down the hall and flung his arms round her, fastening himself to her like a limpet. 'Libby's disappeared,' he wailed. 'Maybe she's not going to come back. Just like Dad.'

'Don't be silly.' She ruffled his hair, wondering in passing what she'd done with the nit-comb, as she struggled to walk towards the kitchen, slowed down by his weight. 'Of course she's coming back. All we've got to do is find her.'

'Suppose she doesn't want to come back?' He squeezed tighter.

'Don't worry, she will.' Whatever she was feeling, she had to be positive for them to get through this. Scaring Fred wouldn't help.

'But if she doesn't, can Olly and Richard come round like they used to?' His face was hopeful under the hall light.

'Freddie! I've come home to find Libby, so let's do that. Come on, you can help.'

'How?'

'Well, stop thinking the worst for a start!' She kissed his forehead, unhooked his arms and held his hand, aware that there was something unpleasantly sticky on his palm. They entered the kitchen to find Maureen sitting at the table, the phone list from the fridge door and her diary in front of her, the phone in her hand. She gave a wan smile of welcome. To Christie's shock, she saw that her mother's eyes were glassy with tears and there was a slight but definite wobble to her chin. Maureen's struggle to stay in control was betrayed by the catch in her voice as she said, 'Thank God you're back at last.'

Christie let go of Fred's hand and went to the sink to wash off what turned out to have been a large smear of strawberry jam sandwiched between them. She inhaled, staring into the gathering dusk outside, trying to muster the strength she needed. Going to pieces wasn't an option.

'Right, Mum,' she said, adopting a brisk, positive approach that she hoped would brace Maureen. 'Show me who you've called.'

'Everyone, Christine. I've called everyone.' Maureen gestured towards the list of numbers. 'She's been missing for over two hours. We should call the police.'

'Mum! Stop it! I'm sure she's not missing. It's just a question of finding her. I'm going to start by ringing them all again.' She could feel her panic returning.

'She's been upset ever since Saturday when she overheard you say you were stuck with her.' Maureen sniffed quietly. 'She's run away, I'm sure.'

Christie didn't respond to the accusation. 'Well, then, I'll run after her,' she said, simultaneously wondering how much Libby's no-show might have to do with Maureen's old-school ways of bringing up children. Perhaps she'd fancied an evening without being made to eat everything on her plate for once. But suggesting this would hardly help the situation. Instead, she added, 'Why don't you do Fred some fish fingers or something while I ring round?'

Twenty minutes later, she'd spoken to every parent and child she could think of who might know Libby's whereabouts and had drawn a blank. She refused to let herself dwell on the worst-case scenarios, involving online grooming, violent strangers or secret boyfriends, that were crowding at the edge of her mind. While Fred and Maureen argued about how much tomato ketchup he could have, she ran through all the places again where Libby might have gone. There must be something or someone she hadn't remembered. As the argument at her elbow grew louder, she longed for a sane adult with whom she could share this, someone who would be clear-headed in a crisis, who would help her decide what to do. All at once, she knew who she had to phone.

She ran up to her office to escape the frayed tempers downstairs. The number was branded into her memory. She dialled quickly. Her heart missed a beat when she heard Richard answer. A feeling of blessed relief swept over her as she heard his voice, warm and measured. Gripped by a terrible fear for her daughter that she hadn't allowed herself to feel until now, she began to cry. She ignored his obvious surprise when he heard who was calling and quickly, tearfully, explained what had happened.

When she finished, he didn't say anything for a second. Then he took control. 'Hang up and call the police immediately, Chris. We've got thirty people here tonight so it'll take me a few moments to pass over to Tom the night-time manoeuvres we're running for them. Then I'll come straight to you.'

'I didn't mean—'

But he had hung up. She looked at the phone, paralysed by the jumble of emotions that were chasing round her head. Then she roused herself and dialled 999 to report a missing child.

*

Richard arrived a couple of minutes before the police. Christie was waiting for him, watching the drive through the sitting-room window. As soon as she saw the lights of his Land Rover, she tore out of the house. He drew up, leaped out and, without shutting the driver's door, ran towards her. As he enveloped her in a great bear-hug, his familiar smell, the comfortable feel of his jacket against her cheek, brought more tears to her eyes. She fought them back, not wanting him to see.

The dark quiet of the lane was shattered by the screech of a police car's siren and a flashing blue light. With a rattle of gravel, the car swerved down the drive and pulled up next to the Land Rover, missing the open door by an inch. Two uniformed police got out, a man and a woman. Christie and Richard broke apart, and Christie showed them inside.

The next half-hour assumed a nightmarish quality. The police were brisk, thorough and sympathetic, but their presence gave an unwanted significance to Libby's disappearance, now she was being recorded as officially missing. As they talked to Maureen and Christie, Fred's eyes were wide with unease. Questions were asked. Replies were given. Calls were made to the local station. Walkie-talkies crackled. Notes were taken. Libby's room was searched, her laptop switched on. Christie poured her mother a stiff brandy, hoping it would calm her. Ted arrived to take her home. Promises were made to let her know as soon as they heard anything. Richard said little, but his presence gave Christie the courage to cope.

While the policewoman took Fred off so he could show her how to play tennis on his Wii, Richard and Christie remained at the table with the policeman, mugs of cold tea and an untouched plate of biscuits in front of them. Random awful possibilities churned through Christie's mind: she could no longer hold at bay various newspaper stories she'd read, and the desperate parents of missing children she'd interviewed or seen giving grief-stricken press conferences. She picked up a biscuit, thought better of it and returned it to the plate.

'You don't think someone might have . . . ?' For the first time, she began to articulate her worst fear.

'No,' Richard stopped her. 'No, I don't. I'm sure there's an explanation we haven't thought of.'

'Thank you for coming.' How small her voice sounded.

He put his hand over hers. 'What did you think I'd do?'

'I don't know.' All she had known was that he would do the right thing, whatever that was. And, unlike her, he hadn't hesitated. He had dropped everything at work and come round immediately. She was aware that the policeman beside her had begun to fidget in his seat. He cleared his throat and excused himself to join his colleague.

Left alone, the two of them sat in a silence that was broken by the tick of the station clock and Fred's triumphant shouts from the sitting room as he won point after point.

'This is impossible,' said Christie, standing up. 'I can't sit here doing nothing. Perhaps we should go out, drive around and look for her.' She reached into her bag for her car keys.

Richard caught her hand. 'You're in no state to drive. I'll go.'

The idea of sitting alone, waiting for news, was even more unbearable. 'No,' she said. 'Perhaps we've missed something in her bedroom. We could look together.'

He nodded. As they left the kitchen, the phone rang. Christie stared at it, unable to move, wanting but not wanting to hear whatever news there was. Richard took a step back and picked it up. 'Mel? You have? Thank God. I'll pass you over.' With a relieved smile, he held the phone out to Christie. 'She's got Libby.'

Christie grabbed the phone. 'Mel? Where are you?'

'At home. I went for a drink after work and got back ten minutes ago to find Libby sitting, almost frozen to death, on my doorstep.'

'How the hell did she get *there*?' Never had it crossed her mind to call Mel or even to consider that Libby might have gone to London.

'You brought her here the first time you did *Top of the Class* – she remembered the way. I told her she could come whenever she wanted, so she has!'

The swell of relief that almost swamped Christie was tempered by a swirl of anger. 'Put her on. I could kill her.'

'Take it easy,' Mel warned. 'She's upset. She thought I wasn't coming home and she's scared. Giving her an earful isn't going to help.'

'Mum?' Libby's tearful voice came on the line.

'Libs! Thank God. Are you all right?' Her anger vanished as quickly as it had come. 'You scared the living daylights out of me. I'm coming to get you.'

Libby didn't challenge her. She sounded tired and vulnerable, like the twelve-year-old girl they all sometimes forgot she was.

When she put the phone down, Christie could imagine her sister and daughter sprawled together on the floor cushions in Mel's tiny green bohemian living room, surrounded by the weird and wonderful bits and pieces she'd gathered together over the last few years. She could imagine why Libby loved being there, with such easy access to the city, compared to being in their draughty old house, stuck out in the sticks – but, like it or not, this was her home: the place where she belonged. Selfish child. Why hadn't she thought to call anyone? When she looked down, her hands were shaking.

Richard picked up her car key from the table. 'I'll take you. But you'd better tell Maureen the good news first while I deal with the police.'

They were soon heading towards Chiswick, Fred slumped asleep on the back seat. The calming sound of Radio 3 filled the car although, above it, Christie could hear Mel's voice in her ear, as clear as if she were sitting right behind her. 'Come on, sis. This is your chance. Libby's been found. There's nothing you can do about the interview with the PM now. So for God's sake say something. He's right beside you. A captive audience, if ever there was one.' But as the adrenalin wore off, Christie was overcome by sleep, her eyelids so heavy she couldn't stop them closing before she had time to say anything. She woke twenty minutes later, by which time they were on the motorway. She turned towards Richard, watching his profile strobed by the light of oncoming cars. The light accentuated the planes of his face, his slightly bent nose. His Adam's apple moved as he swallowed. He stared ahead, absorbed in the music, giving no clue to what he was thinking. Mel's voice returned: 'Now! Say something now! You won't get another chance like this.'

'Who's Marianne?' she blurted, and kicked herself for such a random opening gambit.

He glanced at her, surprised. 'Why?'

'Just curious.' Come on, Christie, she encouraged herself. You can do better than this.

'My sister. She's been staying and helping look after Olly while Tom and I have been setting up some new endurance programmes for the unsuspecting punters.'

So Maureen's innuendoes had been way off the mark. Christie still might be in with a chance, after all. Encouraged, she covered her small smile with a hand and looked out of the window. But, she corrected herself, harbouring hopes that Richard would change his mind was pointless. What had happened this evening could only have confirmed to him that he'd been right to disengage himself. This family's too much trouble for any man, she thought sadly.

'How did you know about her?' he asked.

'Mum mentioned her. She thought she was my competition. She'll be so disappointed.'

He laughed, breaking the tension. 'Sorry about that.'

'I'm glad.' She turned to him again. 'I'd hoped we weren't quite done, although I know tonight must have confirmed your . . .' She didn't finish the sentence because he lifted a hand to stop her. His eyes didn't leave the road.

'It's hard for me, Chris. It's taken me such a long time to get to this point and I don't want to mess things up for you or for me.' He stopped as if he was working out what to say next.

She waited.

'I didn't want you to feel sorry for me or to put you off. A screwed-up ex-soldier is impossible to live with – as Caro will tell you. Being in the services changed everything for me. After what I did, what I saw in Iraq, I used to wonder whether I'd ever be able to make contact or communicate with real people again. No one understands what goes on in a war zone. You see and experience such dreadful things. So you carry them round in your head. The nightmares take years to go.' He paused.

Christie said nothing. He had never opened up to her like this before. The darkness in the car and the sense of intimacy felt as she imagined a church confessional must.

'Christie, these are things I've kept to myself for a very long time. Caro really tried to help me when I got back, but I couldn't find myself, let alone her hand of love to hold on to.'

Christie sat very still, every nerve tuned in to him.

'Caro and I were childhood friends, always kept in touch after school, and once I'd joined up. But I let our correspondence drift while I was in the Gulf . . .' He stopped and was silent for a full minute. Still Christie didn't speak.

'After I was demobbed, I came home and we bumped into each other at a friend's house – the rest is history. We married, which pleased our families. But, if I'm honest, marrying was just an easy option. I was numb inside and it felt like the right thing to do. Poor Caro. She deserved so much more. It's testament to her that we're still friends. When she had Olly, I kind of woke up. Here was a perfect miniature human I was responsible for. I tried to be the husband Caro wanted but it was too late. A colleague of hers fell in love with her and she left me.

'Thank God we never argued over the sharing of Olly. Eventually I did see someone, a therapist, who helped me find my way back to me. He said it was very common for soldiers to have a form of post-traumatic stress syndrome – horrible label, but there you are.

'So, I know what it's like to be scared and not quite handling things. I got frightened when I saw what a mess we could make of Libby's life, and I didn't handle that well either, did I? When we met, you'd obviously had your own problems, and I had no idea what you thought about me. You seemed way out of my league, running your own life, starting a new career in TV.'

She gave an ironic laugh.

'To be honest, if Mel hadn't persuaded me at Christmas . . . Well, you know the rest. But . . . however much I want to be with you, and I do, I've messed up enough lives without adding Libby's to the list.'

The pieces of the jigsaw fell into place. 'But Libby's problem isn't really with you. Can't you see that? It's with me,' Christie said, tentatively placing her hand on his thigh. How was she ever going to get him to understand? 'You were right. She's pissed off with me, like any teenager is with their mother, but at the same time she's scared that I'll love you more than I love her.'

'Love me?' He sounded so hopeful. 'Even when I've been such an idiot?'

'You haven't. I love the way you think of the children and . . . I love you.'

For a few moments they said nothing, letting the music flow round them as they thought about what had been said.

'Christie Lynch, I've fallen in love with you too, big-time. These last few weeks have been as painful as I can remember. I really thought I'd blown everything. You, Libby and Fred, Mel and even your mother have got under my skin. I've missed you so much, missed making love to you, missed sitting in your bloody cold house, missed just seeing your silly face.'

'Does that mean Olly and me are going to be brothers, then?' piped up a small voice from the back seat.

Richard and Christie exchanged a secret smile in the dark.

29

The first thing Christie noticed as Mel opened her front door was the scent of cinnamon and cloves from a candle burning on the hall table. Then she noticed something sweeter in the air. She took a second to recognise the smell of toasted marshmallows, the nostalgic stuff of many a wet Saturday afternoon in their childhood. She hugged her sister and went into the sitting room to find Libby kneeling on a cushion in front of the fire, holding two wooden skewers over the flames, each holding two marshmallows. She looked untouched by the distress and upset she had caused as she turned to give Christie a sheepish grin. The tears of earlier on had disappeared.

'Can I just finish these off? They're nearly done.'

Christie sank down beside her, putting her arm around her shoulders and kissing her temple. Feeling her daughter relax against her drove home her immense relief at finding her, and simultaneously made real her fear of never seeing her again. She would never have recovered had something more serious happened.

'Never, ever run away again without telling me, Libs. You scared us all to death.'

'If I'd told you, then it wouldn't have been running away, would it?' Nick's unarguable logic once again. Libby removed the caramelised sweets from the fire and put them on a plate, then hugged her mother, repentant. 'But I didn't mean to scare you. I just wanted to see Mel. I needed to talk to her. My phone battery ran out and then it was dark and I thought Granny'd be cross.'

'She probably would. But that would have been better than making her so worried we had to call the police.' She squeezed her hard. 'And I had to leave work and miss out on my big interview with . . .' She heard Mel quietly clearing her throat: a not-so subtle reminder of what was important here. As if she needed that! When she looked round, Mel was standing in the doorway, staring at the floor. Behind her, Richard was taking in the shabby-chic Moroccan-brothel look that was Mel's sitting room.

'We just had to finish off some things we began talking about last time,' Mel said. 'That was all, wasn't it?' She crossed the room and picked up the plate to offer everyone a marshmallow. 'Libby's a bit clearer now about some things than she was, aren't you?'

Self-conscious, Libby nodded as she concentrated on loading another pair of skewers. 'Kind of. Yes.'

'Have you guys had any supper?' Christie wondered, the taste of the marshmallow making her realise how hungry she was.

'Not exactly.' Mel gestured towards the packet of sweets and two almost empty hot-chocolate mugs. 'Libby had a cheese and strawberry jam sandwich first, though.'

'Well, let's go home and get something.' said Christie. 'Smudge is missing you, Libs.'

'Thanks for having me, Auntie Mel. Can I come back soon?'

'Of course you can.' Mel kissed her on both cheeks. 'Just remember to tell someone where you're going next time. Including me.'

*

In the car, Christie sat in the middle of the back seat holding Fred's hand on her left side and Libby's on her right. She watched the houses they were passing, registering the number of for-sale signs, so happy that the kids were being brought up in the fresh air of the country rather than at the side of an arterial road out of London. Then the abandoned interview with the PM drifted into her mind. How had Gilly done it? Let it go, she said to herself. Just let it go. Some things are more important than work. Much more. She gave Libby's hand a little squeeze.

'Why couldn't whatever you wanted to say to Auntie Mel have waited until the weekend?' she asked.

'I told her about what you said to Granny,' Libby replied, soft but accusing nonetheless. 'All about you being stuck with me and me making choices for you.'

'Oh, Libs. You know I didn't mean it quite the way it sounded.'

'That's what Mel said, too. She said I should let you decide about your life because you wouldn't do anything without thinking of me and Fred first.'

'But *I*'ve told you that time and time again.'

'It's different coming from her.'

Christie had nothing to say to that, but she understood. Sometimes the same words took on a new significance when they came from another direction. A fresh point of view could shed light on a familiar problem, if you let it.

'I think it's time I said something. May I?' Richard caught Christie's eye in the rear-view mirror.

She nodded, realising he hadn't said a word since they'd arrived at Mel's.

'Perhaps I should have said this earlier, but now seems as good a moment as any. Libby, you know your mum loves you and Fred more than anything, and anybody?'

Libby made a face, then grunted and looked out of the window, but left her hand in Christie's.

Richard refused to be deterred. 'And tonight's made me realise how very fond I am of you too.' He stopped, momentarily embarrassed by his own straight speaking.

Christie sat rigid, wishing he'd picked a better time for this, unable to anticipate Libby's reaction.

'Not just of Fred but of you,' he continued. 'I'll never be your dad and would never try to be him, but I do love your mum . . .'

She gave a little gasp.

'. . . and I love you two kids, so . . .' He glanced at Christie in the mirror again as if assuring himself of her encouragement. '. . . I'd be honoured if you think Olly and I could be part of your family. There. I don't expect you to say anything now but have a think about it.'

As he finished, his shoulders relaxed and, even though the car's interior was no longer lit by streetlights as they hit the motorway, Christie thought she detected quiet satisfaction on his face. She glanced at Libby, who was staring at him, clearly as surprised as Christie was by this unexpected confession.

'Yeah, well, OK,' Libby muttered, self-conscious. But she left her hand in Christie's. That must be a good sign.

'Thanks. That's all I ask.' He returned his concentration to the road, tapping his fingers against the steering-wheel in time to a tune he had begun to hum under his breath.

Libby shifted across the seat, and manoeuvred herself so her head rested on Christie's lap. She closed her eyes as her mother lovingly stroked her hair. Within minutes, she had dozed off.

As soon as they got home, Christie made them all scrambled eggs, then encouraged Libby and Fred straight to bed, even allowing Libby to take Smudge with her – an unprecedented treat. Instead of returning to work, Richard called Tom to say he wouldn't be back until later. While he cleared the table, Christie went upstairs to say her good nights. Fred was already sound asleep, lying on his bed still in his school uniform. He half woke to be cajoled into his pyjamas, then went straight off again the moment his head hit the pillow. Libby was lying on her back in bed, eyes shut, Smudge curled in a ball on her chest, purring loudly.

As Christie tiptoed through the clothes strewn over the floor to turn off her bedside light, Libby's eyes opened. 'Mum?' she whispered. 'I am sorry. And I'm sorry you had to come home from work. You won't get into trouble, will you?'

'Don't worry.' Christie straightened the duvet without dislodging the kitten. 'You're way more important to me than some silly interview. I'll be fine. We'll talk about it in the morning. Love you.' She kissed Libby's forehead and switched off the light, at the same time dislodging a pile of hair slides and nail varnish from the bedside table.

'And you know what?' Libby's face was hidden as she fumbled around on the floor, attempting to pick up her bits and pieces in the faint light from the landing. 'I do think Richard is kind of OK. You're not going to marry him, though, are you?'

If the question hadn't been asked so seriously, Christie would have laughed. As it was, she said, 'We've got a long way to go before anything like that. And if it was ever a possibility, you, Fred and Olly would be the very first to know. Pinky promise?' They twined their little fingers in the family gesture.

She had just got downstairs and was taking a longed-for glass of wine from Richard, bursting to tell him he had been granted Libby's grudging approval, when her mobile rang. Worn out by the day's events, she was about to disconnect when she saw Sam's name on the screen. After answering all his questions about what had gone on since she'd left the studio, she asked about the interview with the PM.

'Haven't you seen the news?' he asked, evidently astonished that she hadn't.

'I haven't had a chance. What's happened?'

'Turn on Sky News right now, then call me back.'

Mobile in hand, she dashed into the sitting room and turned on the TV to find a report showing a major train crash outside Leeds that had happened in the late afternoon. Local hospitals were working flat out to cope with the injured. There had been twenty-five fatalities, with another ten people on the critical list and countless others injured. The prime minister had flown north to support the victims and their families, and on the day of her controversial speech announcing the dismantling of the NHS, she was discovering for herself exactly how vital the health-care system was to the country. She was filmed looking extremely shaken, refusing to answer the shouted questions of journalists. In the studio, the political editor and various pundits including the shadow health minister discussed the tragedy, speculating that the prime minister would surely be forced now to find the necessary funding for the NHS, thus making a spectacular U-turn in recent government policy. If she didn't, she was surely hammering the last nails into her political coffin.

Intrigued, Christie rang Sam back immediately. 'So? The interview? What happened?'

'Postponed,' he said, triumphant. 'Gilly was spitting tacks. I wish you'd seen. She was so pissed off at missing her big chance that she stormed off as soon as the show was over. Didn't even visit the green room to say thanks to the poor sods who were drafted in at the last minute to fill. We had the runner-up from *Britain Can Sing* and Brando Black, who's just completed a world record for walking on his hands. No one from the government would step into the PM's shoes. And, of course, there was plenty of live reporting direct from the scene.'

'But you said "postponed"?' She took a first sip of her wine.

'I'm guessing she might agree to come on again when she decides whether or not the lady's for turning. Whatever she decides to do about the NHS is going to need some spin, if she's going to save any face at all.'

So there is a God, Christie thought as she lay back on the sofa. Or if not, something else must be watching over me. A day that had gone so spectacularly off piste hadn't turned out so badly, after all. In fact, thinking of Libby's change of heart towards Richard, things were better than they'd been that morning. He came in from the kitchen with the wine bottle and topped up their glasses.

'What a night.' He sat down heavily, as if he was never going to get up again, his long legs sprawled towards the fireplace, his arms out to the sides.

'What you said in the car . . .' Christie reminded him.

'What about it?'

'Did you mean it?'

'No. I was only joking.' He watched as her face changed from anticipation to surprise to disappointment, then relented. 'Of course I meant every word. If you want us to be together, so do I. The last few weeks without you have shown me that. How do you think Libby's taken it?'

As she told him of their conversation, he sat up, energised, leaning towards her. 'But that's terrific. You were right and I was wrong. All she needed was time.' He reached out a hand to her. 'So, Mrs Lynch, will you entertain the idea of a relationship with a war-battered veteran and his son? They come as a convenient two-for-one user-friendly package.'

She laughed. 'Of course I will, you idiot. I can't think of anything I'd like more.'

30

By the weekend, the household had reverted to normal. Fred's fears for his sister and Libby's contrition over her disappearance had soon vanished into the ether and they were back to their usual bickering. That Saturday, Christie heaved a sigh of relief as Maureen accompanied Libby to London to meet Mel, who was taking her niece shopping and to the V&A to look at the fashion collection. At the same time, Richard had driven Fred and Olly to visit the lambing sheds at a neighbouring friend's farm.

Without them, the house was wrapped in a blissful quiet. Taking advantage of everyone's absence, Christie was going to use the morning for the long overdue chore of sorting out her finances with Ted. With her TV7 salary keeping her going, she'd allowed herself to put everything else on the back-burner until now. At lunchtime she was expecting Lily, who had phoned the previous afternoon to ask if she could come out to see Christie at the weekend. 'I've got something I need to show you, and I can't show you here.' She had sounded slightly panicky, as if she was anxious to get off the phone, and wouldn't be drawn on whatever it was she was bringing with her. Christie couldn't imagine what could possibly demand such secrecy but had been forced to contain her impatience. Her accounts would provide the perfect preoccupation.

With a few hours to go before Lily would appear, she brought down all the paperwork from her office: receipts she had stuffed into a drawer, pay slips that had lain by a ring binder without being filed for months, the contract from Drink-a-Vit, and her diary, in which she'd kept a record of the sums she'd understood she was to be paid for the various engagements Julia had negotiated for her. By the time Ted arrived at ten thirty, scraps of paper were littered over the kitchen table. Her attempt to compare her records with those from White Management, which had arrived in the post from Lily, was still very much a work in progress.

Ted was dapper in a pair of gold corduroy trousers that were balding at the knee, a slightly too tight green sweater and a leather-elbowed tweed jacket. Despite his sartorial shortcomings, Christie still felt rather underdressed in her leggings, boots and a large sloppy jumper. His few strands of hair were Brylcreemed to his scalp and there was a distinct gleam in his eye as he anticipated getting to grips with Christie's finances. However, when he saw the paper chaos, the gleam dimmed. Disorganisation was not what he was used to. But he shook off his dismay and, with a cup of tea and a plate of assorted biscuits at his right hand, rose manfully to the challenge. His scuffed briefcase contained a brand new block of squared accountancy paper, three perfectly pointed pencils, a sharpener and a large white eraser. He took them out, snapped the case shut and placed it on the floor at his side, then laid everything he needed in a neat row in front of him. This was a Ted Christie had never seen before and, despite herself, she was impressed. After a concentrated hour or so, they had managed to impose some sort of order on her affairs.

Then Ted looked through the White Management file, his spectacles perched on the end of his nose – he resembled a character in a Dickensian counting-house. He punctuated his concentration by pinching his top lip between his thumb and index finger and pulling it. Occasionally he'd tut and rub out a line of figures, then urgently reconfigure them in his spidery hand.

After a while, feeling like screaming with boredom, Christie gave up waiting for him to pronounce and went out into the garden. Although there was still a chill in the air, the spring sunshine was bright and the leaves were just beginning to emerge, smothering the branches in a gauzy green. Beneath the trees, drifts of daffodils nodded in the breeze while, in the flowerbeds, new shoots were pushing through. There was going to be a decent show of tulips, especially in the pots on the terrace, while elsewhere the hellebores were in full bloom and leaves were coming through on the swathes of wild geraniums. This was Christie's favourite time of year, when winter had packed its bags and spring was knocking on the door. Her garden was coming back to life.

She heard her name called from the french windows. Ted stood framed between them, his sleeves pulled above his elbows, his cheeks flushed, the breeze lifting his comb-over from his head in a single sheet. He hurriedly patted it down. As she approached him, she felt a shiver of apprehension. From the look on his face, this was not going to be as straightforward as she'd prayed it would be.

'I've been through the lot,' he puffed. 'In fact, your records are quite thorough, just disorganised – don't worry, I can give you a few pointers to help you keep them tidy in future.'

'Great,' she said, trying to inject the word with the enthusiasm she didn't feel.

'But they simply don't tally with White Management's. A couple of pages seem to be missing from those, by the way. In certain instances, the fee you've noted in your diary doesn't correspond with the payment received. And it would help if I knew when their cheque runs were – then I could see whether any further payments are due and whether the rest went through when you were expecting them.' He scratched his head, disturbing his hair again. 'I wouldn't want to put the cat among the pigeons, but it looks to me as if there's been some sort of fraudulent activity going on. I'd say, from what I've seen, that you're definitely owed a considerable sum of money.'

'Oh, God, Ted. Surely it's a mistake.' Faced with her worst suspicions, she didn't want them proved right. The last thing she wanted was to be the person forced to blow the whistle on an opponent as formidable as Julia. 'They're a well-respected management company. They'd be mad to risk their reputation.' And yet, and yet . . . She recalled the stories of Ben Chapman's money worries and of Gilly allegedly badgering Julia for funds.

He rocked back and forth on his brogues. 'They probably don't do it to all their clients, just a select few: those they think may not notice or who can afford not to. And they probably don't do it consistently, in the hope that such dealings might be missed or, if found, dismissed as a mistake. I've seen this sort of thing a couple of times before, when a company's "borrowed" clients' money to pay off their own debts.'

'Really?'

He nodded. 'I'm afraid so. They usually refund the money later when they've squared their books and before anyone's noticed. That may well be what's happened here.'

'If you're right, what the hell am I going to do?' Christie could feel panic swelling inside her.

Ted, however, was calm and surprisingly reassuring. 'For the moment? Nothing. Let me take these away to double-check. Then we'll talk. You don't want to make any false accusations without more proof.'

Checking his watch, he refused the offer of another cup of tea – the bar at the Legion would be open by now, the chess-boards set up and waiting. She waved him off, confident at least that her affairs were in good hands and that, whatever the outcome, Ted would shed light on what was going on.

Minutes after he had left, she saw a silver Fiat Punto turn into the drive with Lily behind the wheel. Moments later, Richard and the boys followed her. Christie hardly had time to greet her visitor before Olly and Fred spilled out of the Land Rover, describing in gory detail to anyone who'd listen how they'd seen two lambs being born. 'And then – and then,' Fred shouted, 'we went into the kitchen and I fed a black one with a bottle. It was well sweet and its tail was wriggling like crazy.'

They both giggled, then raced down the garden to the trampoline, leaving Christie to introduce Lily to Richard. She took them round the house and into the repaired conservatory. The new white paintwork gleamed in the sunlight and the windows shone. They sat in the creaky rattan furniture, which Christie had covered with blankets to protect the cushions against Smudge attacks. Richard offered to get them a drink, which they both refused, before he disappeared inside.

'The suspense is killing me,' said Christie. 'What have you got to show me?'

Lily was clutching a Jiffy-bag she'd brought from the car. She pulled out several A4 photos and passed them to Christie without a word. Richard returned with a can of beer and sat beside her as she flipped through them. Her interest gave way to uncomprehending surprise as she took in a series of images that were all of her, caught when she was looking her worst, among them the shot taken outside Angela's consulting room and the one of her and Richard in a clinch on the alpine balcony. And there were also some she hadn't seen before, of her and Libby standing by the car at school, of her and Richard walking together down the street, of her standing at her front door.

'But these are all of me! And they must have been taken by the paparazzi. How have you got hold of them?' She passed them to Richard so he could see while she looked to Lily for an explanation. 'Why have you brought them here?' The evidence that someone had been spying on her made her feel insecure, as if she had lost control of her life. She could more or less cope with the photographers she could see, but being photographed secretly was a much more disturbing invasion of her privacy.

Lily sat on the edge of her seat, twisting the end of her scarf between her fingers, unable to meet Christie's eye. 'I, er . . . I found them.'

'Obviously. But where?' Christie took the photos back, squared them up and slipped them back into the Jiffy-bag.

'On Julia's computer.' At last she looked up, her face pale and worried. 'I opened the file by mistake while I was hunting for a photo for another client. I shouldn't have been on there at all.'

'That's impossible.' Christie put the Jiffy-bag on the seat beside her. 'How on earth would she have access to all these?'

'There's only one way,' said Lily, quietly. 'The photographers must have given them to her.'

'They wouldn't *give* them to her, would they? They'd want to be paid.' Christie wasn't sure she liked the picture that was emerging as, slowly but surely, the pieces began to fit together. 'But there's no reason for her to pay them, is there?'

Lily shook her head miserably. 'The file was marked "Star Features".'

'One of the big photographic agencies,' Christie explained to Richard, and waited for Lily to explain more.

'I think she may be involved with them . . . as a partner, perhaps.'

'But why? That goes against everything she stands for, surely.'

Richard appeared puzzled as he prised open his can of beer. 'Damage limitation?' he suggested. 'If she has them, no one else does.'

'But they do, though. We've seen some of them in print. That's what I don't understand.' She took them out of the bag again. 'Look. This one – and this. Remember when we came back from France?' Then the last piece of the puzzle slotted in place. 'Unless she's the one who's been placing the stories in the press and making money from the photos.'

'But she's your agent,' Richard protested. 'That really doesn't make sense.'

'I know. But she did say something about keeping my profile up while the show was off-air over Christmas,' Christie remembered. Could Julia really have been responsible for placing those stories? As improbable as it seemed, she had been one of the very few who knew of Libby's troubles and where Christie and Richard were taking the children at half-term. 'But I can't believe she'd stoop this low.'

'Why would she?' Richard remained the voice of reason as he tried to follow Christie's train of thought.

'To have control over me. To undermine my confidence and make me grateful for her skilful management.' The idea was so ludicrous that she almost laughed.

'That's just daft. She'd ruin the credibility of the show at the same time.'

'Not if it meant Gilly could come riding to the rescue.' Christie spoke carefully, as if she was thinking aloud. 'It would make her return to the show all the more welcome and, let's face it, newsworthy. She'll look more golden than ever by comparison. As will Julia by association.'

'Don't you think that's being just a tiny bit paranoid?'

That word again!

'Let's ask Lily, then. She knows Julia far better than either of us. What do you think?'

Lily had been chewing her lip, staring at her lap as she listened to them. At last she came to life. 'I've racked my brains as to why she'd have them and I can't think of a good reason. I don't want to, is the truth. But I know she does occasionally leak stories about her clients to the press.'

'Really?' muttered Richard, disbelieving.

'I've heard her,' Lily insisted. 'Julia will trade one client off against another if it works to her advantage. She's certainly not above persuading an editor to spike a story that'll harm one client by giving them a scoop on another. I'd never have dreamed you'd be one of them, though.'

Christie remembered again the way the Marina French and Grace Benjamin scandal had conveniently broken after she had let slip her anxiety over Libby to Sarah Sterling. Julia had been so certain that she could prevent anything damaging appearing in print. But if that was true, why had she turned against her now? Christie could think of only one reason. She had been asking questions Julia didn't like. That had been made quite clear. To react by destroying Christie's credibility could only mean that she must be protecting herself against something. But against what?

'You know that I've been chasing her about the money I'm owed,' she reminded them. 'Perhaps that's got something to do with it.'

'Darling, you're getting hopelessly carried away.' Richard took a swig from his can. 'Too many detective novels.'

Nettled, Christie wanted to knock the indulgent, masculine smile off his face. She leaned forward as a new theory presented itself to her. 'No, listen. I've had a couple of conversations with Frank about how Ben Chapman had money problems too. He told Frank that was what he wanted to talk to Julia about on the night he died. And Frank heard Gilly moaning about her cash-flow. Ted's just been going through my books and he's fairly sure he's found some "fraudulent activity" – that's exactly what he called it. He's taken them away to make sure.'

'From paranoia to conspiracy theory. You're beginning to sound dangerously unhinged.' Richard laughed as he crumpled the empty can in his fist.

'I'm serious. Three presenters of *Good Evening Britain* with money problems and one common denominator – Julia. That must be why she set me and Gilly up against each other. If we'd been friends, we might have rumbled her. Do you think this is completely crazy?' she appealed to Lily, who had been looking increasingly disturbed as the conversation progressed.

After a moment, Lily spoke. 'Not entirely. Put like that it does sound a bit far-fetched, but if you haven't met her . . .' she looked at Richard, who shook his head '. . . then you have no idea what she's like.'

'It beats me why you both got involved with her in the first place, then.'

'Because she's charming, convincing, successful and smart,' Christie explained. 'Her reputation in the business means she'll advance you as fast as she can. I was flattered when I met her. God, how naïve was I?'

'And I thought I'd learn everything I needed to know from her.' Lily was as quick to justify herself. 'But I didn't sign up for anything like this.'

'Too many things have happened for them all to be coincidences – the missing money, my forged signature, Gilly's hostility, these photos, the press campaign against me. Julia must have planned everything for her own ends. But if only some of this was happening to Ben and he died . . .' Christie began to articulate her thoughts, which were moving in a very unpleasant direction.

'You are not about to be next,' Richard said firmly, as if he'd read her mind. 'Everyone knows his death was an accident. Don't even go down that road . . . or I *will* have to have you certified.'

'OK.' She gave a small smile. 'I agree that's a bit melodramatic, but the existence of the pictures on Julia's computer proves to me that she's been acting against my interests, and I don't like that one little bit.'

'Well, what are you going to do about it?' Practical as ever, Richard asked the one question to which they all wanted the answer.

'I'm not sure. I don't want to confront her until I've got more evidence. She'll sucker me without it. I'd better wait until Ted gets back and then I'll decide.' She clenched her fists. 'But she's not going to get away with this.'

'Spoken like a true warrior.' Richard patted her back. 'Now! Any chance of a bite of lunch? The boys were starving when I last spoke to them.'

'The soup!' Christie leaped to her feet. 'I forgot all about it. Come into the kitchen while I heat it up.' She picked up the Jiffy-bag to put it at the bottom of the stairs to take up to her study later.

As Lily got up to follow, she noticed the copy of *Gone Too Soon* that was lying on the side-table. She picked it up and flicked to the illustrated sections, looking at the pictures documenting Ben Chapman's life. 'Have you read this?'

Christie stood beside her, and Lily angled the book so they could look at Ben's portrait together. He gazed back at them, relaxed, his arm around his golden retriever. 'I've just about finished it. I stopped when I got to the police reports on the death, though, because I wanted to read them when I had enough time to concentrate properly.'

'He was such a nice man,' Lily murmured. 'So sad.'

'I don't know why but I feel that he's holding the key to something,' Christie said. 'I thought that maybe I'd get a bit closer to whatever it is if I read about him.'

'And have you?' Richard asked.

She could hear his sceptical amusement as he slipped an arm around her waist. 'Not yet,' she said.

'Give it up, Chris. I'm sure you're reading too much into all this.'

'I don't think so, and I don't think Lily does either, do you?'

'No, not really. I wish I did.'

'I know you're unhappy about all this,' Christie said to her. 'It's going to make it difficult for you to go on working there, isn't it?

'Yes, it will.' Lily was thoughtful. 'But you're right. I'm unhappy but I'm not surprised. I showed you the photos because I knew she shouldn't have them. I can just about put up with her temper and her put-downs if I'm learning about the business from her, but I don't want to work for someone who lies and cheats to line their own pocket.'

'What will you do?'

'Look for another job, I guess, but I can't afford to quit without somewhere else to go. And, until I have, I'll keep my ears and eyes open for you. I can't promise I'll find out anything more. You know what Julia's like. But I will try.'

At that moment, Fred and Olly appeared at the door, demanding food. With their appearance, the subject of White Management's dealings came to a welcome close and the five sat down to lunch.

31

Waiting for Libby and Fred to come down to breakfast on Monday morning, Christie leafed through the *Daily News*. To her surprise, four or five pages in, she found a profile on Julia, fresh home from LA. God knew what strings she must have pulled to get into the paper so close to its going to press. The piece was accompanied by a large photograph shot in her office. Christie poured herself a second cup of tea, then considered her agent, noting her almost translucent complexion, the perfectly cut skirt and blouse that flattered her body (obviously no stranger to some eye-wateringly expensive personal trainer), and the wide leather belt that cinched her waist. Her arms were folded, her sleeves pulled back to reveal a chunky gold bracelet, and she stared out at the reader, chin high, gaze challenging, with an indecipherable smile playing on her lipsticked lips. She was the image of a no-nonsense, professional woman who would take no prisoners. I want you on my side, she seemed to be saying, but if you're not – beware.

With five minutes to go before she needed to start hurrying the children, Christie turned her attention to the article itself, in which Julia began by crowing about her successful US trip.

> ***Über-agent Julia Keen has a new star shining in her galaxy. While in LA recently, she signed up Lola Nussbaum, co-presenter of*** Showbiz Daily. ***Known for her combative style and willingness to speak her mind, Lola has attracted a huge fan base and is thought to be responsible for making*** Showbiz Daily ***one of the most watched programmes on American TV. 'She is an astonishing woman,' confirmed Ms Keen. 'Of course I had heard of her before coming to LA and I'd seen what a natural she is on screen. When we met, we instantly hit it off. I'm proud to be representing her. I think we have a great future together.' Insiders say that Ms Keen is on course to make Nussbaum millions of dollars by turning her into a global superstar. She is said already to be in talks with Jack Bradbury, head honcho at TV7.***

Christie guessed that they must have tacked this bit to the beginning of a feature that had otherwise been ready to go before Julia left for LA. How hell-bent she must be to prove she was back in the game, having kept a respectfully lowish profile since Ben's death. And how familiar her words about Ms Nussbaum were. Only a year ago, she had been saying the same sort of thing to Christie, and now look. The piece went on to talk about Julia's stellar career, how her work was her life – 'I live, breathe and dream it' – and then she went on to dismiss the clients who had left her and to big up those who had stayed with her since the 'dreadful tragedy' of Ben. Most notable, of course, was

'. . . darling Gilly. She has always been a total star. It's been such a pleasure to work with her particularly in contrast with one or two newer clients who are still so insecure that they find it difficult to let go and trust me completely. That's so essential for a good working relationship. Of course it's usually just a question of time until they let go. It's only the rare one or two who don't, and then, sadly, we have to part company.'

Christie shuddered, as if Julia was issuing some kind of warning directly to her. She had already skimmed over the break-out box in which were listed Julia's most high-profile clients, with a few words summarising each one – no surprises there. Now she glanced down, reading more carefully, until she found herself at the bottom.

Christie Lynch – latest signing whose unstable home life is reported to be in conflict with the demands of her TV career.

She stared at it, fuming. Julia would never have let this page go to press without having copy approval. She must have let this description go through unchanged, yet again confirming that Christie was some sort of loose cannon whose future was uncertain. Once her contract with TV7 was up, who would want to employ someone so notoriously unreliable? The statement confirmed to her that Julia was waging some inexplicable personal vendetta against her. She looked up at the clock. Seven forty-five. She folded the paper, put it into the recycling (best place for it), then went to the bottom of the stairs and yelled, 'Libby! Fred! If you don't get down here right now, there'll be no breakfast. And, Fred, don't forget your football kit. It's in the bottom of your wardrobe.'

She returned to the kitchen as what sounded like a herd of elephants clattered down the stairs. She heard the rat-tat-tat of things being dropped onto the hall floor, then footsteps, and Fred came in, bright-eyed, to pull out a chair with a screech before he hopped up onto it. Libby was right behind him, blurry with sleep, pillow creases still visible on her cheek, her tie hanging loose round her neck. Slowly, she parked herself opposite her mother.

'Did anybody have a shower?' Christie knew the answer but asked anyway.

'No point before football and then we have one at school. One's enough in a day, I think,' said Fred, matter-of-factly, emptying almost half of the packet of Sugar Puffs into his bowl.

'Fred! Don't be so greedy,' objected Libby, as she took some for herself. 'I'm having one tonight. I'm quite clean,' she protested, in response to Christie's look of doubt. 'I am. And I've done my teeth – which is more than *he* has.'

Breakfast was eaten in minutes, then Fred was dispatched to reacquaint himself with his toothbrush, and all the bags and coats and shoes were retrieved from where they'd been dumped. After one false start, when Libby had to run back in to get the history textbook she'd left in the sitting room, they were ready to go.

Arriving at the school, Christie was alert to the possible presence of snappers but saw no one: no light glinting off a camera lens, no car drawing up near hers and no one jumping out to follow them. In other words, if she put Julia to the back of her mind, a good start to the day.

She took the long way home, avoiding the main roads and detouring along the country lanes. Although the roadside was puddled, the sun had come through, and even with puffs of cloud being chased across it, the sky seemed bluer and the grass greener than they had for weeks. Fields were crowded with sheep, lambs suckling their mothers, romping by their side or standing, leggy and lost, baaing for rescue. The blackthorn was beginning to stud the hedgerows with tiny white flowers.

She was so engrossed in the beauty of her surroundings that, as she turned into her lane, she narrowly avoided a car speeding towards her. She pulled in close to the hedge and stopped as it edged past. The sun was in her eyes but she caught a glimpse of the driver, a youngish man with slick dark hair. He seemed familiar, but she couldn't place him. As he slid past without acknowledging her, he raised his hand to lower his sun visor. She noticed his bitten fingernails. Idiot! What did he think he was doing? She turned to catch his number plate but he had turned the corner and disappeared.

By the time she arrived home, Christie's breath had more or less returned to normal. But as she got out of the car, she was immediately aware that something was wrong. The miniature conifers (much easier than those annuals that insisted on dying) in the pots by the door stood to attention, but the door was very slightly open. Hadn't she watched, and heard, Libby slam it shut? She remembered biting back a telling-off about how the glass in the ox-eye window would break. In which case, Richard must be paying a surprise visit or Maureen had arrived early and whoever it was had let themselves in. Of course, that must be it, she told herself. Except their cars weren't here. Neither was anyone else's.

The door swung open at her touch.

'Hallo!' she called, putting one foot over the threshold, then hesitating. 'Anybody there?'

Silence.

She armed herself with an umbrella from the coat stand and, feeling a little more confident, edged towards the kitchen, keeping her back against the wall. Everything was exactly as they had left it, except that Smudge was on the table licking the milk out of Fred's bowl. She shooed him away – he hopped between the untouched yoghurts and fruit and over the open jars of Nutella and peanut butter, knocking a spoon onto the table. The noise echoed round the room.

'Hallo!' she tried again.

Still silence.

Feeling braver, she checked the other downstairs rooms where, as far as she could see, there was no evidence that anyone had been into them. The only possible explanation was that Libby hadn't slammed the door as firmly as she'd thought. However, even though she had convinced herself the house was empty, she needed to muster a bit more courage before she went upstairs. She'd seen too many movies with intruders looming on landings and bodies falling backwards, lying in crumpled heaps at the bottom of staircases. She decided to make herself a cup of coffee first.

Still armed with the umbrella – just in case – she took the paper and her coffee to the study. She pushed the door open and stood there. Had she really left her desk like that? She would readily admit to not being the tidiest of people, but even she . . . Smudge! The kitten must have got shut in there – but he was downstairs now, and no one had opened this door since she'd left the room last night. One of the children, she thought. Libby or Fred must have come in, even though they'd had it drilled into them that, without her permission, they did so on pain of death. No, they wouldn't. She went over to the desk. And then she saw.

Lily's Jiffy-bag containing the photos was missing.

She took her mobile and rang Richard who picked up immediately. 'Morning, my love. What can I do for you?'

'You didn't take Lily's photos home with you last night, did you?'

'No. Why would I?'

She explained what had happened and, for the second time in a week, he advised her to call the police. She assured him she could cope and that he needn't drop everything to run to her side again. Despite himself, he couldn't hide his relief that he didn't need to leave Tom to cope with the day's business.

When she hung up, she slumped down in the old leather

chair, slopping some coffee onto her jeans and cursing as she rubbed her leg. If Richard hadn't taken the photos, then who had? Who else had known they were there? And why would they want them?

Before she got any further in her deliberations, the phone rang. She answered, thinking it would be Richard calling back. Instead it was Lily. Christie could barely distinguish what she was saying between the sobs and sniffs, although she gathered it had something to do with Julia.

'Take your time,' she encouraged the girl, and sipped some coffee. 'Whatever's the matter?'

Lily managed to compose herself before hiccuping and gulping through a description of her morning. 'I wanted to be in first, to make absolutely sure everything was in order, but Julia was already here when I got in at eight thirty. She was sitting at my desk, logged on to my computer, going through all my work. I could see she was furious. She didn't say good morning but blasted straight into a criticism of the way I'd booked Jed Cleaver for a speaking engagement. Him arriving late was nothing to do with me: the organiser gave me the wrong time. But she wouldn't listen. She started saying she couldn't trust me, that she didn't like the way I handled the clients in her absence, that I wasn't professional enough. That was so out of order. I've worked really hard to prove I can handle the responsibility while she's away and nothing's gone wrong. I thought she'd be pleased with what I'd done but she couldn't even bring herself to say thank you. In the end, she said that as hard as she'd tried – *she'd* tried! – it wasn't working out any more, so she wants me to put everything in order and clear my desk.'

As she spoke, Christie could hear indignation bringing strength to Lily's voice. 'So where are you now?' she asked.

'In my office, with the door shut. I'm the only one here, apart from Julia. Even Lenny's not in yet and he's usually first.'

Christie immediately pictured Lenny: young, gelled black hair, smart but with badly chewed fingernails. The driver she'd met in the lane? Could it have been him who'd broken into her house to reclaim the photos?

Lily blew her nose. 'I'd pretty much decided to hand in my notice anyway, but her getting there first makes me feel as if I'm not in charge of my life – and I hate that. That's why I'm so upset. That and the fact that she's finding fault where there isn't any. But I'll get another job, something better.'

'Of course you will.' Christie had no doubt that a girl as enthusiastic and efficient as Lily would land on her feet. 'Has anyone said anything about the photos you gave me?'

'Why would she?'

'Well, someone's stolen them,' said Christie. 'Someone must have been watching the house and broken in when I took the kids to school.'

Lily gasped. 'You're joking?'

'I wish I was, but no, they've gone.' She heard the door open in Lily's office and Julia's voice, imperious as ever: 'I need to see you, Lily. Now.' The door slammed.

'I'm sorry – you heard that – I can't talk now. But could I come over this evening? I may have more to show you both.'

391

'Of course. Come about eight thirty. I'll be back from work by then, Fred'll probably be in bed, and Rich will have had time to get over here too. And, Lily, do be careful.'

*

Lily arrived half an hour after Christie had walked through the door. She was tired, having spent an afternoon of frantic preparation for a last-minute story on the mystery shooting of a businesswoman in a supermarket car park. But the show had gone well. To her surprise, Lily was not the crushed and miserable soul she had been expecting. On the contrary, there was a definite purpose in the younger woman's stride, and determination in her expression. During the course of the day, she had obviously gained strength from somewhere. She was carrying an A4 manila envelope. Christie looked at it, but all Lily said was, 'You'll see.' She laid it on the kitchen table.

'I've agreed to stay with Julia until close of business tomorrow on the condition that she gives me a reference,' she said. 'I know she only needs me there while she finds a replacement but there are one or two things I want to finish off, so it suits me too. She's making a mistake by underestimating me. I talked to Dad, who explained exactly what my rights are – not that I really have any.' She shrugged. 'But he gave me the confidence to face up to her. I wish I'd talked to him sooner.'

'I know that feeling,' Christie empathised. Just as they sat down, Richard came through the door.

'Just in time.' Christie smiled. 'Lily's got something to show us.'

Lily put her hand on top of the envelope she'd brought. 'I've been thinking a lot about what we talked about on Saturday. At least I know that I absolutely don't want to work for someone who I now realise hasn't got one ethical bone in her body.'

Christie was surprised to hear Lily condemn Julia so whole-heartedly. Until Saturday, she had given the impression that she would go to the stake for her employer, for the sake of her own career. This was quite a turn-around.

But she hadn't finished. 'What you told me reminded me of something that happened to Ben, so I decided to do a little research of my own while Lenny and Julia were out of the office. I went in yesterday and photocopied some stuff that I think you may find interesting.'

Christie was willing her to get to the point of her visit as Lily slipped some sheets of paper from the envelope and laid them out so they could all see them. 'I remembered hearing that he was unhappy over a payment he hadn't received for an exclusive shoot with *OK!* that Julia had set up for him.'

Richard tutted with mild disapproval. Christie shushed him and leaned forward, interested.

'But I also remembered that someone had tipped off the paps so that Ben was photographed when he came out of a private clinic after having some liposculpture. That broke the exclusivity deal – no other photos were to appear in the press that month.'

'Ben had work done? *Really?*' Christie could hardly believe what she was hearing.

'Yes. He was a lovely man, but he couldn't say no to Julia and she encouraged him to look his best, whatever it took,' Lily explained. 'Anyway, as a result of those pictures appearing in the press, his exclusivity agreement was broken and Julia told him that *OK!* would halve his hundred-thousand-pound fee.'

'What's this got to do with us?' Richard asked, as impatient as Christie.

'Look at these.' Lily pointed at the papers. 'I've photocopied the agreement with *OK!*, the letters that accompanied the payments to Ben and the relevant pages from the White Management bank statements. If you compare them, you'll see that *OK!* did in fact pay the full hundred thousand. It was banked by White Management three days later, but, in the end-of-month cheque run, Ben was only paid fifty thousand, as Julia had told him he would be.'

'But how do you know that the balance wasn't paid later?' asked Richard, as he turned the papers round so he could read them for himself.

'In the first place, any payment to a client is always made in full immediately, or within the month anyway, less the commission. But in the second, I looked through his file and there were no payments made between then and his death, a year later, to suggest that's the case.' She sat back, watching the effect as the couple grasped the implications of what she was telling them.

'My God . . . So, given what Frank told me, Ben could have been going to confront Julia about all this,' Christie suggested. 'And, given how badly she's reacted to me asking a few questions, we know she'll have been more than furious.'

'Easy, Chris,' warned Richard. 'Don't get carried away.'

'There's one more thing that I've never told anyone,' said Lily. 'The night Ben died, I called Julia at home.'

Both Christie and Richard sat motionless, intent on Lily as she spoke.

'I was panicking because the *Sun* had called me to say they were running a story about Lucy Smyth-Burton, an actress client of ours. They were claiming she'd been arrested on drug-related charges. I had no idea what to do. Julia took ages to pick up – that's unusual in itself – and, when she did, she sounded incredibly distracted and upset. When I asked her what was wrong, she said she'd dropped her BlackBerry into the pool.'

'Well, that's enough to make anyone suicidal.' Richard's joke was meant to ease the tension between them but Christie just muttered at him to shut up. She could feel the intense gut excitement she remembered from the outset of her career when she was chasing a good story, and sensed she was close to the kill.

Lily carried on: 'I didn't speak to her again that evening and, of course, the next day, the news of Ben's death was everywhere.'

'What time did you call her? Christie asked, her investigative hackles rising. 'I think I'm right in remembering that in Ben's biography it said that although the police weren't called until two thirty the next morning, Ben had been dead for several hours. Julia said she'd gone to bed early, leaving him to amuse himself.'

'You're not going to suggest she was up all the time and murdered him?' Richard put his hand over Christie's. 'You don't think the police might have worked that out for themselves?'

Christie took no notice. 'As I read it, according to the inquest Ben died between ten thirty and eleven. Did the police know about your call?' She looked at Lily.

'Julia didn't want me involved so she told me to forget we'd spoken since she'd dealt with the *Sun* – our conversation wasn't important. Especially in the light of Ben's death. I thought she was really generous to think of me like that, so I did what she said.'

'But what time was it?' insisted Christie, despite Richard's nudge.

'Well, late, I think . . .' Lily hesitated. 'I'm sure I'd had supper when the *Sun* called and I rang Julia straight afterwards. But if you really think it matters, I could check. Julia insists that I keep records of all calls. We keep the tapes and phone bills for five years, filed in the records office, and I keep my own bills at home too, just in case.'

'But this is crucial,' said Christie, rapidly adding two and two together. 'If she was lying about being in bed, then perhaps she is implicated in his death, after all.'

'And perhaps she's not,' Richard reminded her. 'She could quite easily have spoken to Lily while she was in bed and dozed off afterwards.'

'True,' she conceded, almost disappointed that her theory might not work. 'Either way, I don't like any of this. And one thing's for sure, I don't want her as my agent any more. I know too much. I'd rather lose the money I'm owed and start again with someone else.'

'At last,' sighed Richard. 'I thought you'd never make the decision. Will you write to her tonight? Please?'

'No.' Of one thing Christie was certain. 'I have to do this face-to-face. Don't look so dubious. Nick always said you shouldn't shy away from the conversations you dread most. He was right. I'd feel I'd let myself down if I didn't do this.'

'In that case,' Richard could see that her mind was made up, 'after all I've heard, I insist on coming along as moral support. Besides, I'm dying to meet this monster for myself.'

They agreed with Lily that she would check her phone records for the exact time of her call. Meanwhile Christie would call Julia and ask if she could meet her after work the following day. The last few days had made her certain that she didn't want Julia in her life any longer than was necessary. But before she got rid of her for good, she had to sort what business she had left with her. More than that, she was determined to find out, with Lily's help, what had really happened the night Ben Chapman died. The journalist and crime-fiction addict in her had to know. The sooner she straightened this out, the sooner she could get on with her new life.

32

Hearing Julia's smooth, unsuspecting tones had made Christie's insides turn to jelly. To think that this was the woman who had once so impressed her, for whom she would have rolled over hot coals to win a coveted place on her talent roster. She had believed that being represented by someone with such a reputation could only be good for her. How things had changed. She had learned so much. She had tried to keep her own voice pleasantly neutral as she requested a meeting for that evening.

'Ah, darling! I wondered when you'd call,' Julia had replied. 'We need to talk, don't we?'

Christie was shaken by Julia's directness but had kept her voice under control. 'Yes, we do. Seven thirty tonight, Julia.' She hung up.

Now, here they were, Richard and Christie, walking from where he'd parked the Land Rover to the White Management office. Even though she was wearing her red coat and Richard's arm was around her waist, pulling her into him, the night air was chilly against her face. As they turned the corner, the familiar glass-fronted office building loomed ahead. They halted outside the front door, looking at the uniformed doorman who was deep in a book.

'Are you sure you want to go through with this?' Richard asked, dropping his arm and turning to face Christie.

'Positive.' She took a step towards him, so their bodies just touched. 'I've got to finish this off properly. Thank you for coming.' She kissed his cheek.

'Well then, let's put this show on the road.' He pushed the door open, stood back so she could go first and sign them in at the desk, then walked with her to the lift.

Although she appreciated the sense of security having him at her side gave her, Christie was slipping into a zone of her own as she braced herself for the meeting ahead. She couldn't get the call Lily had made to her that afternoon out of her head. She now knew that Lily had spoken to Julia at 10.43 p.m. on the evening of Ben's death. That meant Julia had almost certainly been awake when Ben died. Whether she was in bed or by the poolside, or somewhere else in the house, it looked as if she had lied to the police. Why do that, unless she had something to hide?

The front office was empty, the receptionists' desks tidied and the magazines straightened on the table in the waiting area. Christie led the way down the corridor without a word, rapped twice on Julia's door and opened it.

Christie heard Richard gasp as they walked in. Julia, resplendent in a tight lavender dress, was rousing herself from the sofa and slipping on a pair of vertiginous black peep-toe Louboutins. Slightly flustered to see that Christie hadn't come

400

alone, she recovered herself to offer them a drink. They refused but she went ahead to pour herself a vodka-tonic before walking across the room to greet them.

'You didn't tell me you were bringing company, darling,' she remarked, extending her hand for Richard to shake.

'This is Richard, Julia,' Christie introduced them. 'I didn't think you'd mind if he came with me.'

'Delighted to meet you at last. Are you sure I can't tempt you to something?' She looked up at Richard through heavily mascaraed eyelashes.

'Nothing, thanks. I'm afraid I'm driving.'

'How nice. Your very own chauffeur, darling. What I wouldn't give for one.' She smiled slowly at him, then turned her attention to Christie, who was alarmed to see Richard succumbing to Julia's charms. He was staring at her like a rabbit caught in headlights. Not part of their plan at all.

'Now, perhaps we should let Richard sit in Reception while we discuss this little bit of business?'

Christie's resolve strengthened. 'Actually I'd prefer him to stay and listen, if it's all the same to you.' She was relieved that, at the sound of her voice, Richard's attention had returned to her.

Julia inclined her head, not quite disguising her surprise. 'Of course. Come and sit down. I don't think you've been here at night?'

Christie shook her head as she and Richard took the sofa. The view was the best she'd seen it as the lights of London twinkled before them, a glittering carpet that stretched into the growing darkness. But this was not what she'd come for. She waited while

Julia placed her ice-laden drink on a glass coaster then sat in the chair, kicking off her shoes again and tucking her feet underneath her before straightening her dress and gazing at them. Kittenish was the word that came unbidden to Christie's mind.

Before anyone else spoke, Christie took the initiative and began, just as she and Richard had agreed she would. They had decided that she shouldn't waste time by mincing her words but come straight to the point. She could feel her middle finger-nail digging into her thumb, distracting her from her nerves, as she spoke. 'Julia, I've seen the contents of my White Management file.' She spoke over Julia's perplexed 'How?'. 'I'm afraid they prove that someone at White Management has been defrauding me. Drink-a-Vit paid me thirty-five thousand pounds in November. That's ten thousand more than you told me I was getting. You've only paid me a fraction of that sum while all the time, when I've been asking you where the money was, it's been sitting in your account. Apart from that, you told me you were signing contracts on my behalf but in fact someone's been forging my signature.' She stopped for a second to take in the effect this was having on Julia, who was sitting absolutely rigid in front of her. Gaining confidence, Christie continued, 'I don't know what's been going on but I'd like you to assure me that you'll be paying me the full sum owed to me. My accountant will be in touch tomorrow. I know that I'm not the only client you've treated in this way. I've got evidence that you defrauded Ben Chapman too.'

There was no masking the shock in Julia's eyes that swiftly transformed into fury, as she muttered, 'Lily!' under her breath.

Richard's attention was now one hundred per cent on Christie. She could feel him willing her on. 'And I can only assume from the jpegs of me on your computer – the ones that Lenny broke into my house and took back yesterday morning – that you must have been supplying them with stories to the press. Why? Why would you do that to one of your own clients?'

Julia seemed to be picking at a spot on her skirt, buying herself thinking time. Then she took a large swig of her drink. 'Sure you won't have one, darling?'

Christie shook her head.

'Pity.' She took a sip. 'Of course I knew you had prints of the jpegs. It wasn't hard to work out that Lily had found and copied them. And what would she do with them, except show them to you? I'm not an idiot. But, yes, you're right, I did give them to the press. Being a partner in Star Features has always worked to my and my clients' advantage, on the whole. But if you're looking terrible and you come out of places where you'd be wiser not to be seen, you've no one but yourself to blame. And you've got to admit that your profile is much higher as a result.'

Christie couldn't believe that Julia would even try to justify her behaviour. Although she had rattled her cage, the other woman had regained charge of herself as she went on smoothly, 'As for the accounts, this is terrible news to me. I've nothing to do with them. That's Lenny's gig. The contracts are sent direct to him. He signs them and organises the payments. All I see is the receipts.'

That couldn't be true. Julia was too much of a control freak to let anything go by without her sanctioning it. But without evidence Christie could hardly argue the point. Despite Richard's warning cough, she couldn't keep quiet. 'I haven't come here to listen to you blame your staff. I wanted you to represent me in good faith, but you've cheated and betrayed me. You won't be surprised to hear that I'm going to find someone else to represent me.'

'At last!' Julia unfolded her legs and sat straight, smoothing her skirt. 'That's music to my ears. I've had the best out of you anyway.'

'Hang on a minute . . .' Richard cut in.

'Darling, tell your muscle man to butt out. This has nothing whatsoever to do with him. Now, unless I'm mistaken, I think we've finished.' She slipped on her shoes, stood up and began to walk to the door, confident in having had the last word.

'Not quite. First, I shan't be leaving until I have your assurance that I'll be paid everything I'm owed – and there's just one more thing.' She had to ask it. 'What really happened the night Ben Chapman died?'

Julia stopped dead. She turned to them, a fleeting expression of alarm crossing her face. 'What the hell do you mean?'

'Exactly what I said. What happened?'

'I have no idea. I was asleep . . . it all came out at the inquest.'

Christie could see Julia's mind ticking over as she tried to work out the reason behind the question, so she took her advantage and delivered her final blow. 'Indeed. But you seem to have omitted to tell the inquest about the call you took from Lily at ten forty-three, when you told her your BlackBerry had fallen in the pool. Unless, of course, you were sleep-talking.'

Julia laughed uneasily at the poor joke and swept her hair back in a gesture to cover her discomfort, but her top lip had begun to glisten. Christie felt a glimmer of satisfaction at having caught her out at last.

'Yes, I got a call.' Julia went to stare out of the window.

The other two held their breath.

'He was dead.' Her voice changed. She sounded distant, almost as if she had forgotten they were there and was talking to herself. 'But his death was nothing to do with me. He slipped. I couldn't do anything . . .' She turned as if she'd remembered their presence, regretting having said too much, then turned away again.

Christie was shocked to realise that Julia was struggling to master tears. She pressed home her advantage. 'So you were there?'

'I was in the pool, yes.' Julia pressed her forehead against the window, her body sagging. 'We'd had a lovely dinner but I could see he had something on his mind,' she said, in the same faraway tone as before. 'I suggested he needed to relax in the Jacuzzi. We went to the pool and changed, but decided to swim first. I was first in but he stood by the side of the pool, looking down at me. He started asking awkward questions about a silly magazine deal. What a moment to choose. He was so handsome and I know I could have done so much for him. We could have been great together. I stroked his feet and kissed his toes. He laughed at me – he gazed down at me and laughed. As he turned away, I grabbed his ankle and he slipped. I'll never forget the crack of his head on the edge of the pool. Blood everywhere. That was it. There was nothing I could do.' She paused as she brought herself back to the present. Then she spoke again, as self-possessed as ever: 'I'm not a murderer. It was an accident, just as they found at the inquest.'

'Then why wait four hours before calling the police?' Richard was as mystified and shocked as Christie by this unexpected confession. They had both imagined that Julia would deny the call or at least try to defend herself. Instead she had buckled immediately. If anything, she'd seemed almost relieved at being able to release what she must have kept bottled up since that night.

But as they watched her, the old Julia reasserted herself. She took another drink before she answered.

'I would have rung them straight away, of course, but I had to think of all my clients, not just Ben. It was for their sake. Do you think I wanted him lying there all night? You have to understand,' she appealed to Richard, with an automatic flutter of her eyelashes, 'many of them would still be waiting tables, waiting for their big break, if it weren't for me. They need me. Unlike Ben, who turned out to be just plain greedy. I'd made him plenty of money. Why did he need more?' She asked the question as if hoping one of them would give her the answer. She closed her eyes. 'What does it matter when I called the police? He was dead. That's why I'm telling you what happened.'

'How can you be so certain nothing could be done?' Richard insisted.

At last Julia crumpled, sniffing into the Kleenex that she ripped from the box on the table. 'I've lived with the sight of him falling ever since. The stupid boy could have had everything but he rejected me . . .' She paused as she took herself back, then cleared her throat, remembering once again where she was. 'But you don't need to tell anyone any of this. Knowing won't make any difference now. Raking it up again will only upset his family.'

'Upset his family! Is that all you can say?' Christie was incensed. 'Don't you think they deserve to know the truth about how he died? Of course we have to tell the police.' She ignored Julia's sound of protest. 'Apart from the truth about Ben's death, they should be looking into the way you run your business.'

'This really isn't necessary,' Julia said wearily. 'Nothing will bring back Ben. As for any financial irregularities, they all lie at Lenny's door. I've told you that. Listen to me, both of you, please.' Her eyes widened and she placed her hands together as if in prayer. 'What you're proposing to do will ruin my business – ruin me. But without me, you wouldn't have got to where you are so fast, you really wouldn't. And there are all my other clients who rely on me for their livelihood. If Lenny's been fiddling the books, you have my word that I'll get rid of him and square anything outstanding myself – with my own savings, if necessary.'

In that moment, she sounded so plausible that Christie glanced at Richard, unsure. His eyes were on Julia, equally uncertain of what their next step should be.

'Please,' Julia added softly. Not an afterthought but a final request. She knew she was at their mercy.

'I don't know,' said Christie, hesitating. She didn't want to be responsible for destroying anyone's life or career – not even

407

Julia's. Who was she to sit in judgement over someone else? If Ben's death was an accident that had just happened differently from the way the world believed, was it better to let the matter go? Perhaps Julia wasn't entirely to blame for the company's business dealings. Perhaps Lenny really was responsible for forging signatures and embezzling client payments. But if that was the case, why hadn't Julia worked that out weeks ago when Christie had asked her about her own money worries?

'Let me at least talk to him, before you decide what you want to do. That's not unreasonable, is it?' Julia interrupted Christie's train of thought. 'I should have treated you better. I should have looked into your cash-flow problems immediately and I certainly should have discussed my PR strategy with you.'

They faced each other: Julia contrite and seeking forgiveness; Christie torn between wanting to punish her agent for what she'd done and a desperate wish to let all this go and put it behind her. She didn't want revenge on Julia: she wanted nothing more to do with her. That was enough. Richard was keeping a diplomatic silence, waiting to follow her lead. She looked at Julia: pathetic, broken, desperate. Christie made her decision.

'All right. Talk to Lenny.' She got up and, Richard behind her, headed for the door. All she could think about was getting out of there, away from her now ex-agent. They walked briskly to the lift and returned to the Land Rover in silence, each listening to their own thoughts. They didn't speak, even when they were driving through the streets. While he concentrated on the road, Christie stared out of the window, going over what had just happened. Unable to get the image of Ben lying dead out of her head, she went through everything Julia had said and her own reactions. She remembered Frank and his friendship with Ben, his suspicions of Julia, and what he would say if he knew what they had just heard. She didn't allow herself to speak until they were well on their way home. Then she broke the silence. 'What the hell was going on in there? I was so taken aback by her admitting what had happened to Ben and she's so damn persuasive. What was I thinking? I've let her off the hook.' She banged her fist on her lap.

'She had me convinced too,' Richard consoled her.

'Of course she did. She's an actress – a bloody good one.' She remembered Frank's account of meeting her at drama school.

'No shit, Sherlock! Should we have walked away and left her?'

'No, we absolutely shouldn't. We've got to go to the police. If we don't, we're just as guilty as she is.' And I'll never be able to look Frank in the eyes again, she thought, or come to that, myself. 'I'm going to call her and tell her.'

'Is that wise?'

'Maybe not but . . . What are you doing?'

'Turning into this service station while you decide.' He followed the road as it curled left then straightened out into a wide, half-empty rectangular car park surrounded by tall straight trees. He pulled into one of the marked spaces. In front of them stood a brightly lit, modern rectangular building with a roof that fanned protectively over the entrance. The last thing Christie wanted was to thrash this out in the company of strangers, so they agreed to stay in the dark of the car, the occasional head-lights panning over them.

'Is it or isn't it the right thing to do?' persisted Christie, anxious to have his support now that she had made up her mind.

'Completely the right thing to do,' he agreed. 'But what I'm wondering is whether you really need to warn her.'

'Despite everything, I do feel a kind of weird loyalty to her. That probably sounds mad to you.'

He nodded. 'Yup.'

'I know she's done terrible things – she must have arranged for Lenny to steal the photos just to frighten me off – and that there's no way she wouldn't know what he was up to, but like her style or not, she has done a lot for me. Can you understand what I'm trying to say?' She knew how absurd her reasoning must sound.

'That's another thing I love about you, Mrs Lynch – your some-times misguided sense of fair play.' He kissed her as she aimed a punch at his arm. 'You must make the call. Now.'

'No. Tomorrow.' She was adamant.

Decision made, they drove home.

*

Her call to Scotland Yard the next morning was brief. The duty officer listened to what she had to say, put her on hold, then returned a few minutes later to ask if she would come in as soon as possible for a meeting with DI Webster, who had been in charge of the Ben Chapman case.

That done, she called White Management. No reply. Surprised, she called Julia's mobile. Again no reply. No voicemail. Nothing.

33

By the end of that week, the abrupt closure of White Management and the disappearance of Julia Keen and Lenny Chow were headline news. Grainy CCTV grabs had been printed, showing Lenny at Heathrow before he boarded a flight for the Far East. But he had flown the coop long before the footage had been found. Of Julia, there was no sign. She had vanished into thin air, leaving her clients in disarray.

After listening to Christie's claims, with the promise of witness statements from Richard, Ted and Lily, the police had hot-footed it to the offices of White Management. On the locked door, they found a notice reading 'WHITE MANAGEMENT CEASED TRADING AT MIDNIGHT.' Inside, the office had been cleared of any potentially incriminating evidence: the computer files were wiped, the shredder was overflowing. Julia and Lenny must have been up all night. An immediate alert was put out for both of them and search warrants issued for Julia's properties. The housekeeper at the Kensington house was as bemused as everyone else, denying any knowledge of Julia's whereabouts. The half-bottle of gin that she'd enjoyed that night had knocked her out so she hadn't heard Julia return home, empty her desk, pack a bag and grab her laptop. Judging from the upheaval in her bedroom and study, that was clearly what had happened. The house in the Cotswolds was locked up, curtains drawn, the Mercedes CLS still in the garage.

Eventually a taxi driver came forward to say that he had received a call from the Kensington house at six thirty that Wednesday morning. He had picked up a middle-aged woman wearing a heavy coat, headscarf and dark glasses and taken her to St Pancras, where she was assumed to have boarded Eurostar. Later Julia would be identified on Charles de Gaulle International Airport CCTV but, without the name under which she was travelling, her destination was never found. She must have had her escape route planned, just in case, for months.

Frank couldn't disguise his pleasure as Julia was revealed in her true colours, every day bringing a new revelation. Her extraordinary and unscheduled disappearance had stimulated a media feeding frenzy. Not least was the speculation surrounding her ability to adopt a second persona for travelling – which was her true identity? Ben's death filled the front pages again, especially when minor soap star Janina Terry stepped in for her pound of flesh by admitting that she had been paid by Julia to take the heat off her after Ben's death by lying to the press about his drug-taking and 'unusual' sexual predilections. Former clients stepped forward to air their hitherto unspoken grievances. Gradually it became clear that Frank's suspicions had been right: Ben's death had taken a hidden toll on White Management. With the defection of a few key high-earners, the company's turnover had dropped while the cost of Julia's lifestyle and Lenny's family in Malaysia had not.

The shortfall could only be made up by embezzling more of their clients' earnings. With no danger of any comeback, previously silenced relatives claimed their five minutes of fame by association, selling stories that shed new light on Julia's past.

Ten days after the news had broken, Frank and Christie were sitting together in the green room over lukewarm stewed coffee, Frank still alight with Julia's downfall. On the table in front of them, beside some empty cups, lay an open copy of the *Daily News*, containing an exclusive with a sharp-featured cousin of Julia's who had materialised in Liverpool.

'Look at what it says here.' Frank began to read aloud from the paper. '"Julia Keen's childhood of crime." Apparently, when she was six or seven, she and her mates were sent out to wash cars but they doubled what they were told to charge and pocketed the difference. So that was where it all began. She kept that under wraps like everything else. Sorry, love,' he apologised to Lillybet, who had come in and was attempting to retrieve the empty cups. He shifted sideways, causing a couple of newspaper pages to drift to the floor. He bent to pick them up. 'I'm only sorry she isn't here to face the music. Ben deserved that.'

'I guess we'll never know what really happened between them,' Christie mused, watching a thin brown scum form on her coffee as she added a bit more milk. 'Although I did get the impression that she was telling the truth at the end and she was a little bit in love with him.'

'But she's a consummate actress. You agreed,' he objected.

'I know I did, but even so, for a few moments she did seem quite genuine. And now we'll never know. And I'll never get the money she owed me. Thank God TV7 hadn't paid me for *Top of the Class*.'

'She's probably on the other side of the world by now. A touch of plastic surgery – to which she's no stranger, as we know – and she'll go unidentified for the rest of her life. Even Gilly's delighting in her downfall. Have you heard?'

Although Christie knew that Gilly was readying herself for an earlier than scheduled return to *Good Evening Britain*, she'd had no contact with her since they had crossed paths the day Libby had gone missing.

'Didn't you see the *Sunday Planet*'s photos of her holidaying *en famille* in La Gomera? They did her no favours – very post-baby blubber. Not a good look, let me tell you. And they even ran a story with the not-so-subtle suggestion that Derek might be putting from the rough. You know, Chris,' he said, seeing her confused expression. 'A friend of Dorothy? First of May?' She was obviously none the wiser so he added, exasperated, 'On the other bus? . . . Gay, for God's sake, woman. Anyway, the point of all this is that she's discovered it was Julia who tipped off the paps and sold the story, pocketing a mean seventy-five K for herself.'

So she and Ben weren't the only ones who had been defrauded in the interests of shoring up White Management. Golden-girl Gilly must be feeling pretty sore that Julia had left her high and dry. Christie almost felt sorry for her. But when she said as much, Frank was quick to dismiss the idea. 'Gilly, high and dry? Come off it. She's no more high and dry than an alcoholic with a bottle of vodka. She's going to be back here all guns blazing, if only to prove that she doesn't need Julia any more than Julia needs her.' He licked his finger and dabbed at something on the toe of his pristine white Converse.

'God help us all.' Sam flopped into one of the seats beside them. 'I've just heard that we're staging a great comeback fest for Gilly in a couple of weeks' time. I thought your contract held you for another three months,' he said, desperation in his voice.

'It does, but with a get-out clause that allows for Gilly's early return. I'll be doing two or three days a week again until she's back full time. But you know what? I need a new start. It's been a great experience, but this life isn't really for me.' She didn't want to admit to them how much she was looking forward to spending those extra days at home with the children and Richard, without the pressure of an evening show. Although she had agreed to stay on for several more months, Gilly had insisted – if the rumours whirling down from Jack Bradbury's office were to be believed – that her return was imperative if the morale of the show was to be held together, not to mention the 'media-damaged' Christie. It didn't take a genius to realise that this was star-speak for 'I'm a celebrity fed up with a home full of nappies and nannies. Get me out of here!' Well, each to her own.

'Did you know, thanks to Derek, we're doing a Secret Squirrel?' Frank asked, using the code-speak for something so secret that most of the crew were kept in the dark until the very last minute. That way, nothing was likely to be leaked to the press. 'He wants to spring some sort of surprise on the beloved mother of his children.'

Sam groaned. 'The idea makes me sick. That woman's got Jack Bradbury wound around her finger. Anything they want, they get. D'you know the details?'

'Not yet. All I know is that a horse is being smuggled into the scene dock.'

'You're joking?' Sam and Christie gaped at him in disbelief.

'No. God knows what he's planning, but no doubt it'll be something tasteless and over the top.'

*

The Friday of Gilly's grand return dawned at last. Christie was in the studio, but Vince had long ago warned her that she was to take a background role. In the circumstances, that was where she was more than happy to be. The show went like a dream. There was a section of filmed tributes from a host of stars, all professing how thrilled they were to have Gilly back. Then Gilly dazzled viewers with a succession of interviews, one on post-natal depression and how to avoid it. 'Never lose sight of how important *you* are and what *you* want from life' was the selfless summary. She had clearly found it worked for her. A fashion feature showed pictures of her modelling skin-tight kid-leather dungarees without a hint of a baby tummy. Anyone with a pair of functioning eyes would see that the photoshopping had been extensive. Finally, she enjoyed a girly chat with the health minister about the improved NHS midwifery services – not, of course, that she'd have been seen dead using them.

Throughout the show, Christie and Sam sat shoulder to

416

shoulder on the second sofa, admiring her brass neck. They knew that running across the bottom of the viewers' screen was a crawl that had been removed from the studio monitors, announcing, '*GOOD EVENING BRITAIN* WILL BE SPRINGING A SURPRISE ON GILLY BEFORE THE END OF THE SHOW.' As the end approached, they began to let out their breath. Too soon.

With only four minutes before the credits rolled, the scene-dock doors slid noisily open. Everyone turned as a masked man rode into the studio on a grey horse led by Jeremy, the gorgeous young scene hand who had once been lusted after by Frank and even, possibly, Derek. Christie hoped the public wouldn't be too affronted by the lengthy tracking shots of Jeremy's bum as Frank's camera lingered where it shouldn't – at least, not for a prime-time audience. Jeremy raised his hand to help the mystery guest from his steed. Gilly, acknowledging that this was a stunt especially to celebrate her return, was on her feet, blushing and giggling, at the same time chirruping about how happy she was to be back, how unnecessary any surprise. The horseman, resplendent in tight white jodhpurs, a frilly shirt and a wide-brimmed black velvet hat with a long white feather, leaped from his steed, helped by an equally well-dressed Jeremy, and stepped towards her.

A sort of bargain-basement musketeer, thought Christie, as she watched the proceedings with astonishment. She had never seen anything like this. Neither, judging from their expressions, had anyone else in the studio.

The horseman swept the hat from his head and bowed low. As he straightened up, he handed the hat to Jeremy and whipped off his mask. The gasp that went up from the crowd could surely have been heard across the country without the aid of microphones.

'Derek!' Gilly extracted a lacy handkerchief from her pocket and dabbed at her non-existent tears. She was a past mistress at milking the audience. Then, clearing her throat, she spoke to camera: 'And this, ladies and gentlemen, is the man who has walked by my side through the good and the bad: my wonderful husband, Derek.'

There was a smattering of applause as she moved to kiss him. But Derek, with a look that would have crushed a velociraptor, took a step back, dodging her embrace. 'I've come here to say something.' He glanced at Jeremy. Gilly was expectant, hands clasped in front of her.

'Gilly – you're an amazing woman, and for the past ten years, I've loved our crazy journey through life. However, life's full of surprises and this is mine to you.'

Gilly was staring at him, thrilled, as she anticipated the next bit.

'I've come here tonight to wish you every success in the rest of your life, but to tell you that you deserve the truth. I can't live a lie. I'm leaving you . . . for Jeremy.'

This communal gasp exceeded the first. Christie and Sam, aware that they were still on camera, could feel each other holding back the nervous laughter that was welling up in them. Christie felt huge sympathy for Gilly. For Derek to choose to come out on camera was one thing, but to dump her in such a public way was worse than cruel.

The credits had begun to roll but the entire gallery, like everyone else, was fixated on what would happen next and, rather than cutting away to anything else, the camera remained on the tableau in front of it. Gilly gave a little scream, then drew herself up to her full five foot two and a half, looking like a cobra about to strike (helped by the curious ruff collar on the dress she had chosen for her return). She moved her arm, then two sharp cracks rang out, like pistol shots, as she slapped first Derek, then Jeremy. A second later there was a third, as Jeremy slapped her. And a second after that, the three of them were rolling about on the floor, scrapping. Around them stood the crew, either with their mouths open in horror or roaring with laughter. Laughing loudest of all was Jack Bradbury who, for the first time Christie could remember, had deigned to grace the studio with his presence to welcome back his 'golden star'.

*

No one would ever know what Julia might have made of this shaming scene, but thousands of miles away, a lone woman sitting on a golden beach under a huge orange and green parasol, reading a British newspaper, raised her cocktail glass to her glossy lips and toasted the mortified Gilly. But it was the head-line on page two that made her smile: 'WHERE IS JULIA KEEN?'

*

A couple of months later Christie and Richard were on their way to the Ivy where they were meeting Maureen and Ted.

Christie wanted to treat them both to a special lunch, at the same time celebrating the start of her and Richard's new life together. Maureen had been in a fever of excitement ever since she had known she was to be allowed to set foot in 'Christine's world', as she insisted on calling it. Christie suspected that she was hoping to catch a glimpse of Jack or, even better, Gilly so that she could give them a small piece of her mind. She was hardly short of opinions on everything that had gone on, particularly Gilly's spectacular return to the show.

Since Derek and Gilly's public showdown, Gilly's star had risen in the TV firmament. The viewers had shown their sympathy by providing sky-rocketing viewing figures. They had no need to know of the bank of nannies who were employed to look after Gilly's luckless triplets and kept hidden behind Gilly's front door. As far as the world knew, or at least those who were interested, Gilly did her level best, struggling to cope on her own. The tears she could switch on so readily came in very handy when anyone doubted her fiction – they were designed to convince, and most often did. She had recovered with almost indecent speed from her public humiliation and had hungrily adopted the role of wronged wife that, in PR terms, had proved a blessing. Julia would have been so proud.

Christie looked around the restaurant, praying that Gilly wouldn't be there. Her prayers were answered.

The *maître d'* showed her and Richard to their table, discreetly positioned at the side of the room, out of the gaze of the other diners. 'Do you remember the day you first came round, just after I'd got back from lunch here with Jack Bradbury?' asked Christie, her attention half on the menu. 'You'll be having the caviar, I take it?'

They laughed.

'Well, the Champagne anyway,' said Richard, as the sommelier hovered. As he moved away with the order, Christie looked thoughtful.

'I'll always remember Julia sitting at that table over there, and the way she came over to check how we'd got on the moment Jack left. What an operator. I can't help wishing I knew where she's got to. That was quite a disappearing act.'

'Forget her, Chris – please,' Richard begged. 'Haven't we had enough of her to last a lifetime?'

'I know, but think what it would be like to track her down.'

'Don't even go there, Sherlock!' He smiled. 'Her or me? That's your choice.'

'Spoilsport! You know there's no contest. I'd take you every time.' She leaned across the table to kiss him.

Just then, Maureen and Ted hove into view. She was dressed for the occasion in a neat black knitted suit and a purple silk blouse with a neck-tie, plus shiny patent shoes. Her eyes darted round the room, taking in her surroundings, imperceptibly slowing her step when she caught sight of someone famous, no doubt making mental notes with which to regale the bridge circle, her reading and Pilates groups. Behind her, Ted was immaculately turned out, trousers creased, shoes shining, blazer buttons gleaming, his round face perspiring slightly as he followed Maureen to the table.

421

Within minutes, they were seated and all four were raising their glasses in a toast. 'To the future!'

Christie pulled a white envelope out of her bag and passed it across the table to her mother. 'A thank-you for everything you've both done for me.'

As she pulled out a ticket folder, Maureen was rendered as near to speechless as she had ever been. She uttered just one word: 'India!' Ted beamed at her, his glass stilled between the table and his lips.

'Thank you.' They spoke together as Ted reached out to grip Maureen's hand. Embarrassed at this far too public display of affection, she snatched it away.

'It's a pleasure,' said Christie, amused. 'This is the very least you deserve for everything you've put up with. And, by the way, we've got one more thing to celebrate.'

All eyes were on her, her audience wondering what she was about to say.

'Max, my new agent, has been amazing. He's secured the next series of Top of the Class for me but, best of all . . . drum roll, please . . .' she paused for effect '. . . he's only gone and got me the Woman's Way job.'

'No!' gasped Maureen, an avid radio listener for whom, like so many women, Woman's Way was an essential part of her day. 'But you said the interview went badly.'

'Well, what do I know? Apparently they liked me, so now I'm the new voice of midday radio. I won't have to worry about what I wear or what I look like any more – no one can see me.'

Maureen shook her head in despair.

Christie laughed. What they didn't need to know was that the deal Max had secured for her meant that at last she and the kids had some real financial security and that the debt Nick had incurred to help his parents would eventually be paid off without them ever having to know it existed. How pleased he would have been.

'And guess what?' Christie hadn't quite finished.

Richard smiled. 'You know we've no idea. Just tell us.'

'The PM has agreed to be my first interview. An exclusive on the health of the nation, to be followed by an in-depth on being a woman in Downing Street.'

'You don't regret leaving *Good Evening Britain*, then?' asked Richard, aware that the life they were planning to lead together wasn't an easy fit with the glamour and glitz of full-time TV work.

'Not one bit,' Christie reassured him. 'Gilly and Sam are welcome to it. I love *Top of the Class* but that's enough TV for me – for the time being, anyway. You know, perhaps we should raise a glass to Julia.' She registered their surprised expressions. 'She's gone, true, but without her, I wouldn't have learned half as much as I have and none of this would have happened. To Julia, wherever she is.'

Then, turning to Richard, she raised her glass. 'But, most importantly, to us.'

THE WONDERFULLY WITTY NEW NOVEL BY FERN BRITTON IS AVAILABLE NOW!

Each year, the Carew sisters embark on their yearly trip to
the family holiday home, Atlantic House, set on
a picturesque Cornish cliff.

Prudence, the hard-nosed businesswoman, is married to
the meek and mild Francis, but she's about to get a shock
reminder that you should never take anything for granted.
Constance, loving wife to philandering husband Greg,
has always been out-witted by her manipulative sibling,
but this year she's finally had enough.

When an old face reappears on the scene, years of
simmering resentments reach boiling point, but little do
the women know that a long-buried secret is about to
bite them all on the bottom. Is this one holiday that
will push them all over the edge, or can Constance
and Pru leave the past where it belongs?